The buzz on Erin Kell *Shadow*

"The search is over for your next book. If you're looking for a must-read this summer, look no further than *Shadow Bound* . . . it's an absolute original."—*B & N Book Club*

"A highly promising debut!"—*Romantic Times*

"I just love it when I find a debut author who wows me. Erin Kellison has written a mind-blowing first novel, full of fae, death, darkness, wraiths, and, of course, love and romance that triumph over all."—*The Good, the Bad and the Unread*

"In a word . . . outstanding . . . *Shadow Bound* is sure to captivate even the most reluctant readers and keep them turning pages into the wee hours of the morning."—*Romance Reviews Today*

"*Shadow Bound* is a shockingly good read."—*All Things Urban Fantasy*

"*Shadow Bound* is Erin Kellison's debut novel, and wow! Just wow. I just did not see this book coming. It's such a wonderful surprise to open a book not really knowing what to expect and end up completely loving it."—*Fiction Vixen*

"This book was amazing. . . . I absolutely cannot wait for the author's next book in the series, *Shadow Fall*!"—*My Overstuffed Bookshelf*

"A rare gift for words."—*Southern Musings*

"*Shadow Bound* is unlike any other reading experience I've had to date. It's a fast-paced, heart-pounding, gut-wrenching, nail-biting, awe-inspiring thrill ride that will leave you begging for more and more."—*Lovin' Me Some Romance*

"This book had me saying 'wow' . . . you could almost drink in the words."—*Parajunkie*

"Other paranormal romance writers should take note, Erin is the future voice of this genre."—*Fiction Flurry*

"Mrs. Kellison's debut novel is a hit, delivering a suspenseful and thrilling book that will keep you up way too late just to see what happens next."—*Dark Wyrm Reads*

"Richly imagined, fast-paced, and engrossing."—*Discriminating Fangirl*

"From the minute I started reading it I couldn't put it down. This book takes on a different view of the paranormal, one I hadn't read before. *Shadow Bound* is a fantastic combination of romance, urban fantasy, and suspense."—*The Book Girl*

"Ms. Kellison has crafted an intense urban fantasy tale with just the right mix of romance and suspense. The fast-paced plot takes readers on an emotional roller coaster, and this eerie and dangerous world won't soon be forgotten."—*Dark Faerie Tales*

"I was hooked until the very end."—*The Books I Read*

"Fans of dark drama will be captivated by this intense new series."—*Romantic Times*

"A fascinating urban romantic fantasy."—*The Baryon Review*

"As well as hot romance, Ms. Kellison can deliver scary. . . . A truly terrifying ride of mystery, action, and the supernatural." —*Tina's Book Reviews*

"Dark and brilliant."—*Anna's Book Blog*

SHADOWMAN

ERIN KELLISON

ZEBRA BOOKS
KENSINGTON PUBLISHING CORP.
http://www.kensingtonbooks.com

ZEBRA BOOKS are published by

Kensington Publishing Corp.
119 West 40th Street
New York, NY 10018

All Kensington titles, imprints and distributed lines are available at special quantity discounts for bulk purchases for sales promotion, premiums, fund-raising, educational or institutional use.

Special book excerpts or customized printings can also be created to fit specific needs. For details, write or phone the office of the Kensington Special Sales Manager: Attn. Special Sales Department. Kensington Publishing Corp., 119 West 40th Street, New York, NY 10018. Phone: 1-800-221-2647.

ISBN-13: 978-1-4201-1896-4
ISBN-10: 1-4201-1896-X

First Printing: September 2011
10 9 8 7 6 5 4 3 2 1

Printed in the United States of America

For Matt, again

You know why

Acknowledgments

Thank you so much to everyone at Kensington, especially Alicia Condon, for being the amazing editor that she is. I depend on your insight and magic. And to Jessica Faust, agent extraordinaire, you do so much and are always there. To KC Klein, Nora Needham, and Tes Hilaire, for standing by me, and, oh yeah, excellent critiques. To Brian Anderson, for his expert information on all things tactical and for demonstrating on my husband. Any mistakes are mine. To my bedrock, my friends and family, who buy my books, sometimes in quantity. To Mom, who passed them out to anyone who would take them. And to Celia, Big C, Cornelia, aka Super Beta—hugs and love for everything.

Fate is a three-faced witch named Moira. Maid, mother, and crone, Moira weaves the patterns of humankind's life threads so that each intersection seems prescribed from the first wail of birth. So subtle is she that humankind invokes her name at moments large and small, sad and joyous, as an answer to or explanation of events—*it was fate, destiny, kismet*—when that is not always the case.

The irony is that Moira is one of the fae, and therefore has a far more circumscribed existence than any human being. Her scissors may be sharp, but she hasn't yet discovered the power to set them down, as has Shadowman with his scythe.

And she is bitter because no matter how tightly she ties her knots, mortal free will can loose them again.

—TALIA KATHLEEN THORNE
The Shadowlands Treatise

Prologue

Shadow throbbed, twisting and irregular, in the corners of the hospital room. Seething with welcome, the ribbons of darkness crept past the cluster of too cheerful sunflowers on the far table, through the quietly humming machines, toward the bed where Kathleen lay.

Not long now. Shadow had always been close, but soon the dark stuff would claim her.

Beyond the filmy layers, on the Other side, the knotted and craggy boughs of Twilight trees swayed. Fae whispers rose in an inarticulate *hiss* and *tick* as they drew near to the thin veil between the Shadowlands and the mortal world, looking on. Waiting in heightening anticipation.

Not long at all.

Kathleen squeezed her sister's hand, urgency giving her the strength to make the squeeze hard. She drew deep on the oxygen at her nose and said, "Don't let them kick you out of the room."

Maggie's lips went tight. Her O'Brien red hair had gone frizzy and she had more makeup under her eyes than on top. Her sister reached above the hospital bed with her free hand and switched the light off.

Shadow coursed into the void, but Maggie, as ever, was oblivious to the churn around her. "We've been over this," she said. "You need to get some sleep now."

In fact, Kathleen could barely keep her eyes open. With Shadow so close, so intent, she needed to be rested and ready for when the time came, but getting Maggie's cooperation was too important; it was part of being ready, like the intensive care neonatal room, prepared for delivery, the on-call doctors, and the machines to warn the nurses if she declined rapidly. All the rest meant nothing without Maggie's agreement. "You need to be there to make sure that the baby comes first."

"I hate it when you talk like that." Maggie looked away.

Lately Maggie couldn't meet her gaze, which was why Kathleen needed this last assurance. Just in case. "You know it's what I want."

The baby's heartbeat *shush-shush-shushed* rapidly over the monitor. Kathleen focused on the sound and used its promise to draw another difficult breath.

She could see Maggie's profile: her sister's jaw clenched, her throat working silently.

When Maggs finally spoke, her voice was rough. "And what about you, huh? You can't think that . . . that . . . I'll just let you . . . You're my *sister*." Maggie braced her free hand on her knee and worked for breath as well, lowering herself into the chair.

"I'll be okay." *He'll be waiting for me.*

Maggie turned back, words tumbling in a sob-clogged accusation. "You could *fight*. You could *try* to get through this. At least you could try."

Kathleen inhaled through the tightness in her chest to speak. "I *am* fighting. I *am* trying." She was giving everything she had to see her daughter safely into the world. She had no illusions about what would come after. How could she with the room darkening, the Shadows reaching farther with each passing moment? But she had no fears. Not with *him* near. Her gaze flicked to Shadow, searching for him in the glossy layers. When she didn't find him, she returned her attention to her sister.

Maggie frowned hard, shaking her head. Eyes blazing. "Not for yourself, you're not."

Kathleen heaved for air again. "Maggs, you know this is for me, too. This is better than I could have ever hoped. I'm happy. Please let me be happy."

How could she possibly make her sister understand when it was so hard to speak? When the dark stuff filled her lungs and choked her breath? Her own heart monitor started jumping, its beeps closer together. Likewise, the baby's *shush-shush* increased, the digital number climbing.

Instantly, Maggie was on her feet. "Kathy, I'm so sorry. Honey, just breathe. In and out. In and out." She exaggerated the action on her behalf.

Kathleen concentrated on the flow at her nostrils, willing the good air to feed her blood, move her heart, and keep her baby growing for just a little while longer. Twenty-five weeks was the golden number, but every day gave her baby girl a better chance to survive. Every day was another 3 percent, that's what the doctor said.

Maggie visibly swallowed, her face reddening as she nodded and blinked back tears. "Okay. Don't worry about it. The baby first, like we agreed." She swiped at her cheek. "I swear I'll be here. I won't let them budge me from your side."

"The baby's side," Kathleen corrected and managed a smile, her eyes fluttering closed. With Maggie's promise, her hold on wakefulness weakened and sleep sucked her down.

"But I'm going to hope for you, too," Maggs said, her voice following Kathleen into slumber, the firm grip on her hand never loosening.

Flying. Her favorite kind of dream.

Kathleen skimmed the topmost branches of the trees— higher!*—then burst out over the eastward cliff of Sugarloaf Mountain to careen into a turn above a storybook patchwork landscape. The air smelled sharp and summer sweet as she rushed headlong into the dazzling blue. She filled her eyes with the color until her heart could hardly bear more.*

Dizzy, she cast her gaze downward, to the rocks she'd picnicked at with her family when she was little. The scene was recalled in wondrous detail from the murk of her memory. Lush trees, dark green. Screaming bugs. Grassy patches, with large, white boulders. Rocky, rooty trails leading off in a couple directions.

Mom was laying out their lunches, waving away interested bees, while Dad dumped excess water from their cooler. Her sister, Maggie, inched closer and closer to the steep drop, yelling toward the woods, "Kathleen! I can see our house!"

The dream suddenly morphed, and Kathleen was seven years old, headed on foot into the tall red and white oaks on the mountain. Old, dusty leaves crumbled underfoot. The fragrant, humid air cooled as she moved deeper into the forest. Her heart skittered in her chest and stars pricked into her vision, but she didn't care. The trees were sparkling and sighing and swaying. Like magic.

"Stay away from the edge, Maggie," Dad called from somewhere behind her.

Kathleen quickened her pace, picking her way over the

jut and hump of tree roots. If Mom or Dad saw her, they'd make her go back. Sit down. Rest.

She was sick of rest. Of new treatments for her heart. Ever since she was born, something had been wrong with it, a condition *named with big words she never wanted to learn. But she knew what they meant: She might never grow up.*

It was much better to explore the woods than sit bored. She'd have all the time in the world to sit bored at home. Later. This was her chance. How deep could she go before they'd come after her?

Excitement made her breath short, her heart glub-glub *before settling again. An adventure at last!*

The air around her shimmered. The shadows shifted from patchy grays and blacks to purples and blues. The colors of a fairy tale. Beckoning. Drawing her into a story.

I'm a princess, lost in a magical forest.

She stumbled on a loop of root. Her heart glubbed *again. Once, hard. She had to check her breath, but she wasn't going back. Not yet.*

Silvery, tinkling music, like from her jewelry box, filtered through the trunks. It was that Disney song she loved that her mom said was really Tchaikovsky.

Coming from . . . that way . . .

She veered off the trail onto the leafy, trippy ground. At the edge of her sight, strange forms darted among the trees. Breathing became easier, the air sweeter. Made her head buzz.

She lifted the skirt of her gold, bejeweled dress. Because that's what she'd be wearing. Gold and jewels and a tiara with diamonds sparkling bright.

Deeper, deeper into the pretty purple. Her heart was strong here. This was where she'd meet her prince.

Within the darkening trees, the shadows unfolded like

shiny black crows' wings, and there he stood. He had long, silky black hair. He was tall and had way more muscles than her dad. His eyes were black-black in a sharp and serious face, but he didn't scare her. He could never scare her. He'd been there all her life, guarding her dreams.

Her Shadowman.

"Kathleen, love, go back," he said, voice urgent.

"But I feel so good. I want to play!"

The shadows behind him started to turn slowly, bruising with stormy eruptions. His dark cloak trembled and snapped on the surface. Tendrils of darkness curled around his legs and arms. One inky strand circled his neck.

"Kathleen, you must turn back now," he said. "I can't hold Twilight from you long."

"But it's so pretty here."

The trees shivered in the gathering storm. Chattering whispers filled the air. And at the edges of her vision, swift, glittering movement among the trunks. Faeries, everywhere.

"It's a lie to trick and take you before it is time," he said. "Wake up!" The shadows surged, and Shadowman flung out his arms to hold them back. One of his hands gripped a long staff, topped by a curved blade that glinted in the colored light. A scythe.

Death.

Oh, God! The baby!

Kathleen whipped around, looking for the mountain, the rocks, her parents. But she was in her hospital gown, her bare feet shuffling in the velvet earth.

Trees surrounded her, dark trunks thickening, branches stretching into a tight, dense canopy, its scent intoxicating, muddling her mind. Where to go?

"Run!" Shadowman shouted, his voice tight with strain.

Kathleen bolted, the frigid darkness licking at her heels and chilling her bare legs. But there were only trees and trees and more trees, pressing in to block her path.

Too soon! *She had to get back. Had to deliver her baby before Shadow could take her. She had to find a way back to life, if only for a few moments.*

"Maggie!" she screamed.

"I'm right here," Maggie said. "I won't leave the baby. I'll keep my promise."

Pressure crushed Kathleen's chest. She gulped for air but was drowning anyway. Her heart clamored wildly. No amount of forced calm would stop it.

The hospital room was a chaos of movement. Nurses, doctors, blurring around her. Maggie was a flash of red hair to her upper right. The young doctor, Cotter, was there, a green mask over his face, gloved hands lifted, waiting. A new machine was wheeled into position next to her and a strange man tugged on her IV.

". . . acute pulmonary edema . . ."

She was lying flat, where before she had been at a slight incline. Something pricked, burned. "The baby," she said, but her voice was a rasp. *The baby!*

". . . congestive heart failure . . ."

"There was no way this baby was ever going to make it to term," a nurse was saying. "Someone with her condition never should have gotten pregnant."

"Shut up," Maggie bit back. "You don't know anything."

Kathleen's vision sharpened as the forest grew around her. Twilight had followed her into wakefulness as her crossing neared. Trees speared the hospital room, floor to ceiling, invisible to all but her. A woodsy scent filled her nose and soft fae voices whispered excitedly. It was a place of magic and dreams, of fantasy and nightmare. There was no escaping its Shadows, not for anyone. No eluding it for long, even with Shadowman holding the darkness back. Everyone eventually had to travel the dark tunnel formed by its trees.

She'd been at its brink all her life.

"Kathleen," Shadowman said, a murmur at her ear. Of course he would be near.

"Not yet," Kathleen begged soundlessly. Heart failing, her lungs filled with fluid. "Please."

Maggie leaned in, face blotchy and white. "Honey, it's time. The baby needs to come out now. Stay with me, okay? I need you, sis."

She veered out of view as the doctor brushed something across the mound of Kathleen's stomach. The world blurred as the colors of Twilight became more distinct—deep vermillion, raging magenta, violent indigo. Static roared in her ears. Her heart clutched. Sensation both numbed and heightened in a frightening electric fission. A change.

Not pinned to a table. Not drowning. Not gasping for air.

Held.

Shadowman's arms tightened around her. Touching her for the second time in her life. His skin brushed hers. His hair tangled on her shoulder. His breath was warm at her neck.

Their first union had led to this moment, when he had crossed to her world, disregarding fae laws so they could be together, to touch just once. They'd stolen time, defied Fate, and created new life. She had never regretted it. Not even now.

With the Twilight forest behind her, Kathleen looked on the world through a thickening veil. Her mortal body lay collapsed on the operating table, eyes glassy, unfocused. A doctor worked at her belly. His hand disappeared into her skin.

". . . she's in asystole. . . ."

"Kathy!"

The doctor eased a small form out of her womb. The baby filled his palm, her skin tinged slightly blue and smudged with a whitish paste. Her face was scrunched, beautiful, while her pink tongue touched air.

Her baby. Her little love. *Talia.*

A wail rose in Kathleen's throat like gorge. She reached out her arms, straining toward her child. *So small!* Kathleen's fingertips grazed the mortal world.

But Shadowman held her tight against the wall of his chest. Into her ear, he said, "Forgive me."

"Please let me hold her." The separation from her child was a vacuum of pain in her chest. Every nerve screamed in protest. Her marrow burned while her skin went frigid. There was no heart pain like this scoring need, no injury or disease more vicious than tearing her from her child.

His lips moved against her cheek. "You know I cannot."

How could he be so cruel? Did his cold fae blood spare him this pain? The child was his, too.

Kathleen turned to face Death, bitter recriminations on her tongue. Shadowman looked down on her, his gaze filled with sadness.

"She'll live," he said. "Even so small, her lifeline is strong."

"I want her. She's *mine*. Don't take me now," Kathleen said. But Death had walked by her side since she was born, holding back the Shadows. She'd always known that one day she'd have to cross. She'd known that bearing her child would part the veil. She'd fought for this very moment.

Kathleen whirled back to view the receding world. Maggie was standing sentry next to the nurse, watching her siphon mucus out of the baby's nose. Prick for blood. Enclose her in a preemie unit. Her sister looked back once toward the action at the operating table, face gray, eyes aged, but she followed the child out of the room.

"The babe is strong," Shadowman said. "Like her mother."

Kathleen would have crumpled to the ground without his firm hold. "I want to know her. I want to be with her. It's not fair!"

She trembled uncontrollably, gripping his arms for support.

Shadowman was quiet too long, and a new horror bloomed in Kathleen's mind. She went very still. "Is she like you? Or like me?"

The fae were bound to the Between world, the twilight Shadowlands. They couldn't exist on Earth, or cross Beyond, like humankind, to the Afterlife.

"She's both. A half-breed. Our daughter has a foot in each world," he said. "No one knows what she will become."

"So I may have lost her completely?"

"I don't know."

"And when I cross, I'll lose you, too?"

His silence answered her.

Pain turned to rage. Strength surged within her. "Nuh-uh. No way. I'll have you both."

"I warned you before." His face was in her hair, and she knew he was memorizing her. Taking everything he could before he passed her on to the Hereafter. The trees around them were already stretching into a dark tunnel to oblivion. They had only moments left.

"Yeah, well, I'm not going to accept it."

She felt a sad chuckle against her body. "Your spirit has always awed me."

"I'm not letting this happen."

"It has already happened." He took her face in his hands, traced her lips with his thumb. "It is the way of the three worlds."

Kathleen shook her head. "I was supposed to die when I was a kid, and I lived to bear my own," she said, "so I think I can handle this. What we need is a plan."

"How I love you." His gaze searched her face, fierce longing tugging at his black eyes.

"The most important thing first: You look after our girl. Keep her safe."

Just uttering those words sent fresh pain roaring through her.

He put a hand to her chest, as if to stop the hurt. "Shhh. Yes. How could I not?"

Faery whispers rose on all sides. The air thickened with magic. Kathleen felt Shadowman shift, drawing his cloak around her. They turned together to face the dark canopy, the tunnel to forever. A bright spark glimmered in the distance. The Afterlife.

Kathleen steeled her nerve. "And I'll find a way back to you both."

Chapter 1

Twenty-eight years later

Firelight dazzled Shadowman's eyes. Acrid smoke scorched his nose, throat, and lungs. His hands were blistered by his work, the muscles of his neck and shoulders knotted with strain. But no matter; what Kathleen suffered was far, far worse.

How could it be that she, of all mortals, had been consigned to Hell?

Channeling all his strength, he brought the hammer down and rang the anvil with the force of his blow. The note held, high and piercing, reverberating throughout the cavernous space of the New Jersey dockside warehouse. White sparks flew from the glowing hunk of iron and winked out in the depths of his fae Shadows, now churning around him.

Filtering through his memory, a scrap of talk from the fateful meeting that changed everything, her soft voice laughing with irony: *Fancy you being afraid of me.*

Yes, fancy that. *Afraid.* And yet he'd been present nearly

every day of her life, the veil between life and death made whisper-thin by her weak heart.

It had begun simply—the soul fire of Kathleen as a child had been golden bright, drawing the curiosity of many of the fae, even him, the darkest of them all. For how *curious* that her soul should burn so bright when her heart was so very compromised. A moment in the presence of her warmth, and Death was transfixed.

He'd watched her grow, fight and cry, watched her grit her teeth as she willed her heart's rhythm into the beat of life.

And in spite of that ongoing labor, her dreams had been more vivid, more controlled, than most other humans' sojourns into Twilight. In dreams, she'd directed him into elaborate schemes of great daring in her imagination. She was a master of the sword, and together they vanquished evil, she never stopping for breath or blood.

And if Shadow had sent nightmares to terrorize her sleep, he had commanded peace. Nothing would harm her while he was present.

At first she wished for a magic cure, of stars and fairy dust—though no fae, not even him, could ever heal the flesh of a human. Her hopes later fixed on a handsome doctor, who promised miracles he also could not deliver. And so time passed.

Then one dark, hopeless day, the woman Kathleen turned her gaze toward Shadow, the knowledge of her fate in her eyes. And her gaze fell on Death, her childhood Shadowman, still watching from across the veil. He'd been more transfixed than ever.

Death afraid of a mortal woman. Yet, for her, he had then and would now again dare anything. Shadowman focused on the timbre of her voice, the light humor, and heaved the hammer upward again. He concentrated himself into his grip on the shaft and jarred Shadow with another sharp, hot strike. The iron flattened, tapering just so.

I wish we could talk, she'd said as she worked at her painting. Art had been her solace, and what else would she have painted but Twilight, the faery world on the other side of the shadows. Her pale profile had gleamed in the wan light of her bedroom. Her tone was filled with warmth. A voice across time. An echo in the dark.

After all, what harm would it be to speak with her? She was so close to passing from the mortal world regardless. Why not cross that divide first himself? Let her see him, really see him, before all chances were lost? Shadow was so cold; Kathleen was radiant. What would it be like to *feel* that warmth, just once?

Shadowman rotated the hammer in his grip to use the tapered head to shape the end of the spear, the decorative tip of the vertical bar to the gate he forged. It needed to be razor sharp, all violence and cruelty, as was the nature of the haunt to which the gate would open.

Please touch me. I want to feel something real while I can, she'd said.

And so he'd crossed when he had no call to do so. He had broken a cardinal law of nature and trespassed where he did not belong. For Kathleen.

Mortals view Death as they conceive him: ghoul, priest, demon. Kathleen had made him her dark prince from her fairy tales, even knowing his true nature—the Grim Reaper. His duty for all eternity was to transport souls across Twilight to the Hereafter. Yet, even as she'd fought against that inevitable passage, she'd embraced him. Bid him come closer, her emotions coursing through Shadow and into him. Her intent was a revelation. Her touch changed him. Changed everything.

He grasped the wooden haft of the hammer tight, but he could feel her soft mortal skin under his hands again. The satin glide from the slope of her waist to the swell of her breast. He stroked his thumb in the hollow at the base of her throat, then followed with a brush of his mouth. Her back arched. Heat flared between them, a fire for the ages, far beyond the sear of his forge. His death-tuned senses had perceived the clamor of her heartbeat, and now he held the memory of the wild rhythm in his head and used its passion to strike the glowing piece of metal on the anvil.

Together they had created a child, Talia, now a woman with a family of her own and a strong protector by her side. Talia had fought a nightmare scourge of wraiths to come into her own fae power.

Now there remained only the second part of Kathleen's last wish, to find a way back, a way to be with them both.

Death thumbed the edge of the metal with his other hand, found a slight thickening, and lifted the hammer again. Taking a deep breath, he gathered his intent, focused his mind on the object of his creation until he shook with power, then brought the tool down. . . .

The shadows stirred.

Sudden weakness diminished him.

The hammer slipped from his grip and clattered to the floor.

Shadowman panted, dismayed, as he regarded the hammer. It was hard enough to create and sustain the corporeal form of a human body. But to hold the hammer, *that* hammer, took all of the power, will, and memory within him. The tool had been created by angels and was near unbearable to a fae's touch.

Kathleen!

The last time he'd dropped the thing, it had taken him hours to lift it again, and by then, the fire had died. He gulped the smoky air and roared at the heavenly object.

"Sorry," a voice said.

Fae Death brought his head up and jerked around to find Custo, the angel who'd given him the damn hammer in the first place. Custo always seemed to be present when Death needed him, but most especially when Death did not. Like now. Custo's olive-gold skin was lined with veins of Shadow, which meant the angel had the power to cross through fae Twilight to any other place on Earth, including this warehouse. But it was the angel's light that had banished the death shadows just enough for Shadowman to lose his grip on the hammer.

Too late, Shadowman detected the even beat of the angel's mortal heart. *Damn the boy. What does he want now?*

Shadowman tugged on the shadows hovering like storm clouds around the angel. Immediately the darkness delivered an echo of Custo's emotions: Curiosity was dominant, but anchored by determined control and personal conviction, though what that conviction was, Shadowman could not fathom. The fae could sense feelings, but thoughts were the purview of the divine.

Bare-handed, Shadowman lifted the spearhead from the anvil and plunged it into the glowing coals of the forge. The fire leapt into red-gold curls, but the skin-crackling burn did not signify. Not as Death finally let cold Shadow take him, succor and restore him.

"What do you want?" Vitality pulsed through Shadowman's form with old magic. As always, he could not escape the distant call of his discarded scythe, the hoary blade clamoring from the twilight Shadowlands to be lifted in place of the hammer.

No. Never again. He was done with death.

Custo crossed fully from Twilight into the mortal world. His pale inner light pushed the darkness of the room back, revealing the scarred floor, old piles of discarded rope and rotting crates, the dingy windows of the warehouse. "I . . . uh . . . came to see . . ."

Shadowman knew the moment Custo's gaze hit the gate. Death watched the angel's eyes narrow in examination, then widen in horror. Custo stumbled backward, his fear pervading the space. Shadowman could taste it, bitter and sharp, could smell it, rank, could feel the terror that made Custo shake.

"Oh, God," Custo said, breathless. "What have you done?"

Death crouched to protect the hammer where it lay on the floor. He brought his deep cloak around, as if the fae folds could possibly hide something divine. Custo could not have the hammer back. Not when the gate was so close to completion. Not when he was so close to Kathleen.

"You told me yourself that she is not in Heaven," Shadowman said. "And you gave me the hammer. What did you think I would do?"

Custo shot him a look of acute alarm, his green eyes deepening to black. "It was a favor. I didn't know what your purpose was. I can read only mortal minds."

Shadowman could sense the angel's inner conviction transforming into a pressing intent to act. The shadows of the warehouse floor roiled as Custo added, "The fae are, as usual, utterly obscure and insane."

"Fae Shadow runs in *your* blood now." Death drew on the silky darkness, sucking the magic into his being, though Shadow could not possibly help him lift the hammer. Lifting the hammer took concentration and time. Shadow was a different kind of power, impulsive and sudden.

Custo sighed. "Yeah . . . well . . . I guess you have a point." From an affectation of easy stillness, he leapt, the fae ascendant in the blackness of his eyes.

Death twitched a finger, and midair, the Shadows struck Custo down with a sickening head crack to the concrete floor. The boy would have been much better off using his angelic gifts. Shadow would forever and always obey Death first, even the small portion of it that ran through Custo's veins.

Custo brought a hand to the floor and grunted as he pushed himself up. "Be reasonable."

Reasonable? There was no such thing. Not in a universe that had consigned Kathleen to Hell, when *he'd* been the one to rend the boundary between the worlds. *He'd* broken the law that bound the fae to the Other side. *He'd* stepped into her room to view her painting. To speak with her. To touch her. If anyone was at fault, it was he.

Shadowman grabbed at the hammer. His hand passed right through it.

Kathleen! he thought, and tried for the hammer again. The tip of his finger budged the shaft slightly. So close . . .

Shadowman thought of her pale face, her gold hair, her violet eyes, but it was the memory of her smell, tinged with the chemical musk of her paints, that helped him close his hand around the grip of the hammer. He forced all his strength into his clenched fist. Mass, that contrary mortal magic, had always defied the fae.

Custo stood, shaking his head, and regarded the gate again. "You can't think for a moment that The Order will suffer that . . . that . . . *thing* on Earth."

"That *thing*?" Death mocked, standing again.

"The Order would call it an abomination."

"And what would you call it?"

"Seriously fucked up."

Shadowman gripped the hammer, a tool of the angels. With it, he could forge the gate. Barbed and brutal, the gate's only decorative element was a few spare flowers, the kind that could grow in the harshest, darkest clime. Three wrought-iron, triangular petals were folded close to guard the core. The blooms were his desperate hope, a symbol that Kathleen could endure beyond, her soul bearing the empty pitch until he could find her.

"Are you going to tell them?" Death asked.

"I'm part of The Order," Custo said. "The angels can read my mind. I couldn't hide this if I wanted to. And I don't. We've had enough trouble dealing with the last forbidden passage you created between the worlds. Wraiths are still plaguing humankind. There's a war out there. Don't open up a way even more dangerous."

Shadowman glanced at the gate.

kat-a-kat-a-kat-a-kat, the gate answered, trembling on its posts. The gate had been talking to him like that since it had been mounted.

And he knew he could not wait to retrieve Kathleen from Hell. There was no higher purpose in her presence there that he could fathom. No order or justice to her damnation. He broke the law, but Kathleen suffered in Hell. There was nothing to do but fetch her back.

"Look ahead, if you can," Custo said, the green forcing out the black in his eyes. His urgency, thick and pungent, saturated the shadows. "I beg you to look ahead."

Shadowman gripped the hammer tighter. The gate was nearly complete. Soon, very soon, it would be ready. The fae existed in the now, the present moment, but he could see that far into the future.

kat-a-kat-a-kat-a-kat

The gate already clamored to open.

"What do you think a gate to Hell will do to the mortal world?" Custo's burnished skin gleamed in the dark. He was all angel now, fighting once again for the people on Earth. "If you can pass through it, what do you think will come out our way?"

Nothing good, that was certain.

So Shadowman answered with a question of his own. "And if it were your Annabella?"

Custo went silent, breathing deeply, thinking of the beautiful ballerina who was his wife. It didn't take long for his mouth to twist.

"It hurts you even to think of it, yet Kathleen is there, right now."

Custo closed his eyes. "There has to be a reason . . ."

". . . for her to bear pain and despair unending?" Shadowman's arm ached with the burden of the hammer. The sinews and muscles strained to hold it, but he held fast to his human form. He had a gate to finish. "And you could tolerate this for Annabella while you had the means to save her?"

"Oh, God. I gave you the means. Oh, shit." Self-recrimination threaded through Custo's distress. "That makes *me* responsible."

"Then see it through."

kat-a-kat-a-kat-a-kat

Shadowman turned to regard the gate. At his side, Custo did the same. The potent menace coming off the thing was palpable. Shadow shimmered against the hell-throb of his creation. A gate to Hell, forged by Death.

Shadowman felt the moment Custo came to a decision, his hard resolve overcoming the wilder emotions.

"I begged for a day once, and that's what I'll give you," Custo said. "Then I swear I'll bring the angels. We will rip it apart, even if you, Kathleen, or . . . or . . . even Annabella are behind it. It is wrong. You fae obviously have trouble telling the difference."

kat-a-kat-a-kat-a-kat

Right? Wrong? Shadowman didn't care. Death, by nature and necessity, was numb to such considerations.

"I don't require your permission, boy." The pain of his grip on the hammer crawled over his shoulder.

"Mark my words," Custo said, summoning Shadow to depart. "The angels are coming."

"Mark mine," Death returned. "I'll have her back."

Chapter 2

A rustle in the brush snapped Layla Mathews's attention from the quiet hulk of The Segue Institute's main building to the dense trees on her right. *Wraith.* She held her breath, willing her heartbeat to silence, lowered her camera, and put a hand to the gun ready on the earth in front of her. *Steady . . .*

She waited for movement. Strained for the telltale screech that meant trouble.

Keep it calm. . . .

But heard only the *kat-a-kat-a-kat-a-kat* of the now chronic tinnitus in her head.

Nothing. Her gulping heartbeat slowed.

Seconds passed. A breeze hit the November trees, and the leaves chattered in the wind.

Still nothing.

Okay. Back to work. She was going to get a photo of Talia Kathleen Thorne if it killed her. A clear shot, in high-res. The follow-up segment to her wraith series wouldn't be complete without it.

Thick trees and tangled thatches of undergrowth concealed Layla's crouch. Adrenaline still flashed through her veins now and then, but her tush and toes had long since gone numb. She hoped the adrenaline would make up for her stiffening body if trouble found her, and she tried not to think about how she was meeting it halfway.

The Segue Institute, located deep in the West Virginia Appalachians, might seem too peaceful for a war zone. But she knew better. The wraith war was one of long silences, broken with sudden, violent terror, but she was going to get the photo she'd come for, frigid wraith-infested mountain or not.

kat-a-kat-a-kat-a-kat

Layla shook her head. The metallic, rattling sound in her ears had been driving her crazy for a while. Had to be a side effect from the blow to the head she'd taken in Tampa, trying to get some video inside what she thought was an empty wraith nest. The nest was not so empty.

kat-a-kat-a-kat-a-kat

She focused on her target. Shadows pooled around the renovated turn-of-the-century hotel that now housed Segue, though the ineffectual sun was directly overhead. It kind of reminded her of an Escher drawing of a castle: The veranda stairs plunged into a bent twist of darkness, the darkness giving way to whitewashed, starkly delineated walls, which took a sharp turn into darkness again. It was an upside-down kind of building. Tugged at her mind. Tugged hard.

"You're seeing things, Layla," she said to herself. The cold wait had to be getting to her. She squeezed her eyes shut to clear her vision. Now, of all times, she needed to stay alert and grounded. No trips to la-la land.

An early, three-hour hike from Middleton, a climb over an unguarded section of Segue's surrounding wall, four hours kneeling in the scraping underbrush, and still no sighting of anyone, specifically Talia or her well-known husband, Adam Thorne. *The Global Insight,* the online journal Layla worked for, had many photos of Mr. Thorne on file, as Thorne Industries maintained a high-profile presence at events and charities. But it had only one of Talia, a blurry screen capture of an Arizona alley fight with a wraith. A faint tilt to her eyes was discernable, as well as the woman's ultrafair coloring, but that was about it. Talia Kathleen Thorne was an enigma, a ghost, and Layla's obsession. She would stay all night if she had to.

She needed one crisp photo to accompany Adam's when she broke her story: These were the people at the heart of the wraith war. Wraiths, the monsters of the modern age, had mutated from normal *Homo sapiens* to some superstrong, fast-healing new breed. Violent and predatory by nature, they attacked their human counterparts, even those they once called friends and family. The spread seemed to have stopped, but the terror continued. All indicators pointed to Segue, yet the government had granted the institute what seemed like unlimited support and power. Was Segue the world's salvation, or the source of the modern plague?

A flicker in the distance had her raising her camera again. Screwing the telephoto lens in place. Focusing.

Someone exited the building and strolled to the high white railing that edged the wide patio.

No. Two someones. One, dark and masculine, had to be Adam Thorne. The other was so pale as to be barely visible against the white of the building.

Yes! Layla knelt up, waiting for the moment when the profile of the woman would shift, when Talia would face the trees.

Layla needed only a second, and she'd have the shot.

kat-a-kat-a-kat-a-kat

The noise jangled in her head, but she ignored it. *Any . . . second . . . now . . .*

kat-a-kat-a-kat-a-kat

She squinted into the viewfinder, as if sharpening her vision would reduce the annoying rattle.

And nearly jumped out of her skin when a branch snapped behind her. She whipped her head around, dropping the camera to the safety of the strap around her neck.

Behind her stood a man and a woman, both with buzzed hair and lots of muscles defining what appeared to be some kind of body-skimming black combat gear. They both had an automatic rifle strapped to their torso. Their steely gazes were set on their quarry: her.

"Uh. Hi." *Oh, shit* was more accurate. At least they weren't wraiths. She nudged her own gun under the leaves, out of sight. How could she have missed their approach? She was seriously going to have to get her ears checked.

Layla scrambled up from her kneeling position, brushing earth and twigs off her knees. The camera bounced hard on her chest. Time to put her cover story into effect: lost hiker, now found. Pray they'd go for it. She put an innocent and bewildered expression on her face.

"Ma'am," the female security guard/soldier/scary lady said, "are you aware you're trespassing on private property?"

Yep. Layla gave what she hoped was a disarming shrug and said, "I'm sorry. I had no idea. I was hiking and got kinda turned around."

The woman's lids dropped a fraction. "There are no

public trails within twenty miles. And this facility is bordered by a wall."

"I— I don't like to stick to trails. Too confining. I'm more of a free spirit. And the wall just made me curious." Layla's laugh came out shaky. *Please don't feed me to the wraiths.* "Gets me in trouble sometimes. But point me in the right direction, and I'll be out of here."

"Afraid we can't, ma'am," the man said, his tone final.

"I promise I won't come this way again." Her blood surged, and her bladder cramped. Here was the moment to fight or flee, and she suddenly needed to pee.

Not good.

The man ignored her. "You'll have to come with us."

"Are you going to call the police?" Actually, calling the police wouldn't be too bad. Law enforcement would be much better than whatever Segue could do with her.

"We're going to need your camera, too." The man stretched out his hand, ignoring her question.

Damn. The time stamps on the digital shots would quickly prove she'd been there for hours, not the MO of a lost hiker. To come so close . . .

She held on to the camera and switched to grit. "So I snapped a few shots of the building. It looked cool. Is that a crime?"

"Now," the man said. "Or I will take it from you."

Double damn. No time to pull out the memory card. Layla removed the strap from around her neck and handed over the camera. Wasn't like she could refuse He-man and She-ra. "Will I get the camera back? It was expensive."

"This way," the woman said, turning back into the woods as she took up the lead. The man maneuvered to take up the rear.

"Where are you taking me?"

Neither answered. *Crap.*

Layla swallowed hard and followed.

Agitation bounced like a bright ball in Layla's stomach as she followed the male soldier through the ground floor of what used to be the Fulton Holiday Hotel and was now The Segue Institute. She hadn't counted on getting inside the castle. *Inside* was a scary place to be, but the soldier didn't know that she knew it, so she kept her expression modulated to suit her cover story—anxiety mixed with I-want-to-see-the-man-in-charge self-righteousness. And she had in fact requested to see him.

They passed through several sparsely furnished connected rooms. Afternoon sun fell through tall, arched windows. The effect was lovely, elegant. Her imagination flashed with a scene of fancied-up, turn-of-the-century hotel patrons chatting, strolling, taking tea, a ghostly twist of time. She could almost hear violins, the murmur of voices.

When they reached a set of beautiful, paneled doors, she asked for the twentieth time, "Where are you taking me?"

The guard kept his square jaw shut, his ruddy face neutral and composed.

Great. She could see the headline: JOURNALIST DISAPPEARS IN THE APPALACHIAN MOUNTAINS. The last piece with her name on it would be an obituary.

The guard tapped a code into a panel at the door, and she kept an eyeball on the pattern of his fingers. He typed fast—six digits, the first two a five and a three, the rest obscured by a sudden shift of his body.

He was definitely not buying her story, though she had the sweaty, bedraggled ponytail to prove it. She couldn't help it if she got "lost." If she "wandered" onto the property of a private research facility. If she "happened" to shoot a photo that would've accompanied an article that revealed Segue for what it was.

She attempted to peek around the door before entering, but the guard none too gently nudged her inside. As expected, he closed the door on her plaintive "But, sir, I . . ." and locked her in.

No luck (or pity) there.

Layla turned and surveyed her prison. The room was large and solely furnished with a long table of some dark, varnished wood, surrounded by sleek office chairs. The table probably cost a mint, but then, Adam Thorne had a mint to spend. The rest of the room was similarly Thorne-fabulous, moldings edging the walls, as well as ornately framing the flat expanses all the way to the high ceiling. The floor was made up of glossy wood squares, diagonally arranged in alternating deep and lighter tones. A ballroom with a conference table. Okeydokey.

She shrugged off her backpack, dropping it onto the floor, swiveled the nearest chair out from the table, and collapsed into it. Chairs were lovely things. The long-dry film of sweat that coated her skin cracked with the movement and she caught a whiff of herself. Wow. But very lost hiker–ish.

Now a wait while they decided what to do with her.

kat-a-kat-a-kat-a-kat

Layla leaned forward, her elbows propped on her knees, and massaged her temples. If this kept up, she was going to have a raging migraine.

She lowered her hands and noticed the pale pink band of skin where her engagement ring used to be. A pang of sharp regret hit her hard. She never should have said yes.

Sure, she cared for Ty, but . . . But she couldn't help who she was, and she couldn't change either. Calling it off had been the decent thing to do. She had the engagement ring reminder to show for it, and this one she couldn't take off.

The only thing left was work. Work kept her focused, her mind from wandering, which was becoming a problem. Work was important. She raised her gaze to the ballroom door. She had no patience for waiting. Too long, and she'd begin to *see* things.

On cue, the door clicked and opened. Thank goodness.

Layla was startled to recognize Adam Thorne, the man himself, as he strode in.

She started to rise, but he waved her down, dragged a chair out from the table, and lowered himself into it. He was tall, a little too lean, and had a handsome face lined with stress and worry. Exactly how the man who bioengineered the wraith disease should look—except for the handsome part.

Still playing lost hiker, she sat slowly back into her chair, twitched a smile on her face, and innocently asked, "Can you please tell me where I am? The man who escorted me to this room wouldn't answer any of my questions."

Thorne lifted a brow. Not buying her story either.

In the spirit of plausible deniability, she forged on. "Though, naturally I am very grateful to have been found. I'd been lost for hours. . . ."

Thorne shook his head slightly, raising a hand. "Ms. Mathews, save your breath."

Layla closed her mouth, heart stalling. He knew her name, which she hadn't yet given. The jig was officially up.

"What would possess you to wander unescorted on

private property you know very well is dedicated to wraith research?"

Layla straightened to cover the sudden tremor that ran over her body and lifted her own sarcastic brow in spite of the rapid pounding in her chest. "You let them out to roam the woods?"

"I don't need this today," Adam muttered. He cocked his jaw while he regarded her. "For the record"—he gestured to her backpack—"do you need a little notepad to write this down?"

"I think I can remember," Layla answered, narrowing her gaze as the zaps in her brain got faster. If he wanted her to take notes, he wasn't likely to feed her to the wraiths today. Just give her the official line and then the boot.

Right. She wasn't about to let him off that easy. Not the man who'd released a pandemic on the world. *How to pin him?*

"As our press release clearly states," Thorne began, "Segue researches wraiths and other paranormal phenomena. We have the cooperation and backing of the United States government, as well as formal agreements with seven other countries. We are a target for wraith attacks, as any intelligent person in the know might surmise." He smiled slightly. "Now, once again, why would you roam the private property—in a wild, wooded area, no less—of an institution dedicated to eradicating wraiths?"

"I was drawn by the building's beautiful architecture and fascinating history," she answered as the wheels turned in her head. *Where to start?*

"I'm trying to save your life here."

Layla gave Thorne another smile. "I can take care of myself, thank you."

"All evidence to the con—"

Ah! "What was The Segue Institute's *original* mission?" she interrupted. She didn't expect him to fess up to the calamity of the wraith disease and give her the data to show the world, but maybe she could make a little headway, a small dent in his smug reserve.

Thorne blinked his confusion. "I'm sorry?"

"When you paid a whopping ninety-six million to found Segue nearly eight years ago, what did you plan to do with the place? Do you have a mission statement from that period?"

He frowned. "What are you getting at?"

"The time line established by the World Health Organization places the first cases of the wraith disease at seven, *not eight*, years ago." Layla watched Thorne's face subtly harden. Hit a nerve there. She pinched. "Segue's formation predates the WHO's wraith disease time line. So what were the good scientists at Segue up to during the year before the outbreak?"

Thorne shook his head. "The WHO's time line is off by several years. The wraiths were already firmly entrenched by the time I started Segue. Segue's primary mission has always been to research wraiths."

Layla cleared her voice delicately. This part was fun. "But you just said that you are working in *cooperation* with the U.S. and international governments. Why wouldn't you give the WHO the most accurate information? Presumably others are doing their own research, and identifying ground zero for the wraith outbreak would be critical to those efforts. Why would you, in fact, hamper them?"

Thorne's lips parted but no sound came out.

Gotcha. And so easy. Damn, she was good.

"What you don't know is a lot," Thorne said, standing.

"I hope you don't publish that nonsense and feed public hysteria. People are scared enough." To the closed door he called, "Kev!"

As if she didn't know the mood of the people, with monsters on their doorsteps, their children at risk. Her story was for them. "I'm here to learn."

"I have neither the time nor the patience to educate you," he returned.

The guard was back. Interview over. She could sit there like a dumb rock or meet Thorne at eye level.

"This way, ma'am," Kev said.

Thorne's eyes were cold gray. Last chance. "When you experiment on wraiths, do you consider them to be human test subjects or something else? What protocols do you follow? I'd like to see the wraiths you have here in captivity."

"If you want to see a wraith, Ms. Mathews, you will surely meet one, up close and personal. One last time: I advise you to stop looking."

Which was how Layla found herself on a small Segue plane headed back to New York. They must have known she'd been hunkered down in the woods for a while. Someone from Segue had had the time to go to the inn in Middleton, pack her bag, and have it by her seat when she boarded. With her camera.

How thoughtful.

Layla pressed the power button and queued the saved images. Of which there were none.

Not so thoughtful. She turned the camera off and stuffed it in her backpack.

Seated across from her was a young woman in a

mood more foul than her own. The woman was in her midtwenties and was very pretty in spite of dull black hair with too long blunt bangs over hazel eyes. Her gaze was heavy and angry.

The woman responded to no verbal overtures—*How are you connected to Segue? Do you know the Thornes? Have there been local wraith attacks?*—so Layla finally rested her head back to enjoy the incessant, teeth-grating *kat-a-kat* between her ears.

At dusk they landed at a private airstrip somewhere in Jersey. A cab was waiting to take Layla into the city. Thoughtful again. Segue's heavy boot would take her all the way back to her apartment.

She was just getting in the vehicle, shivering in the gusty, frigid November evening air, when she felt a poke on her shoulder. She turned to find the creepy-moody woman from the plane, her features stark, eyes vivid in the diffused evening light. The contrast punched the woman out of reality, made her gleam with some kind of strange soul aura.

Either this woman was *not* normal, or Layla needed to go back on her meds. No more putting it off.

The visions had plagued Layla all her life, usually occurring at the worst moments when she'd have to strain to ignore whatever hallucinations popped up in order to look normal herself. They seemed so real. Ultrareal. Like now. This weird woman was surrounded by pulsing black light. The aura was part of the impression, but Layla could feel it as well, as a pressure on her chest.

Layla squeezed her eyes shut. Two times in one day. This was really bad.

"You pissed off Adam, right?" the woman asked.

Layla opened her eyes. The soul-glow was gone, thank God, so she answered, "I sure did."

"And you want to find out how the wraiths got started, right?" The woman had been on the Segue Express; it followed that she knew about Segue's work.

Layla straightened fully. "Yes."

The woman glanced over her shoulder, back toward the small airport, nervous. "The public doesn't know anything. I mean *anything.* And why the fuck not? Because Adam-fucking-Thorne says so."

"What doesn't the public know?" Layla wasn't cold at all now.

"And what burns me is that I actually helped that man once. Him and his wife. And now he's got my sister under lock and key."

This got better and better. "Is she a wraith?"

"Abigail?" The woman looked at her, hesitating as if Layla were stupid or crazy. "No. She's sick. Adam's got doctors all over her. And last week some Navajo medicine man."

Layla tried to get her back on track. "What doesn't he want the public to know?"

But the woman ignored her question. "Try the docks. I think he's there."

"Adam?" He was in landlocked West Virginia. "Which docks? Where?"

The woman smiled bitterly. "No. The one who started everything."

"Started what? How?"

"And if you live long enough to break this story, you put my name in your article. I want that controlling bastard to know."

The bastard had to be Adam. "Which docks? Who started it?"

"I want him to see my name in black-and-white. Zoe Maldano. If you survive"—Zoe laughed there—"you tell the world how this happened, and you put my name in your article."

"Yeah, sure, but . . ." Zoe was already striding toward another car, sleek with Thorne money. She slammed the shiny door shut and was taillights before Layla came out of her surprise.

Docks. Adam or someone else was there. And they had information on how all this—the wraith disease?—started.

Layla's head was spinning. She had to get home. Get on her computer. Find out who Zoe Maldano and her sister were, and if there were any links between Thorne or Segue to some docks. The vague reference *docks* would probably need a whiteboard of its own.

The taxi dropped her at her walk-up in the East Village. She tried not to look at Tyler's boxes as she entered her apartment. Maybe it wouldn't hurt so bad if he'd pick up the last of his stuff. Three weeks and the boxes still blocked the door. He hadn't wanted his ring back either. Hadn't even tried to understand what she herself couldn't explain. Three weeks, and she was still so sorry.

Layla dropped her backpack on a box and shuffled into the living room. If she recalled correctly, there was no food in the fridge—Tyler had done the grocery thing—and she was too tired to wait for delivery.

The dining table–cum–desk was covered with her notes, the adjacent wall tagged with photos of possible wraith sightings. At the center was the blurry image of Talia Thorne. Talia, whom she'd give anything to interview up close and in person.

Talia.

Still, two leads in one day: a several-year shift in the wraith disease time line and a motivated informant. Layla smiled. She'd do her research and connect the dots. Then Adam Thorne wouldn't be able to boot her anywhere. Nope. He'd be forced to answer some real questions, and his wife, Talia, would finally have to come out of her shadows and face the light.

kat-a-kat-a-kat-a-kat

Layla gripped her head. Phantom sounds. Visions. She just hoped she could keep her head on straight long enough to tell the story.

Chapter 3

Finished.

The hellgate shook on its posts with a loud, metallic bone rattle that filled Shadowman's mind until he was near mad with the sound. He let the hammer fall from his hand, its impact with the floor mute. All world noise was silenced, overcome by the hideous clanging of the gate.

The *kat-a-kat* morphed, deepening in meaning with new vowels and consonants, and became intelligible, commanding, *Open me!*

The words carried a compulsion that slid cold and coercive into his thoughts, urging him to step forward. To put his blistered palm to the handle. To test the resistance of the mechanism with the weight of his hand.

After the labor of the gate, opening the doorway would be so easy. There would be a strange pleasure, a dark *rightness,* in answering that call: Make a thing; use the thing. Simple.

But Shadowman turned his face away. When he crossed that cursed threshold, he had to be a seethe of intent. He'd enter Hell as fae Death, with Shadow at his back.

Open me!

Not now, Shadowman answered, *but soon.*

At long last, he allowed his weary corporeal body to shred. The atoms of his bone and flesh evaporated into clinging smoke that hovered, man-shaped, in the air, and then dispersed into the deepest corners of the warehouse. His consciousness opened and spread with the loss of his body. It was a relief not to bear the burden of that mass. Mass, the substance and magic of mortality, was difficult to manage for a fae, even one as canny as Death.

In his native Twilight, strength would have come quickly, but he could not leave a passage such as the gate untended. Some weak mortal would find and open it. Instead, he was forced to wait, impatient, as silky layers of Shadow reached through the variegated patches of light and dark, cast by the fire, to cloak him in power again.

He could hear the roar of the fire echoing within the empty warehouse space, the mournful bellow of a ship on the river beyond the docks, and the soft pats of a trio of footsteps moving down the street, the bearers' heartbeats an overlapping, near-tribal drumming of life. The gate's *Open me!* was reduced to an insidious whisper in his mind.

Yes, insidious and perilous. Damnation was infested with devils, twisted souls of those who'd spurned life and love and hope for evil and destruction and pain. Once cut from mortality and delivered to the Hereafter, they existed in agony, suffering eternity by torturing each other.

Soon, Kathleen. I will rescue you.

The heartbeats quickened when they neared the warehouse. The atmosphere became tinged with burgeoning mortal fear. The unease rapidly escalated to terror.

Shadowman cast his attention outward, away from the gate, beyond the walls of the warehouse, to find a young woman pursued on the street by two swarthy thugs. The lust coming off the men reeked like rotted fruit. The woman held her keys like spikes through the fingers in her fisted hand. Her fear pervaded the area like a wild, living thing.

Open me! the gate called in his mind. Death ignored it and observed the woman.

What could have possibly driven her to wander this street, amidst the industry and violence of the docks?

Calloused by eons of experience, he watched as she picked up speed. Death could sense the threads of her life glowing in the ether around her, drawing her toward her final destiny. The lines formed a strange map, forces urging her this way and that, subtle tugs that drew the pattern of her existence to intersect at this point, at this moment.

Why here? Why now? Irrelevant.

A shimmer of dark faelight broke over the dun of the street, visible only to him. A glittering sleeve, a sweep of glossy gold fae hair, the twinkle of madness in an eye. Moira. Fate leered toward him, girlish and laughing. Moira had three faces, but she preferred the young one best. She leaned with her sharp scissors toward the woman's lifeline. Death caught the glint of the silvery blade as the mortal's lifeline was cut, her thread in the tapestry of the world at its ragged end.

It happened to everyone.

The woman must have sensed it herself. She cast her eyes up to the sky, praying no doubt, and strained for breath. Moira had already departed from the world, her work done. The woman, of course, had sought a higher power. Her gaze arced from God to over her shoulder, her mouth parting as she met the hot eyes of her pursuers.

Would she stumble and fall, as so many others had throughout the centuries?

No. The woman leaned into a run. A hopeless flight.

Death marveled as she gathered her terror to her and bore down on it as she ran. Curious that a spirit should burn so bright when closest to death.

Kathleen's had as well. Bright and bold enough to pierce Shadow.

But, like Kathleen, this woman would die. She had to. Moira had cut the thread of her life. It could not be undone.

One of the men, dim by comparison, reached out to grab her jacket.

The woman spun and planted her spiked fist in his face.

Good girl. Fight your Fate, then. Cross in a blaze of glory.

The man reeled back, one hand going to his bloody cheek, the other still clutching her sleeve. The men's lust was threaded with a heat for murder, like a sticky tar to stain the soul.

She peeled out of her jacket as the first man grabbed her flying hair, jerking her suddenly back. She raised that spiked fist again as she shifted her weight. He stopped her at her wrist, and Death grinned in appreciation as her shift of weight moved into a vicious knee to his groin.

She managed four steps before the other man struck her at the back of her neck. She fell, skinning her palms and chin on the pavement. He grabbed her by the ankle, dragged her back to them, and heaved her up by the waist of her pants. Though she kicked and bucked, he pinned her arms with one of his.

From her gut she screamed, a sound that ripped through the atmosphere of the deserted street. The man put a fat palm over her mouth and nose.

Was Kathleen fighting this hard in Hell? Did her spirit still burn bright, or had she dimmed with hopelessness?

The men looked this way and that for a place to enjoy their prey. One tried the door of the warehouse. He kicked at the knob, breaking the lock and splintering the frame.

With a flex of power, Death compelled Shadow to slam the door and bar their entry.

If the hellgate could infiltrate *his* mind—*Open me!* it rattled—then the mortals would be utterly overwhelmed by it. And he was still too weak to fight an army of devils.

When the warehouse door didn't give, the men looked for an alternative. They spotted and quickly agreed upon an alley not far away.

The woman's heart beat as fast as a newborn child's, *shush-shush-shush*, but her eyes were hard. Death could sense the clockwork of her brain, though he had no idea what she thought to do.

She had to know by now it was hopeless.

Hopeless. The word was poison. And today of all days, he could not permit its pollution within the three worlds, not when he fought its contamination himself.

He couldn't save the woman. She would die, if not by these devils in the making, then by some other means, and soon.

One of the men cursed as she bit his finger, and he slapped her face.

If Death had his scythe, he would have cut her quick. Ended this without her experiencing the indignity of the attack. But he would not touch that weapon again; it would keep him from Kathleen. And he was done with death.

The only thing left was to save her, though he would do her no favors by prolonging her demise. It would come, and there were forms that were worse than the one these men intended.

Still. This would take little effort. With cowards like these, almost none at all.

Shadowman cast his attention down the alley, where it terminated on the other side of the street. He found a heap of refuse topped with a length of metal. With a finger of Shadow, he nudged the piece to fall. It clattered on the ground.

The men stilled. The woman's shirt was up above her breasts, though an undergarment kept her nakedness from their eyes.

"Anyone there?" one of the men called.

Death answered by flicking Shadow toward a dank heap of cardboard.

"It's only a rat," the other man said. But they both stared down the alley, eyes squinting for signs of movement.

Rats would be fitting. Death organized the darkness into a swell of vermin, a river of scrabbling claws and gleaming eyes, and then sent them coursing toward the men.

"Fuck!" one shouted, shrill, rearing back, and landed on his backside when the woman gave him a hard kick to his chest. Then he fled, swatting at the Shadows scampering over his body.

The other had already ducked out of the alley and was running down the street, glancing over his shoulder, with no care for his friend.

Done.

When both were gone, the woman slowly sat up, squinting into the dark.

A long moment passed, her fear and anger dissolving into an acute sense of isolation and vulnerability. She pulled her shirt down, drew her limbs in, and made a ball of her body, hands gripping her head. Visible shivers wracked her. Tears streamed down her face, and she wiped her nose with a knuckle.

She snorted at herself. "Ty was right. What the hell am I doing?"

Hell, indeed. The gate went *kat-a-kat*.

"I swear this story is going to kill me."

She rested her head against the brick. Black smudges winged from her eyes.

It was time for the woman to go home. To see her loved ones. To make the most of the hours or days he'd won her with Shadow. The only other person for whom he'd held back Twilight had been Kathleen. How fitting that he should do it again on the eve of Kathleen's liberation.

The woman examined her skinned palms, then used the wall to stand. After stepping to the end of the alley, she peeked around the corner. Shadowman noticed her gaze drop to her discarded coat. A lick of anger had her straightening. She glanced both ways, then walked resolutely to the fallen material and picked it up. She retrieved her dropped keys as well, refashioning the spikes between the fingers of her shaking, fisted hand.

She couldn't possibly be thinking of continuing on, could she? Was she deranged?

But she seemed frozen in front of the building, eyeing the facade.

Perhaps the hellgate had her in its grip.

The woman put her free hand on the knob and tried the broken door, bitterly muttering, "Thanks for opening it for me, guys."

Shadowman waved a hand and compelled darkness to hold it shut again.

But she effortlessly pushed the door open anyway.

* * *

Layla swallowed hard and opened the busted door. The cold knob soothed the skinned heat of her palm, but it didn't ease her fear-cramped stomach or get rid of the deep ick of the men's touch. That would take a long shower. Or ten.

At least she'd be able to hide in there if those assholes came back. Not smart about her gun, though, which was still in the woods somewhere around Segue. There had been no wraith attacks near the docks, but she hadn't considered normal violence, everyday predators. Not smart at all.

She dabbed at her chin. It wasn't bleeding, but it sure stung. And if those guys hoped she hadn't gotten a good look at their faces for a police report, they'd picked the wrong girl. Noticing details was her job. She could and would give a description down to the mole above one guy's unibrow and the tat on the other's hairy forearm.

The memory of his hand on her mouth made her nauseated. Common sense told her she shouldn't be there, especially not alone.

If I get through today alive, I promise to get therapy.

kat-a-kat-a-kat-a-kat

Maybe the shrink could help with that, too.

Light from the street fell into the interior, but it wasn't enough to get an impression of the space. The air smelled faintly smoky. She swiped her hand on the walls near the door, felt a kind of humid griminess, but no light switch.

Good thing she had a backup. She fished in her jacket pocket, produced a small flashlight, and pressed the button. The flashlight had a strong but narrow beam, so she had to cut the darkness to get a hint of what was around her.

Her immediate vicinity was dusty and bare. Rope. Some chain. Rotted wooden pallets stacked in a corner.

Whatever had been there once had been cleared out long ago. Except for the *kat-a-kat* in her head, the warehouse was silent.

According to Zoe, she was supposed to be looking for a person. A *he*, in particular.

He who? Another disgusting street thug? Layla doubted it.

Research hadn't helped and Zoe was nowhere to be found for further questioning. This dockside warehouse was the nearest of Thorne's considerable assets to New York City. If this wasn't it, she could try a couple other places farther away, but she wasn't hopeful. The lead was simply too vague.

"Hello?" she said, but her voice didn't carry. She wasn't keen on shouting either. The place felt claustrophobic despite its size. Much better to tiptoe forward, then run like hell should anyone appear.

She moved farther, swinging the light left and right. Just more empty, dirty space. The smoke thickened in the air as she progressed. Above, to one side of the building, was a row of high windows. Even though it was midmorning, no light seeped through them. Spooky.

Metal debris clanged underfoot. She swished the light to her feet to find a curling, black piece of metal.

Curious, she toed it. The piece rolled to the side. The curls became open leaves around a strange, wrought-iron flower.

She stooped and picked up the creation. The flower should have been cold, like the weather and the room, but it was warm, near hot. It was heavy too, larger than her palm, and clearly made by hand. A black flower, delicate and . . . wicked. A treasure left behind as junk.

When she brought her attention back up, she noticed a low-licking fire, its glow barely lifting the press of darkness. And nearby an anvil, flat and wide, with a horn on one end. On its surface lay a hammer.

A blacksmith's workshop. On the New Jersey docks. In one of Thorne's warehouses. It made no sense whatsoever.

"Hello?" This time she called loud and clear. The smith had to be near. No one would leave an open fire unattended in this old building.

kat-a-kat-a-kat-a-kat answered her. This time it wasn't in her head.

Shocked, Layla turned, and though the warehouse was matted with shadows, she could easily see a gate looming black and beautiful before her. The iron portal shook on its posts. How could she have not seen it until now? The sound should have been audible from the street.

Even to her untrained eye, she could tell that the gate had been crafted by a master. The vertical pieces were tall, barbed spears, made for war. But laced among the black shafts, giving them structure and support, were twisted vines. An occasional gorgeous bloom, like the one in her hand, faced outward.

The gate trembled, as if alive. Her bones trembled with it. She tried to turn away, but her stiffened muscles wouldn't obey.

kat-a-kat-a-kat-a-kat

It called to her, had been in her head for days. She knew now that it would never let her go. It was *made* for her.

Never alone again, it said.

Her eyes teared. She felt exposed, the hole in her chest so easily revealed. She crossed her arms over the pain. Ty had tried to fill it, had offered her a fantasy of children, a happy life without the drive of her dangerous work.

kat-a-kat: Never alone.

But Ty wasn't the answer. He was just a nice guy. And she was his challenge.

Home, the gate promised.

The gate knew her. If she opened it, her isolation would be at an end.

The darkness around seemed to shift, as if something or someone was coming—the street thugs or dreaded wraiths even—but she couldn't so much as lift her flashlight to pierce the dark.

Her deepest wish could come true.

kat-a-kat, the gate explained, and Layla understood perfectly. The gate was meant to be opened. Why else make a gate, except to open it?

The shadows churned, whipped, and lashed.

Layla dropped her flashlight and stretched out her hand as she stepped closer. A turn of that twisted, black metal and her lifetime longing would be at an end.

"Don't," a man said in her ear.

Where he came from, Layla had no idea and didn't care. His urgent, low voice was compelling and familiar, but the pull of the gate was stronger.

"It is evil," he explained.

"Can't be," Layla answered. Her every cell quaked with expectation. She took another step.

The man's voice came out of the shadows. "You fought those men on the street. Fight this."

kat-a-kat: Open me! Now!

Layla shuddered, eyes tearing again in awe of the livid creation. There was no way to explain this feeling. It was much easier to keep it simple. "I don't want to fight it."

Shadowman knew he never should have saved her. Meddling with Fate always had repercussions. The woman should be dead in the street, her body slack, her soul just entering Twilight.

And now she was clearly going to open the gate to Hell. The thing must have insinuated itself into her weak mortal mind.

Death gathered Shadow to him until the mass of darkness snapped and thrashed in his grasp. He sent it rolling toward her, to crush her, to knock her from her path to the gate.

If it had any effect, she did not let on. Her reaction was the same as it had been at the door. The same as with his repeated attempts to impede her progress through the warehouse. She was impervious.

He could not use Shadow against her and didn't have the time to figure out why.

There would be no retrieving Kathleen if devils poured out into the world. He was work weakened, gate plagued, and he didn't even have his scythe.

He'd kill her himself if he had to. And with the gate's control over her mind, he most likely would.

Shadowman poured his strength into forming a body. Lungs to move air. Tongue and teeth to shape words. Hands to throttle her with. The body he created was the one most familiar to him, the one created from Kathleen's imagination, the hero of her dreams. Better still would have been the terrors other people made of Death. Monsters of deepest nightmare. Something to scare her into submission.

"Don't," he repeated in her ear. His spine cracked into place. His legs assumed the weight of a man.

But her arm was already outstretched. Her hand gripped black metal. The cursed lever turned.

He threw himself toward the gate as her weight shifted back.

The woman turned to face him, still gripping the metal behind her, her confusion and terror bleeding into the shadows. Where before her heart had calmed, now it raced again. "I . . . I'm sorry."

A queer deathlight lit her features, illuminating, stripping away the mortal coil of her life, shining through her fresh, pink flesh as if the atoms had little substance at all, revealing her soul.

It cannot be.

And Shadowman slammed the gate shut again. Held it closed with his greater strength while the woman trembled in the cage of his arms, her lips parted, breath frozen mid-inhalation.

But too late. Something *wrong* was in the room with them. A presence edged with bloody menace. A devil.

Shadowman almost didn't care, not as the woman got her first good look at him. Her mind functioned as all other mortal minds did, remaking Death to her conception of him, and for once in almost thirty years, his Shadows nearly obeyed. Such was the power of mortals. Shadowman had held Kathleen's conception of his physical form, her dark prince, since their meeting. Kathleen, who had named him. Kathleen, who had loved him.

But now, this woman . . . here, today . . . threatened to shred him completely and make him over to fit *her* idea of Death.

Of course he had to forgive her, escaped devil and all. He had to forgive her everything and damn himself, holding on to his favored body with every iota of power he had, lest the woman see a beast and know his true nature.

No wonder his Shadow could not stop or harm her. His Shadow had ever sheltered her.

Kathleen was not in Heaven. And Kathleen was not in Hell.

She'd kept her promise. She'd found a way back. She'd

traded her memories for a slim chance, a small hope that they'd meet once more.

Shadowman's gaze raked the woman's face, memorizing her new features. She had wide-set, gray eyes in a narrow face, a small nose, defined cheekbones and jaw. Sweet, full lips. Dimpled chin. And a mess of light brown hair waving to her shoulders.

He gripped the gate to Hell for a little calm.

Kathleen was not dead.

She'd been reborn.

Chapter 4

"How did you find me?" The blacksmith's gaze roved her face. Firelight cast a flickering band across his features, but Layla could make out slightly tilted black eyes, tensed with strong emotion. Her heart stumbled in reaction; the intensity of his gaze was painfully familiar and cut straight to her core. A sudden fierce burn rushed along her nerves, so when he shifted to stroke her hair, her shock allowed the intimacy.

"I don't know what you're talking about. I didn't mean to—" She was shaking with confusion. The attack on the street must have been worse than she'd thought, because the rattling gate, the strange blacksmith, the impenetrable dark . . . She was used to her visions, fighting them, compartmentalizing the real world from the aberrations she saw from time to time. This was different.

"Kathleen. Tell me you remember." His voice was husky.

She felt his fingers lightly stroke the side of her cheek. Where he touched, sensation spread, sensuous and enticing. Her blood sang as heat flooded her, humming through her system in a gorgeous awakening of want and need. This was too much, way too much, so she turned her head away.

The gate behind her breathed against her body, a living thing. *Throw me wide.* The voice hurt her head. *I was made for you.* This wasn't right; gates did not speak, did not simmer with life. She understood that now and gritted her teeth against the compulsion to obey.

"Be at ease, Kathleen," the man said. "You've nothing to fear. I'll take care of everything."

She gave a tight shake of her head. This, at least, she knew, and it was a start at getting things straight. "I'm not Kathleen. You must have me mistaken for someone else."

And she could take care of herself; she had since she was a kid. She found her spine and slapped his hand away from her face to prove it. What had gotten into her? She didn't know this man, and he certainly didn't know her. Why did his open arms seem like a haven of safety and comfort?

"I am not mistaken." His lips curved into a slight smile. A smile. Here. In this black hole, with this . . . this *thing* burning at her back.

The man was out of his mind, and so was she to respond. She had to be very clear. "Get the hell away from me."

The smile grew fierce. "Same spirit."

Drugs. It had to be. Something in the air was causing her to hallucinate. That's why she felt this way. She needed to get out of this smoke, breathe clean, industrial smog and rancid river, and then maybe her head would clear. She peered into the darkness beyond him. The exit, she hoped, was that way.

kat-a-kat: You'll be alone forever. Throw me wide.

"No!" Though she didn't know whom she answered. If she could just get out. Find her car. Then maybe—

"Shhh. Be still." The man raised his hand again, but

hesitated, holding it in the air over her heart. Or maybe he wanted to cop a feel. What was it with men today?

She gripped her flashlight, but found she held the iron flower instead. Fat lot of good that would do her unless she could knock him out with it, then . . .

. . . *then throw me wide.*

Yes, then open the gate wide.

A sudden bright light caught her attention, a door opening in the dark. So white-bright it made her eyes tear. What now?

"Damn fool angel," the blacksmith growled under his breath.

Angel? He was absolutely, unequivocally stark raving—

Layla didn't have time to dodge the swift caress of his fingers to her forehead. "Sleep," he commanded.

Even as her mind sparked with anger against his touch, her legs gave in a watery whoosh and she fell into darkness.

Shadowman caught Kathleen's fluid drop and lifted her against his chest. Elation had him humming, trembling with excitement. He had to check himself so he wouldn't crush her body.

"That her?" Custo asked as he approached. His gaze quickly flicked to the gate, hardened, then returned to Shadowman.

"Yes," Death breathed.

Custo's doubt and impatience infused the crowded Shadows. "Then why is she mortal? And why is she out cold?"

"I cast her into sleep so the gate wouldn't plague her

while I dealt with you. And she wasn't in Hell after all." Shadowman drew deep to inhale her scent; under the cloying perfumes of modernity was tangy, feminine sweat, turned slightly with fear. "She came to me."

Custo's doubt redoubled and his brow lifted. "If you build it, she will come?"

Shadowman frowned. The boy was laughing at him.

"Talia is twenty-eight." Custo jutted his chin toward Kathleen. "Shouldn't she be in her fifties?"

The woman in his arms was indeed young, fresh, new to the world. "She was reborn."

"Reincarnated? That's very rare. Damn near unheard of. Are you certain it's her?"

Shadowman did not deign to answer a second time. As if he wouldn't recognize the woman who'd changed everything for him. Kathleen.

"Okay, it's her. Bully for you." Custo's gaze moved to the gate. "So that thing wasn't necessary after all?"

"The gate drew her, did it not?"

"Next time make a compass. Leave Hell and its devils alone, please."

A sear on his senses told Shadowman there were more of Custo's kind massing outside the warehouse. The jumble of heartbeats confirmed it. They had come for the gate, but somehow he knew they'd refuse him Kathleen as well. They could not have her. He'd fight them if they tried to take her.

"They're coming," Custo said. "You'd better get her out of here."

"The gate?"

"We'll take care of it. No way it's staying here, vulnerable." His gaze dropped to Kathleen. "And I think your attention is going to be elsewhere."

The boy was ever naive. To transfer the keeping of something so drenched in power could never be that easy; such creations were bound to their maker. The gate would have to be *unmade,* which was a great deal more difficult than merely dismantling the metal.

But the angel would have to learn that the hard way. Shadowman would take his reprieve to be with Kathleen. To help her remember. She had to remember.

Shadowman reached into the darkness, parting the veil. "The hammer is on the anvil."

He watched as Custo strode over and gripped the hateful tool.

Now only the devil remained, but Shadowman could deal with it on his own. The devil would wreak havoc with any it encountered, and so needed to be put down immediately. Otherwise, Kathleen would blame herself for the lives it took.

But Custo need not know about that either. Knowledge of the devil would prolong the angels' stay.

Death stepped into darkness, his woman clutched at his chest.

"Wait," Custo called.

Shadowman paused but didn't turn.

"Where can I find you?"

As if he would ever let that happen before he was ready. "I'll be in Shadow."

How to begin? How to help her remember?

Shadowman laid Kathleen on the soft earth under the glittering boughs of the dark trees. Fae voices murmured on the rise and gust of the wind.

This incarnation of Kathleen would have her own idea

of Death, created by this life's experiences, fears, hopes for her future. Of all that, he knew nothing, and so could not chance revealing himself.

At least in Twilight, Shadow sustained him. His form would be easier to hold. He filled his essence with the dark stuff. He'd need every bit until she remembered him and what they were to each other. *Please.*

Her sickroom? Kathleen had loathed it.

Then where? What could possibly reach her? He'd have to work quickly. Too long in Shadow and a mortal would go mad.

He cast his gaze down. Kathleen's head was tilted to the side, her lips were slightly parted, and her eyelids fluttered as she dreamed. The wavy swath of her hair gleamed gold in Twilight. Her hips were turned, narrowing her waist and accentuating the swell of her breasts. She was Sleeping Beauty all over again.

And then he knew. Kathleen's fantasy when she was a girl. He'd start there, where he'd been her hero.

Layla woke in fairyland. She raised a hand to her groggy head but stopped short when she saw the princess sleeve with pointed cuff of the—her gaze examined the rest of her attire—gaudy yellow princess dress she wore. There was a slight weight on the crown of her head, and she knew, given the atrocity of her getup, that it had to be a tiara. Or, hell, worse—one of those satin cones they sold at the Renaissance Fair, ribbons coming out of the tip.

Obviously she was asleep and in the middle of a nightmare.

Fact of the matter was she'd been working too hard. The signs had been there for a while. The events of the last few days only confirmed it. Her recent breakup hadn't helped either. If she didn't let up soon, she was going to have a nervous breakdown. Considering all the things she'd been seeing lately, maybe this was it.

She struggled against the billows of fabric to stand on two feet. She didn't know, but could guess, that she was wearing some sort of slippers completely unsuited to a dark and dense forest. Her waist was cinched tight with a wide ribbon, the bow blooming from her backside.

Maybe when she was three she'd have enjoyed a dress like this, all princess and fairy tales. But not for long. Weak damsels in distress that lay around waiting to be saved made her want to scream. She hated feeling weak. Helpless.

"Okay, Layla, wake up," she said aloud to herself.

She scanned the area but saw only crowding trees and darkness. The trees were weirdly familiar, as if she'd seen them all her life, but couldn't place where. Among them, like an ashen vampire, tall, narrow, and wrapped in a cloak, was the blacksmith from the warehouse. At least, the tortured gaze was the same, resting heavy and soulful on her. Shadows still concealed the rest, but somehow she could guess that his body would be dreamworthy. All that physical labor at the fire, pounding metal day in, day out. Yes, very nice.

She ached with a beat of need, as if part of her were already leaning toward him, but she held herself back. She didn't have that easy, warm-comfy feeling of bed. She couldn't recall making it home from the warehouse, much less outside the building to her car. The dream, like the dress, felt like a trap. She'd learned a long time ago to trust her instincts.

"Wakey, wakey," she sang, eyeing the blacksmith while denying the coil winding tight in her pelvis.

"You don't remember." The man sounded like he was in pain.

No, so tell me. "Remember what?"

"Anything. Your life as Kathleen."

Kathleen again. This *was* a nightmare. "For the last time, I'm not Kathleen. I'm Layla Mathews. *Lay-la.*" She exaggerated that last bit with her mouth. How could she want a man who didn't even know her name?

"Lay-la." His rough, wounded delivery made her wonder about this Kathleen chick. The woman had obviously broken his heart.

"Listen—"

"No." He swiped the air with his hand. "I was mistaken. This is not the way to reach you."

Now they were getting somewhere. Layla sighed relief.

"We will just have to begin again," he said, and darkness inundated her vision.

Shadowman patted Layla's cheek to wake her. Layla, not Kathleen. *Layla.* The name was made of tip-of-the-tongue sounds, rather than the throat pull of his beloved. So different. How could she be different?

He closed his eyes and drew what strength he could from the earthbound shadows. The gate had cost him much. Reforming his body had cost him more. Holding it for any length of time would be very, very difficult.

"Come now," he said. "Wake." He'd crouched near Layla's fallen form and gently lifted her shirt to bare her skin and the white undergarment that snugged her breasts, though he knew doing so would embarrass her later. He should have sent the human vermin who'd attacked her deep into the river and let the ghosts within the flows grasp at the rapists' limbs until the men drowned. Too bad it wasn't their time.

Layla turned her head in the alley dirt.

"You're all right," he said to counter the confusion billowing out of her. The woman had a strong mind and a stronger will. He could not blot out the memory of the hellgate or Kathleen's fairy tale, however brief, but he could make her doubt they had ever really happened. They would seem like dreams to her. Would she succumb to this adjustment in her reality?

"Mother of—" she groaned, her lids lifting as her face contracted in a wince.

"They're gone now," he said. Long gone.

She laboriously shifted up onto an elbow, then must have perceived her partial nakedness, because she scuttled back toward the concrete wall pulling her shirt down. Expression tight with shame and anger, she said, "Who are you?"

Simple question, yet he had no answer to give. Kathleen's "Shadowman" would sound absurd to Layla's ear. Instead, he asked, "Can you stand? My place is just there." He lifted a hand toward the warehouse. "You would be comfortable, and we could call"—this was a gamble, for he had no modern contrivances to make good on the offer—"for aid."

She lifted herself along the wall to standing and held up the palm of a scraped hand. "Just stay back."

"I will not harm you." He allowed her a very small distance between them. "We can summon the"—what did they call them in this age?—"police."

"Police." She nodded agreement, visibly swallowing. "Police would be good. Those guys can't have gone far."

He gestured to the building.

"Right." Layla lurched into a walk, glancing once furtively over her shoulder and murmuring, "Had the weirdest nightmares."

"You hit your head." He felt her internal denial, then a surge of determination as she attempted to collect her confused impressions into some other order. The gate, her moments in Kathleen's fairy-tale fantasy—yes, with a spark of desire that made him fight a grin. Then her frustration. The only reasonable answer was the one he was giving her, and Layla, he'd discovered, preferred reason whereas Kathleen lived for dreams.

She stopped at the door, gaze dropped on the knob. What had been broken, he'd used Shadow to make whole again, though only in appearance. He had no lasting hold in the mortal world. Now he was using everything he had to hold his body.

She stepped back, shaking her head. Disquiet and confusion infused the air. "I don't want to go in there."

Of course she didn't. The last time she had, she'd faced a gate to Hell. Touched it and released something evil. But the gate was gone, now in the angels' keeping.

"You need to sit down," he said, reaching around her and twisting the knob. He pushed the door open to let her view the changed interior.

She startled, swayed, and grabbed for the door frame. He would never let her fall.

"You had better go inside."

Still she hesitated. This was the moment she would have to decide what was real and what was false. Would she hold to the memory of the bare, dirty space and the hellish gate, or would she take this more reasonable illusion, made from a glossy image in a moldered magazine scrap: "Bachelor Pad Goes Old World."

"Who did you say you were?"

"I'm an artist," he answered. That's what Kathleen had been.

"I meant your name."

He had none to give but Shadowman and variations of Death, neither acceptable. He needed something else, and fortunately he had a great catalogue from which to choose—the names of the souls he'd taken into his keeping, however briefly, as they crossed from the mortal world, through faery Twilight, to the Hereafter. One stood out: a fighter, a leader, a gambler, and cunning enough to challenge Death.

"Khan."

Layla snorted. "As in Genghis?"

Yes. But instead he lied. The fae were excellent deceivers. "It is common enough where I come from."

And so he became Khan, artist. It was much better than the alternative, Death. If he could not control his Shadows, that's exactly who he would be.

Layla stepped over the threshold, looking around to take in the trappings of his residence. He had to admit, the style, drenched in the memory of the old world, suited him. The furniture was framed in thick, scrolled wood. The fabrics were rich with deep color: burgundy, royal blues, and burnt golds. A large medieval tapestry hung on the wall, its roaring lions and crest faded with time. Candlesticks littered a nearby table, upon which a map was unfurled, the unknown expanses of sea and land marked by monsters. Holding the corners down were a stack of books and the sculpted head of Buddha, the "awakened one."

Layla wrapped her arms around herself. "How can you live here? Eventually someone's going to rob you. Aren't you afraid you'll be murdered in your sleep?"

Khan smiled. "I am in no danger. For the most part"—*you being the exception*—"I've been left alone. May I ask why you ventured into such a dangerous area?"

"Insanity." She fidgeted in place, worrying the frayed neckline of her shirt. "You didn't happen to see my coat or bag outside, did you?"

He had, and he'd put them aside. "No."

"Well, can I use your phone?" She looked around again, as if searching for it.

She'd chosen reality, and now he had to produce it. Khan reached for Shadow and mentally exhaled, and the object materialized in his palm. He lifted the phone, as if from a pocket, and held it out, saying, "Really, why are you here?" He needed her to acknowledge some small part of their connection, the pull that had drawn her to him.

She took the phone, concentrating on its face. "Wraiths. I'm doing a story on them."

"I don't understand." The gate hadn't called her?

"I'm a journalist. I got a lead that the source of the wraiths might be here, so I decided to check it out." She hit the buttons with growing frustration. "How do you power this thing on?"

Wraiths. The cursed empty husks of used-to-be people. They plagued his daughter and her family but would not venture near Death. They'd given their souls for immortality, but he could still cast them out of the world. This warehouse was likely the safest structure on Earth from wraiths.

"I think it's dead," she concluded. Of course it was; the phone was a good facsimile, but he could not simulate the energy it required, nor the signals she needed it to send. "Do you have a landline?"

"I'm sorry, I don't." If indeed she came for information

on the wraiths, another great power had to have directed her his way. Because he could not believe, not for a moment, that she was here by chance. Not his Kathleen.

"Well, is there a pay phone nearby? Without my keys, I'll need to call a locksmith or tow truck for my car."

"What car?" The source that had brought her here had to be a formidable power, the same that had cut her lifeline, even as she was delivered, once again, to him. Moira.

Layla half turned toward the door. "It's just up the block."

He gave a little shake of his head. The vehicle was there, but his Shadow concealed it.

"Oh no," she said, whirling to the door and out to the sidewalk, staring down its length. Her hands went into her hair, disbelief and anger radiating out of her. "Stole my piece-of-crap car. My camera was in there. Damn it!"

Fate was meddling in Kathleen's life again. And thus their story would begin anew: Kathleen, no, *Layla,* on the brink of death, and he, powerless to stop it. But this time, Layla had no idea who or what he was.

"I think I can help," Khan said. This Layla was a resourceful woman. Sooner or later, she would find a way out of her predicament. Probably sooner.

"Not if you don't have a phone, you can't." Her smile was at odds with the irritation that sparked around her.

"I meant the wraiths," he clarified. If information would hold her here, so be it. "I know who made them, and why."

Layla took a few steps back inside the warehouse. "Excuse me?"

Her gut told her that Khan was just saying what he thought she wanted to hear. He'd have to offer something solid before she'd believe a word he said. Something was off about him, about the room, about her memory. She didn't always trust her senses, which occasionally produced some odd spectacles, especially lately, but her instincts were usually dead-on.

Khan stripped off his slim-fitting black leather jacket and tossed it across a fat chair. The long-sleeve gray shirt beneath was molded to his body, while the cut of his slacks skimmed over his admirable physique. His build was long and tall, thickening just enough for bulk and tone. His features were foreign, almost Asian, uncanny eyes glinting, but with Western dimensions and sculpting. And in this light, his skin had the faint teak of some other nationality.

Again she was aggravated by a sense of displaced familiarity. He was beyond hot—he was lust-cious—so if she'd seen this man before, she was sure she'd remember him. She'd sure remember the curl of want in her belly and the finger tingles that urged her to stroke his ridiculously long hair. He wasn't even her type.

"You don't believe me?" He raised a brow. The tilt of his head sent that black hair sliding over his shoulder, and she had to admit it suited him. Some women might like it. Some men, probably, too.

She shrugged. "I'm listening."

He hesitated, as if choosing his words carefully. "I can't tell you much, as most of what occurred must remain secret, but I will say that the spread of the wraiths halted two years ago because Talia Kathleen Thorne killed their maker."

Layla's mind briefly flashed blank in shock, then worked furiously to assimilate and judge his statement. The wraith spread did seem to halt about two years ago. But the rest? Talia had killed someone? Could it be true?

Was that the reason Adam Thorne kept her hidden from the public?

"You know Talia Thorne?"

"Certainly." He smiled a bit. Drew out the moment as if to prick her interest.

"How?" Her interest was pricked already.

"I'm her father."

Rose Petty dug her nails into a rotting wood post, slipped on the slimy wet mud, and buried splinters in her hands and bare feet as she climbed from the river. She crawled onto a ratty dock on her elbows, her hands too bloody to hold her weight, and collapsed into a fetal position. Her naked body quivered in the chilly air and her teeth chattered *kat-a-kat-a-kat-a-kat.*

Stupid, stupid. She never should have made for the river. The burn of her reformation had been excruciating, but no water could possibly douse it. She'd only drown herself and die forever. That's what you risked when you came back. Soul dead. Even Hell was better, not that she'd ever belonged there. If she'd screamed it once, she'd screamed it a thousand times: There'd been a mistake. She had to do those things. It was self-defense. She didn't belong in Hell.

Never mind. She was out now. No rivers. Lesson learned.

Her new body shook with the cold—*kat-a-kat-a-kat-a-kat.* Her muscles cramped in contraction. Gooseflesh swept viciously across her skin.

Warm. She had to get warm.

Trembling, she pulled her feet beneath her, pushed herself up a bit by her wrists, and careened to standing.

Docks. An empty gray expanse lay before her, dotted

with orange and blue cargo containers piled up among rotting pallets, decaying in the cold, wet air.

She needed clothes. Shelter. Food.

She wiped her running nose on the back of her damp arm and stumbled forward. Across the lot she could make out a door. An office.

Okay, knock on that door, get help. Get warm, she told herself.

Sheeeiiiiit, nice little piece of ass.

Rose turned, belly clutching, and put an arm across her breasts and a shaking hand splayed at her crotch as she looked for the voice. Saw no one.

Pretty titties, too. Gots to get me some o' that.

What the—? She stopped herself before she swore; a lady didn't swear, no matter how pressed. But this was too strange: The voice was in her head, though not hers. Like maybe her mind got wired wrong when her body reformed itself. Or maybe she just came back different.

Her gaze flicked from glinting window to dull doorway, but she found the source sitting in a car, lighting up a cigarette. A paunchy old man, skin going yellow. *Tsk. Tsk.* Probably too much drink. Had to be him, what with the way his beady eyes stared at her. Maybe this mind-reading trick was okay. Might just be useful. It revealed what she already knew. That he was no gentleman. He was sick and low to think of her like that.

Girl's got all the right parts.

How dare he? Anger ran hot through her veins, warming her just enough to loosen her stride. A woman drags herself naked and bleeding out of the river and the man can't get off his lazy behind to help? Maybe lend his coat? She could get sick and die (forever).

His clothes would do. He certainly didn't deserve them. The car meant shelter and transportation, too. Get her out of this awful place. She limped toward him, dropped her covering arm and hand when she got near the car so he could get one last good look.

Gonna get lucky, lucky, lucky.

The man mopped his reddening face. Licked his lips. Rolled down the window.

Come to papa.

It was self-defense all over again. He screamed a little, which was only human. Even with all the dark acts she'd seen in the fires Beyond, she really couldn't blame him.

Chapter 5

The eyes. That had to be it, why he seemed so familiar, why she couldn't shake the sense that she'd been here before. Those slightly tilted eyes were the same as Talia Thorne's. "You're Talia's *father*?"

Khan took a seat in one of his big chairs, leaned back, arms wide on the rests, and crossed his legs with an ankle to the other knee. Big chair, but he managed to dominate it as a king does a throne. Arrogant. "I am."

Layla kept the skepticism from her face. *Father* would put him in middle age, and he sure didn't look it. Either he kept himself very well, or he was lying. Nevertheless, her informant, Zoe, had been right: there was something to be learned about the wraiths in this dockside warehouse. That Khan knew to drop Talia's name was proof. She played along. "Do you know who started the wraith war?"

His expression darkened. "Yes. I am responsible. I and I alone."

Disbelief mellowed the pop of shock that hit Layla. Zoe had said she'd find the source here, too, but . . . this guy? Really? "How?"

He sighed. "You would not understand."

"*Try me.*" Layla felt his gaze on her, searching, debating. She wanted to press but let the silence work for her instead.

"No," he finally answered, and she swore inwardly. "Explanations will not work. Not with my family, not with the wraiths. You would have to stay with me and experience it for yourself."

Stay with him? "But why? You know I'd have to expose what you've done." *What you* claim *you've done.*

He smiled, a slow pull of his sensuous mouth, heavy with meaning. "I doubt very much you'll do that."

Oh, please. Yes, she could admit that on some level she was attracted to him. Fine. But nothing was going to happen.

"I'm sorry. I have to write my story in good faith, as the facts present themselves." There was too much shoddy reporting going on about wraiths already, some of it resorting to paranormal explanations, which simply didn't cut it. Wraiths were the product of a disease, not a supernatural event. Period.

His face grew serious. "Do not misunderstand me. You can reveal whatever you like. I believe, however, that you will choose to refrain. Sometimes a little deception is called for."

"You still haven't answered my question. Why would you want to do this?"

He leaned forward, braced his elbows on his knees, gaze sharpening on hers. "That's one of the things you'll have to find out. The most important of all."

Layla stepped back, considering. She didn't trust him, or his offer. And especially his motives. But she didn't have anything left to lose and no reason to go home. "So you want me to stay with you . . ."

". . . and I want you to promise that you will see your story through to the end. That you won't run from what is revealed until you have all your answers."

"Will I meet Talia Thorne?"

"It stands to reason; we'll be staying at Segue."

Now he was talking. If he wanted to seduce her, he should have led with Segue. Talia was the ungettable get. For her, Layla would agree to almost anything. "When?"

"Now." He stood and approached. "But I want your promise that you will see this through. You will discover things . . . uncomfortable to your sensibilities. It will change you."

Layla had to tilt her head to look up at him. Meet Talia today. Yes. Okay. And if he didn't produce, she'd have reason to back out. And all she'd have to do was endure his melodrama.

"I agree."

"Swear it."

"I swear I'll stick with you until I learn the truth about the wraiths, provided that I meet Talia Thorne today." How he was going to pull that one off, she had no idea. Talia Thorne was in West Virginia and they were in New Jersey.

That familiar smile tweaked his lips again. "Done."

A moment hung in the air between them. Layla didn't have a good feeling about this. Not at all. Her palms still smarted from her skidding fall during the attack. Her sweater was dirty, the neckline pulled out of shape. And without her phone and gun, she was unarmed. At least at Segue, she'd be a lot closer to her Glock, though she didn't think they'd let her out to fetch it.

They'd need to get to the airport soon. The police report would have to wait. Tomorrow morning, for sure. Her attackers could not be left to prey on other women.

Khan made no motion to get his own car keys. Layla prompted him with a drawn out, "So . . . ?"

"Yes. So." He inhaled a slow breath, then asked with an air of great deliberation, "Do you believe in magic?"

Layla never answered questions like that.

"Of course you do," he answered for her. "Or will, shortly."

Something flickered at the edge of Layla's vision. A free-standing mirror, gilt framed. She hadn't noticed it before. Weird.

"I imagine you need your things?"

Layla shrugged. Would be nice.

"Where do you live?"

As a rule she didn't tell sources or strange men where she lived. She answered vaguely. "New York City."

Khan gestured to the mirror. "Well, let us go and get them."

Layla stood in place. Yeah, she wanted to go, but it seemed like he wanted her to look in the mirror first. When still he hesitated, she ducked her head for a quick, obligatory peek. As she pulled back, what she'd seen registered.

Not a silvery, reflective surface. The mirror was full of dark trees. Familiar trees. She knew those trees.

Layla stepped directly in front of the glass to get the full effect. The trees had realistic depth, though the coloring was fanciful, as if deep jewel-toned light emanated from within them. Actually, the setting reminded her of her silly princess dream. Hadn't Khan been there, too? *Weird.* The mirror had to be some sort of plasma screen. A moving window. She could get her computer monitor to look like a fish aquarium, and she'd seen similar things in futuristic sci-fi movies.

"Is this your art?" He must have found a wooded area

with more than a touch of mystery, lit it just right, then filmed the trees for an extended period of time. Created the interface. "Does it show other places, too?"

"Come," he said. His hand dipped through the surface.

That she hadn't seen. Made her heart clutch, anxiety roll over her. She gritted her teeth against it but felt the first prickle of sweat anyway.

Not again.

She'd seen a lot of uncomfortable stuff that went away with a hard blink and firm shake of her head, so . . . there *had* to be a reasonable explanation for this. It was a wicked technological effect, that's all. She'd be fine when she figured out how he did it.

She stepped closer herself, fingers ready to touch. She held up her hand against the screen, reached. Her hand—*oh no*—tingled and joined his on the other side. She felt him move closer, his hard chest at her shoulder as his free arm circled her waist. They were almost dancing, and she fit against him perfectly. Her skin tingled at his nearness, her blood warmed. This was starting to be a problem.

"Don't pull away," he said, then stepped them both through the surface.

The trees seemed real, but she only had a passing impression of them. A deep, layered scent, heady. A hurtful longing ripped at her heart. Whispering voices filled her head: *Remember!*

But the single step carried them into the middle of a city. New York. Across the street from Central Park.

They'd been in one place . . . and were now in another. Impossible.

Her knees gave, but Khan held her up and pulled her into a close embrace. This couldn't be real, couldn't be happening. This went beyond occasional hallucinations, maybe to a complete psychotic break.

She dropped her head on his chest to blank out the city street. He smelled good—dark and woodsy like those trees, and masculine, with something sharp and exotic besides. She smothered the impulse to put her arms around his neck and hold on tight. Wait, she *was* holding on to him tight. Maybe a little bit longer . . .

If she could just take a deep breath, everything would be okay.

"Magic," he said into her ear.

Layla shook her head in denial. Couldn't be.

"It is," he said with that honey-dark voice. "I would have taken you directly to your residence, but I do not know where you live."

She choked on a sarcastic laugh. "You can't use magic to find out?"

"Would that it worked that way. I'd have found you sooner."

Layla noticed the amused glance of a middle-aged man walking briskly with a paper under his arm, as if she and Khan were canoodling in public. She pulled away, straightening her clothes. Without his arms, she needed a coat. The city was freezing.

"So we teleported?" Maybe he had some superadvanced technology, like from an alien civilization. Maybe that was it.

"I would say we *passed.*" He held out a hand to invite her back to him. "Is it so hard to believe in magic?"

Kinda, yeah. Magic belonged to fairy tales. Life was based in reality. Growing up as a foster kid, she'd learned that the hard way. Shunted from home to facility, she'd been forced to abandon any and all daydreams, all hope for a bit of magic. It was too painful when those hopes were dashed over and over again. Things were what they were, and nothing more. Even her hallucinations were just a chemical imbalance, a defect probably caused by her addict mother during pregnancy. Reality was cruel, but she could trust it. How could she possibly believe in magic?

"Then you're like, what—a wizard?" She took a step back. The space between them chilled her more than the winter weather. That she was already halfway home, in semifamiliar surroundings, helped her keep her composure.

"I warned you that your perceptions would be challenged." He reached a little farther toward her. "This is just the beginning."

Layla didn't budge. Perceptions challenged?

No, no. It was way worse. More like . . . perceptions confirmed. Because if this guy had a magic mirror, then maybe all the weird shit she'd seen throughout her life was real, too.

Oh, God, she was going to be sick. She couldn't think about that possibility.

"The wraiths—are they infected with a disease or . . . or . . . are they magic?"

"Magic."

"And Talia Thorne?"

"Magic."

Legs suddenly weak, Layla ignored his hand entirely and lowered herself slowly to the sidewalk. She wrapped her arms over her breasts to keep warm. This changed everything.

A young woman walking by gave her a wide berth, but her sweatered Shih Tzu yipped briefly before being yanked on its way.

"What about Adam Thorne?"

Khan towered over her, tall and dark and now very dangerous. "Not magic."

Figured.

She focused across the street into the park, gazing at the break in the low stone wall where the sidewalk led into patchy November-stricken grass. Some guy stood at the edge, staring at Khan. Beautiful, dark haired, model perfect, the guy was positively glowering with his ice-pale eyes. He must have seen them come out of "magic" nowhere.

She had the urge to ask the stranger if what had happened was real. What it looked like from his perspective.

But Layla felt Khan's hand under her arm and she followed his upward pull. He was returning the other man's glare. "We go."

"What?" Layla tripped into a walk, dragged along. "Is he magic, too?"

"Not exactly."

Layla had to double her stride to keep up. "Wraith?"

"No," Khan ground out. "Something else. Where do you live?"

Ahead, an outrageously beautiful woman, blond and glossy, turned in a doorway and stared as they approached. Her intensity burned. Khan pulled Layla into traffic to cross the street before they got too close.

"And her?" Layla was getting scared. Magic everywhere. A taxi horn blared at them.

Khan didn't answer. He halted midway across the street as a lovely child with huge expressive eyes emerged from the throng on the other side. The maturity in his perfect, guileless gaze was piercing and unnatural. Layla looked up the street to find perfect person after perfect person emerging from the stream of otherwise bland and ignorant pedestrians. A car jerked and made a new lane to get by Khan and her.

"Khan?" Layla flipped her gaze to the other side of

the street. A watcher here, another there. Oh, God, she was going to lose it.

"You have nothing to fear," he said.

Yeah, right. The whole world had just turned upside down.

A screech sounded behind her, and she turned as a car jockeyed to get ahead of a bus. Bumpers touched, scraped, crumpled while a wave of traffic poured through the intersection, a light turning green. Cars collided with earsplitting force, and a Chevy suddenly fishtailed, its hulk careening toward her position.

"Kathleen!"

Layla's senses foundered as darkness broke into the world around her. Faraway screams of alarm warped in the air, and she had a sickening sense of displacement. Attachment to her body seemed suddenly tenuous, the exotic, woodsy scent again filling her head. She was drifting, separate, her tether to the world loosened.

And then she was standing on the sidewalk beyond the accident, Khan's arms around her. It felt so good, so right, against him, as if some part of her could finally rest, while her nerves vibrated with excitement. A new sense of street orientation was slow in coming, so she clutched at his arm and managed a breathless question. "Magic?"

His answer was an affirmative low growl. The tightness of his returned embrace told her that he was deeply disturbed by the sudden danger as well.

"I thought you needed a magic mirror to get from one place to another."

"No," he answered. "I didn't want to scare you the first time you touched Shadow."

"Still scared, though." She panted with shock, trying to recover her equilibrium. The accident involved no less than five cars, but the speeds hadn't been great, so the only lives at risk had been those of the bystanders, most particularly her. Close call. If not for Khan, she could have been seriously hurt.

The strangely perfect people who'd been watching them had disappeared, though the sidewalks weren't so busy that they could melt into the crowd. It was as if they were never there. She'd have dismissed them from her mind entirely, and even had a niggling inclination to do just that, if not for Khan holding her tightly, proof that magic was all around her. That was twice she'd been transported now, and she didn't feel drugged.

Layla swallowed hard as she watched people emerge from their cars to check the damage and yell at each other with wild gestures. "So this magic thing?"

"Yes?"

"It's everywhere in the world?"

"More so than ever."

"And everybody just goes around oblivious?" *Except, maybe, me?*

"Most are aware on some level." She felt him lower his head to her shoulder. "Each must experience it for himself or herself sooner or later."

"I want to know everything. I mean *everything*." The blood now pumping through her veins had way more to do with this incredible revelation than with her near miss. This was huge. Way bigger than the wraiths. This was her life.

"You will learn if you stay with me."

"Right now."

He chuckled softly against her, the movement teasing her wayward senses.

She didn't see what was so funny. This knowledge was

momentous. She could not conceive of going through another day without a full understanding of this unbelievable power and its influence on the world. On her.

She gripped the arm he'd circled around her waist and glanced over her shoulder. "Do it again."

Khan got them as far as her neighborhood, and then they walked the "little ways down here" to her home while he responded to her rapid-fire questions.

How did you learn to use your power? *Came naturally.* Do you cast spells? *No.* Can you do anything else? *Like what, for example?* Kill a person? *Yes.* Kill a wraith? *Certainly.* Guess lotto numbers? *What are those?*

He didn't elaborate on the nature of Shadow; she'd see it soon enough for herself and he didn't want her to fear him. Her continued regard was already wearing away his power, and he had been weakened to begin with. If he wasn't very careful, very controlled with his appearance, she would know Death.

She spoke her thoughts with her questions. ". . . I get the secrecy thing—I mean your kind has been burned at the stake and drowned and who knows what other horrible deaths—but do you blame us? Well, I guess you do, but still . . ."

Khan didn't correct her mistaken assumptions. No fae had ever been killed by fire or water; those were mortal deaths. The fae existed out of time and place and could not do anything as transformative as *die*.

Her street was lined with buildings of ugly gray or red brick. Attached were metal landings ascending the exteriors, each connected by deathly narrow stairs. The area lacked soul, the spark of creativity, but at least it seemed clean. It smelled better than many a human road he'd traveled in his time.

A small scrap of a park opened up across the street. A group of little girls in heavy coats sat in a circle around a blindfolded child who waved her arms to locate one of her playmates. The children forming the circle chanted:

Dead man, dead man, come alive
Come alive by the number five
One, two, three-four-five
Dead man, come alive!

Again, the human preoccupation with immortality. Did it start so young?

Layla heard it, too. "Can you bring someone back from the dead?"

Khan withheld a bitter laugh at the irony of the question. Kathleen had come back from death, hadn't she? Her soul burned bright right beside him. And then there was the devil, escaped from Hell, now at large. "It is possible to return into mortality, but none are the same as they were upon their passing. Death is change."

A yellow vehicle, garish for the gray day, waited in front of the next building, its back lights an impatient, glaring red. Toward this building, Layla turned, saying, "This is me."

She stopped at the door, mumbling, "Crap. My keys."

No doorway had ever blocked Khan from his quarry. A twitch and push of Shadow and the door swung open.

"Damn handy," Layla said, her wonder mixing with her unease. Already she was growing accustomed to the idea of magic. The human adaptive capacity was staggering. The rapid pulse of change would shred many a lesser fae.

No wonder few could hold on to the form of a body long in mortality.

Layla marched up the stairs before him, took the short hallway on the second floor to a door that already stood open. She rushed inside. "Ty?"

Two mortal heartbeats accelerated within the apartment. A myriad of emotions flooded the air, most of which Khan didn't like. One in particular he found he hated, which was a revelation.

"I was hoping I'd catch you," a strong, male voice said. "If we could just . . ."

Both Layla and "Ty" looked over at Khan when he entered.

Ty was in the full power of youth and physical maturity. Eyes clear, blood thick, the light of his soul shone with purpose and self-assurance. He took a step back from Layla, which proved he was intelligent, too. "Sorry. I didn't know you had company." Ty's tone suggested extreme irritation, but the emotion coming out of him was now distinctly one of hurt.

Too bad. "If you could just *what* with Layla?"

A dark, near-violent sensation hummed beneath Khan's skin, but he could not name it. It quickened his Shadow heart, though.

"Speak with her," Ty answered. His shoulders went back as he drew himself up.

"Khan," Layla said with a note of warning. "This is my friend."

Ty glanced back to Layla. "Friend? Three years and that's what I am to you?"

She shook her head in frustration. "I want to talk, Ty, really I do, because there are things to say. But I can't right now. I'll call you as soon as I can."

A muscle in the boy's jaw twitched. He jerked his head in Khan's direction. "Are you with him?"

Khan smiled *his* answer.

Layla scowled. "Not like that. He's just an informant for my story."

"Your story. So you're still out there trying to get yourself killed? Fine." Ty heaved a sigh, but anguish still poured out of him. "Don't bother calling me until this is over. Then maybe we'll have something to talk about."

Ty stepped toward the door, and Khan allowed him to pass, his estimation of the mortal now at dust. Layla said nothing but watched while Ty turned the corner out of the apartment. Her silence followed the tread of his feet down the stairs and only broke when the downstairs door slammed shut.

"You didn't have to be a jackass," she said.

"Get your things."

But her chin dimpled with fury. "The last thing I want to do is hurt him any more. So thanks."

Her reasoning was insane. "You seek out wraiths, and he leaves you to do the work alone? If he cared, he'd be by your side to see that you do not get attacked on the street, dragged into an alley, almost raped, almost killed. And you don't want *him* to get hurt?"

Layla's mouth compressed with obstinacy. "He didn't know where I was, or what I was doing."

"By his own admission, he had an idea. And he left you to it."

"It's not his job to shadow my every step."

That's right. It's mine.

She swiped a hand across her eyes. "And I'm my own person. He's tried to stop me, but I felt that the story needed to be told. I can't seem to let it go. Leaving was his way of taking a stand, of showing me how much he loves—"

"Don't." Khan couldn't bear for her to finish the sentence. There was no defense for such inaction. How long had she braved the deathless ones alone? She'd have been dead and "Ty" would have preserved himself. "Get your things. We go."

"Fine," Layla bit out, leaving the room. Khan stood fast against the gale of anger behind that short word and almost lost cohesion as he battled for control. He'd been weakened by the gate already, and by Layla even more so.

An enlarged but blurred image of Talia was pinned to Layla's wall, and its presence steadied him. Amid the clutter of her life, the urgency of her story about the wraiths, Talia was at its center. Talia, her daughter. Talia, *their* daughter. The thought cooled Khan and allowed him to shift his gaze from the picture on the wall to take in the rest of her home.

Papers and books littered every surface—table, couch, counter, floor—with an odd empty pocket here or there, the places for her body as she worked. There were few personal touches. A framed photograph caught his eye. The image revealed the break of dawn reflected on a worn, urban doorway, the citrine colors of morning simmering on its surface, making new what was old, regardless of the peeling blue paint. An artist had to have snapped this shot, one with the vision to thumb her nose at Time as she captured a moment of magic. It was signed Layla Mathews, but it bore the stamp of Kathleen's soul.

What was she doing following wraiths when she should be at her art?

A sudden cry brought him swiftly into the room. A large bag, spilling with possessions, sat on a messy bed. Layla was on her knees on the floor, her head in her hands, breath hitching, broken. She screamed again as a loud, metallic *clang* sounded. The molecules of the room shuddered outward from a point of impact: her.

What was—? No!

Her scream devolved into a low moan as Khan gathered her into his arms and threw his head back to curse Heaven. The angels had no idea what they were doing. They rarely did. And the bitter irony was, Khan himself had given them the means to Layla's destruction.

What Rose needed was a good deed. A big one. Something to prove, should she be caught, that she didn't belong *there*. Because she didn't. She'd been forced to take care of some rather ugly business from time to time, but that wasn't her fault. She had a right to defend herself, didn't she? A good deed would prove once and for all that she was good, because that's what she was—good.

kat-a-kat-a-kat-a-kat

First thing, though, she had to wash the blood off her hands—those women at the Walmart were just *rude*—and then find Mickey. According to the newspapers, twelve years had passed, but she was sure he'd been faithful. Would probably be at home in Macon, missing her. Mourning her. On the drive down, she'd make a plan for a good deed on a far larger scale than what had transpired at Walmart. And how selfless of her, too, because others might not understand what had just happened and *blame* her instead. Selfless, that's what she was, especially since she was so plagued by the rattle in her head.

Rose turned into a strip mall parking lot and made for the Starbucks. She dove into the bathroom first thing, locked the door, and stripped off her shirt. She'd had it all of half an hour—a modest turtleneck, fall flowers embroidered in a pretty turn over the breast—and it was already stained with red splatters. The sticky red was on her hands, too, but she had to make do with just water, as the soap pump was out.

The smell in the room was a little strong. How people could be so lazy about their work, she didn't know. She had half a mind to . . . well, there was no time now.

She used her nails to scratch and scrape at the black lines under her cuticles. Evidence was such a trial. One hand was a little worse for wear. At first she thought the knuckles were just swollen from the fight, but the bones seemed different, too. Longer. The muscles were corded and sinewy, the fingernails coarser. Didn't look right. That hand, her bad hand, she'd have to keep carefully hidden, or else people would stare.

Reasonably clean, she drew on another of her new shirts, a lovely pale yellow, like her sunny nature.

When she emerged, a coffee was waiting for her at the pickup counter. As she walked out the door a customer yelled behind her, "Hey, that's mine!" but Rose paid him no mind. She made a point not to respond to uncouth behavior like shouting. His mother should have taught him better. If he persisted, Rose would.

She got back in her car feeling much refreshed and looked down the street for signs of a freeway entrance. Somewhere along the way she'd have to dump the body in her trunk before it started to smell. Unclean things, bodies. Maybe it'd be quicker to leave the car instead and find herself another, something roomier that didn't smell like cigarettes. She didn't want to keep Mickey waiting. Twelve years was enough, sweet man. A green sign directed her to I-95 heading south.

But the *kat* in Rose's head said, *That way!* West. *Go that way!*

And then she knew what the sound was. She should have recognized it at once. The rattle had to be the gate. No matter how far she ran, she'd never be free of Hell.

kat-a-kat: That way!

No. She accelerated to exit the intersection. Before morning she could be in Mickey's arms.

kat-a-kat: Obey me. Turn. Now.

It really wasn't fair. All she wanted to do was get back to her sweetheart—*twelve years!*—before she was caught and sent back to the bad place. And here the bad place was coming after her before she could do a really good deed. A big one. Mickey would know just the thing.

kat-a-kat: Kill a woman, and you'll never have to fear that place again.

Rose eased her foot off the gas. "Any woman?" That was easy. Women were everywhere.

kat-a-kat: Layla Mathews.

"And I'll be free?"

kat-a-kat-a-kat-a-kat

Her bad hand kept the steering wheel steady while she whipped the car into a tight turn.

Open, empty road was before her, so Rose closed her eyes. A quick stop, perhaps a difficult moment when she'd have to take care of some unpleasantness, and then freedom. Mickey. He'd be so happy to see her.

Chapter 6

Khan cradled Layla in his arms as a third metallic shock wave hit her. The blast also shredded his Shadows, their frayed edges whipping with the warped currents that wracked her body, the room, the air, but she was shuddering and insensible to his near dissolution. He was Shadow weak, but he still commanded the layers of darkness to open a passage, to permit a final shift to Segue. The danger came from another location, but to that high place, he could not go. His only hope was that Adam could get word to Custo.

Twilight sighed around him, its power briefly suffusing his being. He used the rush to propel himself back into mortality, where he crouched in a large empty room of Segue's main floor, Layla in his arms. "Adam!"

A heartbeat among the many within Segue accelerated, the person moving quickly. Others joined the first, and together they ranged closer. Finally, Adam, jogging down a connected series of wide rooms, appeared. He was breathless, confusion and alarm a static pop around him. "What's going—?"

"Call the angel," Khan rasped. "Tell him to stop."

A handful of other mortals gathered and watched from a few paces back.

Adam frowned. "Is that Layla Math—?"

Layla jerked and clutched at Khan as she was struck again, a reverberating tone ringing out as a hammer rings an anvil. The sound set Khan's teeth on edge, and he willed Shadow to hold his form. She needed him now, in this moment.

Adam was already on his phone. "Custo. Stop whatever you're doing. It's hurting Layla Mathews." A pause, then Adam sharpened his gaze on Khan. "Yes, he's here. He brought her." His forehead flexed with disbelief, his focus shifting to Layla. "You can't be serious." Trouble billowed off him, but he nodded. "I'll be waiting."

Khan ignored Adam as he knelt beside them, making another call on that worldly contraption of his. "I have a wounded woman on the main floor, east side, third parlor. We'll need a gurney." Another pause. "I have no idea what the nature of her injury is."

More heartbeats accelerating. Sudden movement below. One from floors above. But the heartbeat that concerned him was the flutter within Layla's chest. It stammered into a regular rhythm, and he knew, for the present, that she would survive. What other hurts she'd sustained, he could not guess. Her eyes were wide, jaw was tense, skin was white, as she waited for the next blow. A trail of thick blood trickled from her nose.

"Ms. Mathews, help is on the way," Adam said. "What happened to you?"

She pressed her lips together and shook her head. "I . . . I don't know." She ran her fingertips under her nose and the blood spread to her cheek.

Khan helped her to sit. She leaned back, her weight on his chest. Every sinew in her body was tensed.

He felt Adam's attention transfer back to him. "Mind telling me what's going on?"

"I'll leave that to your angelic friend. He knows enough." But clearly not all. What did The Order think they were doing, pounding at the gate without thought or caution?

Layla pulled a breath. "Mind telling *me*?" Outrage roared within her. She pushed away from Khan, her loss diminishing him further, and moved toward Adam. "First Khan says he started the whole wraith business. Then he says Talia—his *daughter*?—killed somebody. Then he shows me magic. Transporting. Strange people in the street." Her words sped up as if she was trying to make sense of it herself. "Next thing I know I'm in a world of hurt. I mean *hurt*."

Adam transferred his gaze to him, a dangerous smile darkening his expression. "'Khan,' is it?"

Khan remained silent under Adam's scrutiny. He didn't have to answer to him.

"I'd like a word," Adam said.

Layla grabbed Adam's arm. "Please. I need to know what's going on. What's just happened to me?"

Adam ignored her request, glancing up instead to signal a couple of approaching mortals, one wheeling a gurney. Khan had bowed over many a stretcher during the millennia. This one was narrow, with railings walling the sides, as if it were part coffin, too. There was no way he would permit his death-touched woman on the thing.

"Will somebody tell me what's going on?" Layla addressed everyone.

"Okay, help's here." Adam stood, fury battering the air, his gaze hot on Khan. "We need to speak privately. And now. In the meantime, our good doctor can look Ms.

Mathews over, though she seems to be recovering just fine and can be on her way shortly."

"It's not safe for her to leave," Khan said.

Adam shook his head. "The question is whether Segue is safe from Ms. Mathews."

"Hey!" Layla said.

If Layla was going to take refuge here, Khan needed Adam's agreement. No, he needed his willing support, and Adam, it seemed, was far from it. Layla, for the moment, could wait; Adam couldn't. And then there were things he had to tend to. One evil thing, in particular.

Khan leaned to whisper in Layla's ear. "You're safe now."

"But—?" Layla sputtered after him.

As he moved to follow Adam, a medic of sorts knelt beside her, pressing gently around her eyes, the bridge of her nose. "Can you tell me your name?" he asked, and Khan almost laughed. Her name had troubled him, too, this day.

"Come on," Adam said, gesturing to the rooms beyond. Khan followed his daughter's husband out of the room, through the connecting passageways to privacy. It pleased him how the place was webbed in Shadow. Not the mundane falls of dark that emphasized normal depth and variation, but the stuff of magic and possibility. Of Between. This was clearly Talia's place. Time lay thick within the throbs, an echo of memory here, a wisp of ghostly movement there.

As soon as he was beyond the notice of Layla and the others, he let his own Shadow loose around him, his illusion of a mortal form relaxing into a body haze that cost him little to hold. Adam could use reminding that he conferred with the lord of the fae, the father of his dark bride, and not one of his underlings.

When Adam turned, he did indeed take a swift step

back. Then he gritted his teeth, steeling his nerve, which also pleased Khan. Talia deserved a strong man. "Custo says that Ms. Mathews is . . ." Adam raised his hands, head shaking, as if he had difficulty completing the sentence.

"Layla is Kathleen, yes." The fact still shot an acute emotion, something sharp and sweet, throughout his body. Kathleen. Found. Kathleen. His.

"Impossible." Under Adam's controlled exterior, he was thick with disbelief and confusion. "You can't possibly expect me or Talia to believe this."

"Yet the fact remains."

Adam frowned his disapproval. "I take it she doesn't know? Or remember anything? Doesn't know who or what you are?"

Good. Adam understood. "She can't know, not yet. She would reject me."

"Yet you saw fit to fill her in on everything else, very likely endangering Talia in the process, not to mention our work here." Adam threw his hands in the air. "She's a reporter. She's been dogging our steps for the past couple years! My favorite piece of hers featured that fuzzy picture of Talia, with the caption WHO IS TALIA THORNE? If she exposes us, Talia will be hounded. Our children will be in danger. And all this in the middle of the wraiths' reorganization! You can't be serious."

"Layla doesn't want to hurt anyone. If she is driven, it is to know her daughter. Surely, the rest is the means to that end. She will reveal nothing when she learns the truth."

"That in some cockeyed, messed-up way she's Talia's *mother*? Why would she believe that?"

"Because it's the truth, because there is a thing not easily broken that binds family across time and space, because Kathleen swore she'd return somehow to find us. And she did just that. She traded her memories to come back. She gave up *herself* on the hope that the connection between mother and child would prevail. That I'd find her. That she could have her family."

Adam shook his head. "But she is not Kathleen anymore. She's *Layla Mathews*, and she is writing a multipart feature series to expose us."

"We will all have to take a gamble, then, to see which of her selves prevails, Kathleen or Layla."

Adam put a hand to the back of his neck, frustration spilling out of him. "Talia will want to know her. Will open her heart to her." His anger turned fierce. "If that woman betrays—"

"I wager she won't."

"How much do you want to bet?"

Khan pulled a grim smile. "I've already bet it all, haven't I?"

He extended himself and felt the tremble of Shadow that was his daughter above and off to the far left. She cradled a bright life close in her arms, while another little one slept nearby. Kathleen's grandchildren. Another gift. "Will Talia be coming down soon?"

"Not until the kids are both sleeping soundly, which actually could be forever."

"I promised Layla that she would meet Talia today."

Adam's eyes sparked with satisfaction. "Sadly, a promise you won't be able to keep."

His obstinacy was going to be a problem and needed to be broken. "Peace, Adam. You don't know everything yet: Like Kathleen, Layla's death is already upon her. I have held back Shadow twice now, but Fate has cut her from the tapestry of life. None of us has the luxury of time. She will die, and soon."

Adam stilled, his driving intensity tripping to a stop. "I'm sorry, what?"

"Layla is going to die soon. It is past her time already."

Adam laughed bitterly. "One of these days, I'd appreciate it if you'd fill me in on how it all works, because as far as I know, Talia's mother had a heart condition and Layla looks pretty damn healthy to me."

"Fate had Kathleen die in youth before, and Layla will follow suit, by violence or by accident. Kathleen and Layla both had the same allotment of time in mortality; they are the same soul. Her measure of life is at its end. We cannot hold her with us long."

"Oh, that's much clearer." Adam shook his head, but the emotion churning the air around him was changing again, taking on the fierce whip of his rising determination. Adam would not allow Talia to lose her mother again, not if he could help it. His eyes had a steely glint when he asked, "And this gate business?"

"Ask Custo. It is in his care for the time being, but let him know that only *I* can destroy it. If he or his angelic host tries, they will only harm Layla."

She must have bound herself to the gate in some way when she'd turned the black handle. He had not considered that eventuality. The destruction of the gate bore a great deal more thought before it was attempted again.

Then there was the devil, a predator in an unsuspecting world. If Custo could be trusted to prevent The Order from dismantling the gate, then the devil was the first order of business. The thing had to be sundered before it could wreak havoc in mortality.

"Keep Layla safe. I will return as soon as I can."

"You're leaving?"

"If Layla may remain here, then I must attend other pressing matters." The creature would be learning the kind of power it wielded, though the thing would ultimately have to bow to Death.

Adam was all resignation now. “I’ll make her as comfortable as I can, keep her out of danger. Where are you going?”

Khan summoned his now sluggish Shadows out of the weak shades in the mortal world. “I go hunting.”

Layla lost the last half of the doctor’s question about her medical history when she spotted Adam’s approach. She stood, pulling at the hem of her sweater, and prepared herself for another boot back to New York. With all the hopping around today, she wouldn’t be surprised at all to find herself back where she started.

“Ms. Mathews”—Thorne held out his hand—“it’s a pleasure to have you back at Segue.”

Had to be sarcasm under that control.

“I want to know what’s going on. And where’s Khan?” He’d promised to tell her everything. He made her feel . . . but she wasn’t going to think about that.

But Thorne shifted his attention to the doctor at her side. “Dr. Patel?”

“She looks like she’s been beat up a little, but I can’t find anything that warrants further examination at this time.” Dr. Patel turned to her. “You let me know if you start feeling poorly, and I’ll take another look.”

Thorne nodded a dismissal to the doc and regarded her again. “Khan tells me that you’ll be staying at Segue for the time being.”

“Uh . . . I . . .” She couldn’t keep up. If someone would just answer her questions . . .

“I understand this must be very disorienting,” Thorne said. His eyes were full of trouble.

"To say the least."

"And Khan is quite the enigma." A little sarcasm there.

"Takes one to know one."

Thorne gave her a half smile with a short chuckle. "I'm going to ask for your patience on those answers of yours. I've got more than a few questions myself. This has taken me by surprise, too."

"What did Khan tell you?" The information disconnect was unsettling, but her sense of displacement was more so. She normally felt like she didn't belong, a remnant from her childhood. Now she felt like the ultimate outsider. Magic? Madness. Where the hell was Khan? Why did she have that . . . that pain attack?

Thorne sighed. Scratched his head. Shrugged. "Some business about a gate. I'll have to make a call before I know what he was talking about."

"A gate?" Layla felt sick to her stomach.

Thorne dropped his arm. "You see one recently?"

In a nightmare. When I was knocked unconscious. But she didn't verbalize it. She'd sound like she was out of her mind. And after today, she just might be.

Another chuckle. "Well, it must be pretty bad."

It's evil, the blacksmith, Khan, had said.

"But not real," Layla replied. "Right?"

Adam gave her a look of extreme patience. "You tell me. You're the one who just passed through Shadow to get here."

There was that word again: Shadow. Khan's term for magic. Just how far did his power extend? Could he mess with her dreams?

"Can you tell me what he is?" Maybe then she'd be able to get a handle on what had happened. If she listened closely she could almost hear that damning *kat-a-kat.*

"So you can put it in your story? Expose him and his

kind to the masses? I don't think so. And anyway, it's not my place."

If Khan and his kind had this much power, the masses had a right to know. "Khan didn't seem to have a problem filling me in."

Adam gazed at her long enough for her to feel utterly stupid.

Of course. Khan had told her only what he wanted her to know. And then he'd delivered her to a place where she could be controlled. She was finally inside the castle of secrets and magic. She'd thought the place was scary before; now she found it utterly terrifying. And no one even knew she was there.

Adam's expression mellowed. "You obviously know quite a bit more than you did a few days ago. And if you hang out here long enough, you're bound to discover more. Frankly, I worry for the safety of my wife and children should you make public certain private matters."

"It is not my intention to hurt anyone."

"I'm saying, be careful."

There was no mistaking the warning that time. Why the hell were they going to let her stay? Just because Khan said so? "If it were up to you, I'd already be on your plane back to New York. Why am I here? What is Khan's hold over you?"

"You jump to a lot of conclusions. It's a dangerous habit."

"Then set me straight." *Tell me something.*

Adam looked down at the floor for a long moment. When he raised his head again, Layla knew that answers would not be forthcoming. "I'll arrange for a room and, uh, give my wife a heads-up that you'll be staying with us. If you're hungry, kitchen's through there. Help yourself to whatever you like. How about I find you there in say"—he looked at his watch—"an hour? I should have everything ready by then."

He'd have to answer her questions eventually, but for now, she let it go.

"The kitchen," she agreed. Felt weird to accept hospitality from him, though. He was supposed to be one of the bad guys. Now she didn't know what to think.

Layla watched in amazement as Adam strode through the large connecting rooms to the elevator. No guards left behind. Just her. Alone.

"Okay, then," she said to break the silence. "Food."

Layla turned in the direction Adam had indicated—couldn't be *that* hard to find—and halted, perspiration slicking her skin with one thud of her heart.

A semitransparent child of eight or nine stood before her, her fancy little dress accented by a large, triangular collar of lace. Her hair was coiled in fat yellow ringlets around her face. Her shiny black shoes stood primly together. Her hands were fisted. But it was the naked loathing and spite in the child's eyes that made Layla go fish cold. She didn't dare breathe.

Ghost. She was seeing things again. The child couldn't possibly exist.

"How dare you bring *him* here?"

Bring whom? Khan? Layla shook her head and took a slow step back from the little girl. "N-no. He brought me."

"The *worst* of them. The *darkest* of them." The little girl wrinkled her nose. "You let him *touch* you."

It wasn't like that, Layla wanted to assure her. Khan just had a way about him that . . .

"This was once a good place. But now it's bad. Bad! *Bad!*" the child shrieked. The black pupils of her eyes swallowed the irises, then the whites. The rounded flesh of her cheeks went sallow and hollow, beyond the cast of illness. The curls unraveled into ratty string as the girl's height seemed to stretch upward.

Layla closed her eyes and willed the specter away. This wasn't happening. She was exhausted and stressed, was all.

"You've got to be kidding me," a woman said.

Layla's eyes snapped open. Young. Black hair, dye job fading and growing out. Bad mood written all over her face. Zoe Maldano.

"Ghost," Layla said, gasping, though the apparition had vanished. When Layla was a kid, she'd told grown-ups about some of the odd things she'd seen. No one had believed her. No one ever believed her.

"Well, duh," Zoe said. "Place is fucking haunted. What kind of shitty reporter are you not to know the first thing about Segue?"

"It— She—" Zoe acted like the ghost was a matter of course. First Shadow, now this.

Zoe raised a dismissive hand as she walked away. "And weren't you going to out Adam and Talia to the world? Wasn't that our deal?"

Layla hurried after her. No way she was going to be left in that hallway, alone again with the demon child. "Can she hurt people?"

"I don't know," Zoe said, slapping a swinging door open. "She doesn't bug me."

"She *hates* me." Layla followed her into the kitchen.

"You're not in Kansas anymore, Dorothy."

No, she most definitely was not. And if this ghost was real, was near ready to spin its dolly head around on its neck, then Khan's magic was real. The awful gate, too? But she'd been *dreaming*. Khan's place was full of all that expensive furniture, not an anvil and a gate.

Nothing made sense.

"Tray ready?" Zoe asked another woman, who was fussing over the stove. The woman was petite and curvy, her short red hair pulled back into two cute pigtails at the base of her head.

"One sec," the woman answered. She lifted a frying pan and scraped some decadent-looking pasta onto a waiting plate. The savory smells of butter and garlic made Layla's mouth water, in spite of the continued pounding of her heart.

"Thanks," Zoe said, but she didn't sound all that grateful. She lifted the tray and moved back to the door, using her hip to ease herself out into the series of connecting rooms. Zoe had to have nerves of steel to cross through those haunted rooms. Nerves of freakin' steel.

The cook put her hands on her hips and regarded Layla. "Adam called and said you'd be over."

Layla pointed toward the door. Zoe didn't care, but maybe this lady would. Somebody should. "There's a ghost out there."

The cook laughed. "Which one?"

"Little girl?"

"Ah. That would be Lady Therese Amunsdale. I've heard of her, but never had the pleasure myself." She walked over and held out her hand. "I'm Marcie. I keep people fed around here. You hungry?"

A normal question. Layla liked normal. She grabbed hold and went with it.

"Starved, but I can fix something for myself." She glanced back at the still-swinging door. Could the ghost child come in here, too?

Marcie waved at her with a dishcloth. "Just sit down. I live to cook."

"She always that unpleasant?"

"Which one? The ghost or Zoe?" Marcie opened the fridge, pulled out bunches of green herbs.

Layla shrugged. "Both, I guess."

"The ghost is supposedly a mean piece of work and can appear as a child or as a grown woman. The child version sounds creepier to me. I've been assured she can't act on the physical world, which means she can't hurt you unless she scares you to death." She looked up from the herbs she was chopping and splashed some of the pasta water into the pan, sloshed it around with more butter and garlic.

"Zoe . . ." Marcie continued. "Well, if you're going to be staying here, you might as well know. She's a sad case. Her sister Abigail is very ill, going to die, I hear. So yeah, Zoe might have an attitude problem, but no one holds it against her. Anyone can see how much she loves Abigail."

"What's wrong with her?" Layla put a hip up on a stool.

Marcie shrugged. "I don't know. Like everything else around here, it's top secret. This place collects odd sorts. And when I say odd, I mean scary. Abigail is special." Marcie leaned in. "I've heard that she can foretell the future, and that it's killing her. I don't know *what* she is, or her sister, for that matter, but they aren't like you and me." Marcie straightened again, her voice rising. "But Zoe takes up the trays and she brings them down again. Sits by Abigail a good part of every day. Sleeps in the same room. She's got a foul mouth, but she's a good sister."

So Zoe's bizarre aura a couple days ago might have been real? Layla didn't know what to think about that.

Layla swallowed hard. "Are there more ghosts?"

"A few. But they're the least of your worries. The wraiths, for one, will scare your hair white in a matter of seconds. First time I heard that screech I just about wet myself. And then there's the fae—" Marcie lifted her gaze. "Well hello, handsome."

The what?

But a man—young, fit—strode around the island counter and gave Marcie a kiss on the cheek. "Make me some, too, will you?"

"Anything for you." Marcie's voice was all warmth. "How's Annabella?"

"Happy. She misses the babies." The man turned and Layla almost fell off her stool. His coloring was unnatural, veins a dark gray driving through olive skin. He was bulky with muscle, like a trim boxer, and beautiful. His green-eyed gaze felt hot and piercing. If not for the strangeness of his skin, he could have been one of those intensely beautiful watchers from the street in New York. Yes, exactly like them.

"You're Layla?"

She nodded. *What weird thing are you?*

"Well, you seem okay now. Adam's call made it sound like I'd killed you." He took a seat next to her, elbows on the counter, fingers laced, head tilted to keep his gaze on her face.

"Killed me?" She tried for a smile, as if to say, *Please don't.*

"The gate. I had no idea I could hurt anyone by banging on it. I am very sorry that I caused you pain." The intense concern in his expression proved the truth of his words.

"So it *is* real."

"You bet. And since I harmed you by trying to dismantle it, I figure you ought to know."

Khan had tricked her then. He'd done something with the warehouse, or her head, which bore some thought. Quiet thought. "I think I'm okay. I don't hurt now."

And actually, she didn't. She only felt hungry—a new batch of pasta hit the pan—and that was about to be taken care of. She would deal with the rest later.

"The damn gate didn't take a dent either." The man gripped his shoulder. "But *I'm* sore."

"Khan made it." Which was to say, he used magic. "So it's not . . . ordinary," she finished lamely.

The man dropped his gaze to the counter and seemed to fight a smile. "'Khan,' huh?"

"Yeah." Why was that funny? "And you are?"

He looked back over. "I'm Custo. It's interesting to meet you, Ms. Mathews. You pose quite a conundrum."

"*Me?*" This from the guy with lead in his veins. Who were these people?

"Adam says you were sneaking around the grounds a few days ago. Well, you got what you wanted. You're within Segue now, God help you. Made it all the way to the kitchen, which means there's no going back." He chuckled. "Least not after tasting Marcie's food."

Marcie smiled over her shoulder at him as she plated the pasta and set it before Layla. "Flattery will get you everywhere," Marcie said with a grin. "What kind of work will you be doing here, Layla?"

Layla noticed the amused arc of Custo's brow. "Yes, Ms. Mathews, how will you be earning your keep?"

He's putting me on the spot on purpose. He knows why I'm here; he just wants me to admit it out loud so Marcie understands, too. Well, it's best to be up front about everything. "I'm working on a feature story about Segue and the origins of the wraiths, and frankly, it might make trouble for some here. But I'm happy to pitch in with whatever needs doing." She gave a game smile and added brightness to her voice. "I call dishes."

Layla waited for warm Marcie to turn cold, but instead she winked at her while handing Custo his plate. "She'll do dishes? I like her already."

"Yes, it's always best to be up front," he said. "I'm glad we agree on that point."

Layla froze, fork midway to her mouth. *Did I say that bit aloud?*

"Nope." He took a huge bite.

Layla carefully put her fork down. *He read my mind.*

Mouth full, Custo gave her half a grin and a howdy-do nod, confirming her suspicion. Marcie had gone quiet, stealing a quick glance at them both, then put dishes in the sink. Her sudden retreat set the butterflies flying in Layla's belly.

Custo looks weird and he can read my mind.

"I can't help the way I look," he grumbled and shoved another bite in his mouth. He chewed casually, at home, without care. As if this wasn't a huge deal.

Layla slid off her stool and backed away from Custo, who went on eating. First Khan, the sudden pain from the gate, then the ghost, now this. She put her hands on her skull to smother her thoughts. Any thoughts at all, but still they came. *So invasive, but don't overreact. He looks weird, yes he does, weird. These people are freaks of nature. I can't help my thoughts, and anyway it isn't how he looks that bugs me. It's the mind-reading thing. No privacy. I have a right to think what I want. Feel what I want. It's what a person does that's important.*

"I hate it myself, and my wife has banned me completely from her brain. I keep telling her that there are times when it could be useful"—he waggled his eyebrows—"but she won't budge."

"Can I ban you from my brain, too?"

He wiped his mouth on his napkin. "Sure. I found out what I needed to know anyway."

What? What did he find out? What terrible thing has he learned about me?

He strode to the dishwasher with his empty plate and placed it sideways in the rack. Dropped his fork and knife in the silverware caddy, too. "That it's best to be up front and that what a person does is most important."

Oh. Okay. That didn't make her sound so bad. But just because he had the ability to read her thoughts didn't mean he had the right. How could Marcie stand it? Layla knew she herself couldn't. With so much power at Segue's disposal, how could they ever have thought she'd be a threat to them? The mind reading alone ensured that she couldn't act against their wishes without their knowing.

He stopped at the doorway. "You've got one thing wrong, though, and it's bound to become a huge problem for you. Considering the players involved, it might even cost lives. Or worse, souls."

What the heck was he talking about? She had neither magic, like Khan, nor extraordinary ability, like Custo.

Custo's gaze darkened. "You're at the boundary of Shadow now. Segue straddles it more than it ever has, even as Adam strives to hold the darkness back. What you think and what you feel here are just as important as what you do. Maybe more. *Temet Nosce.*"

"What does that mean?"

"It's the best advice I can give you, and, sister, you need it. *Know thyself.*"

Now she was angry. "I do. I'm Layla Mathews. I know who I am." Where did he get off suggesting otherwise?

"Oh, okay," he conceded easily. He turned to leave, pushing open the swinging door and tossing over his shoulder, "Then you know you're one of the weird ones, too."

Chapter 7

Once in Twilight, Khan trembled as Shadow dissolved the mortal body he'd worked so hard to hold. He strained to retain a semblance of Kathleen's Shadowman but was too weak to stop the cyclone of his dissolution. The cold, wild tendrils claimed him again, and he became the Reaper, a Shadow-fae consciousness wrapped in darkness. Instantly, the keening of his scythe filled him, the curved blade a hated extension of himself, paining him like a ghost limb.

"So lift the blade again," a soft voice said.

Moira. He didn't look upon the lie of her lovely face. The long fall of gold hair, the youth shining from her sunny skin, eyes that matched the earth's blue sky. Of her three faces, this countenance promised life and health, but her nature was age old and rotten with it. Fate.

She'd cut Layla's lifeline from the fabric of humanity, and he'd stood by and watched her do it. Moira was the inevitable.

"All mortals must die," she crooned. "Even your woman. Only the blade is eternal."

His scythe, *his* fate. A legacy of death.

No. To take up his blade again would sever him forever from Kathleen. He'd take what little time he had with her, with Layla. Moira had already done her worst.

He was here only to reclaim his strength so that he could hunt the creature that Layla had released. He knew the burden of letting loose something evil into the world. He would not have her bear it. And then he would deal with the gate.

A moment here and already he was growing stronger. Shadow may have destroyed the illusion of his mortal body, but it also fed him. He could feel the contrary stuff snapping within, his power redoubling, his darkness deepening.

"The human form Kathleen made for you is lost." Moira laughed. "What will Layla make of you? How will she see Death?"

Only Kathleen had ever made him beautiful, and it had taken every iota of strength to hold that body in Layla's presence. Without Kathleen, he was hollow. The next time he saw Layla, she would alter his appearance according to how *she* perceived Death. At least he'd seen her to safety first.

"You said it yourself: she will reject you, because it is human nature to do so. Life cannot make peace with death. Between the two is Shadow. Bide . . . you . . . *here*."

Moira drew her shimmering skirts aside. Beneath crawled the blinded, ravaged soul of a human woman. Her eyes were sunken, and her hair was balding, long strands still clutched in her own hands from when she'd pulled them from her scalp. She'd died, but because he'd abandoned his post, there was no one to see her safely across to the Hereafter, as was his duty.

"Like so many others, she got lost in the trees," Moira said. "The angels try, but they have not found this one yet.

I keep her hidden; it's so much fun to watch them search." Moira clucked with her tongue, and the mortal looked around in terror. The woman's spirit was dim, flickering with exhaustion. She was losing herself to whatever illusion Moira had trapped her in.

Pity flared within Khan. "Set her free."

Moira's eyes twinkled. "Set her free yourself."

"I cannot. I will not."

"It is your nature, Stormcrow," she said. He had as many names as he had faces. He preferred the one that Kathleen had chosen: Shadowman. Moira shook her head. "And nature always prevails."

Khan smiled to match the sharp flash of her gaze. There was no going back, not now, not ever. The world was different . . . and so was he. But Moira had been trapped in darkness age upon age. She couldn't possibly understand, but he tried anyway. "*I want to change.*"

Moira laughed. "But you are *fae*."

Fae, yes. But not the same as he had been. Kathleen had worked that miracle, and he would not, could not, give it up. To prove it, he lifted a hand and banished the illusion from the woman's mind. He would not help her cross, but he would not leave her trapped, her soul to burn out, either. The kneeling woman froze, double blinked. Blinked again. Slowly her gaze lifted from the root-gripped earth to him.

He'd known it would happen. Could almost sense the order of her mind asserting itself. The perfumed air of Twilight changed its humor, took on a familiar stench. Likewise, his shadows stirred as the woman reformed him to match her mental image. Shadow pulsed, then condensed into a settling roil. Then went still.

And the woman screamed.

The ultimate monster now stood before her: Him. Death. The Grim Reaper.

Moira's laughter rose. "You are as you have always been."

"Perhaps," he conceded. What horror had his form taken? Would Layla see a monster as well? Would she scream? "But I don't choose it."

The words had scarcely left his tongue when he sensed the earth shiver, a great trembling as if it sought to cast off something unclean. The devil.

Khan sent fingers of darkness skimming along the veil. Mortal life sizzled on the other side with flashes of emotion, innumerable voices raised in conversation, layering into a great clamor of humanity. Everywhere soul-lights flickered, some approaching for a cross, though he would not be the one to shepherd them. The angels had better look sharp.

There! A sticky suck of blood, the smear left behind by the devil.

Khan gathered great wings of Shadow to him.

Moira laughed, "Fly, Stormcrow!"

And he did. He had a devil to catch.

He crossed the boundary between the worlds, broke through the atmosphere, and found himself down the street from the warehouse where the gate was created, near the river. An unholy stain marred a spot on the street where the devil had taken its first victim. The kill was not palpable to human senses. The spilled blood had been washed from the street and the smell of fear had dispersed into the wind. Yet the sense of evil remained. Passersby would shudder. Neither animal nor insect would draw near. But the devil was long gone.

Khan cast his Shadow out again. And *there*, again, the creature had taken lives. The devil had headed south, into a neighborhood on the outskirts of the city.

This blot on the world, marked off by yellow tape, was

situated near racks of clothing within a large store. Again, the signs of violence had been cleaned, but the sense of evil could never be completely erased. This store would fail. The building would go derelict.

Khan reached again. Where and how far could the devil go in the short space of a single day? He sought the stain of another wrongful death and found it along a highway. Through Shadow he gathered himself to that spot.

The body was still there. The spirit had crossed.

Khan crouched low to examine the corpse. It had been a quick kill, more to incapacitate than to murder. Across the gut were four long, bloody gouges, like the swipe of a bear claw. The red stuff congealed across the belly. The ground beneath was stained red. A vehicle was parked askew, off the road. It was incongruous with its owner—the metal rusted and dinged, while the body of the man had the sheen of wealth. If Khan had to guess, the devil had preferred this man's car and had stolen it from him.

But to go where?

Mountains rose in the far distance. A green sign just up the way read, WEST VIRGINIA TURNPIKE. And then Khan knew. Of course. Where else would it be headed? To whom would it be irresistibly drawn?

Segue. And Layla, who'd set it free.

Layla sat on the bed, the blankets still drawn but now covered with chicken-scratch notes she'd jotted on a pad of Post-its she'd found in the bedside drawer. The sleek digital clock next to the bed said it was 1:12 a.m., but there was no way she could sleep. The ghost girl had made sleeping ever again unlikely, and Custo's cryptic warning had settled it.

She was in over her head. Khan had promised her

answers, but with the depth of mystery that existed within Segue, answers could easily become a life's work.

But she couldn't go back. How could she live with the knowledge that the bump in the night might just be real? That what she saw might be real? She'd be scared every minute. Going back to her apartment, marrying Ty, and having kids with all this in the back of her mind was impossible. She couldn't even imagine that life now.

She needed to be here. The place, the people, even the magic . . . she'd never be able to shake them. Where she fit in the scheme of things was now the driving question.

The scattered Post-its noted each probable "fact" she'd accumulated. There was no order to her system, and she liked it that way. The happenstance disorganization of her notes allowed her to make unexpected connections that neat lines and categories would not allow. Right now, "mean girl ghost" overlapped with "superhot Khan." Why did the ghost hate him so much? And north of that, "Talia," whom Khan had said killed the wraiths' maker. But hadn't he also said back at the warehouse that *he* and he alone was responsible for the wraith disease? Didn't make sense. She rearranged the notes. Put "Khan" next to "Custo." Now there was a combo. Would Custo be able to read Khan's mind? Something told her Custo had better not try.

A soft knocking sound had Layla crumpling the note in her hand, her heart leaping. She held her breath. She didn't think she could take any more today.

The knock sounded again. Still soft. Tentative.

Someone was at the door. A ghost wouldn't bother to knock, a wraith would bust in, and Khan would simply step out of the shadows.

Layla glanced at the clock. 1:23 a.m. The strange place obviously kept strange hours. She crawled off the bed, scattering notes on the floor, and tiptoed to the small living room of her Segue suite. All quiet. The one-bedroom apartment was lovely—fireplace, flat-screen TV, comfy couches in warm, welcoming tones. It had every possible comfort except peace of mind.

She approached the door and put an eye to the peep-hole. The warped figure of a woman, white blond hair in a loose ponytail, was moving away down the hall.

Talia. Had to be.

Layla jerked open the door.

Talia turned. She was midway down the long corridor to the elevator. "I'm so sorry if I woke you."

Her voice was like her knock: soft, tentative, kind. Layla shook her head to say, *No, I was still awake*, but the words themselves were caught in an incredible tightening of her throat. The late-night hush of the hall roared in her ears. Her sight wavered with the vertigo of an out-of-body dream. *Talia.*

"I saw your light and thought maybe . . ."

All Layla could do was nod. *Yes, any time. I've wanted to talk to you for so long.*

Talia approached, a nervous half smile winking in her eyes. Khan's eyes.

Seems like forever. Where have you been? I've been looking for you. Layla's mind reeled. Talia blurred in her vision and Layla fought to swallow an unreasonable sob.

"I'm Talia Thorne. Mind if I come in?" Talia's tone had a note of apology. "The days get so crazy around here that we might not have a moment alone tomorrow."

Layla swiped at her tears, snuffling, and trying to laugh at herself. "Don't know what's come over me." She held the door wide. "Please, come in." Talia was so pretty. So very pretty. Her eyes—they were more exquisite than she had ever imagined. And she was here. Right now. Layla gestured to the kitchenette. "Can I get you anything?"

Talia's smile grew. "I'm good, thanks. And I only have a minute. The babies are restless tonight. I just wanted to say hi and introduce myself. Couldn't wait until morning."

All the questions Layla had stored in her mind about the wraiths and Segue and Thorne Industries became jumbled in her spinning head. This was the interview of her life, and all she wanted to do was cry. And hug a strange woman. And cry some more. What was the matter with her?

"I hear you've had a big day. Why don't *you* sit down?" Talia made a show of glancing around. "Every light's on in the place, so I expect you're as terrified as I was my first night here."

Layla lowered herself onto the red sofa that faced the small fireplace. "Scared out of my mind."

Talia laughed. "You'll get used to it. The east wing isn't haunted, so you should be able to rest easy here. West wing, on the other hand . . . well, it stays quiet when I'm around. Ghosts don't like me much."

"The little girl ghost doesn't like me much either."

"Then we already have something in common. Why don't we find out what else?" Talia took a seat next to her, her brow furrowed, then leaned over to pull something from Layla's pant leg. She lifted a Post-it. "What is Custo?" she read.

Layla held her breath. She didn't want her story to break the moment. Her story didn't matter at all. This was what was important; she knew that now. Not some stupid story. Talia.

"An angel," Talia answered. "And I mean that literally. As in from the Hereafter. Don't let his rough edges fool you."

Angel. Talia's answers were just as absurd as Khan's were about magic. About Shadow. How could she believe? Considering the day, how could she not?

"Wraiths?" Layla croaked.

"Regular people who gave up their souls for immortality. My father accidentally let something bad into the world, and I took care of it a couple years back. Segue mostly now hunts and kills the remaining wraiths, though"—*big sigh*—"they seem to be reorganizing now, gaining momentum. I should warn you: Segue is not the safest place these days."

The whole world wasn't safe with those creatures on the prowl.

"And what is Khan?" *How can he do all the things he can do? Why do I feel so strange when I'm with him?*

Talia's expression sobered. "Custo and the wraiths—and ghosts, for that matter—all have their origins in humanity, but Khan is of an altogether different race. Khan is fae."

Fae. The word had a lot of meanings, but Talia had to be referring to an abbreviation of fairy. More fantasy stuff. Magic.

But, if what Talia said was true, the fae existed. And if Khan was fae, then Talia had to be, too. Just one look at those tippy-trippy eyes confirmed it.

"It's simple, really."

Layla felt a spark of joy-shock as Talia squeezed her hand for a moment. Layla's heart hammered as Talia took a deep breath and blinked away tears herself. But what had caused the welling of emotion, Layla could not guess. She was near bursting with it, though.

Would it be too creepy if she, a stranger, was to touch

Talia's hair? Layla fisted her hands in her lap so they wouldn't stray. *Yes.* Way too creepy.

"There are three worlds," Talia began. "Mortality, Shadow, and the Hereafter. Mortality is where humanity lives—ghosts are the souls of people who don't want to cross into the Afterlife; wraiths gave up their souls to live forever and have become monsters because of it; mortal angels, like Custo, are the souls of very good people who died and came back to dedicate themselves to humanity's well-being."

"So all this is about life and death?"

"Isn't everything?"

Not necessarily. Didn't have to be. Those stakes were way too high. Why couldn't everything be about beaches or going to the movies or . . . love? Why did she have to be afraid?

"Where does Khan fit in?" *Where do you? Where do I?*

"Ah. Shadow is the realm in between here and the Hereafter. It's the place of dreams and nightmares. It's where all the stories are true."

"His magic comes from there?" *You must have some, too.*

"Yes. In fact, *Shadow* is a much better word than *magic*, because it connotes all the borderland possibilities of inspiration and impulse that the twilight Shadowlands promise."

"What about me?" *Because these last four years—no, my entire* life*—has been a hell of questions and searching and life-ruining obsession. Why? Please, if you're answering questions, answer that one. No one else will.*

"You've been a bit of a traveler through the three worlds. You just don't remember." Talia's expression strained as if to hold back strong feeling. She stood, stepped away a short space, wringing her slight hands. "But some of us have crossed paths with you before."

Impossible.

There was no way.

Layla had crossed paths with *none* of them. She'd been *alone* from the day she was born. Her life had been a misery of foster home after foster home. A stint in some halfway house for troubled teens. A chance at a prep school scholarship. A ruined engagement because she didn't know how to love. *That* was her life.

Now this . . . this . . . madness of a story. Shadow. Angels. Fae.

It took all her effort, but she tried to smother the bursting feeling. She couldn't trust it. No. That feeling always ended in heartbreak. Every. Single. Time.

She couldn't breathe. And what the hell was a traveler between the worlds?

Her heart labored for oxygen. Sounds cluttered her mind: a *shush-shush-shush* with no possible source and the *kat-a-kat* of the gate.

She was going crazy. Freakin' certifiable. She gulped for air.

"Take it easy," Talia said. "You're okay. It's a lot to take in at once."

Layla's eyes spilled over. She tried to inhale again, but she couldn't get anything good because her chest was already full. The space that had been empty all her life was near bursting with a *Yes!* and *It can't be* and . . .

I don't believe any of this.

But when she looked into those faery eyes beside her . . .

"We've crossed paths," Layla had to say. How terrifying to utter those words, but she couldn't feel this way without some kind of . . . of what? A shared history? "I know we have."

Talia nodded. A smile flickered. "Briefly."

"And Khan is so familiar. He acts as if . . ." *As if he knows me already*. Maybe she shouldn't confess the exhilaration that came when he was close. The coil of need that turned in her belly when she looked at him, regardless of his silly hair.

But Talia laughed freely. "Yes. I expect Khan is *very* familiar."

"Then we were—?" Layla meant to say "a couple" but wasn't ready. She'd been "a couple" not too long ago, and look how that had turned out. And now Khan? A . . . a . . . *faery*?

Oh, God, this was not happening.

"You bet."

"And . . . um . . . why did I travel between the worlds?" Layla was afraid to hear the answer. "How?"

Talia shrugged. "I'm not sure." Her face had drained of color. Her black eyes were wide, shimmering with feeling. "But I'm glad you're back. Very glad."

Life and death. If Layla had traveled through the three worlds, particularly to that last one, she'd have to have been dead, then returned to life. . . .

"Am I an angel, too?" Seemed preposterous, but in the scheme Talia had described . . .

Talia shook her head. "No." She backed her way to the door. "But *I* think you are."

Don't go. Not yet.

Layla stood to beg her back.

But Talia already had her hand on the knob. "Now for sure you won't get any sleep tonight."

"What am I supposed to do?" She couldn't possibly go back to her old life, not after today. She'd been lonely before, but now she was completely lost.

"Do? Your story is just getting started. I'll assist you with all the research you need. I've been doing a little writing on the subject myself. Actually, the wraiths are a very good place to start contextualizing the rest."

Wraiths. Right. Her story. Everything else might be upside down, but her story was still valid. The only thing valid, maybe. There was work to be done. A war to cover.

Okay. Research was good. This world-traveler thing . . . Talia, Khan . . . she'd think about all that later. She couldn't handle it now. The confusion. The pressure in her chest.

"Try to settle in, if you possibly can. It'll all work out." Talia opened the door with a quick swipe of her hand across her eyes and let herself out. "In the meantime, welcome to the family."

Khan's Shadow settled at his shoulders with a gasp of relief. Segue remained secure, and he was here ahead of the devil. Layla's heart still beat, even and strong. All was well.

There was time left for them yet.

He sought the familiar form Kathleen had made for him, but it would not come. He organized Shadow into the shape of Khan's body, but it would not hold. It was a futile effort, but he had to try.

He'd found Layla, and lost himself. On the mortal plane, he could now only be Death.

Stretching himself into the dark corners of Layla's room, Khan had to make do with watching. As he'd watched and waited for Kathleen most of her life.

He observed as Layla sat unmoving in the center of the bed, her arms around her shins, her chin on her knees. Bits of yellow paper were scattered around her like petals. Thin eddies of disquiet trailed through the air, weakening as she deliberated silently. The trails cut off when she straightened, as if coming to a decision. Layla brushed the bits to the floor and leaned over to switch off the bedside light. The low-hanging clouds in the sky outside permitted no moonlight or starlight to touch the world, so darkness filled the space.

Kathleen. Layla. Both brave, both willful. Both lacking caution when it was needed most. Both treating with Death. And yet, still different. He'd thought that the soul alone constituted the entirety of a person, but perhaps that wasn't true. What defined her?

It was a question for the angels, with an answer they would not share with the fae. Hence, the great wall that divided their realms, a relic of an ancient war between the races.

Khan extended within the shadows, drew closer, the deepness of the dark a cloak to hide him. He could sense the wire of tension and anxiety that kept her consciousness high, away from rest. But sleep is kin to Death, so with a soft stroke, he released her.

"Please remember," he whispered as she tumbled into fitful slumber.

He followed her down, into Twilight, where he could be anyone he chose.

Talia's voice echoed in Layla's sleep-slipping mind. "Welcome to the family."

But the mouth that formed the words was on the face of some puffy lady who was escorting her down the front hallway of a house. "I'm Mama Joyce," the woman continued with a smile. "You can shorten that if you want."

Layla hugged her backpack tight against her chest to stop her heart from beating so hard. She hated new placements. This lady seemed nice, but Layla wasn't going to call her "Mama." Her mother was dead, and only babies said that anyway, not seven-year-olds. So it had to be Joyce, who did kind of look happy, like her name.

"I have two special-needs kids here now." Layla felt Joyce's soft arm come around her.

Layla knew that special needs *meant like* you. *The arm on her shoulders felt heavy, just like the word* schizophrenia *that she carried from foster home to foster home. Layla still couldn't read (too dumb) but she knew that word. Schizophrenia meant she saw things that weren't there. Meant she couldn't tell the difference between what was real and what was "in her head." Which didn't make sense, because what she saw was* not *in her head. Never in her head.*

"This is a safe place," Joyce said, pushing open a door. In her free hand was a plastic bag with Layla's new medication, handed over by the caseworker. The doctor was "trying something different." But the way he'd said it made Layla's tummy hurt. Like he wasn't so sure after the last "episode."

"Micah and Jonathan have been with me a long time," Joyce said, "and they're doing great."

One of them was in a funny kind of laid-out wheelchair. The boy's body was all wrong, his mouth stretched weirdly to the side like he was trying to tell a big secret. The other boy was kneeling, and he rocked, rocked, rocked his body while he mumbled, Dead man, dead man, come alive, *which was part of a rhyme Layla knew but couldn't remember from where. The room was clean. Smelled okay, too. The TV was on—a kid's show—but the sound was soft. Nothing like at the last house.*

Layla's caseworker had said that Joyce wanted to save the world, one kid at a time.

Somebody needed to save the world. Dark people were

everywhere, squeezed into shadows and trying to get out. And when nighttime came and the shadowy patches grew, the dark people came after her. Their long fingers scraped at her skin, so cold, snagged her hair, and the voices whispered bad things—should be dead, already dead—*in her ears so that sometimes she ended up in a ball on the floor, rocking, rocking, rocking like that boy. One day the dark people would find a way out of the shadows, and then, yep, the world would need to be saved.*

The doctor called it paranoia. Said nothing could hurt her. But when the dark people pulled at her hair, it did so *hurt. She wasn't pulling it out herself, no matter what anyone said.*

Grown-ups didn't believe her, and she didn't believe them. Which is why she stole the knife. She could take care of herself.

Layla's gaze flicked over the room, then stopped. There.

She went tight and cold, and clutched the backpack closer. Joyce had told her something about the boys, but she hadn't heard. Her heart was beating too loud and making it so she couldn't breathe right.

'Cause one of the dark people was right . . . over . . . there. In the big triangle of shadow made from the lamp and a chair.

Which meant the dark people were here, too, in Joyce's nice house. The dark people were everywhere.

The shadow man crouched, dark, dark, dark, his long hair shining like a slick waterfall, as he watched her. But he didn't have greedy meanness in his tipped-up eyes. His eyes were sad.

"What happened here, Layla? Will you show me?"

The dream folded in on her, rolled into a muddle of color, darkening into the night. Walls fell and switched around and stood back up again so that Layla was in a bedroom, still clutching her backpack, but dressed in a nightgown, the cold from the floor twisting up her calves. The messed-up covers where she'd been lying had princesses all over, which was dumb because no one ever really got to be a princess. A new teddy bear was on a kid-sized desk that Joyce had gotten just for her.

"I thought you said she was nonviolent," Joyce argued from way far off. "I can't keep a violent child in the same home as an autistic one. He's making so much progress. I can't help them both."

No, that wasn't right. Mama Joyce had said that later. After the blood.

The room went scary quiet, and Layla made her breathing even quieter. Her heart did that running-away thing that always happened when the shadows came close, but her heart was trapped inside, like her.

Layla's throat hurt to call out for help, but she bit her lips. At the last home she'd called out and got slapped for waking the other kids. And then she'd still had to stay in bed anyway, the dark ones touching, scraping, pulling. She hadn't even been able to hide in the bathroom until morning like she usually did. That was a bad night.

Shhhhh.

Layla stood stone still. Her heart stopped, too. The dark people were coming.

Whispers filled the air—should be dead—*the words all on top of each other.* Already dead.

Why did they say that?

Dead, dead, dead.

Something brushed her cheek.

She could turn the light on herself, run for the doorway, flip that switch, but the dark people would just come back tomorrow and the tomorrow after that and forever. She shook when she thought about it, scared and mad and tired and all by herself.

Tonight she'd show them that she could be mean, too. Even meaner than them. She'd cut them if they reached for her. Then they'd leave her alone.

Layla backed to the window and into the squares of soft starlight. The crisscrosses of the windowpanes' shadow left x's all over her. The floor was even colder there.

Greedy tipped-up eyes gleamed from the closet. From the corners. From under the bed.

Layla unzipped her backpack and reached inside. Found the handle. Drew out the knife. "Stay back!" she said, pointing the blade into the room.

The dark ones smiled and moved forward, their shadow bodies wavering like black water. Closer and closer.

"I said stay back!" Layla jerked her outstretched arm so they'd see what she'd brought.

They laughed. Can't hurt us.

She bet she could. She had to.

Layla squeezed her eyes shut, made herself brave and mean, and slashed the knife through the air.

More laughter.

She slashed again and again. "Never come back! Never, never!"

She slashed for them to leave her alone.

She slashed until the laughter broke with a cry of pain.

And then she opened her eyes.

". . . down the knife, honey," Mama Joyce was saying. Her face was all red.

The light was on. Blood ran from one of Mama's arms. She was kneeling, her good hand out as if she wanted Layla to stay, like a dog.

Layla let the knife clatter to the floor. "I'm sorry . . . Mama."

Mama grabbed for the covers and pressed them to her arm. "Not your fault, honey." Tears ran down her face, so it had to hurt bad. "Not your fault."

Yes, it was. But Layla didn't say that.

"You saw something scary?" Mama asked.

Layla nodded. Bad things. Tears fell down her face, too.

"Are they gone now?"

Layla nodded again, even though she knew they'd be back.

Mama nodded herself. Her face had a worried look on it, the red of her cheeks going splotchy. "Do you know how to call nine-one-one?"

And that's when Mama Joyce gave her back. She had wanted to save the world, one kid at a time. Just not her.

Khan watched from Twilight, the dream shadows of the fae creeping by him into Layla's childhood bedroom. The colors of the dream were bright and harsh, like the intensity of her dread. She was trapped in an old nightmare, one that had the sense of recurrence. Layla had been here many, many times before.

He lifted a hand and cast Layla's mind deeper into sleep, beyond the reach of memory.

Same spirit, same will as Kathleen's. And now, also, the same ability to see through the veil and into Shadow. Or she had once. And here he'd thought that Shadow was a revelation to her. Deep down, she'd known. Deep, deep down, she'd known all along. Of course she had. She and Kathleen had the same soul.

But where Kathleen had seen fairy tales in Shadow,

Layla received nightmares. His fault. The ability to see beyond the veil often attracted the attention of the fae, who would divert themselves by driving the mortal mad. If he'd been in Twilight, where his duty lay, he'd have surely found her. He'd have spared that child her loneliness and pain.

Instead, she'd overcome and found him.

Chapter 8

"I'll meet you there," Talia said.

Layla agreed and hung up the phone. Library, first floor, half an hour. With Talia Thorne. Wow. Layla still couldn't believe it.

Her couple hours of crappy sleep were not enough to clear her exhaustion, but the appointment gave her a jacked alertness.

Talia had been the shock of a lifetime—a kindred spirit. Until now, Layla had believed those were a myth. But as she thought of last night, her heart gave an off-rhythm, double-beat glub. She'd never felt like this before.

More difficult to face was the idea that wraiths might have a viable paranormal explanation after all, rather than the science-based origin she'd been pulling for since day one. Personal bias might have slanted her articles, which made her wince. And here she'd thought she was being so scrupulously neutral. She'd have to ask her editor to hold that last article.

Layla was hoping to see some case files, but Talia said she'd have to be set up on the view-only interactive tablets that accessed Segue's database. So, for now, she'd be going old school and browsing the texts amassed on the library shelves behind her, then later doing some staff interviews with those who felt comfortable sharing their findings. Dr. Sikes's work on wraith cellular regeneration was very high on her wish list.

She intended to get started any minute, but she couldn't rip her gaze from the painting over the library's fireplace mantel, not even to enjoy the fire licking below, though the room was cold.

Trees and more trees, craggy with age and glowing with magic, filled the canvas. The artist's execution gave the forest an uncanny, realistic depth, yet the paint had the texture and surface immediacy of brushstrokes.

As Layla stared into the boughs, her breath grew short, her body hummed, and her nerves crackled. These were Khan's trees, the ones in his mirror, the ones she'd glimpsed when she'd passed through Shadow in his arms. But more than that, she'd seen this place, time and again, though mostly darker, over the course of her life. Thank God, someone else had seen it, too. The proof was right there.

Layla cocked her head. A child was crying close by. Had to be one of Talia's kids, but with each squall, the leaves on the magic trees rustled. The painting, like Khan's mirror, was alive.

She glanced at the corner of the canvas. *Kathleen O'Brien* was written in a loopy script. Talia's mother. So that's why it was here and not in some gallery proving to the world that Layla wasn't crazy. Talia kept her mom close.

Layla stepped back and forced herself to turn away; otherwise, she'd stare all day.

The library was old-fashioned, with dark wood bookcases, thick and deep. Books lined the shelves, their covers faded, the old paper smell prevailing over the wood burning in the fireplace. Three neat cubby desks had laptops ready for use. And centered in the room were two large tables for spread-out work.

Better get started.

As she skimmed her fingers over the first row of spines, an old guy stepped out from among the deeper shelves, a short pile of books in his hand. He was white bearded, disheveled, with a bit of a belly hanging over his pleated slacks. He moved his reading glasses down his nose as he approached, his gaze sharp on her face.

"You'll want to begin with these," he said.

"Excuse me?" Layla had to keep from looking behind her to see if he addressed someone else.

"For background. One of them is mine. It has the most comprehensive review of what you'll be looking for. The bulk of what's out there is just sloppy work."

He handed her the books, and she glimpsed the titles: *The Soul of Man in Philosophy and Social Anthropology* and *Relativism and Rationalism in Paranormal Linguistics*. Talk about taking her work in another direction.

"Um, thank you." She hated initiating introductions. "I'm Layla Mathews, by the way. New here."

"Not so new, from what I've heard." He held out his hand, and they shook. "I'm Dr. Philip James. Talia asked me to get you started. Colic keeps her busy with her children."

Disappointed, Layla turned back to the painting, from which she could still hear the faint cries of a baby. She was used to seeing things, not necessarily hearing them. "You mean they're not down here?"

"No, but I'd not be surprised if you could hear them scream. Their mother, after all, is a—"

A chair went skating across the room.

Goose bumps swept across Layla's body. Oh, crap. Not another one. "Ghost."

Dr. James frowned into his jowls as his gaze darted around the room. "Ms. Mathews, you need to do a lot more reading if you believe a spirit did that."

Layla remembered what Marcie had said. "Ghosts can't act on the world."

"Correct."

"Then what?" She knew of wraiths and now angels, both of whom she'd seen with her bare eyes.

"You, more than anyone, should know. You brought him here." Dr. James crossed himself and took a backward step toward the door.

"Khan? Fae can be invisible?" If it *was* he, there was no need to bolt. Sure, Khan was intimidating, especially with his shows of magic, but as a person, he wasn't that bad.

The light in the room darkened so that not even the fire cast a glow. Okay, that was eerie.

"The fae don't need to be invisible. They exist in Shadow, which is everywhere," Dr. James murmured, then louder, to the room, "My apologies. I meant no offense."

"Khan, knock it off and come out." Way to scare away a great potential source of information.

"No." The sharpness of Dr. James's tone brought her head about. "No," he repeated. "I don't want to see him." He took another step back and gave a slight, but respectful nod toward the room. "I'm not ready."

"But . . . ?" Now Layla was completely confused.

"Call me when you've finished with those." His gaze flicked to the books in her hand, and then he left, footsteps hurrying down the hall.

Layla was alone. She waited a beat, looking into the murk of the room. "Okay, he's gone. Come out. I have a lot of questions for you."

After everything Talia had told her last night, Layla had decided to start from scratch. She needed a deeper understanding of the underlying processes at work within the framework of the three worlds, and how the wraiths fit into the scheme. And Khan still had some explaining to do about the gate.

He didn't show.

"Khan?"

The chair, of its own accord, returned to the table, but slightly pulled out, for her to sit.

"Okay, fine." She'd just ignore him then. Eventually Talia would be down, and she was far more forthcoming with answers than anyone else had been. Working with her would be a pleasure. Besides, Layla had no patience for games, especially as tired as she was. In fact, with all this paranormal business, she was shocked she got any sleep at all last night.

"I am not strong enough for your world right now," Khan said.

Layla whirled back to the painting. Khan stood in the trees wrapped in his cloak, dark and pale. His appearance had the same brushstroke quality, the fine ridges of texture, that comprised the rest of the work. The painting, like his gilded mirror, was a window, a passage to another world. She understood that now. But when she put her hand to the canvas, all she felt was the surface slickness of the dried oil paint.

"Will this do?" he asked.

She'd seen Khan in his vampire pose before—yesterday, when she'd been attacked and knocked unconscious. She'd had a ridiculous princess dream. His look had been the same: solemn, so dark as to be mistaken for shadows, his eyes full of power and feeling.

And come to think of it, he'd been in her nightmare last night, too.

"You were there," she said. He'd been a presence when she was all alone. Because of him, for once, the dream hadn't been as bad.

He gave a rueful smile. "I've been many places."

He was dodging again. "How about in my dreams? If you're not strong enough for my world, are you strong enough for that?"

She held his gaze until he answered.

The smile faded. "I should have been there to protect you."

So he *had* been there in her head. "You can read minds, too?"

"No." He walked forward, shifting the motley daubs of color over the canvas as he moved, then crouched in the foreground nearer to the canvas barrier. This close she could see the brushstrokes on his skin, the fine lines that created his hair, and the swirls of paint that were his shadows. "That is for the angels. But I can sense what you feel—your loneliness, your isolation, even among people."

The soft rumble of his voice was getting to her, and the color smudges of his appearance gave him an old-world romantic cut, though he needed no help in that department. He belonged in those trees, and something about their rustling sway made her want to join him. It was a fantasy, and the accompanying yearning was mixing her up. Again.

"Well cut it out." Her feelings were her own. "All these superpowers are going to give me a nervous breakdown. And by the way, I happen to prefer my isolation."

He lifted a brow, not mocking exactly, but telling her he knew better. "Emotion penetrates Shadow, so I sense the truth. And if you don't want me in your dreams, shut me out. You have the power."

Emotion penetrates . . . ? Well then he had to know she was irritated. "I just say, 'Go away'?"

"That will do."

"Then—" She stopped herself. She'd have made a definitive statement blocking him, but the Joyce nightmare had haunted her for years. The possibility of a good home. The encroaching dark ones. The blood. She just couldn't shut him out.

Layla was shaking again. Better to change the subject.

She floundered to gather her thoughts, then focused on what was right in front of her. "Is the painting under a spell? Or is it another way to your world?"

"You know about my world?" His gaze went very, very serious. And not a little scary.

Layla squared her shoulders. "Talia told me. She said that you were fae and that your kind exists in the Shadowlands, a world between mortality and the Hereafter."

His gaze grew darker still. "Is that all she said?"

"Yes," she lied. It was also much better to stay away from volatile subjects, like the suggestion that she and Khan had been something to each other. "Now about the wraiths—"

"Layla." Khan's voice lowered. "What did she say?"

She winced. Okay, fine. Might as well get it over with. They had to reach an understanding about this, too, if she was going to get any work done. "She said that, um, you and I . . ."

The tension in his eyes relaxed. Then the man smiled, big and dangerous. "Yes. *You and I.* Exactly."

Something about the way he spoke sent a fever burn over her skin. Had to be exhaustion, or she wouldn't be reacting so strongly.

"We were bound together with those words," he went on.

Layla choked. "Like married?"

"That's right. You're mine."

No, no, no. The closest she had come to marriage had been Ty, and she'd known from the beginning that it wasn't right. She went to fidget with the band of her engagement ring, but it wasn't there. Just that white stripe of skin. "I'm not married."

"What passed between us might be lost to your memory, but nonetheless, I swear we came together, made vows in our own way, and created a life."

She shook her head. No. Although, if she was going to be honest with herself, her body had been remembering from the first moment he had her pressed up against that awful gate. And Talia had confirmed as much last night.

"A life?"

Something clicked in her mind. Talia had said, *Welcome to the family*. Layla had thought that Talia was being kind, putting her at ease. Was there more to it than that?

If so, Layla didn't want it. All her life *family* had been a dirty word, an empty promise. A joke. She was all grown up now and still hadn't been able to find her way into one.

Cold anger replaced disbelief. She was so stupid. How had she let herself be conned? All the weird shit yesterday, then Talia's compelling explanation. Now she was related? No. Suggesting it was cruel and twisted. Take an orphan and pretend she's long-lost family, except some upside-down creation where the lost one was the mother? Come on. She wasn't falling for it. What were they trying to do?

Manipulate her and her story. Had to be.

From inside the painting, Khan reached her way. A

current of Shadow emerged from the canvas, rippled through the air like a smoky arm, to stroke her cheek.

She reeled back.

"Believe it," he said.

Of all things, she thought of the gate. If she listened hard enough, she could still hear its rattle, *kat-a-kat,* calling her. She had placed her hand on the lever. And then Khan was there, looking at her with such terrible joy and yearning. He'd *known* her. Had asked her how she'd found him. He'd called her . . .

"Kathleen." Layla's heart tripped. "You think I'm Kathleen."

And when she'd recoiled from him and explained who she was and why she was there, he'd obligingly filled her head with his illusions. He'd said everything she wanted to hear, promised a prize interview with the elusive Talia Thorne. And after one conversation with Adam her welcome at Segue was assured, when Adam had been so vehement only moments before about getting rid of her.

Kathleen O'Brien. Talia's mother.

No.

It was ridiculous.

They were trying to control her.

"Stay away from me." She swatted at the Shadow still hanging in the air.

"Why do you think you were drawn here? Why endanger yourself for the wraiths when there are so many other things you could do with your life?"

She wasn't going to listen. "You guys are screwed up."

Layla gathered the stack of books. She was going back to her room, where she would think of what to do next.

"Layla!"

She walked briskly down the hallway. She'd seen and

experienced enough in the last twenty-four hours to know that the paranormal existed alongside this world, and that she was involved somehow.

But this was too much. This was personal.

The hallway grew dark, but she ignored it. Ignored him. Was it even possible to have a relationship with that . . . creature?

She turned the corner to the elevator just as Talia stepped out. A bright smile lit her face. "You going somewhere?"

"Forgot something in my room," Layla mumbled. The soul ache flared, and not even holding her breath would dampen it. Talia. Her daughter from another life? Riiight.

"Then I'll see you back here . . . ?"

"Yeah, sure," Layla lied and punched the button.

Little lines of worry formed between Talia's brows as the elevator doors closed. Well, Talia would just have to deal. Better yet, she could ask her father what was wrong. As far as Layla knew, he was still down there.

Or, oh, God, maybe he was in the elevator.

She hugged herself tight.

She had to find Zoe. Zoe hated the Thornes. Everyone could see that. If anyone would give her a straight answer, it was she. Although . . . she *had* been the one to tip her off about Khan. Did she even have a sick sister?

When the elevator doors opened she took the right-hand hallway, not the left. To the west wing.

Layla would see for herself.

"What did you do?" His daughter slowly turned to address the Shadow in the corridor. Her pale hair whipped in the churn of her panic.

Do? I told her the truth.

"She just got here!"

And Fate is conspiring at this moment to take her away.

A human man exited his office, blanched in fear of the gathered storm, then darted right back inside.

Talia jabbed a finger in the air and spoke through clenched teeth. "This is family business. I'm going back to my apartment, and you will meet me there. Because I'll be *damned*"—her voice rose, took on the shattering quality of a banshee—"if I'm going to let you screw this up for me."

She turned to the elevator and slapped the button, then waited, glowering in Shadow, for the vehicle to come.

Khan sensed Layla's soul light above, moving briskly. He'd intended to push her, whether she was frustrated or not. She wasn't a weak woman, and they had so little time. Kathleen had taught him how each beat of time was precious.

But he hadn't intended to hurt Layla, and though he tried, he couldn't fathom the turn of her mind that had sent her fleeing from him. It wasn't his claim on her. That had only shocked her. And he knew, though she might not admit it to herself, that she was intrigued and aroused by him. He had only to stoke that fire, and she would be his.

So what had gone wrong? She'd come back to Earth for Talia, so rediscovering her connection to her daughter should only be joyful. An end to her loneliness.

He didn't understand. Mortal men had declared women's minds a mystery. He agreed. Perhaps Talia could shed light in his darkness.

The elevator doors slid open. A long, quiet hallway stretched before Layla, the rug a classic red, beige doors with white trim off to each side. *Crap.* Which floor, which door would lead to Zoe?

She stepped out and knocked on the first one. Waited. No answer. Knocked again. Somebody was going to open up or she'd kick it in. She rapped again, harder. Waited.

Down the hallway, a door opened. A woman leaned out in a bathrobe with a towel turban on her head. "Can I help you?"

Yes. Layla strode over. She wanted a peek in the woman's room. "I'm looking for Zoe Maldano."

The apartment had the same neutral furnishings as Layla's own, though it was cluttered with framed photographs and papers. A coat was thrown over the arm of the couch. The place was lived in, nothing unusual. The woman herself was damp from a shower. The lines on her face put her in her forties. Brown eyes.

"Zoe is on the fifth floor."

"Which room?"

The woman held out a hand, but her expression had turned wary. "I'm sorry, I don't think we've met."

Layla smiled. "Oh, I'm Kathleen O'Brien, Talia Thorne's long-dead mother."

"Is that supposed to be funny?"

"Hilarious," Layla answered, then strode to the elevator again. Fifth floor, this time.

"You've got to go easy on her," Talia was saying. "You just can't blurt this stuff out. It has to be handled carefully." She threw her hands up in frustration and paced to the other end of the couch, where Adam was sitting on the arm. From him, Khan felt her draw strength; her frustrations eased somewhat.

"She came back for you," Khan said. "And she found you. That should make her happy."

But he understood what his daughter meant. Some things took time and some things were best left unsaid. One glance in the wide mirror over a dining table was sufficient to illustrate the problem. His daughter, like every other mortal, had shaped his appearance based on her conception of Death. For her, he was a man of impenetrable darkness, lacking any pigment of any kind, except for his eyes, which glowed red in the reflection. A demon man in a cloak. Still, after all this time.

"She's overwhelmed and confused," Talia argued.

"She knows me. On every level but consciousness, she accepts me." It was consciousness that concerned him most.

"Then court her."

"There is no time." Not when he had to search for the devil as well. The creature should be near Segue already, setting her traps.

"You don't have a choice."

Adam put an arm around his wife, easy in his affection. "You want me to go after her? Do a little damage control?"

From another room, a babe let out a piercing wail. Talia fetched him, and returned, bouncing the infant on her shoulder with a *shhh, shhh, shhh.*

Khan had seen his daughter's children before, little bright lights full of noise and wonder, but Shadow was deepening in this one. The black of his eyes was only the slightest indicator of his heritage, though. The squalls that lifted from his throat already stirred Twilight. Did his mother know?

"Talia, girl, watch that child carefully. Power rises in him."

She stopped bouncing. Her jaw went tight as her concern filled the space. "I know."

"Like you, if he crosses into Twilight, his mortal half will perish."

Adam stroked Talia's arm. "I'll hold them here. I'll hold them both."

"But, Adam," Khan observed, "you have two children, a wife, and only two hands."

A loud crack brought Adam up. "Gunshot."

Layla found Zoe waiting for her outside one of the doorways, so the woman below had to have called to warn her. Zoe was in a holey T-shirt, the curve of one breast visible, and rolled-up Segue sweats.

"Abigail is sleeping. If you make a racket, I swear I'll kill you."

"Apparently," Layla said, "I'm already dead."

"Look, I don't do drama, and you seem unhinged." Zoe made a little scat motion with her hand. "So just turn yourself right around and go back the other way."

"I need to talk to you. Now." Of all the people Layla had met at Segue, Zoe was the least complacent. She had to have an idea about what was going on.

"I have a gun just inside the doorway. Please give me a reason to use it."

"Why did you want me to write an article exposing Adam and Talia? What are they really doing here? Why are they messing with me?"

Zoe leaned inside her apartment and came back with a Glock. "Found it outside last week."

Layla startled, then put two and two together. "That's my gun."

Zoe smiled. "Finders keep—"

And the gun went *crack*!

* * *

Khan was already dissolving into Shadow when Talia begged, voice urgent, "Find her. Please, don't let her go."

It was easy to locate Layla; no soul fire glowed so bright, so sure. She stood inside the living room of another mortal woman, laughing, "How about I show you how to handle a gun, eh?"

Fate had made yet another attempt on her life, but Layla still lived, and she was unharmed.

The woman next to her was young and hale, but her spirit was broken, curious faint trails of Shadow in the air around her. She was wan with exhaustion. And he knew why. In the next room, her kin, a sister, lay propped on a bed. The woman bore an awesome gift, rare to humankind. In ancient times they would have called her an oracle or a prophet and set her up like a queen. Mortal blood and Shadow commingled within her veins, and thus she aged rapidly toward the brink. She would have crossed into Shadow already if not for the devoted hold of her sister, who would not let her go. And so love once again trumped death.

"It's not a crime to want to protect myself," the woman said to Layla. Her expression was rude, her emotion sick with old fear. "Wraiths keep coming, but Adam won't let me have a gun."

"You hold on to it for now; just be careful. There's no standard safety on it, just that little lever on the trigger, so don't rest your finger there unless you mean it." Layla, whose anger had abated, held the gun out. "Go on, Zoe, take it."

"Fine." The girl named Zoe grabbed the gun. "I have to have something." What went unsaid but Khan understood was that she had to have something . . . for her sister. "The world's gone fucking nuts."

"You're telling me," Layla said.

"Oh, give it a rest," Zoe sneered. "My sister's told me about you. I know you're in thick with them and I know why."

"Care to share? Because frankly I'm at a loss."

"It's really not my problem."

Layla turned back to the door, frustration near bursting within her. "Right. Not your problem. Happy times with the gun."

"Wait," Zoe said with a long-suffering eye roll. Khan wondered why everything about the girl was at odds: her body was young, but her soul was old; she expressed one thing, but felt another; she said she hated Segue, but she clung to its security. If she weren't standing there in mortal flesh, he'd think she was fae. "What did June and Ward Cleaver do to get you all worked up? Must've been good, whatever they told you."

Layla faced her. "Basically that I'm related to them. I just need to know if they're screwing with my head. Because if what they say is true . . ."

"It's true."

"But . . ."

"It's true."

"Why should I believe you?" Layla's frustration gave way to acute anxiety, but Khan didn't put a stop to the conversation. If he couldn't convince Layla, perhaps this contrary woman could. "Maybe you're in on it," Layla continued.

Zoe's eyebrows went up. She put a hand to the bedroom door, pushed it open. "Because I didn't actually mean to shoot at you, I'll help you out. Then we're even."

Layla looked inside. The ailing sister lay slack on the bed. She was aged beyond her youth, hair thin and colorless, wrinkled skin hanging loose and dry on her bones. Her lips were cracked, Shadow filmy on the whites of her eyes. But Khan knew Layla could see deeper than an illness of the flesh. For Layla, the veil was as thin as a membrane, and just as transparent. She looked on an oracle for the ages. Layla would see the trees of Twilight looming darkly at the woman's back. She'd see how Shadow breached the matter of the oracle's body, impregnating the pitiable mortal with its capricious and jealous churn.

"That's my sister," Zoe said. "She basically knows everything about everyone, which is why she's so sick. Add Adam and Talia's fucked-up business and she's ready to die."

Layla was silent, her breath stopping as she looked on. Wonder and horror and sadness flooded out of her and into Shadow, and Khan knew she was ready to believe.

Finally.

"I'm so sorry for bothering you," Layla said to the oracle, stepping back.

The oracle's eyes cracked open. "You've finally come," she rasped. "I've been waiting for you."

"Me? Why me?"

"You started all this. You and your fae lord."

Khan caught the rheumy shift of the oracle's gaze as it flicked up at the ceiling of the room, where he watched.

"You mean Khan?"

The oracle grinned. "Khan."

"What about Talia?" Layla asked. "Are we—? Is she—?"

Yes. Khan very much wanted the oracle to answer this question. It would settle everything.

The oracle's smile faded. A tremor went over her body,

but she breathed a response. "Why do you ask what you already know to be true?"

Shadow rolled into the room, and the oracle's eyes darkened, the lids widening in horror at a pressing vision. "Rose is coming," she choked. "Watch yourself."

Confused, Layla looked to Zoe. "I don't know a Rose."

Zoe shrugged, murmuring. "The visions overlap sometimes and don't make sense. Did you get what you came for, or what?"

Shadowman was tempted to see into the oracle's Shadow himself and witness this Rose who frightened her so. Could she be the devil? But Layla was backing out of the room, saying, "Yeah, I think I did."

Zoe closed the door again. "If Abigail says you're related to those bastards, then you are. Goody for you."

"How long does she have?"

Zoe studied the floor. "I don't know. She's all I've got. As long as I can hold on to her, I guess."

A similar conviction rose in Layla, painful in its sharpness, so sweet in its fast-rising hope. She looked to the outer door, as if seeking her daughter, Talia. "Yeah, me too."

And Khan knew, for the moment, all was well. And it would be better still tonight when he could go to her in her dreams. In the meantime, he had work to do.

Someone was cooking, and it smelled like Heaven. Bacon, coffee, fresh bread. Rose wanted to cry, she was so happy. After twelve years of being hungry and deprived, tortured without reason, a home-cooked breakfast was just the thing to start the day, and a new life.

All she had to do was take care of a Ms. Layla Mathews. And Rose would, right after she ate.

The B&B had been a godsend. A sweet Victorian in

the middle of downtown Middleton. The inside was meticulous, woodwork gleaming, and the hand-sewn quilts decorating the walls reminded Rose of her mother. Braided rugs kept the cold off the polished floors. The owner, Grace, was a woman after her own heart.

"How's your hand this morning?" Grace asked when Rose came downstairs and sniffed out the dining room, ready to dig in.

Rose glanced at her bandage handiwork. The proportions were a little off since her hand had lengthened and thickened. Underneath, the yellowish cast to her skin had turned to a bruised, unsightly green.

How provoking of Grace to mention it.

"Just fine," Rose answered and approached the table. The lace runner had been removed and several dishes were set out. The mix of savory and pastry scents made her dizzy. "This looks delicious."

Rose tried not to be annoyed by the woman's thoughts. Right now Grace was thinking, *Just ask her. She's got to be expecting it.*

Grace smiled. "Wait till you try the blueberry pancakes. They'll keep you warm all day. But before we start, how about we settle up? I can run it real fast, and we won't have money hanging over our heads while we eat."

The woman had the nerve to congratulate herself. *There. That wasn't so hard.*

Rose looked at the steaming plate of cakes. She didn't have any money. Not even a credit card. She'd been dead twelve years. Besides, Mickey used to pay for everything.

"I really should've taken care of it last night, but you came in so late and seemed so tired," Grace said, then to herself, *Don't let her weasel out of it.*

Weasel? Rose's bad hand itched and ached, the binding suddenly too tight.

She flashed her dimples. "I don't have my purse with me. When I come down again, I'll take care of it."

No. You'll sneak out.

Grace put a hand to the back of Rose's chair, keeping it tucked under the table. "It's just, you didn't have your purse last night either."

A red haze swept over Rose's eyes. She really, really wanted to do something to Grace. Her hand was burning with it, and her ears were pounding with the urge to act. But the gate had warned against further bloodshed, even if it was warranted. Said she could and would be tracked by it.

Inconvenient. The food was getting cold. Her belly was rumbling.

"How about you just run up and get your wallet."

"How about you put a fork in your eye?" Rose snapped.

No one was more shocked than Rose when Grace did just that. Opaque fluid mixed with blood spurted, then ran down her hostess's cheek. Grace held the fork's weight up, hand shaking, and covered her oozing eye with her other hand. Goop leaked between her fingers.

The screams that followed made Rose ball up one of the nice linen napkins and stuff it in Grace's mouth. Too bad the screams went on in Grace's head.

Helpme, please, ohgodohgod, pull it out! Ohgod, hospital, helpme helpme . . . !

Rose pushed Grace into the kitchen pantry, shut the door, lodged a chair under the knob, and took her breakfast to go. She wore Grace's coat, a classic wool in royal blue, and had Grace's wallet in her pocket.

The old lady in the antique store was harder to push, but after a few forceful suggestions, she handed over the money in the cash register and danced around her store naked like a monkey.

There really wasn't anything Rose couldn't do.

Chapter 9

"What the hell did you think you were doing?" Adam yell-whispered at Zoe as he removed the magazine from the gun. He waved away the soldiers who arrived at the apartment door, and they moved out in short order.

"It's my fault." Layla kept her voice low, too. No one wanted to bother Abigail. "And my gun. I was just showing Zoe how it works."

"Shut up," Zoe said to her. To Adam she stuck up her chin. "I can have a gun if I want."

"Not at Segue, you can't." He tucked the barrel into the back of his pants. "You almost killed Ms. Mathews."

Layla waved. "Still alive, though."

Adam ignored her. "I can't be bothered about what's going on inside when I've got wraiths on my doorstep."

"Then give me the gun, and you won't have to worry about me." Zoe smirked and held out her hand.

Reluctantly, Adam gave both the gun and the magazine to her. "I want you trained. No exceptions. Today." He left cursing under his breath. He shut the door softly, with excessive control.

"You can leave, too," Zoe said, transferring her gaze to Layla. "We're done."

What a piece of work. Layla could've been ticked, but she chose to laugh. "You mean we're not going to braid each other's hair?"

Zoe made a face, and Layla let herself out.

The elevator door at the end of the hall was closing, which was just as well. Layla needed time in her own head before she faced her long-lost family. This next reunion could only be awkward.

She took the hallway at a slow walk, shaken by what she'd seen in Zoe's apartment and the implications for herself. Layla had seen some disturbing things over the course of her life, but nothing compared to the raw transparency of Abigail's condition.

Abigail's body had been limp in her bed, like an old woman waiting to die. She seemed bird brittle, used, her limbs loose. And in her unblinking eyes lurked Shadow, smoldering with knowledge. Whatever Abigail witnessed in the dark churn of her vision about Rose must have been terrifying, the horror of it in the O of her open mouth. And behind her were Khan's trees stretching out of nightmare while the rest of the room was solid, mundane. Abigail wasn't ordinary. There was no denying that she'd been cursed with a gift. And somehow Layla knew Zoe couldn't save her, no matter how hard she might try.

It was a sorry situation, one that Zoe shut everyone out of as she simultaneously grieved for and clung to her sister. To her only family.

And it seemed now that Layla had a family, too, though she had no idea how to handle the revelation. The thought made her chest tight with strange, contradictory emotions that threatened to unravel her. Best thing to do was head back and go through the motions of the day until it felt normal again. Gauge Talia's reaction. Conduct her interviews. Layla already knew what Khan wanted.

"He's gone now. You can play with me," a child's voice said.

Layla stopped dead in her tracks, the fine hairs on her body standing on end. The little girl ghost, ringlets perfectly in place, stood before her. Pinafore pressed. Bows perfect.

"Who's gone?" Layla managed.

The ghost put a hand up to her mouth to tell a secret. "The dark man. He follows you."

Layla looked at Zoe's apartment door. But then she remembered ghosts couldn't act on the world. She should move on down the hallway and get back to her side of the building, and as quickly as possible.

"Play a game with me?"

Layla ignored her. She sidled by the apparition, trembling with cold sweat, and headed for the elevator, *hating* the west wing. How anyone could live there was beyond her.

Then she stumbled to a stop again. The hallway was morphing before her eyes. Green striped paper appeared in place of the beige paint on the walls and the floor darkened, the carpet replaced with a brown runner. Light in the passage dimmed to a soupy murk. Layla glanced back. The ghost girl, strangely, appeared more solid. Layla could almost smell the sticky sweetness of her.

Not act on the mortal world? What the freak did they call this?

Layla took two steps forward, but doing so seemed to enhance the effect of the change. She turned back, uncertain. If she screamed now, would anyone hear? "Zoe!"

"Play with me." The little girl sat cross-legged in the

middle of the hallway, and she tucked her skirt over her knees.

Layla retraced her steps to Zoe's apartment, as if she could adjust time by where she stood in the passage, but the illusion didn't shift. She was stuck. "Khan!"

The girl shook her head, curls bouncing. "The dark man isn't here."

Layla swallowed hard and finally acknowledged her host. "What's your name?"

"Therese. Sit down, silly, so we can play."

Layla didn't want to, but the child might be her only way back. Even as Layla lowered herself to the floor, her stomach turned. She sat cross-legged, too. "I'll play just as soon as you return me to my time."

"Do you know the words?"

Layla wasn't going to get sucked in to her game. "I want to go back to my time. Can you help me?"

"Say the words." Therese gave her sweet smile, then shrieked, "*Now!*"

Scuttling back, Layla said, "I don't know the words."

Therese leaned forward, intently. "Yes, you do. Dead man, dead man, come alive . . ."

Oh. Layla *had* heard that somewhere before.

"Come alive by the number five."

Layla recoiled from the madness in Therese's expression. Sitting had been a mistake. She stood, headed for Zoe's apartment. Anywhere was better than the company of the ghost child.

"Say it!" Therese screamed behind her, then added in singsong, "I'll let you go. Just say: Dead man, dead man, come alive!"

Not likely. Layla wasn't stupid enough to go along with anything about a dead man coming alive, especially on the instruction of a disturbed ghost of a child in a haunted hotel that imprisoned wraiths. There had to be other options.

Layla's skin crawled as she rapped on what had to be Zoe's door.

Please, open. Her heart hammered, tripping over its rhythm. She flushed with heat, then cold. The rhyme was bad news, had to be.

In an overlap of time, a translucent version of Zoe flung open her door and looked both ways down the hallway. She didn't acknowledge Layla.

"Zoe!" Layla called, right in her irritated face.

But Zoe cursed and shut the door again.

"One, two, three-four-five!" Therese chanted.

Okay, Zoe was oblivious, but maybe a fae would be different. If Layla could just find Talia or Khan, maybe one of them would see her and get her out. Right? Was there another way? Fear fuzzed her mind like electricity, her thoughts almost breaking apart into panicky, incoherent bits, but she held on. She couldn't stay here. Here was bad. Real bad. She had to get back to the elevator and the east side, where the ghost couldn't follow. Then find help.

Therese was up on her feet. She stamped her foot, hard. "Dead man, come—"

The space in front of the elevator suddenly punched black. Shadow reached, swirling into the long hallway, like octopus arms in a swim of darkness.

Oh, thank goodness. Khan.

But the voice that spoke was female and shattering. "Lady Amunsdale!"

"She's mine!" the child screamed back.

"She's mine," Talia answered from the void. There was no mistaking the authority with which she spoke. That voice was power, awesome in its cadence.

Darkness pounded down the corridor. It rushed over

Layla, cold and slick, and finally she could see Talia. Her pale hair whipped in the dark wind of her Shadow, her skin glowing with a weird light, eyes full-black.

Fae, Layla identified, and stopped breathing.

Shadow grumbled over the walls, wrecking them and battering Therese in its wake. Layla felt a pang for a child harmed, though she was a mean little brat. Therese was tossed, and when she reemerged, she wasn't a child at all, but a rag of a woman, bitterness lining her expression.

"I need her!" Therese the woman called.

Her reach was perversely long. She grabbed at Layla's shirt with bone hands. On instinct, Layla whirled around to tear off the ghost, but gripped only air, though the ghost's touch clawed at her still.

Layla felt as if her soul was slipping from the moorings of her body. Felt a sudden distinction between flesh and spirit, and she knew she was grasping after the wrong thing. Her soul lifted like a balloon, and she let go of Therese and grabbed hold of herself instead. Two spirits, one body, its heartbeat stalling.

"Leave her be, Lady Amunsdale." Talia's voice had lowered, but its power still sent currents through the warping dark. "Now!"

And Layla slammed back into her body again.

"Dead man, dead man . . ." Therese chanted again, but she lost her scraping grasp on Layla's shoulder.

Layla looked back just in time to see Shadow harry the ghost off on the tide of its storm. The ghost reached toward her, straining in desperate misery, but was swallowed by the abyss at the end of the hallway. In a static suck of sound, the hallway was returned to its modern appearance, Layla at one end, Talia at the other, now looking more human, if very disconcerted.

Forget Khan. What the hell was Talia? Her, uh, daughter? More like Khan's.

"Lady Amunsdale is a pest," Talia said, breathing heavily. "Don't let her get to you."

Layla stammered for something to say. "She pulled me back in time. She wanted me. Why?"

And what the hell had Talia just done? An ocean of Shadow? That bone-shattering voice? Those fae were some serious mothers.

"I don't know. Might be a complication of your reincarnation. We'll have to ask Custo, or maybe my father. I'm more concerned about *how*." Talia inclined her head toward the elevator. "Let's get out of here, have lunch. Puzzle it out together."

Layla's drying perspiration sent a chill down her back, but she boarded the elevator. Talia had to know about the mother-daughter thing. The word *reincarnation* hung in the air between them, but Layla had no idea what to say, so she decided to remain quiet.

"I freaked you out, didn't I?" Talia bit at her bottom lip but kept her gaze on the doors.

"No, no," Layla lied. "We're good. I'm surprised, but good."

"Come on now. I freak everyone out."

"Well, everyone doesn't know Khan. And he spoke to me from a painting today."

Talia laughed, but it seemed forced. "I told him to go easy on you, and here I . . ."

"Don't worry."

"But . . ."

"Really. I've seen crazy stuff all my life and no one ever believed me."

The tension didn't leave Talia's eyes. "Lunch, then, and you can tell me about it."

"Sure." Chances were, Talia would believe every crazy thing Layla had seen.

"Oh, and for the immediate future," Talia said, "it's probably best for you to stick to the east side of Segue."

Layla choked a laugh. "Ya think?"

Khan laid a peace offering at the foot of Layla's bed: her bag from her apartment, so she could be more comfortable, and a pile of fragrant red roses, forced into extravagant bloom. Mortal women were supposed to like those, and he was under his daughter's instruction to court when he wanted very much to take.

For the moment, he left Layla to Talia, who knew better how to settle her into this new life, and lifted out of Segue and into the weak winter sunshine. With Death hanging over the land, the temperature dropped, a hush silenced the afternoon skitter of leaves, and movement slowed. The Reaper was on the hunt again.

The devil was being careful, growing wise to the ways of the mortal world. No smears of wrongful death marked its path, yet it lurked somewhere within the streets. Khan loomed over the village of Middleton. Only an occasional soul was about. They hurried inside, drawing their coats more tightly about them, and glanced over their shoulders as if Death stalked the streets. And so he did.

He checked each house, set children wailing with his passage. He made the dogs howl and the cats arch their backs. The leaves fell more swiftly from the wintery trees as he blackened the streets with his icy search, and he paused only when he chanced upon an angel, leaning on a lamppost in the now failing light.

"She's here somewhere," the angel said, with a wry expression. "Had a little trouble this morning with her. She's been messing with people's heads. We almost had her, but she got away."

"No deaths," Khan answered, or he would have felt the mark. He did not like the angels, but he was glad they were searching, too, and probably limiting the harm the woman could cause on the unsuspecting populace.

"No?" The angels had no gift for death. "Well, that's good news."

"She'll be turning foul, a monster to behold."

"Takes one to know one," the angel returned. He shoved his hands into his pockets and walked down the sidewalk, his back to Death.

The devil, a *she*, was biding her time. It made no sense for her to strike in Middleton now, when Layla was so near. Khan could feel a sense of waiting in the stillness of the air for the moment the devil deemed it right to strike. The angels were here to keep the peace in the interim.

The day, like the eons of days before it, had been swallowed by the night, so Khan returned to the beat of life within Segue.

The roses were in a vase at Layla's bedside.

She paced in the room beyond, wringing her hands. The air was rife with the charge of her nerves, so he drew out a chair that she might sit down and calm herself.

"Khan?"

If her apartment had had any of Kathleen's paintings, he could have given her a familiar face to speak to. But these rooms were like all the others in Segue, similar in their comfortable furnishings, unimaginative in decoration.

He needed another medium and found it in the glass of a window.

He rapped with Shadow for her attention.

She screamed when she saw him there, and he considered her perspective. For her, he was a face in the night, looking in from the dark air some distance from the ground. It took a moment for her heartbeat to slow again. He was rapt with the subtle expressions that played across her face, matching them to the emotion that touched his Shadow: an excited kind of fear, which he liked; a pleasure-coil of interest, which he liked better; and best of all, humor, though it was born of exhaustion. If she could laugh at him, they might have a chance.

"I'm curious," she said, "how you think this could possibly work out."

He pushed for a smile. "You doubt my ability to seduce you?"

And got raised eyebrows instead. "Well, right now, you're a window man, and earlier you were a painting man, and when you're all creepy with darkness, a shadow—"

"Layla!" He cut her off.

She startled, which he regretted, but he couldn't have her completing that thought. So often her mind worked like Kathleen's; they'd both arrived at the same name for him. Shadowman. But names have power, and with it, she would surely know his nature.

Layla sighed hugely, shaking her head. "You should know that we're doomed from the start, and not only because you're, um, two-dimensional right now."

"Anything is possible." He had to believe that, however small their chances. Possibility was the essence of Shadow. "You bid me come to you before. I came. You asked me to touch you before. I answered the call of your desire. We gave ourselves up to each other. We made our own doom, but I'd take it again if you'll have me."

"Well"—she ran a nervous hand through her hair—"while I might be . . . *intrigued* by your interest, and what you claim is our history, I just . . ." As she spoke, she worried the skin on her ring finger and looked away. "This is crazy. Any chance you'll be out in the real world soon? It would be much easier to speak to a body."

His body was the problem. "It may be some time before I can get back. Please continue. You just what?"

"I don't remember you." She sobered completely. "Maybe our time has passed. Maybe you were meant to be with Kathleen, but not so much with me."

"I've searched the whole of your life for you. Been burned by divine light. Breached Hell even." His Shadows grumbled within him. "And now that I have you, I'm not letting go. Our time is just beginning."

He watched her swallow hard. Scrape the skin on her ring finger.

"What troubles you?" he asked.

Her gaze darted nervously away, then back. "Well, I'm sorry to have to point this out, but you're strange. Frighteningly strange."

"Get used to it."

"Yeah, and the bossy, imperious thing . . ." She made a pained face as if looking for the right words. "I'm a pretty independent woman. You say something arrogant, flip your long black hair, and I just want to, uh, mock you, which I think might be very dangerous. And I've had enough danger for today, thanks."

She was right. What he had in mind would be much easier face-to-face. "Go to the bed, Layla, and lie down."

She tilted her head, as if thinking. "See, now, there you go again. I'm not quite sure if you're aware of it since it comes so easily to you. You just commanded me to do something, and I can't see myself complying."

Her words were at odds with her reaction. The word *bed* had sparked a violet pulse deep in her womb. Part of her badly wanted to be in bed. It was her indomitable will and her Earth-centric reservations that tormented them both. They needed Twilight, and now.

"Layla, will you lie down for me? Or will you drive me mad?"

"Those are my options?" she scoffed, goading him.

"I am immortal, yet I do not know how I will survive you."

She waggled her head. "Yeah, and speaking of the immortal thing . . ."

Khan cursed himself. "Lie down."

"Don't boss me."

"*Please*, lie down."

"I don't go to bed with people, or"—she snorted—"*immortal fae*, that I've just met."

"You know me, Layla, or you would not be arguing with me." *Stop fighting, love*. "Your inborn sense of preservation would send you flying from my presence. And yet you stay, and argue with a dark lord of the fae, because you know that, of all mortals, you are safe. I ask you to lie down so that I can share your dreams, so that we might converse a little easier."

She frowned. "You scared the crap out of Dr. James this morning."

"An excellent example of the typical mortal response."

"What are you?"

His Layla was too clever.

"Fae," he answered.

She gazed at him in the window and pressed her lips together, deliberating. "The 'dark lord' part was a bit much."

He bowed his head to concede her point. Nevertheless, a dark lord he was. That much she would have to accept.

"It will be your dream, Layla. You control what happens in it."

"Dream only," she said.

"Yes, of course." What occurred in the dream, however, was entirely up to her.

She went to her bedroom and set herself up primly, head centered on her pillow, hands clasped over her belly, ankles crossed. The coverlet dimpled around her. Her mind was too agitated for slumber, so he waited for the moment her shoulders relaxed, her thoughts wandered, and then he cut her free and let her fall.

Khan emerged in the dockside warehouse where they'd first met. He took the form Layla knew, the body that Kathleen had created for him. In dreams, he could be anything.

The warehouse was done up with the riches he'd copied from the magazine scrap: plush chairs; books; the map flat on the table, held down by the figure of a wooden Buddha, who regarded him tranquilly. Khan found Layla staring into the gilded mirror. Frustration beat the air around her. The glass was murky; whatever she sought eluded her.

"Layla," he said.

The room blurred as she turned, her mind sifting the details of the dream from a new vantage point. He held his body fast as the furnishings settled into clarity again. Dreams were always shifting, always fluid. Beyond this little island oasis, the trees of Twilight swayed.

"I can't find her," she said. "I look and look and look and I can't see anything."

Layla had been searching her reflection, so he could guess whom she was looking for. He approached and skimmed his knuckles across her cheek. "She's here. You're here."

"I'm lost."

Would she even remember their words this deep in a dream? How much comfort could she bring back to consciousness? He didn't know. He bent to touch her nose in an Eskimo kiss. "You're found."

The color of her anguish shifted to intense, consuming longing. The dream, the room deepened, the hues growing harsh, aging. "I don't want to be alone anymore."

"You're not alone. I'm here. Come what may, I'll never let you go again." To prove it, he brushed his mouth across hers.

Fine black lines of anger cracked the room as she became self-aware in the dream setting. It was a difficult skill to master. Kathleen had been proficient at it as a child, and Layla was learning just as fast.

"I need to be able to take care of myself. A ghost attacked me today, and Talia had to save me." Layla gestured wildly to the mirror, where another version of herself now stood, dressed in the gold gown he'd fashioned for her upon their meeting. The gown ill fit the body it covered. "I'm not your precious princess Kathleen, locked in the castle tower waiting for rescue."

On that point, Layla was mistaken. "Kathleen fought the only way she could: she *endured*."

"Yeah, well in this life, I don't sit around." Her dream voice warped with her intensity.

It was the quintessential human struggle: to be the master of one's own fate. Layla didn't know it, but even now she fought a power far greater than a wisp of a ghost. She fought Moira, who inevitably would win.

"A ghost attacked you?" They were harmless.

"Yeah, the west wing freaky child."

Softly, in singsong, a chant began to echo in the warehouse. "Dead man, dead man, come alive . . ."

And Khan grew cold as he understood the threat: the chant was a curse, masquerading as child's play. Layla's lifeline was cut, her time on Earth at an end, and therefore, her body was forfeit. The ghost, clinging to life, sought to occupy it. The chant, *Dead man, dead man, come alive,* was an invitation for her to take over Layla's flesh. And Layla would be cast out, forced to cross or become a ghost herself.

As a rule, ghosts were shallow things, rarely capable of intelligence, just strong feeling: sadness, rage, greed.

This act reeked of design, of a trap. Moira. Again.

The dream hazed for a moment. "Talia got her. I mean, damn—"

Good girl. But Talia could not force the ghost to cross. The "west wing freaky child" still walked the halls of Segue.

"It's me who can't do anything," Layla said.

She squinted back into the mirror, but the figure in the glass was still indistinct, a definite problem. This reincarnation business was messing with her head big-time.

"You have more power than you think," Khan said. "Those in the mortal world have the most power of all."

"Compared to you guys, I have none." And the world grew more frightening and unknowable by the hour.

The dream flashed white, muddled her senses, before settling again.

She turned back to Khan, Mr. Dark Lord of the Fae. He wore black, head to toe. Pants that skimmed over his long, muscled physique. A simple shirt that defined the ridges beneath. And a minimalist leather coat. His hair fell past his shoulders, and as she watched, it braided itself, and the sharp line from jaw to cheekbone was revealed.

What the hell was he?

No, wait. She didn't want to know.

The dream flashed again—Khan was near, then far—

all perspective seemed off. Better to *feel.* That sixth sense overrode everything else.

Feel everything.

She knew she should be screaming in fear, but she was stirring with interest and . . . and . . . tingly, torturous *want* instead. The sensation, right down below her belly button, had never been this strong. Perhaps meeting him in dreamland was a mistake. Fighting this pull was going to be far more difficult here.

"Are you doing this to me? Making me feel this way?" It would be inexcusable if he was.

"No," he answered, but his wicked grin was back. "I can cast an illusion that might terrify or please, but I cannot make you feel anything."

"You can do more than cast an illusion," she said. "I've seen it."

"I can sense the rapid beat of your heart." He circled her in a blur of movement. "And I can sense your emotions. Your dream is thick with them. Shall I describe what you feel?"

The room flashed white again, and it occurred to her that each lightning strike was her desire, crackling in the air around them.

"Well, scared. Doesn't take a genius to figure that out," she mumbled.

He bent his head to her ear, the line of his jaw just touching her temple. Goose bumps roared across her flesh from the point of contact.

"Bright. Wild. Fearless."

Layla trembled. "I'm *terrified.*"

"Of what is going on around you, yes. But not of me."

He remained motionless, standing beside her, waiting. Shadow magic buzzed the air between them, simmering with energy on her skin. And still he waited.

This was a choice, she understood that much.

She'd been responding to Khan from the moment she met him. Khan said he'd been looking for her. Maybe she'd been looking for him, too. Nothing, no man, had ever made her feel like this.

So. Stay on safe ground, or leap?

Lightning struck again. She chose the storm.

She put a hand to his chest for balance, raised herself on tiptoe, their gazes meeting for an electric second, and then she kissed him.

She got his upper lip mostly, full, taut, just at the parting dimple, but then he opened his mouth to adjust in a hot, rasping slide she felt all the way down her body. His arms came around her, gathering her into a tight squeeze that compounded the urgency of the terrible, building pressure between them. The kiss seared reason from her mind. All sense of place, time, even gravity fell away, so that there was only her, now gripping the roots of his hair, and him, stroking her lips with his, her tongue with his. The ache in her abdomen tightened into a fierce, wet knot of bliss-pain. *You and I.* Yes. She got it now. The air rushed around them, silky and sensuous in texture, somehow gliding against her skin as if she were naked. And in a way, she was. His kiss stripped her of all pretense and denial.

"Is this how it was?" She was shaking. Or he was. Or maybe it was thunder.

"Very much so." He shifted his hold so he could look into her eyes. Around them the colors of the warehouse room churned. His expression was near savage with triumph.

She understood that, too. The dream flashed bright white again.

Layla shifted, grabbed his wrist, and dragged his hand

to her breast. She pressed to show him what she wanted, and he laughed against her mouth. Reckless, she thought, but couldn't bring herself to care.

The cloth under his palm dissolved and she was naked in his arms, burning under his hands.

"Khan?" she gasped in shock. This was moving way too fast.

"It's your dream. You did that all by yourself," he said. He drew his thumb across her peaking nipple, then grazed his hand down to the curve of her hip, her thigh, to draw her leg up around him. To bring and tilt her closer.

And here she'd thought a dream would be safe . . .

The air charged again, flickering with a brightness that highlighted the man holding her.

. . . when in a dream she really didn't care about safe.

She grazed his neck with her mouth, mumbling, "At least be naked, too."

And his apparel evaporated into smoke, wisping away from his body.

"How can you doubt your power?" He drew her closer.

None of this was really happening . . . was it?

Layla's mouth dropped to his chest. She curled her tongue around his nipple, her body straining under his hands. She stroked her cheek against the plane of his muscle. Licked the ridge where muscle met bone.

"Khan, please . . ."

"Yes?" And his hold on her thigh shifted, his hand stroking higher to somewhere infinitely more intimate.

She gripped his shoulders as her heart raced. Her fingernails dug into his skin.

The sensations were building, his hands working a magic that burned color from her sight, that propelled her up and up, toward an exquisite peak, so high . . . that Layla woke gasping for air.

Where was he?

Gone.

Or rather, she was.

Disappointment mingled with her need, a bitter combination. She sat up, covers tangled around her legs. He'd been there, right?

And he'd touched her. Or started to. But it wasn't enough. Not nearly.

"Khan?" she gasped. *Don't leave me like this.*

She braced herself on the mattress as the top sheet and cover slowly slid from the bed. Her breath came quick, but it was enough to keep her mind sharp.

"Khan."

The room had been lit by starlight, but now it grew dim and took on a silky texture, sliding sensuous and cool against her bare arms. Like water, it moved around her and she longed to feel the Shadow on her thighs and breasts, at her nape and within her deep places. Longed to have sex with the darkness. Want beat between her legs for him. For a man who had no body to ease the burn.

Shadow rolled over her, and she was both eased back and buoyed up on the torrent. This was better than the dream and would be best if he could be there with her. If she could hold on to him and they could do this thing together.

She held her breath as a hand of darkness tilted her head. Shadow brushed her mouth, touched her tongue. A kiss. And as she arched into the thick air, reaching to grasp something—*someone*—her clothing was pulled down from her waist. Cool Shadow spiraled up her calves to the juncture of her legs. The hem of her shirt fluttered up to bare her breasts, her nipples tight in the pitch of the room.

She shrugged for him, and her shirt was gone, too. It

was just her and her man in the shadows, and she was both terrified and exhilarated at what might come next. No matter what, he wasn't going to leave her wanting, like a dream.

"Khan?"

Shadow seduced her, clinging to her skin, caressing each millimeter so that every part of her was claimed, made known to him. She couldn't hide, couldn't seek a little corner of her mind to be safe and alone. He demanded everything. She could either fight him, a thought that made her zinging nerves quail, or give in. Allow him to take her.

The storm on her senses continued, but he was waiting for her permission. Again.

"Please, yes . . ." She understood now, a little better, why Kathleen had agreed to this union. If he would just stroke harder, reach a little farther, then . . .

Yes! Her mind fragmented as darkness feathered over her, filled her so completely that she couldn't breathe, rocking with the throb of his assault.

Pressure mounted in cool pulses against her swollen flesh. White static hazed her vision in an extended strike of lightning. And she shattered, bright stars swirling in the dark as she trembled in his Shadow embrace.

She was held aloft, the only sound her breath hitching.

Her skin felt tighter, senses overwhelmed, yet still exquisitely acute.

She arched again in Khan's hold, marveling. No human man could ever make her feel like this. She couldn't remember when or how they first came together a lifetime ago, yet the tandem draw and pull of their connection remained. It didn't matter if she was Kathleen or Layla, and he was Khan or . . .

Or . . .

Layla held her breath.

She'd almost had something there. A memory. A scrap of her before-life. A name?

"What did Kathleen call you?" she asked the Shadows surrounding her.

But he couldn't or wouldn't answer.

Cool air swirled around her as she was lowered slowly to her pillow and the bed. The sheet and covers rustled and then were pulled over her, rough on her skin and nipples after the slide of his Shadow.

He was tucking her in.

A brush on her lips. Which was an evasion.

"Who are you really?"

Another brush. She tilted her chin to catch more. To beg for an answer. She'd trusted him with herself, but he wasn't returning the gesture.

He stroked her cheek, and she knew no name would be forthcoming. He kept his secrets to himself.

He was there in the dark, but she was alone again. As ever.

Chapter 10

A shrill series of beeps wrenched Layla out of a dreamless sleep. All the lights in her apartment were on, and the phone was ringing in the front room. Something was wrong. Her apartment was *alarmed.*

She fell out of bed, blinking dumbly, and stumbled through the bedroom doorway to pick up the receiver.

An automated voice said, "A wraith incursion is in progress at the Segue perimeter. Please remain in your room until—" Which cleared her mind completely with a jet of adrenaline. Wraiths? "—you have further instructions. The Segue building is in lockdown for your safety."

The line went dead. Layla dragged a hand through her hair to steady herself. The dregs of sleep were now flotsam in her waking mind.

And then she remembered everything.

What had she done?

Correction. What had she allowed to be done to her? Just thinking of it made her skin heat with embarrassment. She wrapped her arms around herself. Squeezed to extinguish the burn of humiliation. Khan was hiding something from her. Bastard. And he was going to tell her.

"Khan?"

No answer.

She found her sweats, a pair of Segue loaners, and shoved her feet into her shoes. She peeked out her window. It was still dark. All was quiet on her side of the building except the beat of her heart.

"Khan?" She was freaking talking to herself.

Far away, she heard shots fired. Her adrenaline kicked up a notch. What she wouldn't give to see Segue in action.

She tried the front door. Locked. She turned the bolt. Still locked.

Which was dumb. A door wouldn't stop wraiths. Besides, the wraiths weren't near the building, and with all of Segue's firepower, they weren't likely to get close. There was no reason she should be locked inside. This was her story, after all, the only thing keeping her sane. Especially after . . .

Layla dropped onto the sofa, her head in her hands. This was not acceptable. Tomorrow she and Adam would have to come to an agreement. "I *hate* controlling men."

In the silence of the moment, the lock to her apartment door went *snick.*

Khan. So he was still there.

Layla rose, tried her hand on the lever, which now worked.

Very handy trick. "Okay," she said to the air, "but we've got to talk later."

Layla threw open the door and jogged toward the elevator. Damn it, she wanted her camera. Her camera, stolen with her car, and her gun, which was in Zoe's possession. A sense of being followed had her glancing over her shoulder; so Khan had her back. No gun necessary. A sensuous whoosh of darkened air on her skin made her abdomen clench. Yeah, he was there all right. Damn him.

She opened the door to the stairs, which must have signaled something to Segue security, because two steps inside the stairwell and a metal wall of bars came down in front of her, cutting off her progress down the stairs. She turned back just as another sudden wall trapped her in the space, like a cage. It had to be some kind of precaution against wraiths, built along with Segue's renovation. And she guessed it made sense that they'd block entrances and passageways in the event of a wraith attack, but it was hugely inconvenient for her.

Or was it? The teleport thing, what Khan called "passing." She debated for half a sec, then decided. "Do you mind taking me to where I need to go? You know, close enough to see, but not so close I get my head bitten off?"

The stairwell darkened. Layla clutched the railing. A slow stroke of air moved around her body. A rush of Shadow, an embrace of shuddering magic, and she was on uneven earth.

Layla blinked hard against the dramatic shift from Segue light to predawn dark. The horizon was just barely beginning to whiten. The sharp winter air singed her lungs but she didn't feel cold.

Sparks flashed with a volley of automatic weapons fire, startling her heart. She could make out human shapes, but whether man or wraith, she couldn't tell. She picked her way forward, squinting to see. There was movement to her left. The low buzz of a voice. Male. A bunch of men.

Had to be Segue soldiers. One turned, as if sensing her presence.

"Ms. Mathews?"

Adam.

"For chrissake, you should be inside."

"I'm not a stay-inside kind of girl." Reckless was her middle name. Adam had no idea.

Layla knelt down behind them. Adam didn't object. He and his men went back to peering at some kind of army technology that displayed glowy human forms moving across a gridded terrain.

Adam tapped on the screen, which shifted vantages. "Where's Khan?"

Of course, Adam would know how she got there, and so quickly. How else could she get through his security and out of the Segue building, some three hundred yards away?

"Somewhere. He won't show himself."

Adam grunted. Obviously, Khan's behavior wasn't unusual to him.

Layla scanned the woods, letting her eyes adjust to make out a couple of crouched soldiers in the thick brush. Bullets couldn't kill a wraith, but they'd slow it down long enough that a trained team could incapacitate and take it into custody.

"How many?" she whispered.

"At least six," Adam answered. "This isn't a full-blown attack. They're just testing the perimeter with small parties."

"What are they after?"

He flicked his gaze over. "Talia. Always Talia."

The look in his eyes—worry, anger, frustration—made Layla like him for once. Every day he worked to stop the wraiths, crouching in the cold dark to keep his wife and children safe. He was a soldier, like these men, dedicated to a cause. If he was hard and controlling, she guessed he had reason to be.

"The perimeter is secure, Mr. Thorne. One casualty. One wraith in custody. No further wraith-sign."

"Doesn't feel right," he answered.

Could've been the cold, but Layla had that bad, skin-prickling feeling, too. Like she was in the center of a bull's-eye, oblivious to the arrow winging her way. The soldiers at least had night-vision gear. Adam had his technology. She was in a T-shirt and sweats. But yeah, okay, with Mr. Enigma, dark lord of the fae, nearby.

Layla cast her gaze around, though she knew she wouldn't find him, especially in the dark. A wooly group of pines darted from the earth into the atmosphere. She followed them up to the faint twinkles in the sky.

Just in time to see a . . . a *thing*, a body, dropping from above. It altered its trajectory toward her, its length flattening as it descended. So not dropping, flying. It had no visible feet or hands, though its trunk seemed to have mass. Old, ripped clothes hung off its shoulders. Its face was ravaged with decay, mouth open, teeth extended to feed. Wraith, but not wraith.

Layla grabbed the gun from Adam's holster, flicked the safety off, and fired above into shadow-webbed branches.

"In the trees!" someone shouted a little too late. Rapid gunshot report battered her ears.

A roar of wind darkness blew through the air, riffling her hair and blasting across her back.

Her trigger finger stalled as the wraith was caught midair, twisting, almost crawling up the sky. A hideous *crack* broke the quiet as it bent double, but the wrong way, then fell to the earth with the hollow clatter of loose bones in a fleshy bag.

She'd seen a couple of wraiths brought down before. She'd written about the experience. But never had she seen one shredded like that. Had to be Khan at work again. Khan, her door opener, dream lover, and wraith killer.

She searched the sky, heart pounding, breath coming in great puffs of frosty air.

Another *crack*, and she turned, bracing in fear as a wraith fell dead to the ground.

The soldiers fired their guns again, but if not for Khan, men would be dying.

Layla grabbed Adam's arm. "Will they hurt him?"

Adam had dark, hungry glee in his eyes, a sharp smile cracking his face. "Not a bit."

The sky went ashy, the sun finally claiming the day. For a moment, Layla saw a swath of Shadow whipping like a cloak around the silhouette of a man. Khan. He was all darkness, arms outstretched, hands raised, body midpivot in the sky. With a pulse, he dispersed into a gritty ink stain and reformed some distance away, a tornado of black to cast another wraith to death on the ground.

"Show-off," Adam muttered.

Layla was breathless. "How does he do that?"

"Do what?"

"Kill them so quickly, so easily. I've never actually seen one die."

Adam's eyes glittered. "The wraiths are dead already. He just, uh, seals the deal."

The explanation made no sense. It had to be a fae thing, a magic thing.

Adam was up, moving toward Khan's first kill. Which was crazy. More wraiths could be out there, yet Adam seemed perfectly comfortable to move around without cover. His men followed suit. Everyone was confident of their safety in Khan's presence.

Layla craned to look above and all around her. Khan was still nowhere in sight, so she leapt, stumbling through the brush, after Adam to follow the story.

"I want the wraith remains picked up and delivered to the holding cell for examination," he was saying. "This one here first."

The smell was extraordinary, as if the wraith had been long dead. Layla had to cover her mouth and nose with her hand as she gazed down at the dry, yellowed husk of wraith tissue and bone. In the bushes was a swatch of stringy, dirty hair above jellied eyes. The remains lacked cohesion and weren't remotely recognizable as human.

"And to think," Adam said, "not too long ago you were camped out in my woods, all by yourself."

The memory made her wince with a belated realization of how much danger she'd been in. She easily could've been killed.

"What were you really after that day?" Adam took a pair of surgical gloves out of his pocket, put them on, crouched down.

Layla thought of how she'd sat with her camera, willing Talia to step out of Segue. "A photo to run with my story."

She crouched down, too. What did Adam think he could learn from the body? Was it still possible to identify the man the wraith had once been?

But Adam was looking at her. "You traveled down from New York, hiked for *hours* from Middleton, climbed my wall, and waited out in the cold for a photograph?"

"I know it sounds insane." She couldn't believe she'd done it either.

Adam shook his head, his hard expression softening. "Talia was all tears when she got back from visiting you the other night. I think I understand a little better now."

Adam's face was haggard with exhaustion, there was a blood smear at his neck, and by the looks of things, he had a day's worth of work ahead of him before he could rest. And if the wraiths were "testing the perimeter," as he'd said, then he might just be back out there again come nightfall.

A team of men in plastic coveralls joined them. They were masked and carried large, industrial-looking gray boxes, presumably containing equipment to gather and clean up the mess.

"We can talk more later, if you like," Adam said. "I've got to take care of things here now. And you can keep the gun. You clearly know how to use it."

She still gripped the handle, finger light on the trigger. "Segue's safe, then?"

"For the moment."

She nodded, then stood and stepped back to let the team do its thing while Adam managed the situation. Kept the gun in her hand, though.

It was interesting, if disgusting, work. She'd never seen a wraith killed before or been privy to the collection of its remains. Her adrenaline tanking, Layla crossed her arms to dispel a shiver of cold. The sun was over the horizon, the world washed with pink. The smell of the woods seemed to warm, but the temperature didn't. Soldiers walked among the trees and occasionally pinned the earth with a red flag to indicate the location of remains. And somewhere above, Khan was watching. He'd saved her life again.

An image of the wraith diving through the air flashed through her mind. And here the public thought that wraiths were diseased human beings.

"Can they all fly?" The alteration in the wraith's trajectory easily had been the most frightening moment of the battle. And she'd been searching out their nests to discover what made them work. How long would it have taken for her to arrive at a paranormal explanation? Probably forever.

Adam looked over at her. "Wraiths can't fly any more than people can."

Layla understood his reasoning, but . . . "This one did. I swear it."

Adam's face subtly tightened, but he didn't respond.

"Really." No one ever believed the crazy shit she saw. She figured Adam would be different. "Ask Khan."

The cleanup team worked a slender spatula tool into the earth, and Adam turned back to monitor their work. She reeled back coughing when the movement of the remains sent fresh stink into the air. Okay, discussion over.

She shivered again. Her ears ached from the cold, though the sun was bright yellow through the trees. Time to get back, take some notes on what she'd witnessed. She had a vision of a wall of Post-its in her bedroom divided into three parts for the three worlds. Maybe if she asked very nicely, someone would get her a whiteboard and a handful of markers.

As she stepped away, Adam said grudgingly, "I'll check the tapes. Flying wraiths could be a problem."

The trees and growth around her required some clambering and skin scratches before she got the few yards away she needed to feel comfortable calling for Khan to take her back.

"Khan?" She waited like a dummy for him to pick her up in his whoosh of darkness, but that didn't happen. Was he there, and not answering? Or had he gone? Either way, she'd have to walk the whole way back to Segue. Great. His mysterioso business was getting to her. Yet another thing to talk about.

A *pop* above had her whirling, her gaze searching the branches. A resounding *crack*, and she whipped to aim the gun overhead. Wrong move. A great, black branch hurtled downward, and she threw herself into the prickly thatches to escape its strike. Got the skin scraped off her calf and ankle. Lost her shoe.

She panted in shock as the men nearby crashed through the growth toward her.

Her heart wouldn't stop pounding, even as she felt strong hands lifting her and placing her on the cold earth. An army jacket was thrown over her shoulders, warm, while some guy took a look at her leg.

"Damn it, I forgot. . . . By violence or by *accident*," Adam was saying.

"What?"

"Nothing," he bit back. "I just fucked up, that's all."

"I'll live," Layla assured him, though the scrapes stung pretty bad. Whatever spray that soldier guy was using numbed the pain a little. No need to get upset. Just a branch.

Adam scowled, his face going red, so she figured she'd better shut up.

"I guess Khan's gone," she offered.

"Yeah. I wish he'd told me first." Adam gestured to a couple of men—one of whom had been her ruddy-faced escort, Kev, on the day of her ill-planned Segue photo op. "Get her back to Segue. Make sure Patel looks at that leg. She's prone to life-threatening infection, I just know it."

"No, I'm not," Layla interjected. Now he was really going overboard.

Adam lasered her with his gaze.

She put her hands up in surrender. "Fine. I'll see Dr. Patel again. But I'm fine."

"And watch for bears," Adam said to Kev. "If there are any left on the mountain, they're sure to come out of hibernation to be in these woods today with Layla around." To her, he said, "You stay inside, take stairs very carefully, and chew your food well. Talia's not losing you a second time if I can help it."

Chew my food? What?

Layla went very still, the blood in her veins rushing to a stop. Would these people never stop speaking in riddles? "What's going on?"

Adam's frown deepened. He closed his eyes, shook his head. "Never mind."

"What did Khan tell you?" And how convenient for him that he wasn't there to answer the question himself.

Kev and his partner looked confused.

Branch. Infection. Bears. Chew her freaking food? Her stomach turned as she mentally added to the list: assault, car accident, gunfire.

"I'm going to die, right?" That had to be it.

Adam went still and looked at her with those tortured gray eyes of his. Finally, he exhaled. "Not if we can help it. Not again."

There was a resignation in Adam's gaze, a sad kind of premature "You've finally got it." So Layla worked fast to parse the riddle.

She was Kathleen, who had died. . . . Yeah, around Layla's age.

But she was still young. Healthy. She should have *years* ahead of her. This was nonsense. She wasn't going to believe it at all.

Layla looked up at Adam. "How much time do I have?"

His nostrils flared. His jaw twitched. "As far as I know, you've been borrowing time for the past twenty-four hours."

Khan hung in the air like a crow, dark wings stretched over the wood, his eyes keen for signs of the living malice, called wraiths, or their even hungrier brothers, the *wights*.

Wights. They were bound to emerge, for one kind of monster would always beget another. Starve a wraith for long enough so that all humanity is eroded, its body self-consumed with its unforgiving hunger, and you have a wight. Adam's tight boxes wouldn't hold them. Gravity couldn't hold them. They had too little substance to mind mundane restrictions. Yet they were still not spirit, not ghost, and never could be, because they had no soul. Only their appetites drove them.

What Adam needed now was an old technology, one of earth, stone, and magic. A barrow, a grave. Khan would suggest something of the sort to Talia.

The sun was just cresting the horizon. Below Khan, in the forest, Layla was moving with Adam toward the remains of Khan's first kill, the wight who'd almost had her in its grasp. Dead now.

A sear on Khan's skin signaled the approach of yet another race to the field of battle, The Order, shining bright enough to light the bare lawns near the main building of Segue. The wraiths had come for Adam and Talia, but Khan knew the angels were here for him.

He hung in the sky considering their approach. The wraiths were dead or fleeing. Layla was in Adam's care, and yes, the angels had to be dealt with. They had the gate in their keeping. Eventually they would have to ask its maker how it might be destroyed.

After their first failed attempt, he'd been expecting them.

He left the wood, stretched across the sky, and gathered himself before the five angels who were situated on the dried lawn in a V, as if they were geese flying south for the winter. Custo stood in the ranks, coolly meeting Khan's gaze, even as Shadow roiled in the boy's eyes.

Khan did not concern himself with his appearance, as he did with Layla; they all knew who he was. Whatever their individual conceptions of Death, how they conceived the fae entity before them, Khan didn't care. To one he was evil-eyed, skeletal. To another, a dark, horned thing. To Custo, he was an echo of Kathleen's Shadowman, but harsher, more vicious, yet still a man.

The angels' combined presence scorched him, but he

stood fast as his skin flecked, blackened, sloughed into darkness, then repaired itself again. In mortality, however monstrous the form, pain accompanied the burn, but he preferred it that way. It was something physical, earthly, to feel, and thus brought him closer to Layla.

The angel at the head of the V was yellow blond, with pale blue eyes, and slightly pink, fair skin. "I am Ballard," he said. It was an old Norse name, meaning "strong." "By now you know that we can destroy the hellgate you created."

Quiet, somber conviction filled the air around the host—so they hadn't come to *ask* him anything; they'd come to state their intent.

Khan guessed what that was. "No."

"Doing so," Ballard continued, "will take the life of Layla Mathews, a life we know to already be at its end."

"No," Khan repeated, with greater force. He should never have let Custo take the gate in the first place. "You cannot. Such an act would be—"

Ballard held up a hand. "We would certainly do everything in our power to mitigate the pain she'd have to endure. None of us want to cause harm, but we know that nature, in due course, will eventually take her life."

Not if Khan could help it. Not today, or tomorrow, or the day after that. They'd just found each other.

When the sun rose this morning, Khan had thought he'd soon fight a devil. It was a fight he could win without difficulty. In the mortal world, the devil might be stronger, faster, more vicious than humans, but it was still *mortal* and Khan was not.

His Shadow burned, his cloak whipping with his fury.

But never did Khan think he would have to fight the angels. In fact, via Custo he thought he'd found a reluctant peace with them. But if they sought to harm Layla, they sought war. Khan himself would strike the first blow.

"Think a moment," Ballard continued. "Consider the alternative, the worst possible. She is bound to the gate, that much we know. To destroy the gate, she also must be destroyed. What if *the only way* to destroy the gate is to take the life that is bound to it? And what if she should die a random death, her fate bearing down on her, and our opportunity is lost? Should she die and the gate remain, it may never be able to be destroyed. We cannot risk that eventuality. We cannot suffer such a thing to exist on Earth. And let us not forget, she should be dead already. So we return to our first course of action: destroy the gate, regrettably killing Layla in the process. It is the only solution, and after great deliberation, Custo Santovari has agreed to take on this burden, as he was the one to give you the hammer in the first place."

"You speak of murder." Khan looked at Custo, who looked back, steady and sure.

"The devil that escaped Hell has already murdered nine people," Ballard returned. "You should have told us you opened the gate."

Khan hadn't opened it, but he wouldn't inform the angels and give them another reason to harm Layla.

War, then.

He reached long for Shadow and found it plentiful in the break-of-dawn filter of trees. Always at the brink of change was Shadow, ready and available. He'd need it all to fight the angels. And if they died and lost their souls, he would not care. He could teach them evil and darkness the likes of which no devil could contemplate. If the angels harmed Layla, he would do just that.

Ballard lifted a hand. "Hold a moment, before you strike us down."

A black mist rolled across the grass, hissing as it met the shins of the angels. Khan would drown them in it while Shadow strengthened him. No angel was as old and canny as Death. No angel, even of Valhalla, could defeat the Grim Reaper in battle. Without Layla, he would become all his names, marshal the fae and knock down all the walls, all gates.

The angels stood fast, as was their nature.

In the midst of the gathering darkness, Ballard cocked his head thoughtfully. "Do you know how rare it is that the same soul is permitted two lives in mortality?"

Khan gave a fierce grin. His Kathleen, his Layla, could do anything she put her will to. That's how magnificent she was. And these emissaries of Heaven wanted to kill her?

"And to be reborn in a space of time so near to the last is . . . well, it's nothing short of miraculous. As far as The Order knows, it's never been done, and we maintain excellent records."

Shadow darkened Khan's vision. He was filled with it, gorging in preparation.

"We believe she had to have a divine purpose in order to come back to Earth. She had to have some great work that only she could do to be permitted this second chance."

"Layla came back for her child. Our child."

Ballard frowned. "Over the millennia there have been countless mothers who have longed for their children with equal desperation. All of them had to wait. Kathleen, we believe, was no different in that regard."

Kathleen was different in every regard, but Khan's attention was caught. "Then what?"

"We have no idea." Ballard shrugged and smiled in spite of the darkness grasping up his legs, his imminent demise. "These are momentous times, and she was there, with you, when all things changed. So, while it would be prudent to take immediate action with the gate, we will wait and watch with great interest."

Khan stilled, the Shadow rippling with his surprise. "You will not harm her?"

Ballard nodded. "Layla is on borrowed time already. I wish her Godspeed with whatever it is she's supposed to do."

Never had Khan known an angel to lie, yet he was loath to believe this turnabout. But if Ballard spoke true, then for now, Layla was spared.

She was spared.

The Shadow on the earth thinned.

"There remains, however, the problem of the gate and the escaped devil. The Order has some small hope that you, as the creator, can dismantle it without harming Layla. At the very least, we'd like you to try in the event she should suddenly pass and the world be left with a gate to Hell and a devil run amuck."

Khan could not leave her, not with such precious little time they had left together, not with a devil headed to Segue, and Layla's life in the balance. Not with the wraiths and wights bearing down. Not now that he'd known the lost, abandoned child she'd been. "No."

Ballard's jaw flexed at the refusal. "You misunderstand me," he said. "We are running out of options. We want to give Layla the time she needs, but we will act on our own if we must. In either case, the gate to Hell cannot remain on Earth."

Again that conviction pouring out of them. Shadow still seethed across the winter frigid Earth, but they paid it no mind. They were all ready to die.

"Please try," Custo said. "I do not like the alternative."

"As ever, you are a murderer," Khan cut back.

"Shadowman!" It was a new voice, Talia's.

Khan bent his head in the direction of his daughter, who was pushing a stroller across the grass, the babes within bundled for a morning walk. Her arrival was so convenient, it smacked of prearrangement.

"This is not your concern, Talia," Khan said.

"The hell it isn't. I lost her, too." His daughter's face was pale, eyes sad. She'd heard everything: the gate; the devil; Layla's life, now at its end.

"This morning wraiths were falling from the trees," Shadowman said, "and you expect me to leave her here?"

"Is it safe for my children?"

Nowhere was safe for those children.

Talia's gaze grew hot. "Besides, I'd like a little time with her myself. And if this gate business is as *hellish* as I've been told, then you need to destroy it. It's your responsibility."

So indeed her presence here this morning was not a coincidence. It was part of The Order's design for his compliance. Clever.

"Please don't let Layla's life become connected to such a legacy of pain and fear," she said.

"Her life is already at its end, and you ask me to give her up again?"

"Not give her up. Never that." Talia stepped forward. "We'll keep her safe for you. The devil is mortal, so Segue security has a good chance of keeping it out."

By nature, the fae did not age, but Khan felt himself grow old. "A *wight* nearly had her just moments ago, and they are not mortal."

Ballard's interest sharpened. "A draug? Are the wraiths so far along then?"

"Yes, yet another reason why I am needed *here.*"

Talia put her body in front of her children. Her eyes went dark as she, too, drew from Twilight for strength.

Between clenched teeth, she asked, "What's a wight or a draug?"

"Wight and draug are the same, old in the history of the world," Ballard said. "It is a night creature, a wraith starved into an insubstantial corporeal form, so the Earth's gravity does not hold it. They are hungry to feed, but lacking all human mores and intelligence."

"They cannot be caged either," Khan said. "Adam needs to begin digging *barrows*, or graves. Wights can only be trapped in the earth, as if they are buried."

"You are safe enough during the day." Ballard looked away from Talia, dismissing her.

"And I'll be here at night," Khan finished.

Ballard shook his head. "Not good enough. Every second the gate remains on Earth, mortality is in grave danger."

"Mortality depends on Segue, too," Custo said. "Shadowman's solution makes sense."

"Do not think to speak for me, boy," Khan said.

Ballard inclined his head to Custo. "You forfeited your voice in this matter when you gave Shadowman the hammer."

"I like it, too," Talia interrupted, nodding, her breath coming hard with her relief. "Khan with you during the day, here at night."

"The irony," Ballard said to Khan, "is that you should be about your duty in Twilight, ushering the dead. No. I will not haggle the terms of your cooperation. You will come, now, and see to the gate, or we will see to the gate ourselves."

Khan smiled, the plain of Shadow going utterly still. "*You* misunderstand *me*. Death does not haggle. Does not bargain. Does not bow. Harm Layla, and the devils and wights will be the least of your concerns."

Silence reigned over the parley.

Then Ballard's face flushed red to match his anger, but his expression was stone. "For the good of man, I concede."

"Women, too, I hope," Talia murmured.

Khan glanced over at the rising sun, yellow bright. The wraiths were gone; Layla was safe for the moment. Time was short. "I'm ready now."

Layla was about to take a seat in the jeep when soldierman Kev jerked her back.

"Black widow," he said and swatted a big, black, and venomous spider. Once, twice, three times before it curled up its extralong legs and died.

Her time to die? Forget that. But Layla's heart was thumping. The forest bramble gave way to bumpy grass, which climbed to a single-lane access road. Kev took the road at a good clip, and when he broke into the valley, she spotted the castle of Segue.

The sunlight was behind her now, the sky pale blue, yet the building was only partially illuminated. The Escher effect again. Inky darkness crawled up the west wing so that not even the windows reflected the morning. The other part of the building looked solid, lightening with the rising sun.

The sight tugged at her mind, as it had that day when she'd come to snap a photo of Talia Thorne. Something was off about the building. Something wrong, dangerous. It made her feel as if she were small and exposed while a massive, violent storm hung on the horizon, but on a horizon line that Layla did not understand.

This was exactly what she'd been talking about with Talia.

Squeezing her eyes shut, she concentrated on relaxing. On breathing.

All her life she'd fought these kinds of visions. She'd pushed them into the back of her mind and had gotten along just fine. Well, mostly fine. She paid her rent. Got an education. And she had a story to report. If she focused on that, the fever in her heart would quiet.

She opened her eyes and the shadow on the building pulsed. Grasped.

Which made Layla gulp hard. Somewhere inside that building, Talia was playing with her children.

"Don't worry, Ms. Mathews," Kev said. "We're almost there."

She should tell them, just in case. These people dealt with scary crap every day—angels and fae and Shadow and who knew what else. They might even already know the darkness was there and weren't worried about it. After all, Khan used *Shadow* for his magic, and what was that thing on Segue but a great big shadow?

Or maybe . . . She might not be able to paint like Kathleen, but she had the same ability to *see*. And once in a while she could capture what she saw on film.

Dr. Patel, a couple of male nurses, and a stretcher were waiting for her at the rear of the building. A massive loading dock was open for their convenience, and Kev stopped there.

She shuffled out of the jeep on her own.

"I'm not getting on that thing," Layla said, as she passed the stretcher. She left Patel no choice but to lead her through the underfloors of Segue to wherever he was going to look at her calf, which stung fiercely, but was in no way life-threatening. Though the ceilings were low, the corridors were modern, sleek, and white, a startling counterpoint to the restoration on the main floors. Offices and lab space were off to each side. They went through sliding doors to a small clinic.

Zoe was waiting there, irritation communicated in every tense muscle of her body. She pointedly ignored Layla with a hostile drag of her gaze to Patel. "I thought you were coming up."

"I'm sorry," he said, professional despite her demanding tone. "We had an emergency."

Zoe jacked a thumb Layla's way. "Her?"

"Yes, and I'll need to take a look at Ms. Mathews's injuries before I can see Abigail." Dr. Patel gestured to a screen partition. Layla assumed an examination table was on the other side. "In the meantime, I can send one of the nurses."

"I don't want a nurse. I want you. Right now," Zoe said. "And you're wasting your time with *Ms. Mathews.* She's going to die anyway. Abigail's seen it."

Which was the last straw. Zoe was mean, but Layla suddenly felt a whole lot meaner. "I'm not going to die. Not now, not ever. Got it?"

Took a sec for the "not ever" to sound stupid.

Zoe was already laughing in her face. "There are forces at work here that you can't even imagine." To Dr. Patel she said, "Look. Abigail can't keep anything down. It's been twenty-four hours. Twenty-four and a half with"—Zoe tilted her head toward Layla—"*her* drama."

"Ms. Mathews, if you will please . . ."

My drama? Layla had just dodged death for the fifth time in twenty-four hours. And apparently, she was destined to die any second now. A little drama was warranted. And as for forces beyond her imagination, if someone would loan her a camera, she'd show them something that would make them squeak but good.

"I'll be up shortly," Dr. Patel repeated to Zoe, pulling the screen open.

Sure enough, a stainless steel table waited. Layla used her arms to lift herself up, then scooted to lie on her side. Her scratches did not need this much attention.

The clinic door whisked open, and Talia walked in, her gaze dark with worry. "What happened?"

"Oh, shit," Zoe said, "if it isn't Princess Die."

"Nice to see you, too, Zoe."

"Abigail is *starving* and your Dr. Patel is bent on looking at Ms. Mathews's boo-boo."

Dr. Patel was unwrapping Layla's field dressing, murmuring, "Not bad at all."

"Zoe," Talia said, "will you please wait outside?"

"I'm not going anywhere."

Talia took a deep breath, for strength, Layla guessed. "I'm not asking."

That's when Layla noticed that Zoe was shaking, her gaze filling with resentment as she looked at Talia. "You did this to Abigail. Made her sick. Made her use Shadow. She wouldn't be this bad off if it weren't for you. Abigail saved your life, and you're letting her go hungry."

"She has the absolute best care. We've done and are doing everything possible for her. Every recourse has been taken. You know this is true, because you've been by her side the whole time," Talia answered. "Dr. Patel will be up shortly. Sooner, if you leave now and let us take care of Layla."

With a slap, Zoe upended a tray of tools, which clattered to the floor. She glared her anger at them, burning Talia the longest.

Nobody moved, though Layla almost opened her mouth

to tell the doctor to put a Band-Aid on her leg and take care of Abigail. The pain emanating from Zoe was palpable.

"This won't take but a few minutes," Dr. Patel assured her.

Zoe stuck up her chin and stalked out, her hands fisted at her sides.

The door hadn't slid shut when Talia rounded on the doctor. "How bad is Layla?"

Dr. Patel cleared his voice. "She's got an ugly scrape, that's all. I'll keep an eye on her, just in case. Adam seemed inordinately concerned when he called about it as well."

Probably because she was supposed to die any minute now.

Layla felt the moment Talia finally settled her gaze on her, and she was immediately filled with a pressing, bright warmth. It was a mixed-up feeling, so sharp and sweet as to be near pain.

And Khan? Where was he?

"I promised my father that we'd keep you alive," Talia said. "Don't make a liar out of me."

"I'm not dying," Layla said.

"Ever," Patel added, deadpan.

"Well, that's good news," Talia said, grinning.

Layla forced her gaze back on the table. She concentrated on the microstriations in the metal to get her mind off the pressure in her heart. Reincarnation. A family. After all these years.

And somehow too late.

"But I still plan to keep you inside and out of harm's way for the rest of the day," Talia said.

So Talia knew, too. Damn Khan. It seemed he'd filled everyone in, but her.

"You could meet the kids—" Talia's voice broke. "If you want, I mean."

Talia Thorne's children. Her little boys. The shadow hanging over Segue.

The fullness in Layla's chest turned painful, cutting off all her air so that the beat of her heart drummed loud in her head.

A baby smell sweetened the clinic's air. It was a mother smell, too. She concentrated on the pain of her scrapes, let it burn, burn, burn, so she wouldn't embarrass herself. If they were trying to wreck her, completely demolish her, they were doing a fantastic job. Meet the kids, but sorry, any time now you're going to die.

"Or not," Talia said. "That's okay, too."

But Layla could hear the hurt in Talia's voice.

Layla's face heated. Her eyes and nose pricked, ready to embarrass her. Damn it. The pressure in her chest was going to kill her if she didn't do something.

With a cough, she cleared the thickness blocking her voice. "No, really, I'd love to meet them. That would be . . . just . . . great. And then, if you don't mind, I'd like to borrow a camera."

Chapter 11

Khan stood back from the angels as they lowered the gate into a cavern in the mountains not far from Segue. How clever of the angels to find a place inaccessible to humanity, as well as ever steeped in Shadow. Places like this, where darkness had long reigned, hovered on the edge of the Otherworld, its cave-dwelling creatures as skittish and wary of light as the fae.

kat-a-kat-a-kat. The gate demanded, *Open me!*

And how foolish to put a gate to Hell at its mouth.

Another group of angels had rigged a makeshift forge, and nearby, an anvil, black, with a horn on one end, much like the one he'd used to create the gate.

The hammer rested on the anvil. How he hated the slippery, contrary thing, but he'd wielded it on Kathleen's behalf, and now he would wield it on Layla's. Strange how each of her lives echoed the other.

"I found this in the warehouse," Custo said, coming up behind him. Khan felt no sear at his approach. In this place, Shadow was stronger than even Custo's angelic light.

"Leave it, and move out of my way."

Next to the hammer on the anvil Custo placed the black

flower Khan had created as a trial piece for the blooms that adorned the gate. Three petals, one for each of the worlds, surrounded and protected an inner core, a soul. The iron, of course, was black—*black* for deep Shadow, black for Death. He'd welded the flowers onto the vertical bars along a clinging vine. They had represented his hope that Kathleen could survive in Hell, her spirit intact, until he could find her.

Then she'd found *him*.

"I thought you might try the flower first, then move on to the gate." Custo, who'd agreed to kill Layla if The Order found this tactic to be ineffectual.

Khan turned to face him.

"Shadowman, if it wasn't me, it'd be somebody else," Custo said, his gaze steady, though a sick desperation rolled off him. "The gate has to be destroyed."

Khan stoked Custo's discomfort. "Haven't you killed enough innocents?"

Khan knew Custo's past. The life he'd led before his passing had been filled with as much violence as good. If not for his last selfless act as a man, his existence in the Afterlife could have been very different. And now he was preparing to walk the fine line between darkness and light again.

"I gave you the hammer. It's my responsibility." Custo regarded the hellgate and shuddered. "There's no way that thing can remain on Earth, but I don't want Layla to die. I'll help you in every way that I can. Just tell me what to do."

kat-a-kat-a-kat-a-kat

Movement brought Khan's attention around. An angel walked toward the gate. He moved slowly, as if in a dream, sickness and terror in a dirty cloud around him. The angel stretched out his hand toward the handle, fingers reaching. The gate had him in its thrall.

"Bran!" Custo barked.

The angel stalled, confused. Looked around.

And then he was dragged back by two other angels. He went limp, his gaze filled with horror and longing as they moved him out.

No one was impervious to the gate's draw.

Custo turned. "What can I do?"

Khan picked up the black flower and shoved it, barehanded, into the glowing coals of the fire. Heat the metal, bang it down.

"You can take your friends and get out of here."

"The Order will not leave you alone with the gate." Custo shook his head. "Not with your Layla in the balance."

"Fine. Just you then. The rest are to wait outside."

Khan stared at the hammer, taking in its shape and the small line of shadow along the inside of its head and shaft cast by the glow of the fire. He summoned old darkness from the depths of the cave and gathered the cold, wet stuff to him for strength.

He reached for the hammer. His hand passed right through.

Taking a deep breath, he tried for it again. And clutched at nothing.

Shadow billowed off his shoulders in great cracking waves, but still he couldn't grasp the shaft.

"Shit," Custo said under his breath.

Khan could sense the confidence shifting within the angels in the cavern. They would all have to learn patience. Either that, or prepare for war.

"After you gave me the hammer, it took hours to lift again for myself." Hours of acute frustration. Each time he'd had to set it down during the creation of the gate, he'd known it would be a trial to pick back up. "And I did not have a choir of angels breathing down my neck."

"Right." Custo turned to the angels gathered around. "Everybody out."

"He's not to be trusted," said Ballard.

"If Rome wasn't built in a day," Custo returned, "a gate to Hell can't be destroyed in five minutes. Get out or I'll help you out."

An angel lifted his voice to argue, "He can't even pick—"

"Yet he managed to build the gate," Custo shot back. "Get out."

Khan poured his attention into the hammer while the cavern was vacated. The tool was not meant for fae hands and defied his attempts. The power to wield it had come from something else, deep, deep inside him. He searched for that space of quiet, for the time he'd spent with Kathleen. He thought of the red-gold fall of her hair, the shift of her features when she smiled, the natural pink to her lips.

He grasped for the hammer again. His Shadow hand passed through the tool, and he wasn't surprised. It was the wrong tack; he'd try another.

Layla.

He'd held her in his arms, her skin smooth and silky under his hands. Her body, warm like the earth, arching for him. Shuddering in pleasure. He recalled the salt of her sweat, the flash of her eyes. He drew from her dream, the child Layla, his glimpse into her life, her young gaze full of loneliness. Layla who'd needed a protector, yet had overcome her fears to brave wraith nests and Shadow. Layla, Layla . . .

"Layla," he said in an invocation and reached.

The wooden shaft was smooth in his grip.

* * *

Rose hid her bad hand in her lap when she came to a stop at the security entrance to The Segue Institute. The deformation had extended to her thickening wrist. Corded sinew ran down from her elbow across her forearm. She'd attempted to paint her striated and . . . rather *pointy* fingernails a pretty pink, which made her bad hand look a little less disturbing, but a glove would be better still. Definitely before she reunited with Mickey.

She rolled down the window of her stolen delivery truck as two soldiers approached, one on either side. She had half a mind to floor the gas and bust through—*Find her!* the gate said in Rose's head—but the enclosure surrounding the place was made up of thick concrete and metal barriers. At full speed, the truck would crumple like a soda can.

Well, fudge.

"Ma'am? May I see your driver's license?" But the soldier thought, *Trouble*. He looked at the other soldier, who touched something around his throat and mumbled a series of numbers Rose couldn't quite make out. It must have been some kind of code for *trouble*, because his next thought was that it would take ninety seconds for backup to arrive. *Survive*, he thought. She had no idea what he meant by *wraith*.

What was a wraith? It did not sound polite, particularly directed at her.

"If you'll just open the gate." Rose tilted her head, smiled, did a double bat of her eyes. She mentally nudged him with the command. If she pushed too hard, his mind might break like that of the poor fool who'd refused to give up the truck, and then he'd be a drooling baby and no good to her at all.

kat-a-kat-a-kat-a-kat

Yes, yes. She was trying. Some things took a little time, a little subtlety. Movement rustled the trees along the road. The backup?

If this soldier would just cooperate . . .

"I have a truck full of groceries to deliver." She insinuated truth into her sentence and pushed harder. "Open the gate, please."

The soldier blinked at her with bleary eyes. "Can't. The lockdown command was already sent. No one goes in or out until Adam Thorne clears it."

kat-a-kat-a-kat-a-kat

She'd think a whole lot better without the gate in her head. She pushed hard on the soldier. "Well, is there another way to get in?"

He swayed on his feet. "Lockdown."

The second soldier approached. "Sullivan, you're relieved of duty."

Rose guessed her time was up. The gate would just have to wait, and so would the girl it wanted her to deal with. Rose would think her entry through and then come back. Maybe sneak through the woods and climb over the wall. For now, though, it was better to go back than wait and find out what a wraith was and what the backup was going to do about it. She wasn't too excited about being shot at from all sides.

"Mike!" the soldier shouted, as the one outside her truck window fell to the ground. Minds were such delicate things.

'Course the road was too narrow to make a three-point turn easily. And she couldn't very well back down the mountain with the hulking cab behind her. She'd go right off the edge and that would be the end of Rose Petty. Nobody wanted that.

"Let me see your hands!" the soldier shouted at her. More soldiers in strange armor approached the vehicle from the front, angling in groups of two on either side. That was about ninety seconds, all right.

For Pete's sake, this was a bother.

Her bad hand twitched. All right, all right. She'd just have to do this the hard way.

It was late afternoon by the time Layla led Talia around the outside of the west wing of Segue's hulk. Once Talia had put a baby in Layla's arms, she hadn't wanted to give him up again. Both children, Michael and Cole, were little lumps of wonderfulness, so soft, so perfect. The fit in her arms, the sweet smell of their skin—it was its own kind of magic, and she'd been utterly caught in the spell.

She'd spent so much time with the babies that Layla had had little more than a peek at the pile of research Talia had amassed on her behalf. At the top of the stack was a tablet labeled *Jacob Andrew Thorne, wraith*. And here Layla had thought Adam's brother had died in a tragic boating accident. Interesting reading, she was sure. She'd have snatched it up if not for the little tickle of panic about the shadow on the Segue building.

Talia. The babies. The shadow had to come first, before something else happened.

The photo op took them outside of Segue, down the grand front steps, and to the left, along the foundation. Kev and company followed close behind as protection. Adam frowned down at them from the veranda, one baby strapped in some kind of carryall on his chest, the other in a stroller, which he rocked back and forth. Mr. Thorne Industries in the role of dad. She almost snapped a picture of him like that, for Talia.

Layla's neck goose-bumped with the memory of the flying wraith, but she pressed on, leader of the pack. As soon as she rounded the corner of the building's base, the storm of darkness crowded her sight. She reeled back a few steps, cringing, while the rest of the group looked at her . . . yes, as if she were crazy.

"You don't see it." Obviously. Or they wouldn't be standing so close to the shadow.

Talia looked up, squinted, flicked her gaze around. "Where exactly am I supposed to look?"

Hello? It was *everywhere.* Layla took a deep breath. "Do you see any shadows?"

"Little ones. Under the windows?" Talia's breath came in a puff of cold air.

"No. A big, black blotch covering half the building. God, I can even *feel* it."

Talia gave her a sorry expression. Polite, but not believing.

"It's there," Layla said and raised the camera. It was a Nikon D40. Nice, but not as good as hers. "That shadow has been bugging me since I snuck into your woods."

"Layla, I know Shadow," Talia said. "If there were anything unusual here, I'd see it."

Uh-huh. Layla would have to explain. "When I was a teenager I got into a kind of live-in prep school for disadvantaged youth. Northfield." She found the manual mode on the Nikon and set the exposure for maximum contrast. "Took a photography class. The teacher explained about perspective. How every person has a different one. How we all see things a little differently."

"Doesn't make sense," Kev said. "A camera will catch whatever it's pointed at."

Typical response.

"Perspective is not about what's in front of the camera. Perspective is about the eye looking through it."

At sixteen, that brief explanation had been a major "aha!" moment in Layla's life. Maybe the creepy stuff she saw was just her perspective. Maybe she just had to learn to see things another way, and the frightening visions would stop. To a certain extent, it had worked until now.

Kev frowned. Talia looked uncomfortable.

"It's easy: I am simply going to take a picture of what I see, and I see Segue half lost in shadows. What do you want to bet I can catch it on film?"

Layla lay down on the grass, which crunched beneath her, the cold leaching through her sweatshirt to cool her back.

Talia crouched beside her, while Kev stepped back to talk into his earpiece.

The framing required some light to contrast with the shadow, as well as the clear sky overhead. If she was very good, she might be able to capture a sense of castle, too. Because to her, that's what Segue looked like. She inhaled to take in the deepness of the dark and the crisp solidity of the white. The blue above augmented the two, revealing their stark differences, not just in light, but in texture and depth.

She snapped the shot, tweaked her angle, bracketed the exposure, and shot again. Pulled back, one more time. Until she downloaded the images, she couldn't be sure, but she thought she had it.

The viewfinder was suddenly filled with a blur of movement, and then she was hauled up.

"Hey!" she yelled as she made a grab for the camera. Kev's better reflexes snatched it out of the air while simultaneously propelling her toward the Segue building. Talia was already a couple of yards away, almost rounding the corner.

"We've got to get you inside," Kev said as he hurried her up to a jog. "I've just been notified of an attack."

His tone sobered her up real quick. Was it time to die? "Wraiths?"

"Something," he answered. Sounded like a dodge. "We'll have to examine the bodies before we'll know for certain."

The sudden emergency had her blood pounding hard while her skin went clammy. Two attacks in one day. Wraiths throwing themselves against Segue security. How could the Thornes possibly cope with this kind of constant assault? The castle was under siege.

They entered on the main floor of the old hotel. Adam met them in the wide, connected corridor of elegant rooms. Talia already had a baby in her arms and was doing a nervous bounce.

"What's going on?" Talia asked.

"We've got action at the main gate. A woman. Caucasian, about five-two, a hundred pounds, brown hair. Blue coat," Adam said, but wouldn't quite meet Layla's eyes. "She took out six of my men before disappearing. She has to be in Middleton by now or we could track her on the thermal-imaging cameras."

Hundred-pound woman besting six soldiers with guns. Had to be a wraith.

Why wouldn't Adam look at her? "Was it the flying kind?"

Adam finally darted a glance. "You mean a *wight*. We're working on new capture strategies. Barrow-tech. Khan suggested it the other day to Talia, and the angels have confirmed that barrows are the way to go."

The wraith situation was just getting worse and worse.

The public needed to know specifics about this threat—not the rumors and misdirection in the media. The public had a right to know about these monsters, including this new breed, the wights. Layla had no idea how to write her article, one that would instill more fear than hope, but at the very least, knowledge was power.

"I'd like to visit the attack site."

"No."

"But . . ."

"No." The heavy look he gave her shut her up. Adam needed to see to the dead. She respected that. And she wanted his full attention to argue her case about the wights. It was just too damn important. The world was different now.

Then came a wait for news. Layla joined Talia and the babies in the library, close to the action, but comfortable. Talia spread a blanket on the floor and the little ones ogled up at the ceiling or attempted to roll over.

Layla's internal panic slowly morphed through the long minutes into a generalized, slightly sick anxiety that had her jumping every time Adam stepped in the room. She decided to distract herself, snagged a laptop from a cubby, and downloaded the images she'd captured with the camera.

Two shots were blurry. It had been hard to hold the camera perfectly still when she was lying on her back, looking up at the hulk of the building. Another captured the shadow, but the crop of the image made it plausible that something mundane was casting the reaching darkness.

But there was one image that stopped her. *Yes. There.* That's what she was talking about.

Shadow, capital *S*, was cloaking one half of the building. More than that, the building itself seemed to twist out of its right angles as if the walls were trying to shrug out of the darkness. The building was writhing, warped by the dark swamp overtaking it.

At Layla's shoulder, Talia frowned at the image. "My mother was an artist, hugely gifted." She paused, cleared her voice. "I've been watching to see if you have a similar talent. Maybe this is it." She paused again. "I *know* this is it."

Layla shook her head, denying the comparison. "I've never been that much into art." She couldn't imagine creating Kathleen's masterpieces. That gene had definitely skipped her. "But I've messed around with a little photography, when I could steal time."

"You need to steal more; that photo could hang in any gallery." Talia bit her bottom lip as she considered the image. "And I was right there. I didn't see that at all. Your perspective is definitely different."

"But didn't you say that you *knew* Shadow?"

"I can draw from Shadow, like my father. Darken a room. Cloak myself and others. But I can't cross, and I can't use it to create illusion. And I've never seen the Twilight trees my mother painted."

"So what are you saying?"

"I'm saying the veil was thin for my mother. And clearly it's thin for you, too."

"But not for you?"

Talia dropped her gaze. "My mom was very ill her whole life."

Layla caught the subtext: Kathleen had been near death, so the veil was thin. Reincarnated, Layla had that same experience, and now she was set to die, too.

"That's why the ghost could get to me, isn't it?" Finally the attack in the west wing made sense. In a weird way, she was almost a ghost herself, just hanging on for that fateful moment.

Talia reluctantly inclined her head. "Yeah, we think so. I'm so sorry I didn't anticipate the danger. We had no idea."

Layla gripped her shoulders to ease the tension there. "You can't anticipate everything, I guess. And you did scream her into submission, so I'm not complaining. One question: Khan has pulled me through the Shadowlands a couple of times now. He never showed you?"

A side of Talia's mouth tugged up. "He offered, but being only half mortal, I'm too scared I won't be able to cross back. The fae are very limited in some ways. Their world is circumscribed, more so than for humanity."

"How does Khan go back and forth so easily?"

"Ah. Khan's very powerful. Maybe the most powerful. And I'm only half fae."

They started bringing in casualties, and later Adam returned to the library to discuss the findings. Once again, he looked deeply tired and Layla wondered how long he could sustain this kind of constant pressure and concern.

Talia went to him and put her head on his shoulder, lending him her strength.

Layla stood, worried and helpless. "Well?"

Adam sighed. "None of the dead exhibited the telltale wraith bite marks on their faces. The prevailing wounds were claw marks across the belly or throat."

Layla shivered. She'd seen the bodies of people killed violently before, but it always made her very cold and heartsick.

"At least their souls weren't taken," Talia said.

Adam acknowledged this with a weary nod.

"Souls?" Layla asked.

Talia looked over. "Wraiths feed on souls to sustain themselves. The souls become trapped within until the wraith is killed."

The WHO claimed the wraiths fed on a form of metabolized energy.

But, souls?

Clearly the situation was much, much worse. Layla needed to take a look at Talia's wraith research. And even then, she didn't know what to report in her article—if she survived to write one. Khan had said she would agree that a little deception was called for. If the soul part was true, then reporting it to the frightened masses would be like announcing Armageddon.

Layla was confused on one point. "So this wasn't a wraith attack?"

She looked from Adam to Talia, both of whom shot each other glances heavy with meaning.

"What?"

They looked back at her.

"Oh, God, what now? I'm already going to die. What could be worse?"

"Maybe we should wait for Khan," Talia said. "He'll be back tonight."

"You tell me now, so I can yell at him later. If there is a later." Layla gripped her thighs for control.

Talia pulled a chair from a big table and sat across from her. "You know he's been looking for Kathleen since she died." Two worry lines formed between her brows. "Looking everywhere."

Talia glanced over her shoulder at Adam, as if for support, then faced Layla again. Layla had no one behind her. The absence had been omnipresent in her life, but she felt it fresh now.

"Kathleen died, but when Khan breached Heaven to find her, she wasn't there."

Because Kathleen had been reborn as herself, Layla

Mathews, the one who was doomed to die at twenty-eight. Okay, she got that.

"If Kathleen wasn't in Heaven, he was going to go after her in . . . Hell."

Layla flinched. What had Kathleen done to deserve Hell?

"So he built a gate."

Oh, God, the gate.

"And the gate was opened."

"For a second! Not even a second."

"And a devil escaped."

"Like with horns?" She hadn't seen anything like that. But then, it had been so dark. And Khan and been there, so close. Oh crap, she was shaking.

Adam sniffed. "Nope. The devil is a woman. Caucasion. Five-two and about a hundred pounds."

Layla stood, knocking over her chair. "That was *her*!"

"Yep," Adam said.

"She killed those men."

"Yes."

"Because I opened the gate." Stars formed before her eyes. She needed to sit.

"Put your head between your knees," Talia soothed and drew her down, shoved a chair under her butt. "It's going to be all right."

"Not for those guys. Where's Khan?" Layla spoke to the floor. She needed to see him. Now. He was superstrong. Mr. Powerful. He could get rid of the devil woman, right?

"Khan's got a day job now," Talia answered. "Busting up the gate."

"But Custo was doing that," Layla argued.

Adam shook his head. "When Custo tried, he hurt you. If he were to continue, it's likely that you'd die. The hope is that since Khan built it, he can tear it down again."

Layla lifted her face. "Aren't I about to die already?"

Talia grabbed hold of Layla's hand so tight that Layla could feel a heartbeat in the connection. "I lost you once. I'm not letting you go again. Neither is Khan."

"We'll keep you safe," Adam added. "This isn't our first battle against an otherworldly creature. Custo's wife, Annabella, had a real keeper for a while. Bloodthirsty thing, he was."

"But why's the devil here? She's after me, right?"

"Well, yes," Adam said. "It's in her best interests, and the gate's, to get to you. The gate was built for you, and so it's connected to you. The concern is that if she manages to . . . to kill you, or if you die by some other means, like an accident, then the gate will never be able to be destroyed. And since a gate to Hell is not *ideal* for the mortal world, it's necessary that it be destroyed immediately."

Which was what Khan was doing. A gate to Hell? He was the man for the job. He could destroy it. Okay. Fine. She could wait until night.

What time was it?

Talia squeezed her hand again. "The good news is that this devil has no chance against Khan. None whatsoever. We just have to hold out until he gets here, until he finds her."

"What about the babies?" Tears finally spilled. If Talia or the babies or even Adam were hurt . . .

"Segue has excellent security," Adam said. "None of my alarms on the interior grounds has been tripped. You set off a dozen on your first visit to Segue. I think the devil backed off for the moment and is reconsidering her approach. She's not very subtle."

"She's a devil! She doesn't have to be."

This time Talia answered. "A devil is just a bad person who died and was sent to Hell. Nothing more than that, though, like Custo, she very likely has some extraordinary abilities."

"Security cameras got footage of the assault," Adam added. "I've sent a screen shot to the FBI already. If she died recently, they should be able to identify her."

"She's just a bad person," Layla repeated.

"No horns," Talia confirmed. "But very bad."

And Khan could destroy her as soon as he was done with the gate.

kat-a-kat-a-kat: The gate tittered at her, like a metallic giggle.

Layla drew back from Talia. Let go of her hand while Hell laughed, at home in Layla's head.

kat-a-kat-a-kat: Best to give yourself up now.

No.

kat-a-kat-a-kat: You don't belong with them. You belong to me.

No.

kat-a-kat-a-kat: He can't destroy me.

He will. He can do anything.

"Layla?" Talia's face loomed before her.

"I think I'm going to head back to my room." Layla forced a smile. "Take a shower. It will probably be a long night."

"How 'bout I walk you there?" Talia said, glancing over her shoulder at Adam.

Layla felt her lack afresh. She braced herself against the hollow feeling. A little time and Khan would be back. She looked at the painting of Twilight over the mantelpiece. "I need to be alone, but, um, could you have someone bring that painting up?"

Khan's appearance in the window last night was too unsettling and she needed to talk to him. Bad.

The rattle in her mind receded as she fled to her room, but she knew with sick certainty that the gate still stood.

Chapter 12

Khan raised his arm to strike the black flower. Smoke filled his nose and choked his throat. Sweat coursed down his bared shoulders and streaked through the soot across his tensed chest and abdomen. Every fiber of muscle and sinew screamed with the terrible labor of his task.

He'd been at it for hours, until he could sense the shift of the sky from pale blue to the tangerine of sunset. His power grew deeper in the world of darkness, his senses more acute. Yet the flower, heated for the hundredth time in the forge and now dimming from white-yellow to rose red, could not be broken.

kat-a-kat-a-kat: You made me too well.

"And I'll unmake you, too." Khan brought the hammer down on the most delicate, glowing turn of a petal.

Not one atom of the metal moved.

He lifted the hammer again, forced his strength and concentration into his grip so that his fist was black and smoking with Shadow, and struck the flower.

The bloom merely turned on its side with a soft clink, unharmed.

Why wasn't this working? His cause was just as desperate as it had been before. More so, since Layla was so close. Why could he not damage the flower? Why could he not hold her once again? Why could Shadow not overcome, just this once, in all eternity?

A sense of unease filtered into his concentration. Khan turned to Custo, who still crouched, watchful, some way from the forge.

The unease grew to alarm, though Custo showed no outward sign of emotion.

"What has happened?" Khan asked. The boy had better not lie.

A pause, then Custo shrugged in resignation.

"An attack," he said, "a few hours ago. Layla is safe, but others were killed. The devil, *a woman*, was not able to breach the compound, but she disappeared into the woods. Adam's soldiers are tracking her."

As a rule, the world pulled at Khan with myriad death tugs as souls readied for their passing. With a simple inner extension, he could divide himself into infinity to see to each. But he'd been ignoring them now for a while, refusing to meet the call of his duty, the cry of his scythe. An awful thought crept into his mind: What if one of those soul lights was Layla, and he ignored her death, and she crossed without him, to be lost and fed upon in Shadow?

Khan dropped the hammer on the anvil with a flick of his wrist. "I will see Layla now."

Custo stood, glancing toward the opening, beyond which the other angels waited in expectation. "You've made no progress."

"Some things take time."

"You may be impervious to the voice of the gate, but humankind isn't." Custo scrubbed his scalp as if to affect his own brain. "We angels aren't either. I can hear it in my head, and it's saying all the right things. The gate demands to be opened. It will be if it's not destroyed soon."

"Then I suggest you watch over the gate carefully and resist as best you can. I'll be back in the morning."

Khan permitted no argument as his exhausted body evaporated into Shadow. He had to see Layla, had to make absolutely certain that she was well. Custo and his angels would have to wait.

Custo's gaze followed him up to the dark stretch along the cavern ceiling. He called out bitterly, "I don't want to hurt her!"

Custo wouldn't. He couldn't. He might have agreed to the task, might be searching for the resolve required to take an innocent life, but as of yet, he hadn't found it. Right now the poor dog would guard the gate to Hell from harm even if he was struck down by his own kind.

Layla was waiting for Khan, anxiety riddling the air around her. Her hair waved freely, a little wet, to her shoulders, so she must have bathed. She had one of Kathleen's larger paintings propped against a wall. She paced before it, biting a nail, then stopped to search the canvas. She reached her fingertips to touch the shifting trees of Twilight.

"Have a care," Khan said, emerging from the darkest Shadow beneath the boughs. "One good push, and you may cross."

"Oh, thank God you're here. Why don't I cross then, and we can talk like normal people?" Her tone was strong, words coming rapidly. Whatever had happened, she had resolved her fear and was ready to fight. "There's a lot we have to talk about."

He had to quash the stinging *Yes!* that rose in him. In Twilight he could appear however he wanted. Draw her close. Stroke that skin. But . . . "If you physically cross, bring your mind and body across the divide, you will soon go mad. We'll have to speak like this."

He would not compromise her mind, risk her spirit.

"I'm already going mad. Besides, you've brought me through a couple of times already."

"Yes, but I brought you right out again as well. Without me, you would be trapped here. The fae will prey on you." Moira would keep her under her skirts just like that other mortal woman. "Stay where you are. Visit me in dreams."

It would have to be enough.

Her face flushed, and she turned her head to the side, hiding her expression. If at all possible, he'd have reached through the veil and touched her like a man. She seemed so solitary, standing alone in her room, waiting with thoughts crowding her head and no one to share them with. In that way, she was his mirror image.

"Please, do not look away. I would do anything to be with you." She was his beacon in the dark. Something bright to look on in the pitch of his existence. No one shone like her. Nothing illuminated like her soulfire. Yes, he'd do anything. He had already.

She turned back, eyes flashing. Anger flared. "Yeah, speaking of which . . . *you made a gate to Hell?* Who does that? And why would you think Kathleen would be there in the first place? What did I do to deserve that?"

"You laid down with me." She'd accepted him, embraced him, in every way. The tide of that union still moved his Shadow.

"Oh, God." She ran a hand through her hair, gathering it on the top of her head, and gripped her hand in the mass.

"Do you regret it?" That one touch. Human. Carnal. Ecstatic.

"Who *are* you?"

"I am a beast, Layla. The worst imaginable. Can we not leave it at that?"

"Hell no. Not when last night . . . when we . . . I . . . Just no."

"Do you regret it?" he asked again. Her emotions were in turmoil, and yes, regret was one of them, overtaking the others. But regret for what?

"Well, apparently I am going to die." She dropped her hand and her hair fell wildly around her shoulders. "What the hell am I supposed to do with that bit of news? I can't believe it, and yet, I've had too many close calls to deny the possibility."

"We will defy Fate"—*and everyone else*—"for as long as we can."

"Fate. Bullshit. I've almost died a million times now."

"Layla—"

She turned and jabbed a finger toward the canvas. Her voice lowered with menace. "There was a spider."

Khan wished he had the angels' gift to read minds; hers moved so fast.

"And the devil bitch," Layla continued. "*I* let her out of Hell, and she's killed half a dozen people."

Twice that at least. "I built the gate. You were merely under its power. The responsibility isn't yours."

And he had no trouble bearing it. Death was his specialty. "Besides, this life is a second chance for her, too. She could have lived among you humans, tried for peace, respected life, but she chose otherwise."

Layla made an impatient gesture. "Oh, just save it. I swear, around here if it's not one thing, it's another. All of it bad." Her jaw clenched. "The question is: Why's it happening now?"

Her tone suggested she knew the answer, but Khan replied anyway. "Fate."

"No, buddy boy—" Layla sent a glare across the veil. "It all started when I met you."

He shook his head. "But our meeting was predestined. I saw Fate herself on the road in front of the warehouse where you found me." Moira had flashed her scissors. "Fate brought us together."

"Whoa." She held up a hand to stop him. "Fate's a person?"

"A fae. Moira."

Layla made a face. "And who said she gets to decide everything?"

"She doesn't decide." Just like Death didn't decide when someone had to pass. "She does her duty. There is no life without magic, without Shadow. She is necessary to the ebb and flow of existence. Her role is prescribed." It was the same with all fae, in one way or another, trapped by their purpose.

"Well, what about the first time?"

Khan was silenced. To which "first time" did she refer?

"When you and Kathleen made whoopee, was that in the cards?" Her tone was aggressive, the emotion coming off her now distinctly wild.

"No, I broke a law to be with her." The fae were constrained by their natures, their duties, not by destiny. What was she after?

"Give Kathleen a little credit. If you broke a law, she broke it with you. And if she could do it, so can I."

Careful, now. Layla was racing toward a decision. "I don't understand."

"I know," Layla answered, a glint in her eye. "How could you? You're not human."

Her statement opened up a painful yawn of space between them. Fae. Human. They were worlds apart. Only a creature of Shadow would attempt such madness as to love a mortal.

"But because I kind of like you," she said, "I'll let you in on a little secret."

"You 'kind of like me'?" And just that fast, warmth spread through the chill of his Shadow. He could listen to her talk like this always. The spark of her mind combined with the snap of her temper—no wonder her soul was a living conflagration.

"It's called free will."

Oh, that. "Moira is necessarily cunning. Eventually the imperative of death will find you." He knew the imperative intimately. All mortals died. While there was occasional elasticity regarding the moment of their passing, there were never any exceptions.

Did Layla think she could do Kathleen one better? Did she think she could change her fate altogether? Only a soul as bright as hers would dare it. She had no idea whom she was up against.

"Of course everyone has to die. That's not what free will is about. Free will, my fine faery friend, is about taking chances, making the most of each moment."

The heat in her gaze and the swell of building intent told him that she didn't think she'd done enough of it.

"Case in point: Kathleen did whatever the hell she wanted. She lived under a death sentence all her life. And look what she had!" Layla gestured to the painting. "Her art, you, Talia. Don't tell me all that was fated."

Kathleen had pushed the limits of her destiny as far as they could go. She'd held on with spit and drive until the moment she delivered Talia. Yes, Kathleen had lived well.

"And what do you want, Layla?" Was it anything he could hope to give her?

"I want to live. And if I've only got five minutes or fifty years, they're going to be good."

Her claim made him a little afraid. What could she be thinking with that spark in her eye?

"So step back, 'cause I'm coming through."

"Layla—!"

But she was already rushing into the canvas. She couldn't know that he wasn't in the painting itself or that Twilight was as vast as the human consciousness or as varied as imagination. So many souls crossed at the same time, but—*there!*—for Layla the veil went up in violent flames. The denizens of Faery lifted their heads, scented her, pricked their ears to hear her. Trained their dark eyes through Shadow toward her bright light. A mortal had crossed; fair game.

Heedless, she ran into the trees to find him. He, the monster who wanted her most of all.

She had no idea. Twilight was not the place for this. There was no tenderness here.

Khan rolled out of the darkness and caught her in his arms. Arms of a man, like she expected. The arms of the Khan she knew. It took one of her breaths for the rest of him to form and modern clothing to slide over his body. Black, like his Shadow.

"You must go. Your mind will wander here." As he spoke, whispers rose around them. There were watchers in the woods, but the fae would hang back from he who was darkest of all.

She was determined in her arousal. It rolled off her in great, crashing waves, battering his reserves.

"Then we'd better be quick." Her eyebrows danced in suggestion. "You have a devil to find anyway."

She wrapped her arms around him and filled him with

her exhilaration. The beat of her heart in his head, the pump of life was too much to bear.

"Layla, *please*," he begged. Her lust for life would override him. And she thought she had no power.

But she nipped his lip, then stepped back to peel off her shirt. "Right now. Here on the ground."

The ground was not good enough for Layla, especially not with the fae looking on in keen interest, hungry for that spark within her. This was no place for one with a loose hold on life. Since only excitement billowed from Layla, the terror had to be his.

Not here. Not like this. Not where he couldn't hide his nature and keep her safe at the same time.

But she was Kathleen all over again, bent on seduction, but without the heart trouble to limit her headlong pursuit of disaster. Layla's heart beat rapidly in her chest, the tempo echoing in his. The tide of her emotion was beyond exquisite. How must it be to experience it firsthand?

He growled in frustration. "I would have visited you tonight in your sleep."

Please, Layla.

"Yeah, that was good. But I want *you*. And now." She came forward again, naked from the waist up, her skin like alabaster in this light. She buried her hands in his hair. Brought a fistful of strands to her face. "You smell so good. Always so good. Faery shampoo rocks."

"Don't ask this of me," he said, skimming his mouth over her neck. She smelled earthy, fecund, and so blood sweet.

She drew back, looked him in his eyes. "You said you were a beast."

"I am." The worst of them. Even now Shadow crackled with the rise of his want.

Passion darkened her gaze. "Well, let's have it then."

He closed his eyes to hide his alarm. She had no idea what she was talking about, his reckless woman, so he simplified. "You will fear me."

Please don't make me show you this.

Layla smiled. "Promises, promises."

The moment the whites of Khan's eyes bled to black, Layla knew she was in trouble. He lifted a hand into the air and the forest around them went dead silent. A thick mist of shadows filtered through the trees, blanketing them in a soft, impenetrable pocket of stillness.

Considering the dark flex of Khan's expression, Layla didn't think the quiet would last long. She crossed her arms to cover her exposed breasts.

The darkness around her grumbled. Khan only lifted a brow. "Second thoughts?"

She dropped her arms again. "You don't scare me."

"I should." He tilted his head as if straining for control and said with that same aching deliberation, "I try very hard to be gentle with you."

She knew that. A little less care, though, and she might learn something.

"I need to know you," she said. And since each bit of revealed information was worse than the last, this must be a doozy. It wasn't as if she had a lifetime for him to tell her either. Tomorrow she might fall down a flight of stairs, and that would be that.

He looked away from her, into the silent trees. "The fae prey on heedless fools like you."

"I *need* to know," she said. "Do you understand?"

He looked back at her, his gaze black and cold. "So be it."

The low-lying mist whipped into a frenzy, and Layla

flinched, covering herself again. The wind took with it all the jewel-toned leaves and all hint of living things in a dirty, stinging tornado of terrifying brevity. Bare trunks of trees amid a soil of ash were all that was left behind of Twilight. It was utter desolation. A holocaust of imagination. The death of all things.

Her heart clenched at the sight. What was she supposed to learn from this?

She sought Khan, who was suddenly behind her. He put a hand roughly to her cheek, to keep her sight fixed on the ruined tableau before her. What was he trying to tell her?

"Khan?" She trembled, fearing what was to come.

"Please tell me you want to turn back," he said, low, in her ear. "I can still take you back."

"I won't go." Her soul was ringing again with recognition. He was no stranger, yet she didn't know him. She trusted absolutely but could recall no basis for her conviction. She wanted *him*, not the polite enigma who left her roses. Five minutes or fifty years . . . she wanted *him*. Opened for *him*.

"You're a fool," he said.

"Your fool," she answered.

She felt a hand at the waistband of her jeans. A tug and the fabric fell to dust. She was abruptly naked, the powder an inch thick at her feet. Her skin flashed from hot to cold, nipples peaked, belly quivered.

His arm came around her waist, an unyielding band of black at the edge of her vision.

Her shakes redoubled, but she relied on the strength of his arm around her. At least he was close in this terrible place. A lonesome howl of wind lifted the ash, but she knew, strangely, that the sound came from him. He existed here, lost in this misery of gray, unchanging dearth.

She tried to turn, to comfort him, but he held her fast,

and, with a hand to her cheek, turned her face back to the wasteland of Twilight. "Don't look at me."

She was cold and scared, her womb aching. All she wanted was him. The real him.

He braced his legs, sending the ash into powdery clouds. He cast a hand up her thigh. He tilted her hips.

She went liquid hot, throbbing in wait. Her breath halted. Her core and soul braced for an invasion.

"Forgive me." And he thrust.

Her vision blanched winter white, the barren silhouettes of skeletal trees scraping an empty sky. Her senses were utterly overwhelmed, so that all she heard was the beat of her heart, all she smelled was the blood it pumped. He pulled back, then roughly reseated himself inside her. Again and again, she was filled with him, gasping for breath in the wake of his driving rhythm.

A feminine voice from the past broke through her memory into the present. *Can you show me how to go? I don't know. . . .*

And Khan's answering, with infinite gentleness. *I don't know either.*

Kathleen had never known this side of him. Relentless, brutal, a being of staggering power. She'd never known the bleakness in his heart.

The wind carried a wail toward her. The warped voice had no gender—it could've been wrenched from his throat or hers.

Where their first coming together had been a fantasy of sensuality, this was need, a longing accumulated over incomprehensible time. His darkness was alive within her, circling her core, wrapping around her soul.

He could have preyed on her. Drawn from her essence.

She understood that now, the danger of the fae. And she would have let him.

Here, take me. I'm yours.

The rhythm grew faster, harder, so deep she couldn't breathe. Just clutched at his arm around her, trembling toward a rapturous brink. She gave him her weight, trusting him with everything she was. Arched against the broad wall of his chest.

His free hand circled to the juncture of her thighs. Stroked her there, hard and sure, and a little bit cruel.

Her belly went tight. Her womb clenched around him, Shadow, beast, monster, fae. The ground shook and he roared behind her.

She split, awed by an exquisite flowering within that thrilled every molecule of her incongruous body. The winter trees likewise bloomed before her dimming vision, crackling into blue and purple and green, the lushness of life and an ecstasy of color. The sky went violet, stars twirling overhead. Dizzy. Pulsing with magic. Or maybe that was her.

Her trembling gave way to tears, which coursed rapidly down her face. "Khan, please, just let me hold you."

"No," he said. "You've seen enough."

Rose hunched in a campsite bathroom on the cold, concrete floor next to the sinks. There were three stalls in front of her, all in need of a good cleaning. She put a finger delicately to her nose. The bathroom was bad, but with this kind of odor, there had to be a body decaying around here somewhere.

She'd worn out her welcome in town. There were strange folks about, beautiful and hard at the same time.

They almost had her once or twice, but their thoughts gave them away.

And it wasn't as if she could hide in a crowd. The scarf she wore couldn't cover all of the change on her neck and ear, nor the fact that the skin on her cheek had started to yellow and toughen. That arm hadn't taken any harm during the messy business up the mountain, but its unusual alteration was now impossible to disguise.

Would Mickey mind? Not if he loved her like he said.

kat-a-kat-a-kat-a-kat

Yes, she knew she was supposed to take care of other business. She *had* tried to get in, but the security was too tight. She could take care of six men with guns, but taking on more might just kill her. It was better to find a more opportune moment.

kat-a-kat-a-kat-a-kat

If the gate would just quiet down, maybe she could make a plan. Stealing the truck had been a mistake. Killing the men had been worse. Each time she'd been forced to take a life, her body had changed a little more.

kat-a-kat: Follow your nose.

To find a dead body? How would that possibly help?

Follow your nose.

Fine. At least it would give her something to do. The smell was so strong that she was surprised she couldn't see an orange trail of awful in the air. It got more pungent during the hour-long trek through the backwoods of Middleton, and grew positively overwhelming near a circle of campers and mobile buildings that surrounded the halted construction of a row of cabins.

Not just one body. Lots of folks had to have died. This was a massacre or a mass suicide. Maybe their food hadn't spoiled, though.

She was about to open a door to one of the campers

when it opened for her. The enlarged teeth she saw first, pointed like a shark's, but in the gaping mouth of a man. Her bad hand came up in defense, grabbed the ugly man by the skin on his chest, and threw him to the ground.

As she backed away, more fiendish people stepped out of the camper, a few from the buildings, too, all of them slavering like a pack of rabid dogs. And *glory*! if one of them didn't seem to float above the earth, in pieces no less. They stank to kingdom come, so she guessed she'd found her corpses.

Living corpses. None of them had a thought in their heads. Nothing. It was like they were hollow between the ears.

Could it be . . . ? Maybe the gate had steered her straight after all. These had to be the "wraiths" that the soldier at the compound had feared. These creatures had to be the reason for the wall and the guns.

"Friends," she said, "are you what're called wraiths?"

One answered with a lightning quick dart toward her, mouth preparing to bite her head off. That wasn't nice, so her bad hand came up and slashed the man's throat. The rest of his body fell to the ground, a dry husk in the dirt.

The others looked concerned, but more for their own well-being than the pile of skin and bones.

"If we could just talk," Rose said. It'd be better if she could read their minds.

The wraiths formed a bit of a circle around her, prowling with their big jaws hanging low. The floating one shivered toward her but was stopped by one of the others.

Curious.

Steps sounded as a woman descended from the camper to join the group. Dark haired, young. Almost attractive. Her mouth was normal, and she was clean, composed, with a light of intelligence in her eyes. But no amount of perfume—and the woman must have used a bottle—would cover her stink. This one was a wraith, too. The leader, most likely.

"I'm Rose Anne Petty," Rose said, holding out her bad hand, which was covered in wraith remains.

The woman regarded the dead body and then Rose's hand. "What are you?"

This confused Rose, so she dropped her arm. "Why, your friend."

"Are you some kind of angel? Angels can kill us with their bare hands."

Rose blushed and put her bad hand to her breast. Finally, someone understood her. "Yes. Yes, I am."

"What do you want here?"

Wraiths. They might just be her answer. "I'm looking for a place to stay and, if you're willing, for a little help."

"An angel wants help from us." The woman looked skeptical.

"It's an ugly business, really"—but Rose was sure these good people wouldn't snap to judgment—"I've got to murder someone inside that compound up the mountain, but rest assured, it's for a good cause."

"You want to kill someone at Segue."

"Yes."

"They kill wraiths, and are *friends* with angels." The woman wraith relaxed her mouth, and pointy teeth grew in abundant proliferation.

"Well . . ." Rose looked to Heaven for a little help.

But the woman raced ahead. "So you're not part of The Order?"

The Order?

"We had a parting of the ways." She wasn't part of anything.

"Is it Talia Thorne you want to kill?"

Again, Rose was stumped. She didn't know any Talia Thorne. She was after a Layla Mathews.

"Yes." Rose flashed her nicest smile. "Among others." What was one more?

"I'm Daria," the wraith said, then turned to one of the men. "I want a table and a couple of chairs." She glanced at the floating wraith. "And put Thing in the camper with the others so she doesn't bother us."

Thing was a woman? Oh, dear. And there were others?

A table was quickly brought out, chairs respectfully opened. Daria grabbed hers and sat, but Rose waited a moment to see if one of the male wraiths was going to be a gentleman. None came forward, and her estimation of them dropped some.

Rose seated herself and placed her arm on the table so that Daria might get a closer look at her bad hand, just so she would know who was in charge. The bones had lengthened, which made the limb take up the better half of the table, and a bit of goo clung to her pink painted nails. She nodded good-naturedly at the wraiths on her left so that Daria could see how her strength went up her shoulder and into her neck. Rose wanted to make sure there'd be no mistakes from the start.

Daria's gaze traveled the length of Rose's arm and stopped on her drumming fingers. "You are an angel?"

Rose didn't like the question in her tone, so she answered definitively. "Yes. Now, where shall we begin?"

"There's no point. Talia's father is there."

"And why is that a consideration?"

"You must have balls of steel. He's Death."

Rose flinched, scoring the table with her bad hand's nails. "I'll have none of that kind of talk."

"This is a waste of my time." Daria stood. She must

have wanted to stretch her legs, because she couldn't be leaving. Rose wasn't finished yet.

"What do you mean by Death?"

"Talia screams, and the Grim Reaper comes. Simple as that."

kat-a-kat-a-kat: Then make her scream.

And bring on Death? No, thank you. This was a dead end after all.

kat-a-kat-a-kat: The daughter doesn't concern you. Layla does.

Hmmm. Point taken.

kat-a-kat-a-kat: And the rest will be busy with the wraiths.

Interesting.

Rose flashed her dimples at Daria but lifted a hand toward the camper. "Are there more of that kind?"

"Why do you ask?"

"Because there's strength in numbers. And I have a little talent of my own to add to the pot, if we can come to an agreement."

This might just work.

Chapter 13

A rose lay on the pillow next to Layla when she woke the next morning, its bloom fat, bursting with fragrance, and bloody red. She didn't remember going to bed, nor falling asleep, but somehow here she was, waking up alone, blinking at the abundance of color, confused and disoriented.

A normal life had never been an option for her. She'd known that from the time she was a kid. Tried to dismiss it in adulthood. Tried to fake a relationship. She'd felt herself on the edge of something, a high, rocky precipice, weathering the wind and the beat of the sky. She'd been waiting for something, stretching the hours for something. Someone.

Well, now she'd found him.

Was she ready for this? For Khan? Layla gave a weary *ha!* That wasn't even his name.

Could she love him? Did the word even apply? No. Stupid word.

Layla sat up, plucked a petal from the flower, rubbed the satin between her thumb and fingers.

You and I. That's what he'd said, and it was much closer

to what she felt after last night. Witnessing the barren wintery landscape, she got it now. They were never meant to be together, yet were ruined for anyone else. They were a tragedy in the making, careening toward doom.

And she'd take as much as she could get.

The phone rang at her bedside. Layla pressed her palms to her eyes to steady herself. Took a deep breath. Answered.

Talia had a quick message. Adam was about to brief the Segue residents on the woman who attacked yesterday, the devil. The meeting was in the ballroom in fifteen minutes.

Layla made it down in five. It was her devil, after all.

The meeting occupied the same ballroom she'd been escorted to by Kev what seemed like a year ago. A couple soldiers hung in the back, but for the most part, mostly scientists and staff were present. Marcie smiled at her, and Layla returned the smile with a glance at the dishrag clutched in Marcie's hand. Patel and his nurses had taken a seat. A couple other men spoke softly. A woman in a white coat was there, as was Dr. James, with coffee stains on his shirt, but with that direct gaze Layla didn't think missed much. More entered as the minutes ticked by, and Layla guessed there were about thirty people gathered.

No Talia. But then, Layla guessed she already knew what Adam was going to say.

When Adam strode in, the group quieted. He dropped a load of files on the long conference table. "We've got a bad one here, people. Listen up."

He projected on the ballroom wall side-by-side images of a woman. One was a screen capture of the assault on the soldiers at the front gate. The woman's brown hair was flying midmovement. She seemed to be holding a fat stick with short, pointy branches. Or, no, maybe that was her arm. Or her hand. Weird.

In the other photo she was laughing as she posed with an ice-cream cone in front of the Statue of Liberty, a green foam liberty crown on her head. The woman was petite and pretty. Happy blue eyes, a lopsided quirk to a sweet smile, brown hair curling gently around a heart-shaped face. Girl next door. Never in a million years would Layla have feared her.

"Everyone meet Rose Anne Petty, born June nineteenth, nineteen sixty-five, died November twelfth, nineteen ninety-nine. She was murdered in her sleep by her husband, Mickey Alan Petty, who is now serving a life sentence in Georgia State Prison. He claimed during his trial that Rose was a psychopath, had planned and executed the grisly murders of a dozen people over the course of three years, to which he was an unwilling party. The only proof that surfaced to support his claims was an old police report that detailed the torture of neighborhood animals when she was a teen. Rose had exhibited no remorse for her actions but had complied with the community service terms of her conviction."

Adam made eye contact with someone in the back. "Dr. James?"

Layla looked around.

Dr. James had lifted his pen. "Then do we have a new breed on our hands?"

"A devil."

"Ah." The old man's eyes lit with interest. He actually seemed to dig this little development.

"And do our friends in The Order have anything to say about it?"

Adam shrugged. "Just that she's mean and mortal. Enough firepower, and she'll die a second death."

"What is she doing at our front gate?"

Adam grinned. "Admiring our architecture and history."

Layla flushed, remembering that she had given Adam that very same answer when he'd asked why she was lurking in his woods. And she knew it was the closest he would get to identifying her as Rose's target to the people assembled.

"Until Rose Petty is apprehended or killed, Segue will remain in lockdown. You all know that drill by now. In the meantime, we're working to deliver her husband here. He might be able to anticipate her movements or talk her into a vulnerable position."

"He's about to get the shock of his life," Patel said.

The group gave a reluctant chuckle.

"Or if he's very smart, a shot at an appeal to his sentence," Dr. James said. "If she's walking on this fair Earth, he could claim she never died."

"Damn wife just won't stay dead," another added.

"And I thought my ex-wife was psycho," someone else joked.

They laughed as a group now, if a little restrained, and Layla marveled at their response. The meeting broke up, and she waited until she was alone with Adam again.

He spoke before she had a chance to ask her question. "Some of them have been at this for going on ten years. Without a little humor they'd be cracked by now."

"Oh, they're cracked all right."

He cocked his head. "We all are."

She was about to leave when he stopped her with a hand to her elbow. "Hey, I don't suppose you had a chance to ask Khan about your photo, did you?"

Layla blushed. "Um . . . no. He, uh . . ."

"It's fine." Adam shook his head as he lifted a hand. "No details or complicated explanations necessary. I get the idea. Tonight, though, will you? Shadow is a mixed bag, good and bad. Talia's comfortable using it, and

Khan's basically made out of it, but I'd still like to be absolutely certain that we don't have an additional problem on our hands."

"'Kay. Sure. Next time I see him."

"Look, Talia's tied up with the kids for a bit, but if nothing happens in the next two hours"—he scratched the back of his head—"I promised her that I'd show you the wraith holding facility. You can take pictures if you'd like, though if you're going to publish something, I'd like to know beforehand."

He couldn't be serious. "Don't you have stuff to do? Wraiths? Devils?"

"There's always stuff to do, and lately always something new and dangerous to watch out for, but I have been informed in no uncertain terms that you are my first priority. Life goes on."

Had to be Talia bossing the boss.

Adam squeezed her shoulder. "You okay?"

Layla nodded. "I'm going to set myself up in the library with Talia's homework."

"Good girl. Then I'll look for you there."

Layla claimed a whole table, thinking to create a time line of wraith growth and activity according to Segue's records, which were considerably superior to anything available to the general public. The institute was founded to house and study Jacob, Adam's brother, who had apparently murdered their parents shortly after turning wraith. Like Layla, Adam had focused on scientific studies of Jacob's condition, but soon diverged to include the paranormal. Looked like Talia was brought in to use near-death experiences to augment the research.

Yet according to Segue records, Jacob was in no way the first of the wraiths. Adam had detailed accounts that identified murders with indicative facial lacerations and jaw fractures as far back as seventeen years. Seventeen. There were two more from eighteen years ago, but that couldn't be right. And then a list of others, spotty yes, that included possible deaths as far back as twenty years. Twenty-three, if the last record was viable.

And here she'd tried to pin Adam on ground zero.

The WHO was way, way off. This had been a growing problem for a long time.

And who was The Death Collector? Sounded like "debt collector" to her. Was he the first wraith? Or something worse? Layla wished she could ask Talia.

She grabbed lunch—Marcie had made killer pizza—then went back to work. Dr. James stopped by with a handful of her articles, which he'd found on the Internet and printed out. He'd taken the time to read them and highlight all the things she'd gotten wrong. Which meant there was more color than white space. Generous of him.

Talia came in and collapsed into a chair. She looked frazzled, almost in tears over her kids. Seemed Michael, the firstborn, was playing with Shadow. It took all Talia's concentration, all her magic, to keep him firmly in mortality. Adam had kicked her out while they napped so she could breathe. A half hour passed before she got a call. Michael was up and at it again, so she was off.

It was late afternoon when Adam showed. He had good news. An agreement had been made for Mickey Petty's release. Transport was arranged for tomorrow, when things would get very interesting. Adam acted like it was just another day in the life at Segue. Even after Layla's day of quiet work, she was still shell-shocked, but she had the even stranger sensation of fitting in.

The wraith holding facility was a mound of earth like a fairy ring, topped with the same yellowing winter grass. A soldier in some whacked-out supergear stood post outside an innocuous-looking door cut into the side of the hill. Entering took two simultaneous key cards and some weird scan that Adam had to stand still for.

"We used to hold a wraith in captivity under the main building," he said, "but that didn't work out too well."

Layla could imagine.

"We lost three people the day my brother escaped, so now the wraiths are kept out here. This building can be completely sealed off in the event of an attack. We'll have to do some kind of service to dedicate it as a barrow, or it won't hold wights."

"How do you plan to get them down here in the first place?" Seemed impossible to her.

"Launching a new division to work on that problem." He looked over at her. "Wish I'd gotten a look at that one you spotted yesterday."

They took a small elevator down into the earth, which opened into a control room. Inside the fairy mound, technology held the monsters at bay. Three soldiers sat in front of several monitors with sleek computer interfaces. A fourth soldier waited by the elevator.

"Good morning, Rick."

Rick nodded back. "Sir."

Layla lifted her camera. "May I?"

"For your reference only," Adam said. "I don't want to compromise the security or personnel here."

Right. Layla lowered her camera.

Adam signaled Rick. "Open 'er up."

A wide, tall door opposite the control desk gasped open, and a strong puff of fetid air almost knocked Layla over.

"Yeah, they stink all right," Adam said.

The wraiths within must have sensed the change because suddenly a chorus of earsplitting pterodactyl screeches shredded Layla's ears. She braced herself on the wall, her heart racing. She'd heard that screech many times during her coverage of the wraith war, but only once so close. She'd never run so fast in her life.

"There are sixteen cells in the facility," Adam said, "with three wraiths currently in residence, all male. These were nested in Baltimore and apprehended by the police. You might remember, there was a stir about it on the news?"

Layla nodded. Two cops down. She took a deep breath, but her heart still wouldn't slow. She didn't want to go in there. Had she really searched deserted city alleys, abandoned buildings, and dockside warehouses to encounter one? She'd been out of her mind.

Three paces inside, Adam stopped at the first thick, clear window. Considering what the cell held, Layla didn't think the window was made of glass.

Inside was a wraith. Layla had originally come to Segue to look at one, to charge Adam and his wife with bringing this scourge on the world. Now that she had a good look at the real thing, up close so there could be no mistake, she could tell for certain that there was no earthly way any disease or drug had created him.

His face had seemed normal, youthful, just for an instant, but then he crouched defensively. His jaw unlocked and his mouth gaped open while barbarous teeth extended. Normal human eyes went hollow and mad, and his skin turned sallow with a queer, sudden emaciation. There was no way in hell that thing was human.

She'd learned as much from Talia and from her research today, but now the truth was feet from her.

Yes, Segue and the government were lying to the public. An elaborate hoax and cover-up were definitely in play.

But, as Khan had said on their first meeting, sometimes a little deception was called for. Should she broadcast the truth, knowing everything possible was being done? Or should she trust Adam, and let him spin the facts as he saw fit?

It was a problem.

Further, it was a problem both Adam and Talia trusted her with.

Should she take this picture, or let the camera hang around her neck? This was the story she came for, and she had data to prove her claims, but she was stumped.

Adam was watching her carefully. She knew that he knew she was deciding something.

She let the camera hang. For now. "How long has he been here?"

And Adam seemed to completely relax. "We've had this one in custody about two weeks. He's hungry, which makes it more difficult for him to maintain the appearance of normalcy. He'll become hungrier still because The Order comes to destroy them only when all the cells are full. Used to be Khan took care of them, but since he found *other projects*"—an eyebrow went up—"we asked The Order to take over."

"Talia can't . . . ?"

"Not alone, no."

They walked on. The cells formed a neat semicircle, at the end of which was a large space with padded chairs lined up to view an operating room of sorts, which was located behind a transparent wall.

"We started by trying to find a cure. These days the research has shifted to rates of regeneration, identifying variables and any relationship to . . ."

Adam's voice muted as an earsplitting scream shredded

Layla's mind. It staggered her, then brought her to her knees as she gripped her head. A woman's scream, sharp enough to cut glass. The sound scored like jagged lightning. Burned in her mind with horror and fear, a soul cry for help. The scream went on and on, and Layla had to work to remember how to breathe, how to speak, how to tell Adam . . .

A grasp and yank on her shoulders had her standing again, Adam shouting soundlessly into her face. Though she couldn't hear him, his mouth moved, saying, *What's wrong? What's happening?*

"Talia," Layla said, or hoped she said. She forced her voice louder, just in case. "Talia!"

An unearthly shriek of terror filled Khan's mind. He dropped his work at the forge, the hammer sparking with impact on the cavern floor. He crossed through Twilight in a rage, baleful darkness riding his wake. If Talia called, she was in danger. If Talia screamed, she needed Death.

No one touched his banshee daughter.

Layla saw Adam's head jerk around as the lights in the facility changed from clean white to a deep yellow. She guessed the alarm had gone off, too late, though, to alert screaming Talia to danger.

Layla lurched into a run toward the cells, in the direction of the exit, but Adam grabbed her and held her back. He shook his head no. Half dragged her through the double row of seats to the examination room. The facing wall seemed to be made of glass or plastic, but knowing Adam, she was sure it was made of much stronger stuff.

The scream broke off suddenly.

"If she screamed, they're inside," Adam was saying, his voice distant as her hearing slowly returned.

"Then go. *Now!*" Urgency ruined her voice. Layla could take care of herself. She'd seen wraith action before. It was Talia and the children who needed Adam immediately.

"Khan will go to her. He'll already be there. Even now." But Adam's face was lined with pain. "We can't risk you, not with the threat of the gate over our heads. If you die before Khan can dismantle it, the gate will stand forever. It's too dangerous."

"But . . ." How would Khan know he was needed? How could he get to Talia so quickly?

Adam coded open the door to the examination room and pushed her inside. "You'll be safe here. It's wraith-tight, but not a cell. Security goes both ways in this room. Audio only." He rattled off a code. "You can get out if you need to, but don't unless your life is at risk. Wait for one of us to come for you. The soldiers are still up front, just in case. I'm taking the back way."

"Okay." Layla backed away from the door to show her compliance. "Go!"

But he was already pelting around the corner.

Please let him get to Talia.

The door hissed closed, and a deep metallic clang signaled it was secure. Only the voice code, which she had cycling in her mind, would release her now. Drawing a huge breath, she turned to look around.

The wraith examination room smelled brightly foul, like decay covered with bleach. The transparent wall looked out to an observation theater, and considering the thick metal slab and restraints in the room, she shuddered at the thought of what had been restrained and for what purpose. She pitied the wraiths. Was there any coming back for them? Segue research said no. The mutation was permanent.

Layla rubbed her hands on her arms to fight a sudden chill. The silence this deep underground was eerie, almost as bad as Talia's scream. What was happening? Layla couldn't begin to imagine. At least here she wouldn't be a liability.

In each upper corner of the room, cameras looked down on her. And Layla caught the gleam of lenses on the other side of the partition. For once, she was the one being captured on film. She almost signaled her awareness but glanced away instead.

Wait it out. Someone, eventually, would come for her.

The metal cupboards and drawers were all locked, so to pass the time she decided to pick them to discover the contents. The first drawer contained scalpels of all sizes and varieties, what must have been a bone saw, flat metal things—retractors?—a pointy tong that looked like a corkscrew. None of it good. All made her nauseous.

Adam Thorne, what goes on in here?

She decided to keep the rest of the drawers shut.

And that's when she noticed the woman leaning on the transparent wall. One-half of her was girl next door, though blood splattered her clothes, and the other half was reptilian, a lizard claw tapping lightly on the glass.

Khan found Talia backed up into a corner of the nursery, her children crying in her arms. The room was dark with her own Shadows as she attempted to cloak the babies, but there was nowhere for her to run. And she was too clumsy with the children in her arms to attempt a concealed dash. A wight hung in the air, its limbs ravaged, face hollow. Whether male or female, it long ago ceased to matter. Its smell polluted the air. The wight swatted a rocking chair out of the way as it lunged toward Talia's position.

Khan sent a jut of Shadow its way and its maw hung slack, its body gasping into decay, dead, a stain and stink in the pretty room. Adam would take care of that.

The door shuddered. Behind it a wraith, probably the wight's master, attempted entry.

"A moment," Khan said to Talia. Adam's stalwart doors didn't stop him. Couldn't stop darkness. A wind rush of black anger, and the wraith's flesh went slack as well.

Down the hallway, wraiths were a thick press of teeth and menace intent on reaching Khan's daughter and her children. They crawled the ceiling and walls, blocking human escape.

Khan seethed. Where were Adam and the security he promised? Where was Layla?

He briefly sought her light among the souls in the building. She was not present. Not here. Whether that was for good or ill, he did not know, which frenzied him like a sudden madness.

But he couldn't leave Talia and the children to this danger.

Fast. Hurry. Now.

Khan cast dark magic down the hallway to batter the wraiths from their perches. A wraith leaped at him. Khan grabbed his head out of the air, twisted to a double snap, and threw the rot out of the way. He flipped the wraith that dared to land on Death's shoulder to the floor and stamped his skull while reaching for two more of the vermin. He took them each in course, the soulless living husks of once-mortals, wishing for steel to make his progress faster. He ranged through the building, casting them into oblivion.

When all that was left was the reek of corpses, he sent fingers of Shadow throughout Segue to sense for other threats. He found the cold shift of a ghost, and another, and the blazing purpose of Custo, just passing through Twilight, too late to kill the wraiths.

But nothing that could hurt his daughter.

He returned to find Talia sitting on the floor cradling her children against her chest. She rocked them rhythmically. "Shhhh. Shhhh. Shhhh." But her face was fae pale, her eyes large and hot with her own strong feeling.

"Where's Layla?" he demanded.

"With Adam in the holding facility."

For the wraiths to come so far, there had to be another at work. The devil. And here he'd thought she was simple.

Custo burst into the room. His gaze darted about, settled on the dead wraiths. "Holy fuck, what happened here?"

Talia looked up at Khan. "We'll be okay now."

"Yeah, yeah," Custo added. "Go get your girl."

Rose Anne Petty. Devil.

Layla had a hard time pulling her attention from Rose's lizard arm up to the devil's sweet twinkling smile. The flecks of blood on the woman's chin were distracting, too.

How did she get down here? How did she get past Segue's front gate?

Those poor soldiers.

"Can you please open the door?" Rose had a slight Southern accent.

"Sure," Layla said, blinking against a sudden dizzy spell. "Hold on a sec." She looked up at the ceiling to address the security system. "Override code three, eight . . ."

Wait. What the hell was she doing?

"That's right," Rose prompted. "Just open the door. I've so looked forward to meeting you."

Layla wasn't as enthusiastic, but in a dizzy swim, the next number in the code, two, slipped out regardless. She bit her lips. She'd been warned that Rose would have extraordinary abilities. Angels could read minds; obviously devils could manipulate them. How . . . devilish.

Okay. Steady . . . Think.

Layla took a deep breath and shouted, "One, two, three!" Any numbers would do, as long as they were incorrect. One incorrect entry and the system would default to locked. Thank you, Adam.

"Open the door, honey."

"I can't. I just tripped the lock." Layla grabbed the counter to stop the room from spinning.

I'm in a wraith examination cell. It's designed to hold an impossibly strong and supernatural creature captive. It can hold out a devil. Maybe.

"Well, that's inconvenient. Mr. Thorne's security has been difficult before," Rose said. "And here I just painted my nails."

Layla focused on the claw. The nails were in fact a saccharine pink. "Sorry."

Rose's voice turned cold. "You don't sound sincere."

The room hazed. "I'm not."

Rose's eyes glittered and her lizard arm drew back and smacked the transparent wall. Hard.

Layla stumbled back against the counter in surprise, but the wall held. Didn't even shudder with the impact. Thorne security was the best.

The monster claw hit the wall again.

Heart in her throat, Layla fumbled through the drawer for a weapon. She had to be ready. She pulled out some kind of surgical cleaver. That would do.

Rose sweetly tilted her head, as if to acknowledge the necessity of the knife, but hit the wall still harder. Nothing.

She turned, wrenched a seat from the theater, and threw it at the wall.

Nothing.

The transparent partition seemed impenetrable. Layla loved the room. She could even get used to the smell.

"I have a suggestion," Rose drawled, all sugar. "You obviously want to stay in there alone, with the door locked. I understand completely and would love to compromise. How about I stay out here, like you want, and you draw that there blade across your throat."

Again the dizziness, but Layla knew that the wall would hold. She was safe. And Rose's solution sounded so reasonable. Everyone got what they wanted. Layla in, Rose out. Layla dead.

Wait a second. . . .

"Don't worry, honey," Rose said. "You won't even feel it."

Layla threw the knife on the counter. Flexed her hand to get rid of the cold of the handle.

"Look at me, darlin'."

Layla's gaze was forced to Rose's blue eyes. An oily shiver went down Layla's spine. How could someone so nice be so awful?

Rose's voice lowered with compassion. "Honey, it's better this way. I think you know that."

No.

"Besides, you're supposed to already be dead. It's like you're stealin' time, and that isn't good." Rose smiled, then gently said, "Go on now, slit your throat."

No . . . The light of the room warped in Layla's vision.

"I can see that you're strong-willed, and I like that about you." Rose's pretty cheeks dimpled. "In any other circumstances, I know we'd be friends. But right now, you're alone. Just as alone as alone can be."

Layla shuddered.

"Why is that, honey? I think you know."

Because no one wanted her. She'd always been alone.

Rose lowered her head in a confirmatory nod. "That's right. I'm sorry to have to say it, but no one loves you."

So it was true.

They wanted Kathleen back, that's all.

"And no one *wants* you. Why else would you be stuck down here, when everyone else has left the area to the wraiths? Do you even have food? No toilet, I see."

"They were protecting me."

"Oh, honey." Rose *tsk-tsk-tsked* her pity. "Couldn't you just die? Why don't you just die?"

"Stop it," Layla said. "Why are you doing this? I never hurt you."

"You are, though," Rose said. "I have a man who loves me, who's waiting for me to come home. Twelve years he's been waiting, since my untimely passing. But I can't until I deal with you. You've got nobody, and your life is already over. Holding on is just, well . . . it's just sad. Pick up the knife and cut your gosh-darn throat."

Stars filled Layla's vision. *No.*

"I said," Rose's voice took on steely intensity, "you are *alone*. You've always been *alone* and you will always be *alone*. It's better to end it *now*."

The room went white with brightness, blurry and indistinct. Layla shook her head to clear her vision, but the action set the room careening around her.

Layla had thought they cared, thought they understood her—Talia and Adam, Khan, who wouldn't tell her his name—but if they'd left her to the mercies of the wraiths and a devil, she must have been wrong. So very wrong. She'd been wrong like this before.

The lifetime wound in Layla's chest opened. She could see the fissure like a black hole, sucking all her hope for love and family and peace into some dark abyss within that would never fill. How her heart beat against that terrible vacuum, she didn't know. The vortex had her in a grip her small strength had no hope to fight. It held her in place. Her only chance of getting free was to cut herself free.

"That's it, honey. Sooner or later, I knew you'd break."

A knife was right there, within arm's reach. The shiny blade looked sharp enough to slice through anything.

"Won't hurt a bit."

Nothing could hurt as bad as what she already endured. And even the angels had said it: she was past her time. If she'd had a place in the world, it was long gone now.

Layla reached out and grasped the handle of the knife again.

Khan evaporated from the nursery into darkness, slid through the Shadowlands, but did not immediately emerge again on the earthly plane so as to have the advantage over whatever creature, wraith or devil, might threaten Layla.

He found her deep in the earth. She stood, tears streaming from her eyes, with a gruesome, fat blade against her throat, held by her own hand. Her grip shook and thin trails of blood trickled down her neck. Distress colored the air around her. Abject sorrow riddled the shadow of the room.

The devil stood on the other side of a clear wall, not

unlike the veil between Shadow and mortality, and she had Layla's mind locked within her own. Khan remembered this foul soul. There was no other place for her but Hell.

"One. Quick. Cut," the devil urged. Partly she looked like a human woman, but her true self was in the hell limb braced on the wall.

His strong Layla trembled, but held fast. She'd fought for this life, fought *through* this life for a second chance at happiness. It would take more than an order to break her will. Layla's will defined her. No devil could break it.

"You're all *alone*," the devil crooned.

Khan's Shadow turned cold.

Except perhaps if the devil touched *that* fear. If the devil found the Layla who'd been misunderstood and rejected repeatedly as a child. The Layla whose fine, upstanding man Ty could not grasp the forces that drove her to her dangerous work, and left her to it on her own.

Layla's greatest fear was being alone. The devil didn't have to break her. Layla's life had already cracked open her soul.

A blind rage overcame Khan.

From Twilight, he blunted the blade with Shadow. Excised the tool from Layla's grasp. Flung it across the room with a tinny clatter.

The devil's expression sobered. Lost its mock friendliness. Became watchful. Wary. She knew that someone else had joined them.

Layla's empty hand shook midair. Her eyes did not lose the glaze of horror. The knife was gone, but Layla was still trapped. Fear, not the blade, was the keen instrument of the devil.

The devil stepped back from the glass. Her heartbeat

doubled its tempo. Her gaze darted to the hallway. To escape.

As if he would ever let her go after the harm she'd inflicted on Layla. No, the devil would release Layla, and then the devil would die.

She'd been clever to use the wraiths, to use his daughter to buy time, very clever, but not quick enough. A devil against Death? There was no contest. It was hubris to think otherwise.

And she enjoyed fear, did she? Well, Khan had a forever's worth of terror in his Shadow. She'd release Layla all right. She'd release Layla *now*.

Khan poured himself out of Twilight, his darkness a Shadow storm under the earth. The deep magic pulsed with power, with his anger and rage, but he let the devil do his work for him.

Not too long ago, she'd been a mortal. He remembered well the shape she'd made of Death.

The devil woman fell back in awe as he assumed the shape of her ultimate fear. His body took on obscene height and hulk, razored teeth grew in his mouth, talons from the tips of his fingers. His chest grew huge with exposed bone and raw muscle, and his belly cavity was hollow. He was a monster for the ages, his breath a snort of fire, his stamp an earthquake. Awful, to be sure, and utterly unoriginal.

The devil woman screamed. Pitiful noise.

Khan took a breath and shrieked a sound that made her ears bleed.

The devil scuttled toward the hallway like a cockroach. He'd crush her out of this world. She'd be a gut smear on the floor. A mess to clean up, nothing more.

But a muffled sob off to the side brought his attention back to Layla.

Layla, whose clear gaze told him she was free of the devil's fear.

Layla, who now witnessed the grotesque glory of Death: him.

Layla peered beyond the glass, into the observation theater, where a mass of churning shadows had condensed, solidified, shifted through the murky spectrum of the color gray. A line of blackness became the hulk of a chest thickening as something—*Khan?*—formed beast-big shoulders. His features, in profile, were harsh, the menace in his posture severe, cutting, cadaverous.

The sound he'd made turned her blood cold.

Oh, dear God. Her sweat chilled to ice. The pulse of life in her veins stalled. Her vision went dry, too clear, as she stared unblinking at the horror before her.

Death.

That's who Khan was. That was his secret. She should have known it from the start. Every cell in her body screamed Death.

And she'd let him touch her.

Her legs gave and she caught herself on the wraiths' cold slab, quailing against the moment Khan's regard would settle on her.

Please, no. She didn't want to die. Not yet.

She must have made a sound because he turned his horrible countenance in her direction.

Please don't see me. Please don't look at me. Please. I'm not ready. I just found her, she begged inside her head.

But his gaze fell on her just the same.

This was it then. So much time, wasted. Her moment with Talia, over.

She raised her hands and face to stop the inevitable.

She knew she had about as much chance as a butterfly in a hurricane. But she met his hoary gaze. Tried to speak to him with the panic of her soul.

Please.

As she begged, the dry gray parch of his skin rippled, then rolled. He was changing again. His monster body settled and took on the posture of a man, strong and fit and naked, all of him large, legs braced, muscles flexed with power. His features smoothed, cheekbones lifting to structure his tilted fae eyes, black with soul. Shadow eroded the sharpness of his teeth and left him mouthing her name, *Layla.* And in the storm whip of his darkness, his long hair gleamed.

Oh.

Wait. . . .

Something turned in Layla's mind, like a key in the lock of her memory. Her two selves, Kathleen and Layla, merged at a singular point of awareness. Her bones shook with the force of its clarity.

She recognized him as she had on the winter plain in Twilight.

Kathleen and Layla together. She knew him. The word burned bright on her tongue.

Death, yes. But he was more than that. More than "Khan," which was just another one of his illusions, a misdirection for his convenience. Males were such idiots sometimes, even this one.

Layla felt a smile stretching her face. She could never be afraid of him.

How could she have forgotten?

"Shadowman," she said, naming him. At last.

But wedged in the sense of triumph that followed was an unbidden knowledge.

Her smile faltered.

The knowledge was crystalline in its perfection, igniting her mind with a purpose and a task that was hers, only hers. Because of all the people on Earth, only she might accomplish the feat.

She knew why she'd been reborn.

With his name from her lips, all Shadow went still, and with her smile, he knew he was saved.

Fate had woven different lives for Layla and Kathleen, but both women had conceived the same body for him. Would it have been the same had he revealed his nature to Layla from the beginning? Or had this form been fixed in her mind that day on the docks? He didn't know and didn't care. As long as she accepted him.

Her gaze broke with his, flicking to the left. "Devil got away."

The devil was no problem whatsoever. She was an irritation, a splinter, no more. There was nothing that could stop him now that Layla was his. He advanced toward the glass wall separating them.

"Everyone else okay?" Layla took a small step back in her room and was stopped by some cabinets on the wall.

She was still afraid, but the color of her emotion was now mixed with fading exhilaration . . . and tremendous sadness.

"The family is safe. The attack is over." Why was she sad?

He lifted his hands and pushed Shadow against the transparent wall. His darkness insinuated itself into the atoms of its composition, and with a sigh of power, the wall fell to dust.

He didn't even pause in his approach.

Layla gripped the countertop behind her, eyes wide,

her breath coming in short pants. He came to a stop before her, close enough to feel her trembling. "Hello."

"It's, um, good to see you." She spoke to his chest.

"Layla," Khan said. To stand before her without effort filled him with an exquisite joy he'd not felt since he first stood before Kathleen.

"Been all spooky shadows for the past couple days." She feigned lightness. Her sadness was turning to desperation.

"Layla, look at me." He put his arms around her waist.

"I am. You're an inch away."

"A little higher, sweetheart."

Kathleen had been brave and strong, as if her heart pumped courage. And Layla had that same quality, heightened by recklessness. If anyone could look Death full in the face, it was she.

Layla stopped breathing, but her chin lifted. Her gaze skimmed over his mouth, his nose. Found his eyes.

"There you are."

"Adam's going to be mad about his wall." She was shaking harder, and Khan wondered if she realized that she had transferred her grip from the counter to his arms.

"You are my Reason," he said. "Do you understand?"

She shook her head, blinking hard and looking away. He followed the dodge of her gaze and caught her again.

"The light in Shadow."

Her eyes were full of hurt. "Don't say that."

He tightened his hold on her. He had a strange sense that she was slipping away from him, when all should finally be well. "You don't fear me, so what is it?"

The color in her face went ashy, and her heart stilled for a long, awful beat. "I know why I've come back. Why everything is happening right now. What I'm here to do."

She tried to shrug him away but he gripped her hard, her body squeezed against his. He wasn't letting her go.

"Out with it then."

Layla strained again. No use.

"Speak, if you've something to say."

She pulled a little air, steeling herself in his embrace. Met his gaze. She had to force the words out of her mouth, because she sure as hell didn't want to say them. "Shadowman, I'm here to ask you . . . to beg you . . . to pick up your scythe again and do your duty."

The room went silent except for her labored breath.

"You can't mean it." He released her and drew back from this revelation.

But Layla, his woman, his life, nodded her head. "I do. Please, you have to. You won't listen to anyone else, but maybe you'll listen to me. It's why I was sent."

Shadowman shook his head. "I don't want to be Death anymore. You know I can't."

She looked at the floor and had the gall to sniffle. "Please. This is what I came to do. I can't fail. It's too important."

The scythe cried from Twilight, the blade weeping for mortal blood. And she wanted him to answer it? "This place is a grave, and you are not dead," he said. "Let us go."

Rose made quick time across the compound aided by the knuckle push of her bad hand on the ground. *Run, run, push. Run, run, push.*

Shots were fired, but they skimmed by her as she vaulted a wall. Then over a jeep. Then took a gallop at the fence along the perimeter of Segue. Leaped. Swung her body over. Her bad hand and arm might be ugly, but they were lovely in their usefulness and strength. How many times had they saved her now?

She had to get out of there.

She urged her body faster, through the trees and growth and up to a knobby ridge, away from the evil that was Death. She only paused, holding her breath, to listen for pursuit. The night was silent. Trees swaying. Winter wind snaking through the branches. And above it all the cruel, cruel heavens. To allow that thing to walk the earth when she'd been sent to Hell made no sense whatsoever.

Hell had nothing compared to the monster she'd seen at the compound. Nothing.

The world was upside down, is what it was.

What if good was bad and bad was good? They were just words, after all. What if somewhere along the line, the good and bad traded places? And nice people like her were sent to torment, while Layla Mathews's existence challenged the Gate.

Just look at that monster guarding Layla Mathews. Anybody could see that wasn't right.

The world was upside down, for sure.

Rose glanced at the five-fingered claw that was her hand. The transformation had crept over her breast and now fed the pump of her heart so that she was alert, ready at all times.

How far could she get before sunrise? Clear the forest. Steal a car. Run. Run. Run!

Hell was kind in comparison to Death. Hadn't Hell given her everything she needed to survive this harsh, unkind world? She should give thanks. If not for her arm, she'd be dead.

"Gate?" Rose said aloud.

The gate was quiet. For once.

Oh, thank goodness. Not that she wasn't grateful, but still.

She'd better get moving. Put as much distance between her and Segue as possible. The last thing she wanted was to face that monster again.

So she was a coward, so what?

Ladies were supposed to be gentle.

Nothing, not even the gate, could compel her to go back.

Chapter 14

Layla sat on the sofa in her apartment, arms crossed, elbows braced on her knees. She breathed deep so she wouldn't be sick all over the nice rug, but each inhalation just fed the internal fire scorching her chest. Denying the message in her head was impossible, but coping with it now that she had found her place in the world was beyond excruciating. It was burning her from the inside out.

Talia was using the bedroom as a makeshift nursery since her apartment had been battered and soiled by dead wraiths. She stood frozen in the doorway, as if on guard, a baby bottle in her hands. Adam paced on the other side of the room in front of the windows. Custo straddled a turned-around straight-backed chair. And Shadowman glared from the seat across from Layla. At least he'd managed to put on some clothes.

Adam stopped abruptly. "Aside from the scythe issue, what exactly did you remember?"

Layla concentrated on the crisscross grain of the upholstery of Shadowman's chair. She hadn't looked at him directly since delivering her message. Hurt too much. "That the existence of the wraiths is our fault. That souls are being lost to Shadow as fae prey on them when they cross. That he has to go back and restore The Order by lifting his scythe."

"But nothing of what we shared?" Shadowman put in.

She shook her head no. And she didn't want to. What she already felt for him was strong enough.

The wraith thing was beyond ironic. Here she'd spent years of her life trying to learn the origin of the wraiths when it had been she and Shadowman all along. Had that compulsion, that obsession, come from her, or had it been part of her reincarnation directive as well? Layla bet it was the latter.

"First of all," Talia said angrily, "you aren't responsible for the wraiths. Yes, when Shadowman crossed to be with my mother, a fae demon got into the world, The Death Collector. I killed him, so in that case we've cleaned up our own mess. But the wraiths? Do you know what each person had to do to become one? They had to drink a cup of demon vomit. They had to choose it. Becoming a wraith was a deliberate, voluntary act, not some condition spread like a disease. And we're still fighting them. We've dedicated our lives and our resources to that end. So that blame is in no way yours to bear."

Shadowman was silent through Talia's tirade, the weight of his gaze heavy on Layla's near-crumbling defenses.

Apparently the wraiths had colluded with Rose Petty, a dangerous combination that still sent shivers down Layla's back. With Rose's ability to manipulate minds, and wights taking to the air, the wraiths had gotten into the main building. Into Talia and Adam's apartment. Into the nursery.

They must want Talia's children bad.

"Doesn't matter if they chose it or not. The wraiths, a

devil, that horrible gate," Layla listed. She forced herself to meet Shadowman's gaze. He had to understand. "We've been hell on the world and it's time it stopped."

"Layla," Adam said, "the problem is more complex than Khan returning to Shadow."

"No, it's not. It's very simple. Very clear." It rang like a bell in her mind, a horrible clanging that she couldn't silence. It was only marginally better than the hellgate's rattle. Both were the sound of doom.

"If Khan goes back," Adam continued, "what will happen to the gate?"

"The angels will rip it apart," Khan answered, each syllable clipped.

He had to be using Shadow; Layla felt it on her skin, moving against her, stroking and churning like an ocean. Even now he tried to seduce her. It would be so easy to give in and let his cool fury douse the burn inside her.

"I'm sorry to be explicit, Layla," Adam said, "but I have to get this straight. My understanding is that if the gate is destroyed, then you will be killed as well."

She didn't know how to respond to that, so she kept quiet. The important thing was that Shadowman went back to his duty. Her life was over, anyway. That fact was abundantly evident in the multiple near-death scrapes of the past couple days. The sooner this was resolved, the sooner the nightmare would end.

"Custo," Talia pleaded. "Please."

Custo stood and turned his chair back around. "It's extremely rare for someone to be reincarnated. In every case I know of, there has been some great work to be done. The second life itself hardly mattered. Case in point, Layla was born an orphan. I defy you to find the birth mother. Layla never connected with any of her foster families, was wholly raised by a system, and moved through this world almost completely alone."

"It's cruel," Talia said, eyes shimmering.

No, Layla thought, she was on a mission; she just hadn't known it. She'd already had a chance at life, and a good one, as Kathleen. This was about finishing Kathleen's business, Layla's business now. The reality sucked, but there was no changing it.

Adam picked up where Custo left off. "Makes sense. Her work has been dominated by the wraiths and an obsession with Segue. And, she went to extraordinary lengths to get near Talia."

"Why wasn't she sent back as an angel, then?" Talia asked.

Layla knew, but Shadowman answered. "We wouldn't have been able to touch."

Angels and fae were at odds, the light of the first eroding the darkness of the other, which was why Custo kept well back from Shadowman.

Layla's face heated as cool Shadow curled around her in an embrace, caressing her skin and quickening her blood. Sensuous zings ran down her tightening middle to torture her when she had no hope of release. Yes, if she had a choice to come back as an angel, full of knowledge, but not able to be with him, or as a mortal, ignorant and scared, she'd choose mortal every time.

"Kathleen had to have agreed to this business," Shadowman said cruelly, even as he reached out to Layla. His black gaze wouldn't let her move. "She chose her fate."

Which made Layla tip up her chin and push back her shoulders. He had a right to act like a cold bastard. She was asking the worst and betraying him, too.

"What I don't get," Talia said, "is why Khan can't choose *his* fate. He's been Death for forever. Now it's time for someone else to step up. Then he could watch over Layla."

"Angels have been stepping up," Custo said. "But they can't cover all of the Shadowlands—the place is endless. And they can't sense a passing and catch it at the brink. Souls have been lost, and they need to be recovered. Khan is the only one who can do that. His absence is a growing problem."

Shadowman smoldered in his darkness. "He's saying I don't have a choice."

"But you do," Layla answered. "You made one choice already. I'm asking you to make the other one. The idea that some lost soul in Twilight is fading while you and I are off doing who knows what . . . It's obscene."

"No, Layla," Custo interrupted. "You have that wrong, too."

She gave him a look that dared him to prove otherwise.

"I, as well as most of The Order, believe your union with Shadowman was necessary. Because of the two of you, magic has once again come into the world. Art and innovation are in a modern renaissance. The influx brings good and bad, yes, but both are absolutely vital to the well-being of humanity. It was past time. We are at the brink of a new age."

"And the devil?" she scoffed. "I let it into the world."

Custo shook his head. "If the angels of our Order have difficulty resisting the gate, it was impossible for you to resist its pull."

"Even I heard its call," Shadowman said, finally ripping his gaze from her to regard Custo. "And I am Death."

Layla held her breath. There. He'd said it. He might even do what was right.

"You don't have to worry about the devil," Adam said. "She's tricky, but destroying her is a question of firepower, which Segue can handle. Her husband, Mickey Petty, is arriving shortly. We'll use him to draw her out."

That was Adam, trying to work the problem. And everyone else, absolving her of her culpability. She didn't deserve it but couldn't do anything regardless.

"Which leaves the gate," Custo said. "I have to warn you: The Order won't let you pass into Twilight with Shadowman before we attempt to destroy it. If you die before it is destroyed, then it may never be destroyed. Eventually, someone else will be compelled to open it."

The Shadow on her skin turned rough.

"You can look at her," Shadowman interrupted, "and plan her murder?"

"You've made no progress," Custo argued, his mouth drawn into a bitter line. "The devil just took more lives. The Order is going to act, and soon."

"Enough!" Shadowman said, standing. He loomed over her, a dark shadow splitting the room. Darkness smudged out from his skin into smoky wisps in the air. "This talk is futile. I won't comply. Layla, you will come with me, and we will be happy."

This just wasn't going to be a happy day.

Layla stood slowly. It hurt to move with the fire inside and the bell in her head. She was more than a foot shorter than he, but she wasn't scared. Of course he would fight this. He would fight and fight until she gave him no other choice. Her throat was already raw from containing her own screams of denial. She tried for a little lightheartedness. "I warned you about the imperious thing."

"I can't lose you again," he said. His voice had lost all human tone, rumbling low, from a deep storm within him.

She reached to brush his cheek, so beautiful, so severe. "That part you can't control."

"Watch me. I won't let you go."

"You will, or I'll fade like all the rest."

"Not if I can keep you alive."

"Don't you understand?" Layla said. "This is my destiny."

Layla saw Talia duck into the bedroom, but the soft cries from within came from the mother, not a child. The fire in Layla's chest flared. The sooner this was over, the better.

She turned to Custo. "I'll want the rest of the day to be miserable, if that's okay with you."

"Layla, I—"

"Custo, it's fine. I'm fine. At last things make sense, which is a huge relief." And here she'd found Talia, a friend, after all this time. Adam should go to her. Why was he still here in this awful room?

Custo frowned. "That's not what you're thinking. At least don't lie to me."

"What do you want me to say?" Layla snapped. "The bell in my head says this is no-win. I get it. At least let me put on a good face while I try to do the right thing."

Shadowman sent his darkness coursing around her. "I won't let this happen."

Brick wall, and her head was already bloody.

Shadowman pulled her into his arms. "I could keep you safe."

Layla felt a strange stirring of air, and then she was struck by an invisible fist. She cried out, then bit her lip too late for quiet. The sound of metal against metal rang throughout the room. Her weight collapsed into Shadowman's arms and she got a crazy vantage of the room.

"Layla?" He gripped her.

Layla marveled as the gray veins under Custo's skin grew darker. "Fuckers started on the gate without me."

Suddenly Adam was beside her. "They knew you couldn't do it."

"Rose Petty took lives today," Custo said. "The Order won't risk letting in more devils like her."

"Go!" Adam shouted. "Stop them. Buy us more time. Tell them she's willing."

Another blow assailed Layla's senses. Stars sprang into her vision and she smelled the metallic scent of blood, running freely from her nose. The rapid man-chatter kept up around her, but her attention was drawn to Shadowman's face. His eyes had gone full black again, swallowing the whites. Unless he was turned on, that was a bad sign. His form, though solid, seemed to phase out of reality, as if the darkness was filling him to bursting. Very bad.

"Don't," she tried to tell him, but she knew he was beyond that. Beyond listening.

This is the way it has to be. But she could see that he didn't care.

She trembled as a new beast was born before her eyes. Her Shadowman, yes, but filled with a blackening menace that outdid anything Rose could hope to conjure.

The angels wanted Death?

Well, here he comes.

Shadowman took the cavern with a hurricane of darkness. He drew from the depths of the earth where shadows were soaked in black pitch and hurled death at the host gathered before the gate to Hell. Bodies flew back and crashed on the stone walls and the stalagmites reaching up from the floor.

Only Ballard hung on to the gate, his yellow hair whipping in the wind, one hand around a wrought-iron rung, the other gripping the hammer. Though Death bore down, still Ballard drew back and struck the gate again.

They hadn't even given her a moment's warning.

Death summoned Shadow, deeper and deeper, until the cavern walls ran with sightless bugs streaming toward the mouth. Bats screamed through the air in a cacophonous flapping. And the gate rattled with hysterical glee.

Shadowman sent a gale of power and struck Ballard. His head bounced off the gate, bloodied, but he held on.

How valiant. But angels were mortal and this one was going to die.

Death flexed his magic and took to his feet. He hoped they saw a beast. They deserved to meet a beast for the murder they planned. He grabbed Ballard's hair in his hand and bashed his head against the gate. Used his skull like a new hammer. Thrilled toward the moment when white bone would show through.

But his arm was caught by that dog, Custo. "Let me—!" The rest of his words were lost on the wind.

Just as well. Shadowman shook off the hold, drew Ballard back, and struck the gate again. Finally, the damn angel's body went slack, the hammer dropping to the cavern floor. Death tossed the used body aside and turned to the angels, who were regrouping for a fight.

Custo stood between them, eyes black with Shadow, arms lifted, hands flattened to say, *Stop!*

The moment they struck Layla, the angels had taken matters way past stopping.

kat-a-kat-a-kat-a-kat: Open me. I've an army at your disposal.

"She'll comply!" Custo shouted at them. "Layla has agreed!"

"I don't," Shadowman's thunderstorm grumbled.

Another angel stepped forward. "Recuse yourself, Custo. You are blinded by your friendships."

"Layla just found out," Custo said. "She agreed. Give her a little time. . . ."

"There is no such thing as time," Death said. Not anymore. There was only forever. And he would have no less.

kat-a-kat-a-kat-a-kat: I can give you forever.

"Listen to me!" Custo shouted. "Layla found her purpose. She can set things straight. Shadowman will go back to Twilight."

"I will not." For a moment, he had considered it. For a moment, he would have taken the heartbreak, if that was what Layla really wanted him to do. He'd have gone back and done his duty. Now he only wanted his scythe to strike down the angels. His bare hands would have to do.

"Shadowman, please. Listen to reason," Custo said. "It's the way things are meant to be."

Ballard stirred from his collapse on the ground. Put a hand to the cave floor.

Through the air, a gleam of steel flew. A dagger, a weapon of the angels. Shadowman stuck out his chest to accept the impact. No blade could kill him, and in the belly of the earth where darkness reigned, it would not even slow him. The point slid into his heart with a thunk as the hilt met muscle. He grinned against the pain, baring his teeth at the host like an animal. He had only to move his Shadow forward, and the dagger would fall to the ground. And so it did.

"No bloodshed!" Custo implored him. "If you don't want to be Death, don't kill today. Layla wouldn't want it. You know that."

"Your kind struck her first." And now Shadowman could only see death around him. Could only see the wasted bodies littering the cave. A war with Heaven. Endless fighting until the world was scorched beyond reckoning.

kat-a-kat-a-kat-a-kat: Open me, and no one will strike Layla again.

Ballard pushed himself up. His nose was crushed, one eye turned slightly inward, blood streaming down his chin, but his body would repair itself rapidly, as angels were wont to do. Soon he would be whole again. However, like a devil, angels could be killed, and Death could not. Why did they fight when they had no hope of prevailing?

"The time for discussion is past," Shadowman said.

"What if we bury it?" Custo said. "What if I guard it until Layla is old and ready to go?"

The boy was grasping at straws.

Ballard wiped the blood from his mouth and stood. "The risk is too great, the temptation overwhelming. The gate must be destroyed now. We do not compromise with evil or with Shadow."

"Let them at least prepare," Custo begged. "Let her say good-bye."

"The decision is made," Ballard said.

"The fuck it is!" Custo shouted back.

Shadowman bid dark magic to flow through his veins. No one would so much as lay a finger on the gate. "You're right," he said to Ballard. "The decision has been made. Custo, it is time for you to choose a side. Order or madness?"

Custo let his extended arms drop. His chest rose and fell with his breath. Conviction overrode the anguish that ripped his Shadow and Ordered halves apart. "Well, when you put it like that . . ."

And he went to stand next to Death.

"You're a fool." Ballard spit blood onto the ground.

"This won't end well, will it?" Custo murmured.

"No," Shadowman answered. "It will not."

* * *

"Look at me, Layla."

She focused on Adam, who crouched in front of her.

"You feel okay? Like the first time this happened?"

Her head hurt like crazy, but yeah, she'd live.

He held up a finger in front of her eyes, tracking to the left and right. "Patel's been evacuated, or I'd have him give you a once-over."

"I'm okay, and I think we can safely say the gate still stands, too." If she was relatively unscathed, the gate must be. Shadowman had stopped them. She just hoped Custo could keep the whole thing civilized. But remembering the look in Shadowman's face, the darkening of his skin and eyes, she really didn't think civilized was possible. Death was pissed.

"Was anyone else hurt in the attack?" Layla asked.

"When the alarm went off, most were evacuated. Some staff remain, those who were trapped in their rooms, and the soldiers are here. We're still well protected, just not organized."

Layla glanced toward Talia, who was leaning in the bedroom doorway, the black-eyed baby in her arms. "Will the kids be safe?"

"I'm a banshee," Talia said. "If we're attacked by wraiths, my scream will bring my father. Add Adam's firepower and they are as safe as we can make them."

"Banshee," Layla repeated. She hadn't meant it to be out loud. So that was the deal with Talia's voice.

"Yes." Talia returned her gaze, waiting for a reaction.

"I heard you scream," Layla said, recalling that piercing terror. "Down in the holding facility."

Adam craned his neck to look at his wife. "She did hear you, even though I couldn't. She sent me running."

Layla gave a wry smile. "One of the kids has quite the scream, too. I could hear him through Kathleen's painting.

He makes the leaves rustle like there's a wind blowing through the trees. Totally confused me, but I get it now. The veil is thin for me." She felt the smile twist on her face. "Getting thinner by the hour."

"You don't really want Khan to go back, do you?" Talia put the baby over her shoulder and patted his back. The other one let out an angry squall, and Adam went to fetch him.

"For myself, no, of course not." But this was bigger than her. Layla shrugged. "I hate it, but I can't think of an alternative. And at least we can be together there for a little while." A very little while.

Talia shook her head. "I can't believe it. For you guys to find each other again, and now this? It's worse than wights and the devil put together."

"Funny thing is," Layla said as his winter Twilight sprang to mind, "even if he does go back, I don't think he'll last long. He's too far gone."

The desolation he faced filled her with sorrow. The ashy ground, the barren branches, the dirty gray of his unending existence. She'd felt the utter lack for a few moments last night and could bear that nothingness only with his arms around her. The pain of his abject loneliness echoed hers. It had been in his voice, and in that lonesome howl, when she'd asked him to reveal himself. He'd known the emptiness of the future, and the monster it would surely make of him.

Layla wept for her love, for his duty, and for his ruin.

"What do you mean?" Talia asked, both urgency and sadness in her voice.

Layla wiped at the tears that coursed down her cheeks. She lifted a helpless hand. "Maybe twenty-some years ago there might have been a chance, but not now." Layla's throat contracted at the thought of him trapped in his solitude. How long would it take to resolve things with the gate? Before she could hold him? Would he bend, or would he fight? Fight. "I think it would kill the good in him and leave the dark. And then what?"

She remembered the look on his face when he'd held her in his arms, the insane rage, backed by the might of his magic. It was more frightening than the beast who had stared Rose down before he'd changed into Shadowman before Layla's eyes.

"I'm supposed to convince him," Layla said.

"I wish I could help." Worry lines formed on Talia's forehead. "But I don't know how or what to do."

"No, you've got the kids."

A chattery hiss rose in the room, like the sound of a downpour on a tin roof or nighttime bug talk in the middle of a jungle. Segue was exposed to neither of those conditions, so Layla stood, a now too familiar tightness pulling in her chest.

"Abby?" she heard from far, far away, but she didn't recognize the voice. It was young and broken and afraid. "Don't leave me, sis."

Oh, no. Fresh alarm stirred Layla's misery to panic. Not Abigail. Not now.

The wraith attack had precipitated something else, too. Everything was coming all at once, with no time to mourn or say good-bye. All the stolen time was spent.

The living room seemed to warp slightly, and Layla remembered the Shadow over Segue, the twisting lines of the building's architecture. In the rush and danger of the past few hours, she hadn't had a chance to ask Khan, now Shadowman, what it was. And now she didn't need to. *She* knew.

The Shadow was here for Abigail. Zoe's sister was passing. The reason Layla knew this was simple: Soon she would pass, too, even though she had—finally had—people who would try to hang on to her with all their might. This crossing was inevitable, for Abigail and for her.

Order was asserting itself everywhere.

Layla turned to Talia, who moved strangely slow-fast forward, her mouth shaping words, though the sound was unintelligible. Her face had that fae glow to it again, the tilt of her eyes a touch more extreme.

Abigail was putting Segue, and everyone remaining within it, at the brink, too.

"Scream," Layla said. She meant to shout it.

Color in the room suddenly amped, and finally—*finally*—Talia whirled back to Adam, a look of alarm transforming the concern on her features.

And with a crashing rush like the ocean on rocks, Layla could hear again.

Adam opened a drawer and pulled out a handgun. "Where is it?"

He was looking for a wraith or a wight. Layla was shaking her head. "Shadow's coming. An ocean of it. Scream!"

"Won't help," Talia was saying, holding her baby fast to her shoulder. "Have to be in the presence of the living dead, like a wraith, for my father to hear. But if it's Shadow, we should be okay. I'll keep us safe."

"This isn't just Shadow. It's freaking *Twilight*." Where was a wraith when you needed one?

A tsunami of great force was coming. Layla's bones trembled with the gather of its force. Colors bled into others, luscious in hue and wicked in severity.

"What do I do?" Adam's face flushed red, veins popping. The child in his arms screamed in confusion, but the one in Talia's laughed.

"Abigail's passing." Layla's heart clutched at Zoe's

racking sobs amid the deafening roar of magic. If Talia and the babies were overcome by it, they'd be lost to the world, too. Oh, God. "Run!"

Layla got to the apartment door, which burst open, blasted by magic, to reveal the hallway. She held it wide for Adam and Talia to pass as dried fall leaves in storybook gold cartwheeled down the corridor. The smell in the air was all promises, exotic and heady, making her thinking fuzz. Again, it occurred to Layla how Segue hovered on the intersection of this world and the next, the present and the past, fantasy and the ruin of the world.

"Looks normal," Talia said, though stricken with worry.

There was no time to convince them. Layla grabbed her by the arm and dragged her out into the hall. Pushed her toward the elevators. "You've got to get out, or it will take you and the kids, too."

Adam was finally spurred to action. He jogged down the hallway. Layla chased, put a hand on his back to make him run. The hallway stretched and torqued, but Adam and Talia seemed oblivious. They went along on only her warning.

Whispering voices, sweet sounding, begged Layla to wait, to stay, to linger. She slowed, looking back toward the dark swirl of Shadow. Behind the vortex, she knew there'd be trees.

Now, finally, Talia looked back in horrified awe.

"Talia!" Adam shouted. He was at the stairs, holding the door with his body. The stairwell was a howling abyss, the steps a vertical careen downward. The only way out.

And far away Layla heard Zoe's cries, now muffled, as if she buried her face in her hands. One sister, hanging on to the other.

Something about it was familiar, too familiar, and since Layla had no siblings, it had to come from her before-life when a sister made the same soul-scoring sound. The pain stopped her in her tracks.

Adam had his wife around the waist. "Layla, come on!"

But she couldn't leave Zoe behind. That sound, a gut wail of grief, had anchored her. One last thing to do.

And besides, it was time for her to cross, too. Everyone, including Shadowman, knew it. She looked in the direction of the west wing. A bad little girl haunted that place, but Layla really didn't care.

She didn't want to force Shadowman's hand, but the time for choosing was past.

"Get out of here," Layla said, glancing back at Talia. Beautiful Talia. "I'm going after Zoe."

"You won't be able to come back," Talia said, the awful knowledge in her gaze.

"I know what I'm doing," Layla answered. She hoped her eyes communicated as much—especially the "I'm so glad I got to meet you" that was bursting her heart. "And I'm not supposed to come back."

Shadowman would just have to come after her. He wouldn't leave her to go mad. He'd pick up his scythe. Maybe this was the way it was always meant to be.

Zoe's sobs choked off, there was nothing for a moment, and then she screamed. Terror.

And Layla was off at a run.

Chapter 15

Shadowman crouched before the gate, darkness rolling off his shoulders, his cloak. The hammer lay askew beneath him. The dagger the angel had thrown was a silver dart on the ground to his side. Custo crouched as well, his skin riddled with black.

kat-a-kat-a-kat-a-kat: Open the gate. Let my throng deal with the angels.

Shadowman lowered and inclined his head. "You sent a devil after Layla."

kat-a-kat-a-kat-a-kat: I can call the devil back. Set her on new prey.

"You'll do whatever suits you."

". . . man!" Custo was saying. "Don't even talk with it. The gate is not an option."

Everything was an option, since no options were given to him: Here is love, but you can't have her. Here is life, but you can only glimpse it upon someone else's passing. You have great power, but you can't use it to fight for what you want. No liberty? Well, then, *Death.*

"We'll find a way to destroy it," Custo said. "There has

to be a way. A different kind of tool, maybe. A different approach, something the world has forgotten."

Across the cavern, the angels took up position. Ballard, now fully healed, stood in front, his hair matted with blood.

kat-a-kat-a-kat-a-kat

Now the gate laughed. It couldn't be destroyed.

Destroying the portal with heat and tools presumed it was made out of metal, but Shadowman knew different. Even if the black iron were melted away, still it would stand. Forever and ever until . . .

kat-a-kat-a-kat-a-kat

It was maniacal in its glee, riotous as understanding came into Shadowman's mind. A wretched mistake among so many.

The gate was not made of metal, heated and pounded into form. He might have set out to create it that way, but the hammer had defied him, had forced his mind elsewhere. The hammer had required something deep, deep within to lift and wield.

The trick of the gate's construction, then?

Shadowman closed his eyes. A small breath, and already she sprang into his mind. Kathleen at her easel, gazing wide-eyed into Twilight. Kathleen under his hands, giving herself up, even as she seduced a dark lord. Her skin, her hair, her rising breasts as his mouth skimmed their peaks.

The gate was not made of metal. Black, or otherwise.

The gate was made of her memory.

He'd set this trap, and so killed her himself, no matter who gripped the hammer.

kat-a-kat-a-kat-a-kat: You created me to save her. Let me save her. I can save her.

Death before him, death behind him. Every single thing he touched brought death. Even to the one he loved.

He was cursed. If Moira were here, she'd be laughing. Stormcrow, Thanatos, Reaper. You are your nature; you are fae.

I want to change. I need to change, he thought.

kat-a-kat-a-kat-a-kat: Perhaps you think you can end this madness? If you can, pick up the hammer yourself and strike her down.

As if Shadowman could ever strike Layla. Crack her body. Make her bleed. The thought sent a blast of despair through the cave, the deep places in the earth bellowing, *No!* Nor would he let another. Not even if Layla asked him.

His power, his ageless cruelty, stopped there. He was at the end of himself.

Then massacre the angels?

Shadowman eyed them from the folds of his dark cloak. Heaven's soldiers, set on a beast they had no hope to bring down.

Custo shook his head abruptly as if to clear his vision, or to get rid of a bothersome thought. What subtle things was Hell suggesting to him? Mortal minds, even mortal angels, were so weak. Eventually the gate would hit upon just the thing, and even Custo's great soul would falter.

The host advanced. A third broke away to circle and come at him from the left. Another third to his right. Conviction and purpose made them glow.

"I stand with you," Custo said, "but I don't have it in me to kill them."

Of course not. He wouldn't be an angel if he could. In fact, Custo would probably try to save as many as he could, while also protecting the gate. His purpose, like his nature, was at odds.

But Death was no angel.

"I'll do what I have to do," Shadowman answered.

* * *

The walls of Segue stretched high as Layla ran through the center atrium to Zoe's side of the building. The roof was gone, and in its place was a ceiling of nighttime stars, the barren tips of branches fingering their way overhead.

"What do you want?" Zoe's voice echoed, laced with fear. "Stay back!"

A coded door almost stopped Layla, but as she gritted her teeth to find a working combination of numbers, the door itself became transparent, the frame an archway to the corridor beyond.

Fae voices whispered, *Coming, coming, coming, coming*, with each of her panting breaths.

When she rounded the hallway to Zoe's room, brown vines crawled the walls, and standing in the way was Therese, the little girl ghost. Her hands were fisted, and a pout was on her face. Around her was an aura of another time, her patch of space a throwback to the hotel a century before. There, too, Shadow crawled, the climbing vines like stitches hemming the two realities together.

"Dead man, dead man," she began to chant.

"Yeah, yeah," Layla said, and rushed past the ghost. "Old news."

Therese made a grab for her, clawing Layla's flesh and wrenching at the vessel she hoped to possess. Layla felt a jarring disengagement but moved forward anyway, the parasite on her back. Was it even possible for a ghost to animate someone else's body? Layla wasn't sticking around to find out.

The right angles of the floor and walls came apart, the structure of the building consumed by Shadow. Therese's hold turned into a clinging cringe as she found herself at the edge of one world and the beginning of another.

A shrill, startled scream from Zoe, and Layla advanced down the vestiges of the hallway. Either Therese would let go, or she'd be forced to cross, as she should have all those years ago. Zoe had to get out now, or be lost to Twilight. This was exactly the reason Shadowman needed to return to his post.

"Leave me the body!" the child wailed at her ear. "I need the body!"

"No can do," Layla answered. There was power in mortality; Shadowman had taught her that. Maybe it would buy her enough time for him to find her. Too long in Twilight and there wouldn't be much left to find.

An electric wave rolled toward her, and the remains of Segue were demolished, particles lifting into the air like snapping sparks from a fire. Layla could feel the advent in a hum that buzzed her senses and tightened her womb. Heart seizing in terrible ecstasy, she leaned into the crossing.

Therese released her hold, sobbing, "The body!" Her voice weakened with each syllable as she fled the tide, and then she was gone.

Layla ran through the trees in the direction of Zoe's room, the hotel now a thick forest of dark trunks and craggy branches. Roots elbowed out of the earth to stop her progress, but somehow her feet only glanced on the surface as she darted forward.

"Just stay the fuck away!" Zoe yelled, voice low and ripped with emotion.

Over there. A rising bramble blocked Layla's path, and she forced her way through. She could see Zoe and Abigail inside a small, squared-off clearing beyond, not unlike the dimensions of Abigail's bedroom. Zoe, dressed in Segue sweatpants and a T-shirt a couple days past clean, her black hair ratty, stood in front of her sister. Her face was blotchy pale, her eyes were wild, and her expression was equal parts grief and horror. She was braced to fight.

Abigail stood directly behind her in a faded green housedress. Her eyes were hollow, jaw was slack with exhaustion. Her posture listed to the side. The only clue that she was still alert was the whimper that escaped when a swarming cloud of Shadow skimmed her skin, as if seeking a point of entry. A second flitted around her shoulder. A third patch of darkness webbed up her calves.

But Zoe didn't strike at these. She fought the air as if someone or something was in front of her, preparing to attack.

"Get back!" Zoe screamed, swatting at nothing.

Had madness already set in? That quick?

"Shit!" Zoe darted to the side in front of Abigail, who was now overcome with visible shivers. She jabbed. She flailed. But at what?

"Zoe!" Layla called.

Zoe's attention snapped in her direction, but she didn't look as if she believed her eyes.

"I'm coming," Layla said. The thorns on the small branches snagged her clothes and scraped her arms as she pushed forward.

"They're everywhere!" Zoe hollered back. She circled around her sister, grabbing her arm to keep her close, to pull her back from the invisible dangers.

Layla peered into the surrounding trees as she trampled forward.

Coming, coming, coming, soft voices whispered around her. But she couldn't see who spoke.

At the edge of the overgrowth, she felt a wet brush on her neck. A lick. She whipped back to find a creature craning over her shoulder, tall and thin, with backward limbs like a praying mantis's. He was naked, gray, with wagging human genitalia.

"Kiss me," he said, voice reedy.

Layla stumbled and fell into the clearing. The impact jarred her senses, and in the hard blink of the fall, a dozen . . . *things* sprang up around her.

"What the fuck are they?!" Zoe screamed.

Layla skittered back from the insect man, bumped into another. Blue. With sketchy human features on a humping shell of a head. Its eyes lit.

Coming, coming, coming, it said to her.

Layla lurched upright, but now she was surrounded, too. "No idea."

They were queer, deformed creatures, each with some attempt at a human feature on a misshapen body. Their curiosity had a predatory quality, a wow in their eyes, like they'd found shiny toys or treats, and even better, ones that talked. Their wonder kept them from leaping en masse. They weren't fae. Then what? And so many of them.

Layla's breath came quick, heart drumming so loud in her ears she almost wished it would stop so she could hear and think. But then she'd be dead, so maybe not.

"Shadowman!" she screamed.

The creatures recoiled slightly, and Layla took advantage of the brief thinning to join Zoe and Abigail. They stood back to back, though Abigail was all but useless.

Zoe grabbed Layla's wrist with her free hand. "Are you here?"

Layla knew what she meant. "Yeah, it's really me. We just have to hang on. Shadowman will save us."

Any minute now. These creatures had picked on the wrong people.

Coming, coming, coming, they chanted at them, inching closer.

"Abigail—" Zoe began helplessly.

"Don't worry," Layla said. Her chest hitched with the sound of Zoe's pain. "He'll take care of her, too."

Except there was no way out for Abigail. Her body was utterly wasted, eaten away by her tremendous gift. Segue had been her hospice while she declined toward the inevitable. If there'd been any medical recourse, Adam would have pursued it long ago. They were all here because Abigail, so full of Shadow in life, had died and Twilight had come to claim her.

Zoe's labored breaths dissolved into a sob. "It's not fair!"

"Shhhhh," Abigail whispered. "Let me go, Zee-baby."

Zoe swiped tears from her face. "Nope. We're in this together. You and me to the end."

One of the creatures made a fast click with his teeth. Reached bony hands toward Layla. She slapped him back, but the contact blasted her senses. She struggled to keep her balance, blinking away stars.

This could get worse before it got better. Zoe needed to get out. And now. Layla had to convince her to leave while she still could.

"I'll take care of Abigail," Layla offered. "It's my time to go, too."

"I can't. She's all I've got."

"No, you've got a whole life to lead. When Shadowman comes, you need to go with him. This place will mess with your head."

"She's my *sister.*" Again, the sound of an open wound, a heart so ravaged that even if it managed to heal it would be deeply scarred forever.

"I had a sister once, I think." Layla had her own heart scars.

"Did you lose her?"

Layla didn't remember, but that didn't seem right. She

recalled a pressure on her hand and a stubborn refusal to let go, like a tether to life. "I think she lost me."

Light drew Layla's gaze up, glittered in the trees, moved closer. So bright it made her eyes prick and tear. Someone was coming.

The odd creatures around them rose to attention, then scattered into the trees, leaving only their voices behind, *Coming, coming, coming.*

Angels? They'd work, too. Custo could get them out of here. Send word to Shadowman.

Saved.

But from the dark emerged a man of incredible beauty, each step an artful placement. His hair was rich brown, his fae eyes black. He was clothed in gossamer threads, but might as well have been naked for all they did to cover his glorious body. And with the soft smile he threw her, Layla knew that the other creatures might have been part of Faery, but this man was fae.

"Oh, shit," Zoe said.

A young woman joined him. She had magnificent golden hair, a pair of scissors at her waist, and a waterfall of a skirt spilling around her. Gorgeous.

And another female, naked and sleek. She spoke in a fluid language that came out in a kind of running-free verse song.

Scissor Lady answered, while the man settled his gaze on Zoe.

Layla had no idea what the language was, but she understood everything that was said. They were divvying up the spoils. Scissor Lady wanted her.

Shit was right.

Layla hated name-dropping, but what the hell. "Shadowman is our friend. He'll be here any minute."

"Friend?" Scissor Lady asked. "Aren't you his lover?"

Layla pushed her shoulders back. If Scissor Lady knew so much, she should know enough to keep away. "Yeah, that, too."

"He'd have to find you first." The fae man slowly stroked the line of his collarbone. Then his pectoral muscle. He feathered his fingers down his belly. Looked like he'd have a good enough time all on his own.

The naked woman clapped, bouncing on the balls of her feet. "A game! A game!"

Layla was less enthusiastic. They needed time. Eventually Shadowman would come for her. He'd built a gate to Hell; he wouldn't let her lose her mind in Twilight. Right? Right.

"Anytime soon would be good," Zoe said.

But what if he was angry? He had reason to be. She'd demanded the worst, and then forced his hand by coming after Zoe.

No. He wouldn't abandon her like this.

The fae moved forward, barefoot and splendid, gods in their own world. A hunger in their eyes.

Layla needed time.

"Run!" she said. Every second counted. *Where is he?*

She turned and grabbed hold of Abigail's other arm. Zoe was just as quick and they lunged into the trees together. Branches scraped Layla's arms and roots stubbed her feet, but she pushed forward. Running, running.

Which way? Didn't matter.

Just deeper into the trees. One minute, five minutes, as if time had any meaning there.

When Layla looked back, she'd opened no distance from the pursuing fae, who walked at leisure through the trees as if on a stroll.

The forest grew more dense and dark as they ran, an endless growth of magic.

"Shadowman!" she screamed, but the air swallowed the sound.

Her foot caught and she fell, flat bellied, barely breaking her fall with a palm skid to her elbows. She flipped over, ready to fight. Only stupid girls in bad horror movies fell when chased by monsters. At her feet, she found a long staff was the culprit. The straight length of dark wood was so incongruous with the trees that even with the approach of the fae, she spared a glance to see what it was.

At the staff's end was a severe curved blade, glinting in the twilight. It could only belong to one person: Shadowman.

Layla gripped the shaft with both hands and heaved the blade upward. The scythe was sized for the beast in him, huge, wide, the moon-shaped metal an unwieldy weight for her frame.

"You've found his weapon," Scissor Lady said, "but you lack the power to use it."

If he would just come, the scythe would be waiting. All the pieces were here, ready. Where was he?

Layla swung the scythe in a clumsy arc, but the blade passed right through the fae as if they weren't even there.

"Tickled," said the naked woman, giggling. "Do it again."

"We're screwed," Zoe said. "He's not coming. He's not coming!"

Or not coming quickly enough.

Then it was down to fists and feet and teeth. There was power in mortality; Layla just had to find it.

"Poor little girl," Scissor Lady said. She reached out her hand, and in a jerk of perception, she was suddenly right in front of Layla, stroking her cheek. Except Layla wasn't an adult; she was a child again. Lost and alone. "It's safe here under my skirt."

"I'll pass, thanks," Layla answered, stumbling back with revulsion. She shook her head to clear the illusion. To grow back up. Already her mind was going.

The naked woman had a grip on Abigail, while the fae man petted Zoe.

"So many things I want to try with you," he said.

Abigail let up a wail. The naked woman pulled strands of light from Abigail's skin, like ghostly marionette strings. "Feels good."

"We get so few with both the body and soul intact," Scissor Lady said.

"Get off my sister!" Zoe cried.

Layla dropped the useless scythe and lunged for the naked fae toying with Abigail. Tumbled her off and set the creature shrieking with laughter. Layla went to punch the fae in the face, but her wrist was captured by Scissor Lady, who effortlessly lifted her and dragged her some paces away. Layla's kicking legs scored the earth, and her hands swatted the air to find the woman behind her. The effort was wasted.

"Now, pet," Scissor Lady chided, "you belong to me, not her."

Layla was nobody's pet.

The naked woman straddled Abigail's fallen body. Abigail moaned, turning her head to the side. Layla perceived a brief shift, a blurring of flesh and light, of disengagement between Abigail's soul and body, the same that Layla had experienced in the grip of the ghost. Abigail's body was expiring, yet her soul was still pinned between the naked woman's legs.

Zoe was scrabbling on the ground, working for the scythe. The fae man stood back for a moment, making a show of admiring Zoe's backside.

They'd all just have to hold out, endure, until Shadowman came. Kathleen had been an expert at enduring; surely the nugget of that skill was somewhere in Layla, as well.

"You're supposed to be dead, too," Scissor Lady murmured in Layla's ear, as she looked on Abigail's death.

"Not today," Layla said through clenched teeth, jerking hard to free herself. Scissor Lady's clamp on her hand was unperturbed.

The naked woman, still astride Abigail, arched her back and laughed at the sky.

Zoe's grasp found the scythe. She stood, chest heaving, the weapon in her hands. "Get off my sister."

A wind riffled through the trees. The naked fae looked over cheerfully. Ready to play.

A tremor started in the ground. Layla braced in Scissor Lady's grasp, but Zoe didn't seem to notice. Rage burned in her eyes. "I said, *Get. Off. My. Sister!*"

The darkness of the forest convulsed. The scythe gleamed. The tremor rose to a rolling earthquake, and even Scissor Lady drew back, though she dragged Layla with her. Shadow grew dense around Zoe as she bore down on the naked fae woman.

With each step, blackness filled Zoe's gaze. Her expression was fixed in anger, tilting the structure of her features much like a fae's. The force of her feeling leached into her skin, making it shine with an eerie glow.

Twilight was a place of emotion, dark and bright, both extremes on fire within Zoe. Here was the power of mortality. Layla knew she was witnessing a transformation.

Zoe sliced through the air with the huge weapon, and in the rainbow arc of its sweep, the scythe, too, changed to match its new wielder. When Zoe struck down the naked woman, cut the laugh from her face, the scythe was a part of her, mastered by rage and love. The fae gasped into a cloud of Shadow.

Zoe swung around to face the male fae, and in terror and confusion, Layla knew Zoe was the new face of Death. The first soul she'd shepherd would be her sister's.

What about . . . ? "Shadowman!" Layla screamed.

"This way," Scissor Lady said, dragging Layla into the trees. The last thing she saw was Zoe facing the male fae, Shadow crackling at her back.

"Zoe!"

But Scissor Lady put a hand over her mouth. "She'll never find you. Would you want her to? She killed your man Death when she possessed his scythe."

Killed? Shadowman? "That's not possible."

"His power was in his duty. He's left it for too long, and now another has taken it over." Scissor Lady tightened her grip. "He's gone."

"He's immortal." He'd told her so.

"Not anymore." Scissor Lady's mouth curled into a sneer. "Fool."

Layla was hauled through the trees. She caught a glimpse of dark branches, a violet sky, a blazing streak of a star. Her heart clamored as her eyes filled with tears.

Shadowman?

She'd had her chance to save him. A second life to bring him back to Twilight. To steal a moment to love. She'd failed Heaven.

Much, much worse, she'd failed him.

Chapter 16

Decision made, Shadowman settled into a defensive wait. The angels prepared to strike, but they could not harm him. The gate would stand, no matter the cost.

kat-a-kat-a-kat-a-kat: So we'll be friends, you and I.

Hardly.

Custo groaned, trouble pouring out of him. The angels' minds were open to each other. The boy had to know their strategy.

"You need not betray them," Shadowman said. "I know how they will approach. I have presided over many battles over the ages."

"And you call me a mind reader," Custo said, the unease abating a fraction.

"I'd imagine emotion is often more telling."

The angels would attempt a divide and conquer: a contingent to busy Custo, a larger one to busy him, and a third to attack the gate. It would not work.

A long moment of silence, and then, as if on silent cue, the host attacked.

Shadowman thrust a wall of pitch between him and the

gate, and the fast-approaching angels were flung back, bodies skipping on the hard floor of the cave.

Ballard lunged, wielding a blade, Heavenly in origin, so it seared as it sliced, but Death reformed just as quickly, unscathed. Ballard would have to do much better than that. Shadowman hit him, heard the snap of his spine, felt the shock of pain, as the angel flew back. At least the spine would take longer to heal.

A jut of Shadow and the angel grabbing for the hammer flew to the side, taking two more with him. Another burn, quick to heal. A spin, a dart, a thrust of darkness and none were near enough to touch him.

More would come.

Custo held off four of his own kind with no weapon, though the wounds he took soaked his shirt. Sweat and dirt streaked his face, but still he moved and struck with grace and force.

Darkness whipped around the cave in a frenzy. Shadowman cast his mind out once again to harness the storm as it swirled around him.

But . . . the hurricane of pitch did not obey.

He tried again and was instead barraged by cave dust and wetness, singeing his skin. Always in the presence of angels he felt a burn, but he hadn't expected Shadow to go astray.

Well, then.

With his fist he knocked an angel back from the gate. A blow like that should have sent the angel to the far depths of the cave, but he only fell a few paces. And rose to try again.

Something was wrong.

Shadowman took position in front of Hell. Kicked the angel back again. But the burn on Death's skin had grown to a maddening inferno, sending needles of fire deep into his muscles and igniting his bones. Within him, he sensed the rush and pull of Earth, relentless in its reckoning, rapturous in its claim.

His mind was ablaze. His vision blurred with echoes of movement. The pain brought him to his knees, and he screamed his agony, the sound reverberating through the cave.

"The wrath of God is upon Death!" Ballard cried. He darted forward with his silver blade to strike.

Shadowman reeled as Ballard slashed through the air. Felt a strange sizzle. Glanced down. Marveled as blood dripped from a slice across his chest.

Blood.

How? Death could not bleed.

Ballard whirled, kicking Death back against the gate. Shadowman heard a skull crack, but it took a moment for him to realize that it was his head that made the sound. A sharp taste was in his mouth, and the smell and texture told him it was blood. Again.

His blood.

Shadow made no effort to restore him. It lifted away like a blanket of mist, leaving him naked and so cold on the silt of the cave floor.

Ballard leaped into the air, the dagger poised to plunge into Death's heart.

Shadowman raised a defensive arm and wondered again at the flesh of his body. He didn't fear the dagger, couldn't in his utter confusion. He knew in the abstract that the dagger meant death, but he was Death, so it made no sense.

And then Ballard was knocked out of the air by a boot to his gut and dropped like a stone.

"Look at him!" Custo yelled.

Look at whom? Shadowman shook with chill and

dampness. Put fingers to the red on his chest. Lifted his hand to his eyes, as if he'd never seen spilled blood before.

"He's mortal!" Custo announced.

"Who is mortal?"

Custo glanced over, pity in his eyes. "Oh, fucking hell. You are."

Shadowman used the gate to climb to standing. His knees buckled and he slid right back down again. This must be gravity. Earth's breast smelled mineral sweet.

kat-a-kat-a-kat-a-kat: Open me quick before they cut you down. They will use your weakness to destroy Layla.

"But he's fae," Ballard argued, standing.

"I am fae," Death agreed. For once Ballard was right. Most other times the angel was too much of a zealot to think through what came out of his mouth. Passion alone should not put a man in a position of authority.

Ballard lowered his weapon, a look of consternation on his face.

kat-a-kat-a-kat-a-kat: Time is running out.

"Yes," Custo said. "Can't we take a moment to think?"

Shadowman squinted as Ballard pointed an accusing finger in his direction, but he could not get a sense of Ballard's emotion. Dozens of mortals were in this cavern, yet it felt empty.

"This changes nothing," Ballard said.

"Death, a fae, is now a man," Custo returned. "This changes everything."

A man. The word made Death's heart beat faster, a breathless marvel in itself.

He couldn't wait to show Layla. She would mock him mercilessly, and they both would enjoy every moment of it.

Ballard shook his head. "There is still a gate to Hell right there."

kat-a-kat-a-kat-a-kat: Here they come.

Of all times, Shadowman needed strength now, yet he was as naked and clumsy as a newborn foal. Next to him on the ground was the hammer. He reached for it with little hope and was incredulous as his hand closed easily, so very easily, around its shaft. He tried again to stand. Braced his legs apart.

No one would get near the gate while he lived.

kat-a-kat-a-kat-a-kat: Hurry! They will rip us both apart.

"Perhaps he was delivered to us in the flesh so that he might be killed," Ballard said.

The gathered host murmured, considering this suggestion.

"At the very least, this bears new discussion, Ballard," one of the host said. "He can't even stand."

Shadowman had thought the cave was moving, but he guessed it must be him.

"Look at his chest," said another.

Shadowman glanced down at the long slice of his wound. The blood had gone tacky, crusting at the edges. He touched the parted skin, which, yes, did not seem as raw as it had a moment ago.

"Holy shit. He's healing," Custo said. "Does that make him one of us?"

"No," Ballard said, his eyes narrowing.

"But he just fell to Earth. That *has* to mean—"

Shadowman startled at a noise in the mouth of the cavern. All heads turned toward the opening. A scrabble of dirt. A knock of a fallen rock. An unfamiliar man descended, but Shadowman couldn't tell anymore if the person was angel or human.

"Keep it together," Custo said to him, pitched low for warning.

The newcomer had to be an angel, then, and conversing telepathically with the others.

"What? What's happened?" Shadowman questioned.

"Apparently, Adam's been trying to get us a message."

Shadowman shivered under a wash of cold sweat. "Tell me."

"Do you know Abigail?"

"The oracle?"

Custo blinked. "Okay, whatever. Apparently Shadow overcame Segue to claim her."

"Her talent was great." So great it had ruined her youth and aged her body prematurely. Her sister had been holding on to her with everything she had, to no avail. If Abigail wouldn't pass into Shadow, then yes, Shadow would come to claim such a one as her. He was glad Layla wasn't filled with Shadow, or she, too, would eventually be overtaken.

"Well, Shadow got her sister, Zoe, a few members of the Segue staff, and . . ."

Shadowman closed his eyes to stop the name from dropping from Custo's lips.

It dropped anyway. ". . . and Layla, too."

Layla went reeling into a tree as Scissor Lady released her grasp. The wood gashed her lip, and she held on to the harsh throb to keep her mind sharp. It was too easy to lose it here. The endlessness of the forest, the whispers of magic, all of it conspired to confuse and mislead.

"I don't believe you," Layla said. Shadowman couldn't be gone. Death was eternal. He was a constant in the great scheme of existence. Necessary. That was the whole reason why she'd been born a second time, to convince him to do his job or the three worlds and everyone within them would be in jeopardy. For that great purpose she'd given up both him and Talia. A family. Her life. Shadowman couldn't be gone.

And yet she'd seen Zoe change in front of her eyes. Handle Death's scythe when she couldn't. Where was Zoe now? Was she still fighting off opportunistic fae? Hell, all fae were opportunistic.

"It doesn't matter if you believe me, does it?" Scissor Lady gave a sparkling smile.

Layla threw back her shoulders. She'd faced a devil. She'd faced a ghost. She could handle one measly fae.

"So much temper," Scissor Lady said. "No wonder Death liked you. I like you, too."

The feeling wasn't mutual.

"You know, many have tried to thwart Fate through the ages. But like Death, Fate always catches up with you."

She must be talking about the doomed-to-die thing. "I'm still here, aren't I?"

"You've reached the end. I think you know that."

The end, yes. Her mission was at an end, and so was this life. Twenty-eight years of loneliness, and then Shadowman and Talia. Was it worth it? Yes, a hundred times over. Was it worth this final capture by some vain fae? Yes, though she'd bet good money the worst was yet to come.

Layla sought deep inside for the core of her will: the endurance of Kathleen. She'd need that now where she'd mocked it before. It was rooted in her connection to Talia and Shadowman, wherever he was. They were everything she'd ever needed and so much more.

The only thing left to do was fight, though she had no hope whatsoever of survival.

"I cut the thread of your life myself." Scissor Lady raised a brow, as if to coax Layla to some kind of realization.

"You cut . . ." Layla looked at the scissors again.

Oh, crap. This was bad.

Out of Scissor Lady's body, another woman stepped with engorged, exposed breasts leaking milk. She held a spindle in her hands, shining threads wound about her like spider's silk. "Layla Mathews née Kathleen Marie O'Brien. I spun your life."

And this was where bad met worse.

"I measured the twenty-eight years of your life." A third woman, an old woman, leaned out the other side, a rod in her hand. Her hair was a soft patchwork of cobwebs. Wrinkled and bowed, her hands gnarled with age, she seemed the weakest of the three. Until Layla got a load of the Shadow in her eyes.

Maid, mother, crone. And of the three, Scissor Lady was the leader.

This wasn't any old fae Layla faced. This was the bitch of them all. "You're Fate." What had Shadowman called her? "Moira."

"When I say your life is over," Scissor Lady said, "then your life is over. Shall I show you the ragged end?"

"No." Layla didn't want to see it.

"Or would you like to crawl under my skirt?" Scissor Lady swept up the material. "You can bide here as long as you like."

It did look inviting. A dark, close space where she could hide.

The three women circled around her like witchy forest nymphs. At first their feet kicked up tree leaves, the colors dream bright, even in bits. Then they kicked up gray ash.

Smell went utterly dead. The air, cold.

Layla trembled but slowly lifted her gaze and found the treescape transformed into the black-and-white emptiness of Death's heart. The skeleton trees branched like great, ominous cracks in the universe. The ground was a snow of dust. Even the fae women paled, the color contrasts broadening, delineating into the nulls of dark and light.

This was a vast sepulcher for the soul, once Shadowman's, now hers.

"You want Shadowman?" Scissor Lady asked. "Well, here he is."

No, this was the part of himself he'd wanted to cast away. With him gone—*dead?*—this was all that was left.

The brightness filled her eyes and parched her skin like sunburn. She could feel the place leaching from her the memory of color, the stuff of her dreams.

The Fates circled, buzzards awaiting the break of her mind.

Not going to happen.

Layla charged Moira, feet digging into the powder and lifting great billows into the air.

Bring the bitch down like a wraith. Grab for the scissors. Stab.

Her footfalls lifted huge clouds of lazy ash, obscuring the way. And when they thinned, the witch was suddenly on the other side of her, never changing the pace of her stride around her prey.

Layla coughed, choking on the powder.

A wasted effort. Blind violence would accomplish nothing. They were playing with her.

Layla shielded her eyes from the glare of the white. If she could just have a little darkness, maybe she could puzzle this out. A little warmth and her blood might reenergize her nerve.

"It's dark here under my skirt," Moira called. "Warm, too."

No, thanks. Layla pulled her hands away from her face and lifted her chin. Last thing she wanted was to find herself under there.

"You might last a little longer."

Lie.

"You're fading already." The three laughed.

"No. I'm still here." She pushed her shoulders back to prove it.

Moira tilted her head in pity. "You don't even know your name."

Layla blinked stupidly. Wracked her brain. Her heart stalled.

Moira was right. She had no idea.

Shadowman sat in the passenger side of a vehicle, a "Hummer" some angel had called it. The driver said he was going as fast as he could, but Shadowman could still count every tree, dried leaf, and scrag of grass, or so it seemed.

This was powerlessness. Acute, miserable, an agony of utter dependence.

Climbing out of the cave had been a blur of hitching breath and clumsy, bleeding feet. At the mouth, clothes were waiting, though he didn't care if he went naked. He needed to get to Segue. He should have been there already, but Shadow would not obey him.

Mortal? Inconceivable.

He growled his impatience, but it did nothing to hurry their progress down the road.

He'd had to rely on Custo to hunt through Twilight for Layla. Custo. An angel. With his fae blood, he might do better than others of The Order, might be able to use his hunter's nose to scent her, but Shadowman had little hope. Twilight was trees upon dark trees unto Forever, and then still more. Not even he had covered all that ground, because it had no end.

Layla must be mad by now, her mind trapped in nightmare. He could only hope—and what a weak power it was—that no fae had discovered her. If so, finding her would be impossible. Even the lowliest of the fae were cunning deceivers.

"Hang tight, we're there," the driver said, slowing to a stop in front of the white sweep of Segue's main entrance.

Shadowman fought the door to get it open, ended up smacking it with his forearm to blow the thing clear off the vehicle. He cast his gaze around the edifice seeking Shadow, and finding none, he tripped going up the stairs for his lack of care. As far as he could see, the only Shadows on the building were the pale, stretched blotches of the coming break of day.

The door burst open and Adam jogged down to greet him. Shadowman watched Adam's gaze travel the length of his new human body. His expression was stressed with concern.

"It's true, then. You're mortal."

"Where's Layla?" Shadowman scarcely knew his own voice. Everything an effort, the littlest combination of breath and throat and tongue delayed his finding her.

"I'm so sorry," Adam said. If Adam felt sorry, Shadowman couldn't sense it, and so the claim felt empty. "When the Shadow came over Segue, she went to help Zoe with Abigail."

The heat of anger that rolled over Shadowman's skin made him sway. "You said you'd protect her."

"I had to get Talia and the children out," Adam explained. "Layla said you'd come for her. How could I have known you'd become mortal? I didn't even know such a thing was possible."

Shadowman pushed Adam aside and continued up the stairs. The boy was useless. "Where is my daughter? Where is Talia?"

"She's in an outbuilding. This place is too dangerous for her."

"Get her, then. And *you* watch the children."

"Don't talk to him that way," Talia said from above them, a babe on each hip. She looked to her husband, shrugging. "I came in the back. I think the worst is over."

"Be still your tongue!" If the worst were over, then Layla was lost. And the bitter, bitter irony was he'd do anything right now to grip his scythe. To hear its keen and answer it with a roar of his own. He'd bear the endless millennia as Death to see her safely through Shadow to the gates of Heaven. Becoming the Reaper again would be such a small price to pay to preserve her spirit. He should have listened to her when he had the chance. Now they were both lost.

Talia pressed her lips together for a moment. "What do you need?"

Shadowman reached the top of the stairs. "I need a wraith and then I need you to scream like you have never screamed before."

They congregated again below the earth in the prison Adam had dedicated to the wraiths, where Death had revealed himself to Layla, and she had known the purpose to her second life on Earth. The angels they left aboveground, so as not to compete with Talia's call to Shadow. Talia's children were below as well, in a stroller for convenience. That Talia and Adam would permit them in this stinking grave spoke of their own concern for Layla. If this didn't work . . . If he couldn't cross . . .

...devil's games, she had not set the

...rt of mechanical arm conveyed ... Binding metal bands restrained ... a doubled cage crossed its torso. The ...ed until blood dripped down the silver, so ... have known its death was coming.

"Scream," commanded Shadowman, looking over at his daughter.

He could tell Talia's thoughts were turned inward, focused on Layla no doubt, and summoning the required intensity of feeling for the task before her. *Please, child, draw deep*. She took a long breath and then shredded the veil with a shriek, a command, a misery, her arms lifting to her sides, fingers splayed with effort. The sound was a wail of her own pain, a lifetime of loss in the making, a hope found, then demolished. The feeling battered the room with its intensity and set the wraith shrieking with her.

And indeed, darkness swirled in a vortex of magic, a storm of great reckoning to call upon Death. The sound shook his mortal body, atom upon atom quailing, which didn't bode well.

Shadowman dived into the terrible center. Flung himself across the divide between the worlds. But only ended up a few paces from where he'd stood a moment before.

The wraith made muffled sounds of laughter, then cut off suddenly, its eyes wide with fear.

From the depths, the moon scythe gleamed. And soon a figure emerged, a girl, Zoe. The sister to the great one. Her gaze now had the black depth of Shadow, her skin the queer shine of the fae. She gripped his weapon, and when she took in the scene, her face contorted.

"Oh, fuck no," she said, eyeing Talia, whose scream ended abruptly. "Ain't no way I'm coming when *she* calls."

"Give me the scythe." Shadowman held out h

"Finders keepers." But true to her nature, Zoe s thing and did the opposite, handing over the weapo a bored jerk.

He took the scythe and rolled the wood of the staff be tween his palms. Its texture and heft had always been second nature to him, yet it felt unfamiliar now. Too slim and light, the magic absent in his hands. A weak sensation pooled in his belly, dread, and stole what little strength he had.

He closed his eyes to be surrounded with his familiar dark. "Can you give me the power to wield it as well?"

"And how do you propose I do that?" The girl, the new Death, dripped sarcasm.

Shadowman opened his eyes again and handed the scythe back. His head pounded with the simple action. He'd denied the blade too long. It had cried for him from Twilight, begging to be lifted, and now when he needed it most, the thing had abandoned him.

"Do you know what happened to Layla?" Asking this chit for news of such import tightened his skin unbearably. He'd have shrugged out of his new flesh if he could have, but it clung to him, gloved him.

"She tried to help us," Zoe said, her tone barbed. "She thought you would come. She screamed for you, but obviously you weren't listening."

Layla had called his name. She'd needed him.

"What happened?" he snapped.

Zoe's expression finally mellowed to pity. "There were three fae. The one with the scissors dragged her away."

"Moira." Shadowman staggered. His mortal legs would not hold him.

"Who?" Adam asked, reaching out an arm to steady him.

"Fate," Shadowman clarified. "Fate has her claws in Layla."

The worst *had* happened.

Adam turned to Zoe. "Seems you've got his power now. Look for her, will you? Custo is already there. The Order may send more angels as well, but they won't value her soul over any other's, so they may not be much help."

No help at all.

"Layla will be under Moira's skirt," Shadowman said. As if Zoe would ever be able to locate Fate, much less bid the witch to lift her dress. "And she will be gone to madness, her soul light dimming."

He'd brought this upon her. Cursed her and trapped himself in mortal impotence. This was why she had come back to life, to prevent this very thing from happening. He'd been a fool, vain in his power.

"Layla will be under Fate's skirt," Zoe repeated, as if the combination of words made no sense to her. Then with false brightness, "Alrighty."

Death's scythe swung out, and the wraith's head was severed, its body sagging into gore.

As Zoe evaporated into the void, Talia's black-eyed child reached a chubby hand after young Death.

"I'm getting them out of here," Talia said and wheeled the stroller down the hallway toward the elevator.

Shadowman made to follow, his mind rapidly sorting all the places on Earth where the veil might be thin. Kathleen's paintings would not work, if this attempt at Shadow hadn't. But, water had always been a medium of transfer. Fire, too. Emersion or immolation. Or . . .

Adam fell into step next to him. "Listen, I know you've got no love for the angels, but they're an undeniable power that is at least somewhat accessible to us. I suggest you go to their headquarters, where information is more readily available. Maybe they can figure out what happened to you and give you some idea of how to reverse it."

"They will not treat with me," Shadowman said, boarding the elevator that would raise them to the surface. The angels had defied him at every turn, and as a mortal, he lacked the power now to force their compliance. They might even cut him down, if Ballard had his way. Shadowman had to try something else. A *Diné* ceremonial sandpainting, perhaps. Though that, too, would take so much time.

"I bet they will," Adam returned. "Word is you might just be one of them."

There was no way he was a mortal angel. The idea was preposterous.

"Try Luca, Custo's uncle. He's a little more reasonable. I'm sure he'll help in whatever way he can. And, they have their own access to Shadow."

Shadow.

"How do I get there?" New York City, the nearest locus of The Order's power, was miles away. "The last vehicle went so slow."

Adam pulled half a smile. "I think I can move you quite a bit faster than that Hummer."

"Oh, no," Talia said, as they stepped out into the sunlight. "Here he goes."

Adam put a phone to his ear. "Kev, I'm going to need the Sikorsky five minutes ago." He paused, then answered, "Make him as comfortable as you can. I'll be there to speak with him shortly."

Talia rounded on her husband. "What now?"

"One Mr. Mickey Petty just arrived at the compound." Adam turned to Shadowman. "Don't worry about the devil. I'll draw Rose out with her husband and end one bit of this nightmare. That bitch took out fifteen of my men. I mean to see her put down."

Layla would want the devil dealt with, Talia and the family safe.

Shadowman gave a tight nod of assent. He should have stamped the devil out when he had the chance. Another mistake.

At least . . . and how strange . . . he wasn't alone in this. Adam must experience the same weakness and humility of the flesh, and yet, he fought even harder. Talia, just as strong, defended her children. The mean tip to her eyes said she was prepared for more.

What about Layla? Solitary. Forsaken. Facing the worst of the threats upon this family.

A racket sounded in the distance, and suddenly a helicopter burst over the trees. The white body was long, slim, like a dolphin, with twin-mounted rotors up top instead of one. It lowered a short distance away, and Talia used her body to shield the babies from the cold winter gusts it kicked up. Yes, this would go much faster than the box that had delivered him to Segue.

This morning he'd been on the verge of war with the angels. Now he would throw himself on their mercy.

Chapter 17

Layla racked her memory for her name. She couldn't be that far gone. Could she?

"Names have power," Moira said, strolling her ashy circle and maintaining an almost demonic triangle with her sisters. "Which is the reason the fae have so many."

Layla could feel the word in her brain. It was the same maddening sensation that had dogged her since she'd first seen Shadowman. She'd known him yet couldn't place him. Known Talia, too, but couldn't make the connection. Now she was losing touch with herself.

Hi, I'm . . .

And she totally blanked. Damn it. The name was right there.

Layla's teeth chattered. She folded her arms for warmth. This couldn't be the end, yet the trees and ash and cold gray sky attested otherwise. Was this really what she had left of him? The desolation was stealing color from her, too.

He wouldn't want that. *She* didn't want that.

"Take your man Death, for instance," Moira continued. "How many names do you think he's been given over the ages and by myriad peoples, yet his power was stolen by a silly girl now bumbling through these trees." Moira paused in the circle, facing Layla with a question on her lovely features. "And how do you think you will fare if you have just the one name, and already cannot bring it to mind?" She started her leggy stroll again with an audible, and very pleased with herself, "Hmm."

Layla called up the names and faces of her new "extended" family: Talia, pale and fair; Adam, managing everything; the babies, black-eyed Michael and cherub Cole. She hadn't lost them. She recited her phone number, her address, even her computer login. All good.

It's nice to meet you. I'm . . .

Nothing.

Layla drew a deep breath of frigid air and puffed smoke into the winter wonderland. Her nose was doing that prickling thing that came with cold or tears. She'd remember if she just didn't freak out. She was doing this to herself. Had to be. If Zoe could find power, Layla could. She would not let this harpy wreck her. In the meantime, "Stop calling him 'my man Death.' His name is *Shadowman*."

The three sisters sneered.

Wait. Hold it. Just. One. Second.

Death as Layla knew him was gone. Okay, she could take that. He didn't even want to be Death anymore. But was *Shadowman* gone?

Moira and her sisters began their circling again. "Shadowman is a fool to trade power and time for a handful of years."

"He's alive." Heat surged into Layla.

"He's mortal," Moira said, as if he were beneath her.

Layla would take him any way she could get him. Determination beat her heart faster. She wasn't cold anymore. Not at all. "I found a way back to him before. I can do it again."

The old sister looked over. "That life is over."

Good. Layla wanted that life to be over. She'd been miserable and alone for most of it. And then she'd ripped out her heart and told the one she loved to do his duty. Her mission was complete. Yes, she was very glad that life was done.

She wanted a new one, on her own terms. "I'm leaving."

Layla made for the edge of the circle, to a space between one fate and another, but the circle moved with her. Moira smiled. "To go where?"

"Anywhere you aren't."

"Impossible. I am Fate. I am everywhere that you are. I tell you what to do and where to go. Do you think it was coincidence that you found Death in that warehouse? No, I took you there. Or that you rediscovered your daughter? Fate did that, too."

Layla wasn't buying. There was no way in Hell, and Layla knew a little bit about that place now, that this hag was going to take credit for every decision humankind made, least of all hers.

"What about Zoe?" Had she predestined that transformation?

Moira declined to answer.

"I didn't think so." Layla made for the edge again, but the Fates effortlessly followed. "Don't you have anything better to do?"

"Better than you?" Moira tilted her head as if to think. "Not at the moment. I'll tell you what. You figure out who you are, and you can lose your mind elsewhere in Shadow."

Moira inclined her head, and around the circle gilded mirrors appeared, glittering and sparkling enough to make Layla wince. Within their long ovals different people stood as if trapped within the frames. Old and young, all of them female, looked out at Layla, their gazes imploring, *Pick me, pick me*. Some were strangers, faces that seemed only faintly recognizable. An old lady; a young woman; a round, middle-aged housewife. As Layla surveyed the faces, she found several that struck home. Within one frame stood Layla the child, her hair in a ragged bowl cut, arms wrapped tightly around herself. The child was wounded—the pain was right there in her eyes. Then there was a serene woman who had to be Kathleen, long reddish blond hair waving over her shoulders. And across the circle stood Layla as she was today, freezing with the cold, dirty tear streaks down her cheeks. Red nose to match. And still no name.

But at least it was something to work with. A puzzle to sort. A trick to turn to her own advantage.

"Pick one." Moira twirled, arms out, gesturing to all of them at once.

Yes, but whom? Layla's gaze darted from face to face. Was she Kathleen, the one who started it all? Layla took a step toward her, then paused. There was no going back. Kathleen was gone. Well then, what about the adult version of herself in the glass? It seemed a straightforward solution. But hadn't she just said she wanted a new life? Should she then choose a stranger?

She was all of them, and none of them. Who was she? She didn't know. Again.

Temet Nosce. It still made no sense to her. Too bad she hadn't figured it out.

With each cold draw of breath, the people in the mirrors grew less and less recognizable, the madness of Twilight tweaking Layla's mind. In her head was the thick, sluggish feeling that preceded sleep. She bit her tongue to wake herself.

The problem was that Fate had posed the question; therefore, Moira controlled the answer. It was biased, slanted, weighted in her favor.

The faces were blurring; Layla was losing her mind. Or maybe the faces were blurring because they didn't matter.

"It's warm and safe here under my skirt," Moira promised.

Talk about twisted. Layla dismissed her. Maybe the question wasn't so much, *Who was she?* as, *Who did she want to be?*

Layla's gaze darted from person to person. Lonely child, the housewife, beautiful Kathleen, the old lady, the young woman, the present-day Layla. And in a circle before them, the three Fates walked. Maid, mother, . . . crone.

She stopped, gazing at herself—*Yes, that one*—and inhaled the surety of her answer.

In the end it was too easy. So easy she had to laugh, yeah, a little like a crazy person.

Shadowman, honey, here I come.

Moira did a little cancan flourish with the material of her skirt. "I thought you'd last longer. Really, I did. With the store Shadowman set by you, I thought we'd play for a while."

What Layla needed was something to bash in the mirror. Bash it in and get back home.

Her fists would have to do. She tightened both with all the feeling she had left: The fullness of her first meeting with Talia. The tuning-fork strike of her connection to Shadowman. The unlikely fit in the madhouse of Segue. She had a place, a family to call her own, and God damn it, she was going to have them if it killed her.

Moira shook her head. "You can't harm me."

She actually hoped the glass would cut a little, too, and bring some color to this place. "I've chosen."

"Oh . . . ?" But Moira's attention snapped to the circle. The big-breasted sister with the spindle had held out her hand, palm up. Her gaze had gone distant as the spindle stood on its own spinning thread of shining gold, the good stuff. Lots and lots of thread for a long life.

"How?" Moira demanded, settling her fae eyes, now gone malevolent black, again on Layla.

Layla pointed at the mirror image of the old lady. "I want her."

Faces didn't matter. This second life had taught her that. What mattered was soul.

"What, so you can be on the brink of death again?"

Layla grinned like a maniac. "Someday. But to earn all those wrinkles"—her gaze fastened on the crumpled skin, the branches winging the eyes—"all those gorgeous laugh lines, I figure I'll need at least fifty years of laughing in your face."

The mirror was across the circle, but Layla was crazy enough by now to know distance didn't matter. She brought her right fist up, as tight as a stone, and struck with everything she was. She caught the swift flush of color into Twilight, the shrill scream, "No!" just before she leapt through the frame.

Segue.

The helicopter was not as fast as Adam promised.

Shadowman had assumed that time was fleeting, had grasped after it for moments with Kathleen, and then Layla. Now time was a torture of uneven beats strung together and stretched into a warp of perception. Frustration hampered each draw of air and accelerated the thump of his heart. He closed his eyes, seeking peace, but swirls of amoebic light danced on the insides of his lids and his mind was battered by the racket of the rotors. Eons passed more quickly in Twilight than this interminable flight across the land.

And all Shadowman could do was sit. And sit. And sit. While Layla suffered.

This world should have long gone mad.

The yellows and greens and browns of the slowly changing landscape below were tainted by gray. A river of black water broke through the land, and beyond, a great city, barbed with tall buildings.

Finally.

Only then did he realize he'd been fisting his hands so tightly they ached. He stretched them open and stared in confusion at the black web of Shadow gathered between his fingers and against his palms. Shadow.

A push of feeling, and the dark stuff pulsed with faelight.

Oh, how stupid of him. Of course.

"Are you all right, sir?" Kev shouted. The soldier glanced from Shadowman's face to his show of magic.

All right? No. Shadowman rubbed his hands together, and the Shadow dissipated.

But now at least he knew what he was. Would have known straightaway, if not for the panic that drove him.

"We cannot go to the Annex," Shadowman answered.

"Sir?"

Angels. Shadowman snorted with the irony. By now they, too, must have realized what he'd become. They'd striven hard enough to wipe his kind from the face of the earth during the last war between Heaven and Shadow.

He couldn't risk a confrontation with the angels. Not with Layla's soul waning.

"Take us anywhere else," Shadowman commanded. "Anywhere without angels."

The last place he could go was the Annex. Surely, death awaited him behind the gleaming faces of the host. That he'd created a gate to Hell was proof enough for judgment against him.

Stretching his palm open again, Shadowman pushed rage into magic. The faelight sprang forth again.

No, the angels would not welcome him. He had to find another way into Shadow.

He required a quiet, dark place—he slid his gaze to Kev—without an audience. And then maybe, maybe . . .

"Go that way," Shadowman commanded.

He knew just the spot.

Layla crashed into a chair, banging her chin, tripped, and fell on the floor as she crossed the divide between the worlds. It hurt, but she kicked to get free and stand in case another surprise awaited her. She glanced around, breathing hard. Abigail's room was dingy next to the vibrant contrasts of Twilight. Solid, cluttered, with a lingering smell of illness in the air. Dull and wonderful. But no surprises.

She was back. A laugh burst out of her. Holy crap, somehow she'd made it.

Had Adam and Talia made it out with the babies? The thought sobered her up real quick and got her moving.

She tore to the door, skidded to a stop near the console table, where she hoped Zoe had left the gun—yes!—then ran down the haunted hallway. No ghost, but then Layla had a much better hold on life now. She'd seen the shining thread of it herself. At the elevator, the button light did not come on when she pressed. Probably not working.

"Shadowman!"

Layla didn't expect an answer, but he had to be there somewhere. Not dead, not Death. Then what? She didn't care.

The stairs wouldn't open either—one of Segue's inner cages had been triggered again—and since she didn't have her handy door opener nearby, she opted to use her Glock. *Bam! Bam! Bam!* she fired the gun at the ceiling to alert somebody of her presence. If Adam was left at Segue, he'd investigate the shots. It took an interminable three minutes for two teams of soldiers to show up. She dropped the gun and held up her hands.

"Ms. Mathews?"

Yes, duh. A couple of the soldiers looked familiar, but she didn't know their names. "Are Adam and Talia okay?"

One of them spoke into a throat mic. "I'm to take you to them now."

Oh, thank God they were okay.

Five minutes later, research level, and into Adam Thorne's supertechy inner sanctum, Layla was clobbered by an awkward, but beautifully tight embrace.

Talia was crying and incoherent. "How—" String of muffled words. "What happened . . . ? We all thought you were gone!"

Layla herself had sniffed. "Nope." She shook her head. "Well, I was, but now I'm back."

Talia opened a little distance but kept a grip on Layla's arms. "What do you mean 'back'? Khan said you were under someone's skirt. Zoe and Custo are searching for you."

Which made Layla bark a laugh and wipe her cheeks with the heel of her hand. If they knew about Zoe, they also knew Abigail had passed. "He meant Fate. Damn, she's a twisted bitch, but I guess I tricked her . . . and here I am."

Adam came up beside Talia. "You tricked Fate?"

"Goes by the name Moira," Layla said, nodding. She glanced around. "Where's Shadowman?"

"He's *mortal*!" Talia's eyes went wide. "As in flesh and blood. Maybe even angelic. And so worried about you."

Mortal. That's what she'd been hoping for. Kicked out of Twilight. Busted.

"He was en route to the Annex building, the northeastern headquarters of the angels," Adam said, "but he deviated at the river. Landed somewhere near Port Newark. Kev lost him from there."

"What do you mean *lost him*?"

"As in, I don't know where he is." Adam lifted his hands in a helpless gesture. "He doesn't exactly keep me updated on all his movements. All I know is he wants to cross into Twilight to find you. Maybe he found another way."

"But he can't cross on his own, right?" Layla had an idea where he might be heading. It was the only place she could think of. A dark and lonesome place that suited him well. The place they'd met during her second life. *Third time's a charm.*

But not if he was gone before she got there.

"We have no idea what he's capable of," Talia said, shrugging. She blinked hard, but her eyes still shone. "No idea what you're capable of either, it seems. I'm so glad you're back."

"In the meantime," Adam interjected, "we've got Rose Petty's husband here. We were just about to question him as to where she might be heading, what she might do next."

Rose. Right. From one bitch to another.

Layla's high crashed. She knew exactly where Shadowman was. Wanted to jump on him and tell him all about her job well done. But, yeah, she had to deal with her devil first, no matter how bad she wanted to dash to the warehouse.

Rose had shredded her heart and made her weak enough to consider suicide when she had just found everything she'd chanced this second life for. Layla had just tricked Fate. She needed to face Rose down, too.

She took a deep breath for energy. "No. That'll take forever, and I'm in a hurry. I've got a better idea."

Rose had to be quick.

She filled an old plastic bag with foodstuffs from the diner's shelves. She'd skipped the modern (and busy) truck stop directly off the exit and gone for the place with the old-style gas pumps and the peeling yellow paint instead. The diner smelled of petrified cigarette smoke, grease, and mildew, even though the earth was frozen right outside.

Only a local would come here, and even that person wouldn't eat.

Potato chips. Mashed packaged chocolate-covered donuts. The cans of tuna would need a handheld can opener. She dug into the drawers to find one, shifting all manner of utensils, and settled for a screwdriver mixed in with the forks.

She needed enough to get her to Macon without any stops. They had to be looking for her by now. She'd been careless in Middleton, so sure that she'd be able to kill Layla with no trouble. She'd been warned about Death, but did she believe it? No. She'd gotten cocky. Lesson learned. And now she had to hide.

Mickey would take her in, and they'd figure out what to do together. Of the two, she knew she had a quicker mind, but he gave her the sense of calm to use it right. Mickey always believed in her. With Mickey, she could do anything.

She grabbed a handful of plastic dinnerware.

Of course, she'd had to kill the fool behind the diner counter. He'd been drinking coffee and watching the news on the TV mounted in the corner when she came in. Went pasty at the sight of her arm. Maybe if he'd worked harder, the place wouldn't be in such straits. Now he just bled on the floor while morning news anchors chattered on about the weather.

The bags of flour wouldn't do her any good. Some green beans. Rose made a face. Fine. One can, just in case. Her belly had been making noises for hours now, and she had to mind her food groups.

"Citizens of Middleton can rest easy this morning," a reporter said, coming over the television. "A recent crime spree has been stopped with the apprehension of escaped convict Mickey Petty."

Rose's attention snapped up. Mickey?

She dropped the bag of food. With the strength of her bad hand, she vaulted over the counter to view the TV screen.

Sure enough, her Mickey was handcuffed, led by a crew of police officers to a large black SUV. Her sweetheart's hair had gone gray and a little thin up top. His face was covered with at least two days of stubble, skin a little saggy at the chin. And those eyes, the ones she loved so very much, were ringed with puffy pink bags of exhaustion and darting in fear.

"The heroine of the hour?" the reporter continued, following the crowd down the street. "A tourist to our small town, Ms. Layla Mathews."

Layla. The one who played whore to Death. The one who threatened the existence of the gate.

"Ms. Mathews single-handedly took down the criminal."

The whore had the gall to lift her face to the camera and wave. Rose knew that she was waving at her. Mickey never did anything to Layla. Mickey was the soul of sweetness.

Rose's vision went red as a wave of heat swept her.

"Ms. Mathews!" The reporter jogged around the officers to get a microphone in Layla's face.

Layla smiled at the camera as she ducked into the passenger seat of the SUV. "I'm just glad I could be of service," she called out. And then winked for the world to see.

Rose started to shake.

Mickey was loaded into the backseat, a cop on either side. Not that they looked like normal police officers, much less small-town police officers. The gray uniforms they wore didn't fit well, straining at their arms and thighs. Those were some of Segue's soldiers, beefy and stupid.

The SUV took off out of Middleton, heading up the mountain and into the tall trees, but not heading for the jailhouse, as would be expected. Layla had to be taking Mickey to the Segue compound and was telling her so. That *hateful* place.

Mickey. Twelve years! Oh, how the world was cruel.

Rose stamped her foot. Her chin trembled. Tears coursed down her cheeks. She had promised herself that she'd never go back to Segue. Death lived there, the monster of everyone's worst nightmares.

She bit the wide knuckle of her bad hand. Debated. Decided.

"Gate?" she said aloud. The last time she'd called, the gate hadn't answered.

This time the familiar *kat-a-kat-a-kat* rattled her bones.

She looked up at the ceiling as if talking to God.

"Layla's got my Mickey. I'll do anything"—except face that Death monster—"if you help me save him."

kat-a-kat-a-kat: One last chance to kill. Your best chance to kill her.

"No, see . . ." she said. The gate didn't get it. "That m-m-monster lives there. He'll kill me. He'll kill Mickey."

kat-a-kat-a-kat: Death has fallen. He can't touch you. Go get your Mickey. Make the ground run with blood. You have nothing to fear.

"Death what?"

kat-a-kat-a-kat: Death is now weak and mortal.

"How?" She could hardly believe it, though her heart and mind were already halfway back to Segue. No Death?

kat-a-kat-a-kat: He brought it upon himself.

Of course he did. A creature like that. "Then I can kill him?"

kat-a-kat: Easily.

Rose grabbed her car keys off the counter, then dropped them on the pavement outside when she got a look at the Mack trucks at the stop up the street. That red one just turning in, the one with the fire painted on the sides, was muscle on wheels, mean with bulk, like a giant steel boar, nosing the road while its tusks belched smoke. That truck should be able to take the wall at Segue.

A couple of run-run-pushes of her favorite arm and Rose was there in seconds.

She fastened the panicked and wheezing driver to the front grill, just in case those soldiers got the idea to blow her off the road with a missile or something. The driver's ride-along wife, a dumpy sack of potatoes, sat next to her, whimpering in a mess of tears and snot.

Rose let her bad hand do the steering when she got upward of ninety on the straightaway. The growl of the engine stirred her blood. When she hit the turns of the mountain, the narrow two-lane road wasn't big enough for the truck and oncoming traffic. A VW Beetle almost pitched over the edge but managed to skid to a stop.

Middleton was empty when she barreled down Main and took the corner that would lead her to Segue. They had to know that she was coming. That she wouldn't stop. If they thought they could cow her, they were going to get a surprise. She knew their secret: Death was as good as dead.

The gate was retracted, for her convenience no doubt. She followed the lane that led to the main building, but she veered onto the stiff grass in view of the forward-facing windows. No one fired on her, so the man on the grill, still bobbing his head, had done his job. Rose dragged the sack of potatoes out of the cab with her and put a claw to the woman's fleshy throat.

"I'll kill her if I don't see Mickey right now!" Rose shouted.

Movement from a downstairs window. Mickey stepped into view and then was pulled back. Oh, her sweet man.

The potato sack woman dropped suddenly, the whites of her eyes twin sneaks under slightly parted lids. The silly woman had fainted. Rose couldn't very well drag the sack's weight, so she flung her to the side and charged the stairs with her run-run-push, nearly vaulting her to the top in one great thrust. Gunfire bit her, but she couldn't see the source. Invisible marksmen had to be everywhere. Fire scored her cheek and darted into the muscles of her back and thighs to lodge, but she didn't stop. Mickey was behind that door. She could heal later. He would gently tend her with loving caresses.

She punched the front doors with her bad hand and the wood splintered, ripping her skin. An inner metal framework reinforced the entrance, but another strike buckled that, too. This was really too easy. With a victorious step, she was inside. Her knuckles dripped blood in Segue's fancy hallway. She took the left passage, in the direction Mickey had been only minutes before. They couldn't have moved him far. *I'm coming, honey.*

An earsplitting scrape and resounding bang had her whipping around. The entrance was suddenly blocked with a wall of close-set bars. The ceiling abruptly lowered—Rose ducked—but the gorgeous chandelier overhead smacked her in the face, crystals tangling and tinkling in her hair. The floor moved, folded up around her. She swung out with her bad hand, but it didn't even dent the metal. Before she could get her bearings, she was caged.

Metal screeched until booming into final prison position.

That whore Layla immediately stepped out from a room beyond the bars, flicked her gaze at Rose's bad hand, musing, *It's gotten worse.*

She bent her mind to master Layla's. "Release me!"

"It's safe," Layla said over her shoulder, but thought, *Unless she can shoot venom.*

Rose lunged at the bars, reaching her bad hand through to claw Layla's face off. She pushed harder on her brain. "Release me!"

"I don't have the power to release you," Layla said, a little too flippantly for Rose's state. *No single person has that.*

"Well, then bring them all to me," Rose said. She twisted each word with power.

Rose watched Layla close her eyes, her lips tighten as she breathed deep. But she didn't make any move to do what she was told.

When Layla opened her eyes again, she shrugged. "I've

had a little practice with this kind of mental thing: The gate made me open it. You almost made me kill myself. Lost my mind in Twilight."

"Why don't you do as I say then!" Rose shoved as hard as she could, tried to splinter the whore's brain. It had been so easy before.

Layla had the nerve to smile. "Because I've faced far worse than you today. Believe me." The whore leaned in. "You won't influence me ever again. Got it?"

Rose was going to have to kill her. Nobody spoke to her that way. Least of all some trash that wrapped her legs around—

"Can I see her?" spoke a familiar voice. Soft. Loving. Mickey.

"Mickey?" Rose called. She pulled at her bloody sweater. Swiped her hair back from her eyes. Wished she had some mascara to make them pop.

Layla looked beyond the doorway. "You've earned it." *Did the world a favor in my opinion.* "Just keep back from the bars, and remember what I told you."

Rose straightened herself up. Strained for a first glimpse.

Mickey shuffled into view. He wore the faded uniform of a custodian. He must have had to work so hard without her help. His belly had bulged over his pants while she was away.

That's her, all right, Mickey thought.

"You okay?" Layla asked him.

"Mickey, honey"—Rose batted her eyes—"we'll find a way out of all this. We'll be together again. I promise I'll find a way."

Mickey's bushy brows drew together. *They warned me about her arm.*

"Oh, this?" Rose answered, lifting her bad hand. "Well,

yes, it looks a little . . . unusual. But, honey, it's strong. It's kept me alive. Soon you'll think it's as beautiful as I do."

And they warned me she could read my mind.

"Yes," Rose said. "I can. It will bring us closer together."

Don't think it. Don't think it. Don't. Don't. Don't.

"Honey, say you love me," Rose implored. If she was going to be taken away, even for a little while, she'd need to survive on those words.

Mickey jerked his face into the fat at his chin and took a step back alongside Layla. "I'm ready to go."

Don't think it. Don't. Don'tdon'tdon'tdon'tdon'tdon't don't . . .

"Mickey," Rose sobbed. "You can tell me anything. Tell me you love me."

Not that I was the one—don'tdon't—

Layla gestured to a man in front of a group of soldiers. "It's time."

—who killed you.

Rose went very still, her hands, good and bad, gripped the bars. She must have heard Mickey wrong. They'd been everything to each other. Shared their secrets. Sure, they'd had some hard times, and there was that once or twice when she'd had to remind him how to treat her, and the occasional messy business he'd cleaned up for her, but . . .

"Honey?" broke from her lips.

Mickey's face went red. His lower lids twitched, as his brain said, *I put a pillow to your face.*

But now that Rose thought about it . . .

You thrashed and bucked.

. . . she couldn't remember how she'd died.

Never loved you.

"Say you love me!" Rose screamed.

"She was even worse when she was human," he said to

Layla. And with that, Mickey Petty turned his back on her and walked from the room. Stenciled to his jumpsuit was State Prisoner. His last thought trailed behind him. *Worth every damn year.*

Fury exploded in Rose's mind.

Mickey had betrayed her. Mickey had killed her. Mickey had sent her to Hell.

The burn took her whole body, and she shook, gripping the immovable bars for support. She shrieked when her blood turned to acid in her veins. A rush of searing cold washed through her body, snapping and spinning her cells.

"Stay calm," someone called, but they weren't talking to her.

New bone stretched her toughening skin. She threw her head back as the change crunched her features. No more pretty eyes. No more winning smile. The transformation crackled across her other arm, took her belly, her pelvis, her weak leg. Made her strong.

Worse, Mickey said? She'd show him worse. All of her went bad.

Layla turned and asked the lead soldier, "Will the cage hold?"

"It should," he said. But his mind answered, *Thank God Talia and the kids are on their way to New York.*

That was all the hope Rose needed. She launched herself horizontal and kicked a bar with the full force of her altered legs. The bar dented outward.

"She's like a lizard hulk!" a soldier shouted.

Rose jacked her legs at the bar again. It squeaked into an outward triangle, just big enough. Mickey owed her an explanation.

Rose watched as Layla drew a gun from her waist and fired point-blank. Cold-blooded was what Layla was. Shoot a prisoner in a cage. No honor in that.

The soldiers followed Layla's lead. Rose was dinged over and over again, but the only bullet that hurt was the one that pierced her skull. Even that didn't slow her.

Rose wrenched the bar out of place. *Where is he?* She used the bar to bat Layla out of the way.

Where is that liar?

She bounded knuckles, feet, knuckles, feet through the door of a wide, open room dominated by a long conference table. Her husband was backed up to a wall, surrounded by soldiers, which she swatted aside while taking a bullet to the eye. Another bullet bounced around her teeth in her mouth.

Blood made her tongue lazy. Her nose itched from her new foul smell. Rotten. Like her love.

She snorted like a beast in Mickey's face. "You did this to me."

His jelly chin quivered, but he didn't tuck it. Took him twelve years to find his spine.

"You always looked like this," he said. "Now everyone else can see, too."

Rose fought a sob and knew the wetness streaking her face was tears. She could feel the violence gathering around her. Men organizing to kill her, while they thought to protect her murderer. One shouted, "Lie facedown on the floor!"

The room was thick with their mind chatter. One man seemed in control of them all. *Bring her down fast, heart and head*, he thought.

"On the floor, now!"

Heart. Rose punched Mickey's chest to see if he had one. It was a puny, slimy thing, just like him. Too bad it stopped.

Mickey dropped to the floor. Ungrateful man. And here she'd given him her best years.

Something hit her from behind and her left shoulder was alight with pain.

Use the Benelli, a soldier thought behind her.

Rose shuddered as eight successive blasts thudded into her side. She couldn't feel her fingers. That whole side of her body had a sparkly singe kind of sensation that made breathing hard.

If they weren't careful, they might just hurt her.

Mickey dead, now that Layla had to go, the one who started it all. No wonder the gate was so intent on getting rid of her. Layla was poison.

Rose struck the window above Mickey. The glass came out in one funny big piece, with a whole lot of wall attached to it. Another fat shot struck her back, and she was propelled outward, skidding across a wide veranda on a slick of her own blood.

She managed to climb on top of the railing, but shots drove her over the side and into the bushes at the building's base.

"Circle around!" the leader shouted.

They were murderers, all of them, not to face her in a fair fight. If *she* died, her *soul* died, too. The end of Rose Petty. Forever.

kat-a-kat-a-kat: Go back. Kill Layla Mathews. Now.

The gate needn't worry. Layla was going to die. And not because the gate told her to kill the bitch. This was personal now.

Rose made for the trees, loping fast on all fours. The ground exploded beside her, showering her with soil, but she kept going. This was Layla's fault. Run. Hide. Heal.

Oh, Mickey.

That Layla was going to pay.

Chapter 18

The last time Layla had walked down this miserable street she'd lost her life. This time, she had it all in front of her. To her left was a wide concrete slab, and across the way, much farther, a cargo ship, crane reaching over its hull. Massive blue and orange cargo containers had occupied the lot near the warehouse. Now it was empty, and she could see all the way to the choppy, gray river. Parked on the street, to her surprise, was her car. Nobody had stolen it, after all.

This was the place. He had to be here.

A rusted smear of blood near the doorknob made her pause, but the frame was still broken, so she pushed the door open and peeked inside. The place was as dark as she remembered, though now a white-blue light flickered in the depths of the large space, like a fluorescent trying to come on. And then the light went out entirely.

Layla crept forward, keeping to the dark.

An extended male roar of frustration and the light burst into existence again, a plasma of blue violet tossed up into the air, battering the darkness. Magic.

Had to be him. Layla advanced, trying hard to keep

each footstep soundless. That weird bursting feeling almost overcame her again when she saw his silhouette—his tall, strong body braced, one arm extended, palm flat as he coaxed the light to maximum brightness, the other arm outstretched behind him, for balance. His long hair was in a ratty knot away from his face. Poor man was finally learning what a hassle that hair was going to be. No way on earth she'd let him cut it, though.

Shadowman. Mortal?

She was three paces from him, but he still didn't notice. His body shook with the effort he used to create the magic light. From this close she smelled his sweat, dark, a little funky, and totally human. Which made her grin and go warm all over, in spite of the cold.

Screw it. She stepped up beside him, pretending to concentrate on the light, though all of her attention was on him.

"So what are we doing?" she asked lightly, rocking back and forth, heel to toe, on her feet.

He reeled back and the light went out. She thought he fell on his ass, but since she couldn't see, she couldn't be sure.

"You okay, honey?" She tried to keep the laugh from her voice. Really, she did.

A blue flame burst to life, held in his palm while he, yes, was half sprawled in shock on the warehouse floor. Strands of tangled hair fell in his eyes. His shirt, a long-sleeve tee, was ripped on the side, his abs nicely flexed beneath. An unlaced shoe had come off. Didn't look like he knew how to tie the laces.

"Need help up?" Layla held out her hand. The bursting feeling grew painful. Crap, she was going to cry again.

"Layla?" The "la" was hoarse. He'd gone and ruined his voice.

"That's me." Her grin got wider, in spite of the tears in her eyes.

His face grew paler, expression dismayed. The poor man didn't blink, but he did start shaking. How long had it been since he'd had anything to eat?

Layla knelt on the floor, reached toward him.

He flinched.

She softened her tone. "It's just me. See?"

Kneeling on all fours, she leaned forward, their faces close. His black eyes went wide and wild, searching hers. "Hi," she said. And then she touched her lips to his. His mouth was warm, firm, oh so real. She breathed him in, reveled in the return press, and gave him her soul.

He groaned, a lost, hurt sound. And the warehouse went pitch dark again. She was grabbed none too gently, dragged onto his lap, pinned with one tight arm around her, while his other hand roved, maybe checking for all the right parts, before settling at the nape of her neck.

Finally, he kissed her back, mouth moving against hers, devouring, tasting. Pulling back to feather with gentleness, skim satin on satin, before crushing her to him again.

And still he shook, but now he shook them both.

Layla shifted. Scruffed her cheek on his five o'clock beard. Yep. Mortal.

His breath was uneven. His heart was pounding against her.

"Shhhh." Layla squeezed him tight. She'd thought to surprise him, and she guessed she had. "It's okay. You'll be okay."

"I've gone mad, yes?" he said in the dark.

"No, actually, you just went missing"—Layla cuddled closer—"and weren't there for my triumphant return."

"I don't believe it."

She chuckled. “I’ve got two cars outside, my piece of crap, thank you very much, and a Segue loaner. How about we get to a safer location—Rose went full lizard, by the way—and I can convince you there?”

“Are you here? Do you live?”

“Yeah, I’m pretty sure I am. And you bet, I sure do.”

“And Moira?” His voice broke again.

“I tricked her. I beat Fate.” Layla laughed. “Boy, is she pissed at me.”

“But . . . how?”

She pulled back. Arched an eyebrow to tease. “I’ll tell you all about it on the way. Devil’s on the loose. We’ve really got to go.”

Shadowman stumbled out into the waning light of the day. He would not let go of Layla’s arm. He gripped her too hard, and was sorry for it, but he needed to keep her by his side. The feel of her arm in his human hand astonished him.

She should not be here. She should be dead. If he could have felt her emotion, sensed the glow of her soul, he might have thought her return possible, but this absence of her feeling and the surfeit of his own confused him.

Layla hurried them down the street, beyond her old car to a sleek black one behind it, and spoke fast. “Rose couldn’t have gotten this far yet, so we should be okay, but we still need to hurry. If I know about this place, she does, too.”

She held out a black fob and the car answered with a flash of its lights. He’d seen the swift rise of automobiles, but so far, he did not care for them. “Where are we going?”

And wasn’t Adam taking care of the devil?

“New York Segue bunker,” she said, opening the passenger door for him. He should be opening the door for her, like a gentleman. When she smiled, waiting, he reluctantly released her and got in. Settled into the black leather.

She slid into the driver's seat and looked over while starting the engine. "Kev reported you didn't want to go to the Annex to ask the angels for help."

"I had to find you, and they kill my kind," Shadowman answered, and braced himself as she made a tight turn with the car.

Her eyebrows went up as she smiled. "And what kind is that?"

In her expression, he could finally sense a giddy mirth mixed with her determination to get them to safety. She was happy to see him. Welcomed him in any state. Delighted in this particular one.

Shadowman exhaled in relief as the car swiftly accelerated down the street. "I believe I am a mage, a mortal who can wield Shadow. A very long time ago, a mage or two crossed into Twilight. I was trying to do the same to find you, yet I have not had time to master the craft."

"I know why the angels want to kill me, but why would they want to kill you?" she asked.

She seemed so blithe as she talked about her death. As soon as the angels knew she had returned to Earth, they would renew their attack on the gate. But in his mortal state, he could no longer protect her.

"Because while magery draws from Shadow, mages are not bound to Twilight, and can therefore wreak just as much, or more, havoc on Earth as the devil. Long ago there was a great war between Heaven and Shadow. Mages, being mortal, were crushed first, and then the fae eventually bowed to the dominion of The Order."

She shrugged, scrunched her face. "What makes you

think that's still the case? I mean, you yourself said it was a very long time ago."

"I built a gate to Hell. They wish to destroy it and me." Ballard would strike him down right now if he could. And Layla next.

Her expression smoothed. "Good point. No angels, then."

"Eventually they will come for me, but I want to spend as much time with you as possible." They were both mortal, yet in the schema of this callous universe, it was still impossible for them to be together.

"Aside from the gate business, we've got all the time in the world." She sent a quick self-satisfied smile his way. "Got that out of Moira, too. Just about spun that frickin' thread myself."

Very few mortals cheated Death. Fewer still, Fate. Shadowman was astonished, and yet, he believed. To alter a fate was impossible, but if anyone could, it was Layla. Hadn't she promised, upon her first death, that she would be back? Well, here she was beside him, radiant as ever. Dare he hope they could survive it all?

"Tell me everything," he said.

They merged onto a main thoroughfare, traffic moving at a ferocious speed. She told him about the ghost clinging to life, the flight through Twilight, Zoe's mastery of the scythe, which made him again bereft at its loss. And then her capture by Moira, the sisters of Fate entrapping her in his winter.

"Your mind stayed sharp?" That was the first wonder of her escape.

"Oh, no, I was plenty crazy toward the end. But at the same time, everything made a weird kind of sense as well. It was like a nightmare or a dream where all the surface stuff stops mattering and what's important confronts you head-on, albeit in a twisted way." Her gaze flicked to the rearview mirror, connected with something, then regarded the road again.

"Yes," Shadowman said, "Shadow is exactly like that."

"Anyway, I think I've got the hang of it now, though I wouldn't want to vacation there or anything. It did help me deal with Rose Petty and her mind games. Now I know anything is possible."

So it would seem.

"You said the devil would be tracking us." Maybe that's who she was looking for in the mirror. "Didn't Adam slay her?"

"She got away. Talk about a beast. Adam's trying to track her. The Order, too. We're going to stay in the Segue bunker for the time being. Hide out. Eventually, they'll bring her down."

Layla leaned forward, squinting upward to peer at the sky. Then braked hard when she came too close to the vehicle in front.

"It's pointless to track her," Shadowman said. He knew what had to be done. The devil wouldn't stop until Layla was dead, the gate secure.

He'd have to finish Rose himself. Even though he was mortal there was a way, though less expedient than his strength and power as fae Death. Mortals had been making deals with devils since the beginning of time. He'd simply do the same.

An adjacent car, boxy like the Hummer, nearly veered into Layla's space, and she jerked into another line of traffic, cursing, "Asshole!" All her previous levity was gone. She gripped the steering wheel tightly, her back straight and tense. "Hey, can you call Adam on that mobile?"

The car lurched forward as they were bumped from behind.

"What was that?" Shadowman asked. He grabbed the

slender piece of technology from the slot in the dash but had no idea how to use it. Again, he was useless in this world.

"We're being followed, but I don't know who it could be. Only you, me, and Rose know about the warehouse." A drip of sweat rolled down her temple. She puffed her hair out of her eyes.

Cold stole over Shadowman, and he shivered for the first time. Ever. "The angels know as well. They came for the gate, and moved it."

"Angels are bullying me on the road?" she demanded. "They could get someone hurt!"

"They just want me." The Order was taking no chances. A mage had been born, one who'd already brought Hell and death to the world. His cursed gate was his own death warrant. "You simply found me first."

"Well, they can't have you."

The boxy car veered again, scraping against theirs, the sound an offensive shriek of metal on metal.

And still the devil had to be dealt with. Might as well be now, before he lost this last chance.

"Get off this big road, Layla." The calm in his voice surprised even him.

"No way."

"We can't go on like this," Shadowman insisted. "Trust me. Let me speak with them."

"The angels will do what's right. Right?" But she didn't sound as if she believed it.

The truth was, the angels would do what they believed was right, whether it was or not. They had only their own counsel to go by, the good of humankind foremost in their minds. But there would be no doubt: A mage who'd built a gate to Hell would be best scrubbed from Earth. Unless of course, that mage meant to fight a devil first.

"This road is dangerous, Layla," he reasoned. "Let's get off it before someone"—*meaning you*—"gets hurt."

"Custo wouldn't hurt you, and he's an angel," she said, trying to convince herself.

She took a side road, and the guard of surrounding cars followed, yes, like a flock of strange geese. She turned right onto the next street and coasted down its length. This road was wide, surely busy at certain times of day, but just now few cars passed. The buildings seemed gray, passionless, silent, on the sidewalks only a soul or two.

Shadowman noted the intersection ahead. Perfect. "Stop here."

The surrounding cars gave Layla no choice but to stop in the middle of the street.

"Good," he said. "Stay in the car."

So of course she got out at the same time he did.

The angels were exiting, too, their bright, beautiful faces full of doom. Two there, four on that side, another group joining at his back. Ballard at his right. They were men and women in modern dress, all of them armed with Heavenly weapons. And suddenly he was reminded of that first day with Layla, on the city street. Then, too, the angels had stepped out of obscurity and made themselves known. Watching.

He approached Ballard, who momentarily braced himself to strike.

Shadowman glanced down at the battle-ax in Ballard's hand. The haft was long and the silver-blue blade moon arched, though differently oriented than his scythe had been. Still, the handling would be similar. "Might I borrow that for a moment?"

Ballard's brows drew together, his former concentration broken. His upper lip curled. "You think I would . . ."

"I'll need something to strike down the devil." Shadowman shifted his gaze to the intersection ahead, the crossroads, hoping that Ballard would know the lore regarding the summoning of a devil, and understand his meaning. A crossroads was a place where the boundaries of the three worlds grew thin, even that of Hell. From there the gate and its she-devil would hear his call for a deal and be forced to answer. Making a deal with the devil had a very long tradition among humanity that lived on in stories and song, even permeating this young country and these modern times. "I built the gate that let her out. It's my duty. If I am going to fight today, don't you think I'd best start with her?"

Frowning deeply, Ballard reluctantly offered the weapon. "You pursue Hell too often."

"Indeed." Shadowman took the ax and found the weight of the weapon pleasing in his right hand, as he had his scythe for millennia. It did not burn his mortal flesh, as the hammer had Death's. He gripped the haft near the blade, reached to gather his long hair into a bunch, and with the blade cut the lot of it off.

"Don't!" Layla pleaded, too late and foolish. The hair could only be a liability in a fight. And he meant to win this one.

"Thank you," Shadowman said to Ballard. "I'll give the weapon back to you shortly."

He turned at Layla's hand on his arm.

"What's going on?" Her gaze darted from him to Ballard. "What insane thing are you going to do?"

He kissed her cheek. Soft, so smooth. "You humbled Moira for me. Let me do this one little thing for you."

She blinked in confusion.

"Trust me." He strode down the street toward the intersection.

"But—?" she called after him.

He lifted a hand for her patience but didn't look back. A car honked as he took position in the middle of the crossroads, ready.

"Rose!" Shadowman called. The intersection blurred. Time and space shifted out of the mundane. Headlights streaked red and white, hanging in the air. The buildings hazed, wavering as if with extreme heat. The place was both located in the city of the present, and the burnt red dust of a dirt road in Hell, superimposed over each other.

A fae might be able to track a devil by subtle signs of death and evil, but a mortal could not. If a mortal wanted a devil, he must bring the devil to him. At a crossroads. For a deal. Fame, wealth, beauty, . . . love.

Call a devil, and she must come.

Rose sat at the pretty kitchen table of a country home, trying to lift a teacup to her lips. Chamomile tea, with its smooth aroma, always settled her nerves. The china cup rattled against the saucer, but Rose was determined to be a lady. Didn't matter what she looked like on the outside if her manners were excellent.

She managed a sip.

Then spilled a little down her chin when the old man she'd locked in the basement started mewling again.

Rose put the teacup down with a smack, snapping the delicate handle from the cup.

Wasn't her fault he'd toppled down the stairs. He was the one who didn't want her to use his dead wife's best china, when clearly the set was the only decent thing in the cupboard.

She tried to hold the cup between her thumb and first finger but broke the china. The tea puddled on the flower-printed tablecloth. She worked to control her frustration. This would not do.

"Rose!" a man's voice called.

She dried her fingertips on a napkin, her blood moving faster. How did the old man know her name?

No, couldn't be him. The voice had been too strong.

Rose stood, wary. Had the bad people from Segue found her? She'd been so careful in her move north. She'd followed the gate's directions so assiduously. No hot-tempered mistakes this time.

kat-a-kat-a-kat: You can beat him.

Beat whom?

Rose stepped toward the door, and her vision wavered. The house fell down around her, disappearing into red dust, and suddenly she was in Hell again, the burnt desert landscape as dry and unforgiving as fire. In the cracked clay dirt, two roads met, crossing each other at right angles.

A shirtless man stood before her. His muscled chest and tight, rippled stomach made her flash her dimples before she remembered her dimples were lost under thick, sallow skin. His pants rode low on his hips, without a belt, so that the fuzz on his navel directed her attention even lower, which was inappropriate, but interesting. He had a really long ax in one hand, a plaything after the attack at Segue.

"Who are you?" she demanded. "What do you want?"

"I am Shadowman," he answered.

Oh, *him.* Her satisfaction at his newly weakened state was poisoned by his appearance. That the monster should look like that, while she suffered . . . This was exactly the reason why looks didn't matter.

kat-a-kat: He's mortal now.

Better yet, he was that Layla's lover, as Mickey had

been Rose's. So, of course, he had to die. Layla should hurt, too.

"I want to make a deal," he said.

"Funny"—she sneered at him—"I just want to kill you."

"Yes, but if I win . . ."

Rose swiped at his throat, but he dodged back.

"You must hear me out," he said. "If I win, then I want the destruction of the gate to be visited upon my body, not Layla's. I want to die in her place."

"You'll die now," Rose said. "And no one will destroy the gate."

The pretty man shook his head. "Accept my deal, and then we will fight."

kat-a-kat: Agreed. Finish him now, and I will exist forever.

Layla ran toward the intersection, drawing her gun. She tried very hard not to blink for fear that she'd lose her visual grasp on Shadowman, the warping red earth, and now Rose, shimmering before him in the rising waves of Hell's heat.

How did Rose get there so fast? Had she been following that closely? The devil had found a large gold and blue paisley muumuu since Segue. It was hard to tell with all that fabric, but it seemed her injuries had healed and she was as beastly as ever.

Shadowman had no idea how dangerous she was. Layla had already shot Rose point-blank, lots of times. If modern weapons couldn't kill her, what did he hope to do with that medieval ax?

Rose and Shadowman prowled in a circle, intent on only each other. And stranger still, the traffic resumed like normal, passing through on green lights, stopping at reds, oblivious to the fight in the intersection. A bass beat from a car parked at a filthy gas station gave the coming fight an urban rhythm, while the air took on a sulfurous stink that made Layla flare her nostrils. Those turning down Layla's street had to go around all the skewed cars, but she didn't care, and apparently, neither did the gathered angels, who joined Layla to watch. But, damn them, not to help.

"What's happening?" Layla shot over her shoulder to the yellow-blond angel who'd given Shadowman the ax. "I thought he was going to fight you guys."

She gripped her gun, ready to fire, but her instincts told her not to shoot, that the bullet would never—could never—reach Rose, though she was only a few yards away.

Layla put her hands to her head, her body flashing with heat. If she ran into the intersection herself, could she join them in that desert? Had there been a trick to Shadowman's approach? Like some mage magic? Maybe . . .

The angel stepped up beside Layla and blocked forward movement with his arm across her chest. "Stay here," he said. "Shadowman is gone from this plane. A mortal can summon a devil at the crossroads to make a deal, usually to sell his soul."

A deal with the devil? "And the crossroads are in Jersey?"

He smiled slightly. "The crossroads can be anywhere, at any time. If mortals can call on Heaven, they can appeal to Hell, too. We'd have attempted this ourselves, but it is our law that Heaven cannot make any deals with a devil."

And Shadowman would never have suggested this crossroads thing to her or even Adam, not up against a thing like Rose. He'd only risk himself.

Layla flinched as Rose, snarling, swiped at Shadowman. He dodged back, light on his feet. He arced the ax into a shining figure eight, the symbol of infinity, to loosen his wrist.

"He's going to sell his soul?"

"No. Mages don't have souls," the angel said. "We won't know the terms of the exchange until the battle is done and the victor claims the spoils."

Shadowman blurred into a counterclockwise turn. The momentum crossed the ax in front of his chest, and he rounded into a spider cartwheel over Rose's shoulder. He lunged deeply into a graceful, two-handed strike. Caught the devil at her neck, but the blade glanced away when it hit bone.

Okay, so he might survive five minutes, rather than five seconds.

Rose lashed back. Raked his chest with a claw.

He flexed his hips back when she sent a cross-swipe across his stomach.

The ax windmilled as Rose punched, but she was too slow to avoid the quick uppercut to her chin, which sent her strike wild and her snarl up to a high-pitched shriek.

Layla gulped. "Can you help him?"

The angel didn't seem worried at all. "I gave him my ax. Devils do not heal from Heavenly wounds."

"Well, how about giving him a hand?"

The angel finally slid his gaze her way. "Have you any idea how many people over the millennia have fought Death?"

Layla watched Shadowman coolly spin the ax in his palm, as if getting the feel of the weapon. One side of his mouth stretched into a smile. His eyes glittered.

"I'd guess people fight Death a lot," she said. There was too much good stuff in this world to give up easily. So, okay, he'd had plenty of practice.

The angel returned his attention to the fight. "This should be over fast. The Reaper has never been one to draw out a death unnecessarily."

Rose dived at Shadowman, but he spun out of the way, bumped her shoulder with the blunt side of the ax, then whipped the blade into an overhead circle.

"And when he's done with her, he'll fight you?" Layla's heart beat fast.

Rose darted a wicked hand toward Shadowman's throat, which he knocked away with the staff of the ax.

"The gate cannot stand," the angel said, "and mages have a long history of conflict with Heaven."

Layla had known this was coming, must be dealt with. She had hoped that after her win over Fate the problem of the gate might also be solved without the loss of her hard-won life. A cry of denial choked her. She swallowed it bitterly. At least Shadowman had been saved that eternity of Twilight winter. "And if I promise to give myself up?"

The angel turned his shining face to her. "Can you also promise that he won't wage war for you? He was bent on saving you, and therefore the gate, from destruction. He'd have killed us all if he'd had to, on your behalf. Right now we hold Shadow very tenuously in check. We cannot afford an extended battle with him. Can you assure me that he will peaceably allow you to die?"

Layla kept her sights on Shadowman. Her heart quailed, but yes, this time she was certain if she asked it of him he'd agree. She was the master of her own fate, and she would not permit her legacy to the world, to Talia, be a gate to Hell. Not when she could stop it. He'd understand. He'd have to understand.

Rose feinted to one side. Shadowman wasn't duped and tracked her movement with a dodge of his own. Turned. Drew the ax back, muscles rippling into tensed planes and bunches.

Layla's heart stalled. "I'd like the night with him, if that's okay."

She'd requested the same when she first learned why she'd been reborn. Maybe now there would be a different answer.

The ax darted in a downward stroke. Rose twisted, off balance, clawing through empty air. Her eyes took on a panicked plea.

Shadowman's expression went indifferent. The blade flashed. Cut through the red dust hovering in the air. Met flesh.

And Rose's head skipped across the cracked, fiery earth.

The angels were already retreating to their cars en masse. The blond one called back in answer, "Have him bring my ax, will you?"

Layla shifted her gaze to Shadowman, who stood panting, sweat coursing down his tawny shoulders. The ax hung at his side. His shoelaces were undone, again.

Those black fae eyes of his tracked the exodus of the angels, whom she knew he'd expected to fight next, then returned to her, a dark and wary question in their depths.

Chapter 19

Shadowman glanced from his shoelaces to Layla. "Now I make bunny ears?"

"Yeah," she said, flashing her bright smile. "Cross them, just like that, tuck one under . . . right. And pull."

Shadowman assessed his handiwork, then looked up to make his report. "This will take some practice."

"You'll get it." Her gaze slid from his eyes to his hair, and the humor turned to mock sadness. "So pretty, now gone. I had plans for that hair, damn it."

An unspoken agreement hung in the air of the hotel room. They would not speak about what tomorrow would bring. Layla's optimism wouldn't flag.

He'd been introduced to the bliss of a shower but driven to curses by the slippery little bottle of shampoo. The trays of food had been set aside, extra water downed until, yes, as she promised, he felt a whole lot better.

She stood up from the foot of the bed, where the impromptu lesson had been held, she on her knees, and he on the edge. (Not how he'd intended to use the bed.) When she reached for the bag of clothing she'd insisted they buy for him, he stood. Took it from her. Placed it on the couch.

At last Layla went still, as he did beside her. The room fell quiet, except for the bumps and occasional footsteps outside their room. It was so quiet he could hear them both breathe, and he altered his rhythm to match hers.

"I don't think I've ever felt this good," she said.

Shadowman knew she'd arranged something with the angels. That, or they'd never have left them alone with the gate still rattling evil. She must think she was going to die with its destruction, and soon. How much time had she bought them? Considering the angels' urgency, not long. A day? Just one night?

She'd be shining bright about now, as she always did at the brink. He closed his eyes and could feel the heat of the glow between them. It wouldn't do, however, to inform her that he'd taken her place with Rose's death. The new day would begin soon enough.

He lowered his head to her crown and breathed in the sweetness and heat of her hair. She tilted her face up in response, brushing her cheek along his shoulder.

"I should've had you take me on a date." She laughed. "Dinner and a movie. Oh! Or for a drive to the ocean. We would've had time for a little detour. There's nothing like the ocean at night."

Shadowman looked down into her eyes. "Regrets?"

She startled, then shook her head emphatically, gazing back at him. "None. I'm exactly where I want to be."

He brought a hand to her waist, slid it under the cloth of her shirt to the slope of her side. The smoothness of her skin had him closing his eyes again to weather the hard beat and flush of heat that was his new body's response to her nearness. Would Death give up forever for a single mortal day? Easily. Layla had more magic than all of Shadow combined.

His eyes were still closed when her lips touched his.

The contact set off a clumsy avalanche of motion: a sudden shift for better access, a tug of his sleeve, a grasp and salty taste of skin, a confusion of limbs shedding shirts and pants. When he swung her weight around to the bed, he'd lost everything but one shoe, held fast by a gathered pant leg and boxer at his ankle. He kicked himself free as she, naked, scooted back to the pillows, laughing at him.

Then she shrieked, happy, when he pounced. The shock of skin on skin set the room careening, but he didn't care as long as he held Layla. He went for the flushed cleft between her breasts, his hand stroking up her thigh, until her luscious bottom filled his palm. He squeezed, then adjusted the position of her leg a little higher, and knew she liked it when she brought the other leg up to match, sliding her hands through his hair to grip his shoulders.

A taste on the tender underside of her breast, too. He had to breathe deep at the thump of want that fuzzed his brain. A pause to wrestle with his laboring heart. Then he brushed his mouth up to the hollow at her throat, just below her ear, where her life beat against his lips. A long life, which she'd won for herself. He would not allow his cursed gate to take it away.

For tonight, however, she would be his. He was granted this much at least, though it embittered his heart that the time should be so brief. Good thing he wouldn't need the tainted organ after tomorrow.

He moved upward, nipped her earlobe, tasted the smoothness of her cheek, grazed her mouth with his teeth. She wrapped her legs around him and hooked her ankles. Her smug expression told him she didn't intend to let him go. So he pushed her further, cruising his free hand around her hip, and discovered just how much she desired him. The wetness between her thighs told him that, even without the gift of Shadow.

Blood and heat gathered within him into a churn and swell of sensation and need. He tensed everything to speak through a shudder of awareness, so she would understand, too.

"You and I," he said.

"Yes," Layla answered. "Absolutely."

His face was flushed, back tensing, ribs flaring with each tight breath. The slow wave of the motion sent dark currents of rapture through her body. No man ever could have made her feel like this, not when her psyche had already known Shadowman.

Layla pulled him down with her legs and wrapped her arms more tightly around his shoulders, so that his slanted eye was next to her human one, and they could look at each other soul to soul. She guided him to her entrance.

"It'll be okay," she said and adjusted her hips slightly to tease him.

Which made him growl against her. The vibration tickled, so she laughed again. Kissed his mouth, soft and deep. Fine-tuned their fit. Connected.

Which stopped his breath completely; every strand of muscle and sinew in his back, thighs, and delicious ass was strung tight. A damp sheen broke out on his skin. A pleasure groan rumbled low in his chest.

She used her legs for leverage, and took them deeper, torturing them both. A bright pulse of delight gathered deep in her womb, begging for friction.

And he answered with a slow, filling pump.

His black irises widened as he moved again, a subtle

ripple of Shadow in the room. Mage. Right. Problem? Too late now . . .

His hands took hers, fingers lacing, and braced them above her head on the mattress. His shoulders flexed as he balanced his weight on either side of her for total possession. A riot of sensation consumed her mind, body, heart, as he claimed her again. She arched to rub her breasts against his chest.

He drove deep once more. "Layla . . ."

Breeched all barriers, stole her breath, and silenced the world until it was reduced to the pounding in her head. The darkness in the room became a sea of reckoning Shadow. Relentlessly he moved, wave upon wave, quickening his tempo. It was primitive, dark, magic and flesh, a cataclysm, volcanic, creating as much as it destroyed. She'd never be the same, but it didn't matter anyway. When his forehead dropped to touch hers, she sobbed and clenched him tight. An extended shout was ripped from his throat, and she met him with her own lift and fierce cry.

They clung like that, together in the dark, a pocket of the universe that didn't wholly belong to any world. She almost would have begged him to make a little universe of their own, if not for the trouble they'd leave behind.

He let his big body collapse on top of her, oblivious to the fact that she required oxygen to breathe. When she gasped for air, he rolled to the side and took her with him. But he wouldn't let her go. One arm held her fast at the small of her back. His other tangled in her hair at her nape. She trembled, gripping him just as hard, as if a hurricane might blow through the room at any moment and tear them apart, when really they both intended to walk into disaster freely come morning.

* * *

Layla woke to the light snore of the mage known as Shadowman. She'd fallen into the crook of his arm sometime in the night, his muscle her pillow. That's how they would sleep if they could have a future. With him breathing deeply beside her, she'd bet her nightmares would be a thing of the past. Nuzzling, she kissed his chest. He was as warm as the tint of his skin, and very little could have compelled her to leave him, but she had work to do, and only a few hours to do it.

First, a difficult responsibility, sure to frustrate her newfound family. She ducked out to the car to get a laptop she'd borrowed from Adam, then settled into the hotel room's sofa. She titled her article "Wraiths, Shrouded in Secrecy" and spotlighted Segue, the place she considered home. With the emergence of the wights and the reorganization of the wraiths, the public needed to know what the world was up against. She corrected the dates for the first-known cases, referencing murders found in Segue's case files over twenty-three years ago. She vouched personally for wraiths' near-immortality and stated that The Segue Institute had discovered a means to kill them, but she didn't divulge more, to protect Talia and The Order. She described in detail the signs of a wraith kill, and then, after a hard internal debate, revealed what the wraiths fed upon for sustenance: human souls. Denied nourishment, the wraiths became wights, specters of such little substance that not even gravity could hold them. The wights troubled her most now. She went on to state that Segue was also in the process of developing capture and control techniques, called Barrow-tech. And last of all, for fun, she referred questions to Adam Thorne.

As the sky grayed outside her hotel window, she e-mailed the article to her editor, and blind cc'd Adam, so he'd be prepared for the phone calls. Not that the public would believe her claims, but at least she'd done what she'd come to do. People were dying. A new age of magic was upon the world. The Order might strive to reverse it, and Segue might try to control it, but really there was no going back.

Having done her worst, she sought pen and paper (more personal) to write a note to Talia, but after addressing the sheet in her best penmanship (never good), she couldn't figure out what to say, and heart aching, she abandoned the project altogether.

She turned when Shadowman shifted to sit up, his physique glorious in the dappled morning light. "Morning, sunshine."

The black got deeper in his eyes.

All right then, a kiss. Which rapidly turned into more. And even though they had several hours of driving ahead of them, they ended up in the shower together. Breakfast on the road. Doom on the horizon.

The gate started rattling in her head as soon as they turned onto Interstate 81 heading south. She tried the radio to cover the sound, but it was no good. The metallic, angry jangle only increased its volume until she could barely hear herself think. And here she'd been looking forward to talking with Shadowman, to having this last time together. The rattle made her want to turn the car around for a little peace. To save themselves.

kat-a-kat-a-kat: How about just one more day?

Rose and Moira had tapped her deepest fears. The gate was playing a crueler game, taunting her with her forfeited future.

kat-a-kat-a-kat: A day for love.

"I hear it, too," Shadowman said, massaging the muscles at her neck. He must have put some magic into the touch, because she could breathe again. Focus.

'Cause, see, a day would never be enough. Not with Shadowman, warm and vital at her side, not with Talia, friend, sister, and so much more. The gate could only offer portions, which was a cheat. And a mean one. With its destruction, the danger would pass, and Layla would carry the precious memory of love with her beyond. None of the nightmares that had plagued her life. Just a bittersweet joy. She wasn't afraid anymore, just impatient.

She gripped the steering wheel and floored the gas. Angels must have been on the road, parting the traffic, turning the cops' speed guns the other way, because she got up to 120 and stayed there. Adam's car could more than handle it. The tolls were empty, gates lifted, metered exits flashing green. The several hours were cut in half.

When she crossed the state line into West Virginia, the rattle reached a crescendo, so loud she had to grab her head to keep it from bursting.

Shadowman took the steering wheel, while she curled into herself, her foot a brick on the gas. Tears ran down her face as the gate to Hell shook every bone in her body and chattered her clenched teeth. Hateful, hateful thing.

The car bumped off the road and she knew to release the gas. They bounced and skipped into a grassy meadow, gone yellow for the winter, until the car finally came to a stop. She felt Shadowman take her head into his hands. She looked him in the eyes, and the rattle receded a bit.

She couldn't drive like this anymore, and he didn't know how. They'd have to walk, though she really just wanted to throw up.

They got out of the car, and Shadowman took her hand as they made their way back to the road. She didn't notice the waiting van until she was being lifted inside, and then she shuddered into Shadowman's embrace on a bench in the middle. She had identified Adam Thorne in the front passenger seat, expression concerned, mouthing something she didn't understand. She was here, wasn't she? That was all that was important. Custo sat on her other side, his stoic face deep in concentration. The rattle in her mind mellowed to a distant hum, as if that infernal voice had been blunted.

And so they were delivered to Hell, its dark mouth like the gullet of some long-dead dragon, their destination its sulfurous belly. She was handed down into the slippery, frigid black earth. Bones of rock hung from the ceiling and reached from the floor, like fossils from ages past. Electric torches lit their way, and every time she fell, Shadowman's hands were there to keep her upright.

Suddenly the gate was before them, a black throb of iron. Tall and barbed, it loomed larger than ever, its shadows reaching to the ceiling, reaching as if it could go on forever.

kat-a-kat-a-kat: Open me!

Layla swallowed. Pulled herself up. Turned to Adam, who trembled, his eyes going bloodshot as he looked on Hell. Sweat beaded on his forehead. The gate must've been speaking to him, too.

"Adam!"

His attention snapped to her, violence in his gaze. The cords of his neck stood out. His skin was flushed. The man needed to get out of here. Bad.

"Talia, Adam," Layla reminded him. "Your babies. Michael and Cole."

He teared as his jaw worked. Shame brought his head low, but his chest moved in a deep breath.

"Give them my love, okay?" she said.

His nod brought tears down his face. He made to speak, gaze filled with things to say, probably a message of love from Talia.

"I know," Layla answered. Talia had a forever hold on her heart. "I felt it, too."

Adam froze, surprised, nodded again. Though he still faced her, his eyes were drawn back to the gate. Abruptly, he rubbed a hand over his face and turned his back on the thing. Still, two angels guarded him as he started his upward climb.

kat-a-kat-a-kat: Open me!

Layla felt a compulsive pull, like a lash around her soul, yanking her forcibly toward the nightmare. It turned her blood cold, made her limbs feel rubbery, her mind numb. She glanced to Shadowman, who didn't seem to have Adam's trouble.

kat-a-kat-a-kat: Throw me wide!

Or hers, since she was shaking.

"It's time for you to go, too," Shadowman said. "This business is for me and The Order."

Not likely. She looked at the gate again. Its bars seethed, constrained only by the vines that wrapped around them, an occasional wicked flower here, there. That gate was made for her.

kat-a-kat-a-kat: But it is no longer you who will die with me. Open me, save him.

She swung her gaze back up to her black-eyed lover. No wonder he was so calm. He'd bartered his life in his deal with the devil.

"But Rose is dead," she argued, horrified. "You won the fight." She whirled back to the gate. "He won the fight."

kat-a-kat-a-kat: He won the right to die in your place. Will you let him?

No, no, no. She'd thought this through carefully. Had it all worked out.

"You've got to think bigger," Layla said, grabbing Shadowman by the front of his shirt. "I can come back again." She hoped, upon her second death, that she could sign up to be an angel. She'd beg to return to Earth, like Custo, and work with her family against the wraiths. "And you can help Adam with the wights, while I can't."

His arms came around her. "But I made the gate."

"You made it for me!" She gestured wildly toward it. "Even prettied it up."

He shook his head, expression going painfully serious. "The flowers were my hope that you'd endure in that hot place, but you didn't need them. Never needed them. You won your life on your own. You should live it. "

kat-a-kat-a-kat: You'll be alone again.

"Shut up!" she yelled at the gate. She was finished with the alone crap. She had what she wanted, and damn it, she was holding on.

kat-a-kat-a-kat: Throw me wide. You can have the ones you love forever.

"No, thanks," she said. "I got a glimpse of Hell yesterday. It's not for me."

Custo emerged from the gathered angels. Approached. "Going or staying, kiss him now. We'd better get started before someone cracks." He flared his nostrils with a hard breath. "I'm halfway there myself."

Custo walked to the cold, dead forge off to one side. On the anvil lay a hammer and another of the black metal flowers. Probably the one she'd found in the warehouse. Shadowman's hope that she'd endure.

kat-a-kat-a-kat: Will you witness his destruction? Will you watch his body break and bleed for love of you?

No. She didn't think she could. But she still wasn't leaving.

Shadowman lowered his head to her ear. His breath caressed her skin. That one spot warmed the rest of her.

"Layla, it is done. I beg you to go now. I want you to remember last night, not this."

Custo lifted the hammer. The violence of his motion sent the black flower to the cave floor.

Layla shook her head. She couldn't leave him. Couldn't endure this either. That was Kathleen's thing, endurance. Not hers. She'd been broken from the beginning. All her life. Set apart. Yes, alone. And why? So she could betray the only one who'd ever loved her.

And he wanted her to remember last night?

kat-a-kat-a-kat: I've got all your memories right here.

"Help me," Shadowman said.

Took a second for her to realize he wasn't talking to her. Then she was surrounded by angels, ready to forcibly restrain her.

"I'll make it quick," Custo promised, his voice a rasp of soul-deep reluctance.

But Layla looked at the gate. All her memories? The temptation grew silky, twining around her soul. What she wouldn't give for Kathleen's memories. . . .

"The gate has her," someone said.

Years of happy childhood. Family. Her sister. How she and her Shadowman had first fallen in love. The birth of Talia, which now, a lifetime away, still made her heart thump hard with a wrench of timeless connection.

Shadowman drew her up for one last kiss. Even as his mouth pressed to hers, hard, dark, full of passion, the gate spoke in her mind.

kat-a-kat-a-kat: What do you think he made me of? Every strike has a piece of you.

And those flowers, so she'd endure. Hold out, against all odds.

"Get her out of here!" Shadowman roared.

Then he frowned in confusion when the angels drew

back, as if a thought had been shared among them. They looked at her. At each other. At the gate.

Layla knew what that thought was.

Those memories sure would be nice. Better than most of what she had in her head. But Kathleen had given them up for another chance at the real thing. And Layla wasn't about to let it go.

She met Shadowman's tortured gaze. "The flowers, love."

The flowers made the gate, the keeper of the memories, endure as well.

She had to be right because the gate's rattle grew stronger, shaking dust and loose rocks from the cave's dark ceiling and tumbling rocks down the narrow opening at its mouth. The gate knew she had the answer. The angels ducked as the debris rained down. One or two made a dash for the gate, giving in to temptation as the opportunity to open it presented itself in the chaos. These were knocked back by the blond-haired angel and Custo, whose veins had turned to lead.

Layla darted toward the gate herself. An arm went around her middle, whipped her back as a large boulder careened in a blue-black arc of Shadow magic and cracked to the cave floor. She took the hammer from Custo, unafraid of the chaos in the cavern. She was well protected. Always had been.

The tool made her arm buzz with a tingling-glowy feeling. This was not any old hammer.

kat-a-kat-a-kat: Open me! Open me! OPEN ME!

The cave rolled with a great earthquake as she stepped up to the gate. Eyed the first flower on it, drew her arm back with all her might, and struck.

The flower's stem bent, and the petals pointed downward. She liked the flowers so much, better even than her gorgeous red roses. When this was over, she wanted to gather them into a black bouquet. His hope that she'd endure. Well, she was right here to prove it.

She struck again as the ground lurched, and the flower fell into the dirt. One, two, three more . . . no a fourth, right there.

The gate stood naked before her, rocking on its posts.

kat-a-kat-a-kat: He loved Kathleen more.

Layla held out the hammer to Shadowman. "You want to do the honors?"

kat-a-kat-a-kat: Desired her more.

"It would be my pleasure." His expression was savage, violent and ecstatic.

kat-a-kat-a-kat: He'll never—

And the gate was silenced with Shadowman's first strike.

Chapter 20

Two months later

Khan held the thrashing wight at bay, mesmerizing it with an orb of faelight. The creature shivered in the air, as if to shed its flesh, but it could never die. At least, not without their help.

"Easy . . ." Talia warned as she directed Shadow to mask the barrow behind them.

The barrow was an ancient construct redesigned for modern times. The outside was the characteristic faery mound of grass. Inside, a large steel capsule, monitored for breaches, took the wight deep into the earth.

"Now!" Khan shouted as he cast the orb into the barrow.

The wight shrieked after it into darkness. A sheet of steel enclosed the wight within but could never hold the thing. Only earth. Dark, rich soil was dumped onto the silver entrance by a waiting truck. Khan took himself out of the way so that another vehicle could pack the earth hard.

The wight was buried, though it would never rest.

The barrow keeper, a man named Chuck, hopped down

from one of the vehicles. His job was to ensure that the soil did not erode.

Talia joined them, wrapping her arms around herself and stamping her feet. "Did it work?"

Khan was cold, too, but he liked the smoky shapes his breath made against the night sky. "Can you sense death in the air?"

He watched as his daughter inclined her head, turning thoughtful. After a moment she said, "No. All I feel is the cold."

"Then it worked," he concluded. "Let's get you out of this weather." He lifted a hand in farewell to Chuck. They'd gotten to know each other well in the past weeks and would know each other better in the future.

Khan was becoming accustomed to the Hummer. Liked it much better when he was driving and relished the heat the vehicle offered on frigid nights. He took it through the field set aside for the barrows. Climbed onto the mountain road that led to the security gate.

Talia had settled back into her seat. She pulled her woolen cap off her head, and her hair frizzed. "Umm . . ." she began, tucking stray locks behind her ears. "I feel like I should warn you . . . Adam wants to get you under contract for special services to Segue."

Khan slid his gaze to his daughter. Contract. He didn't think so.

"Not that he wants any kind of obligation from you or anything," she said. "He just wants to make sure you are compensated for your work."

"He wants to give me money," Khan clarified. Adam had already hired Layla as Segue's new director of public relations, ostensibly to deal with the "mess" (Adam's word) she created when she sent her article to her former editor. Khan didn't know for sure, but he suspected that

Layla's salary was well above the standard. But then, she was worth every penny.

Talia huffed a sigh. "No. In the real world people get paid for their work."

"My work is pro bono." He smiled over at her.

She shrugged. "Okay, but eventually you might want a house of your own."

He laughed aloud. Had to. "Have we overstayed our welcome, then?"

"No. Of course not. Stay as long as you like." Now she was flustered. "And never mind. I'll tell Adam that you said no."

She went quiet, but another quick glance and he could see the small line of worry between her brows.

"Have no fear," Khan said. "I'll find my own way in this world, as the work with the wraiths and wights permit." He smiled to himself, hope for the future glowing bright and warm within him. "In fact, I relish the opportunity."

Layla was staring at her ringing phone when Khan got back from the barrow field. Her new supertechy mobile was ringing, but she couldn't reach it. The thing was probably lost forever, even though she could see it right in front of her.

She knew Khan threw his keys on the table, his coat over the arm of the couch, but kept her eyes glued on the phone. His arms came around her waist as he, too, regarded Kathleen's wall-high painting. In the foreground, in front of Twilight's magnificent trees, was her mobile. And the number on screen? Her conference call with the Japanese Minister of Defense. Wraith attacks were rising in Tokyo, but the Japanese were slow to accept Segue's counsel as to how to deal with them. That call was a major breakthrough.

"Took a week to set up this meeting," she said. If she looked away, she knew it would disappear altogether.

"Which one of the boys did it?" Khan gathered her close. She rested her head against his chest.

Of Talia's children, everyone thought that Michael was the most troublesome, with his black eyes and his obvious delight in Shadow, but Cole, quiet Cole, could be just as mischievous. And they were still infants.

"I have no idea," Layla answered. She couldn't turn her back on them for a minute. They'd gone from rolling over to scooting within weeks. Exactly how one of them managed to get her phone off the table, she couldn't imagine.

"The call is important?" Khan's voice lowered, and she felt the vibration in her blood. Khan. He'd chosen the name for day-to-day use, but he'd always be her Shadowman.

Layla closed her eyes as he skimmed his mouth up her neck and tugged on her ear with his teeth. Happy tingles spread from the contact, and she didn't think he'd even put magic into it. This was not the way to get work done.

"I'd better go hunt down another phone," she said.

"This late at night?"

"It's morning in Japan."

"Ah."

She turned in his arms. Looked up into his fae black eyes. "Unless you can reach in and grab it for me?"

Khan's magery was expanding fast, probably faster than she knew, which worried her a bit. She'd seen him make a spider bend its legs in death, and then snap, reanimate again.

"And why would I want to get that thing?" His hand slipped underneath her shirt.

"I'll plan tomorrow's date," she offered. The dates were her idea—a way to get him used to this world and a way for them to get to know each other in a normal setting. The bowling had been particularly hilarious, especially

when that little kid suggested Khan play with bumpers. They could never, ever, go back there, which was a pity because there wasn't much to do in a thirty-mile radius. She'd have to come up with something good.

"That won't be necessary." The room darkened. Shadow rippled sensuously through the space. "I've got a better idea."

"There's a wraith problem in Japan," Layla pointed out, though she liked the direction of Khan's thoughts. Was trying very hard not to give in.

"The phone is lost, Layla," he said. "I have no idea how far I'd have to reach to clasp my hand around it, and even if I could, I doubt it would work properly. I suggest a trip instead. Present the wraith problem in person."

Wouldn't that be nice. The likelihood of getting an in-person appointment, however, was slim to none, even with Segue's connections. She'd once had suspicions about Segue and its questionable "paranormal" work. She wasn't shocked to find others shared them.

"I don't want to lose time." And if someone was finally willing to listen to her, she didn't want to lose the opportunity either.

"I meant now."

Layla drew back, but somehow she wasn't surprised. "You can pass through Shadow?"

Passing had been his obsession since the day they'd destroyed the gate. He'd sworn that he would never again be trapped on one side of the veil, she on the other. He'd had enough of that, and frankly, so had she.

He smiled, dark and wicked. "Perhaps it's always been my . . . *fate* to do so, our destiny to always be together." Now Layla was surprised. After all they'd been through . . . "You believe in Fate?"

"Only the kind we make ourselves."

Don't miss SUPERNATURAL, a fabulous paranormal romance anthology, available now!

Desire comes in many forms . . . some dark, some dangerous, all undeniable . . .

In this tantalizing collection, four *New York Times* bestselling authors invite you into the alluring worlds they've created in the Demonica, Guardians of Eternity, Nightwalkers, and Dragon Kin series. Each mesmerizing page will leave you craving more . . .

SUPERNATURAL

"Vampire Fight Club" by Larissa Ione

When a wave of violence forces shape-shifter Vladlena to go undercover, her first stop is a haven of vice—with a dangerously sexy vamp in charge. Both Vladlena and Nathan are hiding something, but they can't conceal the lust that simmers between them . . .

"Darkness Eternal" by Alexandra Ivy

After being held captive by one vampire for four centuries, Kata had no intention of taking another one to the underworld with her. Yet even in the pits of hell, there's no ignoring the intoxicating desire awakened by his touch . . .

"Kane" by Jacquelyn Frank

Kane knows Corrine was meant to be his . . . just as he knows that truly possessing the lovely human is forbidden. But on the night of the Samhain moon, the beast in every demon is stronger than reason, and Kane's hunger is more powerful than any punishment . . .

"Dragon on Top" by G.A. Aiken

Escorting the highborn Bram through deadly Sand Dragon territory will try Ghleanna's patience . . . and her resolve. For Bram is determined to enhance the journey with a seduction no female could resist . . .

A RIVETING ZEBRA MASS-MARKET PAPERBACK!